The Murder Road

The Murder Road

A Cooper & Fry Mystery

STEPHEN BOOTH

WITNESS
IMPULSE
An Imprint of HarperCollinsPublishers

This book was originally published in Great Britain in 2015 by Sphere, an imprint of Little, Brown Book Group.

EPub Edition SEPTEMBER 2015 ISBN: 9780062439239

Print Edition ISBN: 9780062439246

10 9 8 7 6 5

For Lesley, as always

The Murder Road

Chapter One

Eight years ago

THE ROAD WAS wet that night, as it always was when the worst things happened. Rain had turned the tarmac into a slick, dark ribbon as black as any nightmare. A wave of spray splattered his windscreen from the tyres of a Tesco Scania as it ploughed through the downpour fifty yards ahead.

By now the steering wheel felt slippery in his hands and the rumble of the diesel engine had become a monotonous drone inside his head. The nose of his massive Iveco Stralis veered towards the white line as his concentration faltered for a second. He screwed up his eyes against the dazzle of headlights from cars on the northbound carriageway as they glared and flickered through a smear of water beneath his wipers.

He had the heater in his cab turned up full, the fans blasting air to clear the condensation. But the miles he'd already covered today had coated the lorry with dirt. There were still fragments of straw from a farm trailer stuck in a greasy film that his wiper blades couldn't shift. It was like driving blind through a storm of sludge.

There were no lights on this stretch of road, just the flick of a cat's eye, the dark shadow of a tree, the wet reflection from the crash barrier in the central reservation. He was listening to Planet Rock on his DAB radio. It was the only kind of music that made sure the adrenalin was still pumping and kept him awake enough to drive the Iveco through the night, even after a daytime shift. He laughed to himself as a Stones track came on. 'Driving Too Fast'. Except he wasn't, of course. He knew better than to try in a rig like this, even without the speed limiter. He couldn't afford the points if a camera caught him. If he lost his licence, he'd lose his job.

'You're close to the edge. Don't push it one more inch.'

That was what people kept telling him. His boss, his wife, everyone who wanted to stick their interfering oars into his life.

Half a mile past the Macclesfield turn-off, his attention was distracted by a splash of white in the darkness overhead. It was just a car, parked on a bridge over the road. But its colour made it appear to float in mid-air, a ghostly apparition in the rain.

As his truck passed beneath the bridge, he glimpsed two people leaning over the rail. Just a pair of dark outlines, the pale ovals of their faces shrouded in hoods against the rain. It wasn't a night to be out watching traffic, surely. They'd be far better at home in front of the telly, or sitting in the pub with a pint. But some people had nothing better to do and nowhere else to go. He'd given up trying to understand what went on in other people's minds. It was too difficult to figure out, even when it was someone you'd known for years.

His phone buzzed and he glanced at the screen. A text message from his wife. Right on cue.

Where r u? We need 2 talk. Urgent.

She was going on about the same old subject, of course. She would never let it alone. She had never learned that the more she nagged him to do something, the more he felt like doing the opposite. She'd been banging on and on about the same old thing, over and over. He'd tried to fob her off, to say exactly what she wanted to hear. But it still wasn't enough for her. She was really starting to annoy him now.

What hv u done wth all th cash?

He sighed deeply. Today it was the amount of money they'd got saved up in the bank. She wanted a new three-piece suite and there ought to be enough cash to buy it by now. But some of the money had gone from the account. She had no doubt who was to blame. It was always *his* fault.

A red BMW coasted by in the outside lane, overtaking his truck and the Scania with ease, accelerating away until its tail lights vanished into the darkness. Grasping the steering wheel with one hand, he picked up his phone. He began to tap out a reply, awkwardly fumbling at the buttons, his words driven by a burst of anger and exhausted frustration.

The juddering took him by surprise. The vibration under his wheels was the only warning he had that his vehicle was straying off the carriageway. He fumbled at the steering, confused by the phone in his hand, not knowing what to do with it and failing to get a proper grip on the wheel, turning the Iveco further to the left instead of back into lane. Trees loomed dangerously close to the cab as he strayed over the white line and towards the verge. For that heart-stopping moment, his truck was out of control.

And then the lay-by appeared ahead and for a second he thought he was safe.

'Oh, damnation. That was close,' he said.

He sucked in air to breathe a sigh of relief and reached over to put his phone down on the passenger seat.

So he hadn't even begun to brake when the front of his truck hit the car. The impact threw him forward onto the wheel and his phone dropped to the floor as the lorry ploughed onwards, driving the mangled car in front of it. Shards of metal bounced off the road, glass shattered to glittering fragments in the rain, a broken bumper cartwheeled past his windscreen and disappeared into the night.

Then the rear of another truck appeared in his headlights and he finally jammed on the brakes. Too late, of course. Far too late. His wheels locked and his tyres screamed as he skidded on the slick surface. The rear of the parked truck lifted into the air and crashed back onto the road as the car was crushed into a shattered concertina between them.

His air bag deployed as his cab smashed into the other truck. He felt as though gravity had been suspended as the weight of the Iveco's trailer swung it round behind him in a violent jack-knife and swept it into the traffic. Its impetus twisted the cab on its axis and bounced it away from the wreckage, until the tail end of the trailer crashed into the central barrier and shuddered to a halt.

Dazed, he tried to sit upright and push the limp remains of his air bag aside. A shocking pain ran up his leg as he moved, making him cry out loud and clench his fists. The stink of petrol leaked into the cab through a shattered window.

Slowly, he opened his eyes. He found himself staring into the undergrowth at the side of the road, his lights illuminating the trees and the fields beyond, steam billowing from his radiator like fog on the set of a horror film, awaiting the arrival of a monster. His engine was still ticking over, his radio was still playing the Stones. Yet somewhere he could hear the sound of an appalling silence.

Chapter Two

Monday 9 February

DETECTIVE INSPECTOR BEN Cooper paused before he stepped through the open door. He took a few deep breaths, inhaling the smell and the taste of the air. You could tell so much about a house by the way it smelled. Dust and old carpets, damp and broken plaster. A picture was already forming in his head, a strong hint of neglect and hidden corners of dereliction.

Then he detected an underlying odour, a faintly medicinal tang that reminded him of hospital wards. It was something powerful, an embrocation or liniment. Eucalyptus oil or wintergreen, menthol and camphor. Even before he entered the hallway, he would have known it was an old person's house.

'Hello?' he called. 'Hello?'

There was no reply. He pushed the door wider and took a couple of steps into the narrow hall. The old floorboards groaned under his feet. Their creaks echoed in the empty passage, as if the house was responding to his presence.

Two doorways stood to his left and another at the furthest end of the passage. To his right a flight of stairs ran up to the first floor. On some of the steps the carpet had got bunched up and pulled loose from the stair rods, exposing the felt underlay. It was old and worn, and the pattern was barely visible in places. But he could see that something heavy had been dragged down the stairs recently, leaving indentations in the carpet and a long scrape in the wallpaper.

There seemed to be no one here, though the door had been standing open, as if waiting for him to arrive.

'Hello?' he called again.

He headed down the passage, stepping cautiously over a broken section of floorboard, through which he glimpsed a dark void. He pulled out a small LED torch from his pocket and shone it into the gap. Ancient wiring snaked along the floor joists to a junction box that was surely made of bakelite. When was that installed? Probably in the 1950s. It would be considered a death trap now.

He pushed the first door open. This room looked out onto the street. Light filtered in through lace curtains on the window. A few remnants of furniture stood against the walls.

The room was strangely familiar, despite its emptiness. He'd been here before, in a different time, a different stage of his existence. A lot of things had happened since then. Death had come into his life, the way it had to this house.

He stood for a few moments in the centre of the room, gazing at the window, watching the shadows of people passing outside. They were like a distant dream, a glimpse of a world he could never be part of again.

Though the house was silent, the bare walls seemed to whisper and murmur. The room had a life of its own, isolated but contained, like a prison cell. All the things that had gone on in here still whirled around in the dust, a memory of the people who'd lived here continuing to stir the air. A starling whistled in the chimney, a car sounded its horn outside. But they failed to penetrate Cooper's reverie.

He was still standing in his trance-like state when the front door slammed. He jumped guiltily, not certain for a moment where he was or why he was standing in someone else's house. He reached automatically for his ASP, his extendable baton, which he carried deep in a pocket of his jacket, hidden from sight but always accessible.

But his hand fell back. There was no threat. There was a good reason why he was in this house. In fact, he was expected.

'Ah, Ben,' said a voice. 'There you are. So what do you think?'

A balding man in his early fifties was standing in the doorway watching him. Guy Thomson. A flushed complexion and ingratiating smile. Cooper had never liked him, but this was the man he was obliged to deal with.

'How much are you asking for it again?' asked Cooper.

'A hundred and fifty thousand.'

'It's a bit on the high side, given its condition.'

'But there's the garden, of course.'

'True.'

They walked through the rest of the downstairs rooms before returning to the hallway and the worn stairs.

'As you can see, we got all the furniture out,' said Thomson. 'Though some of that heavy Victorian stuff upstairs was tricky. There was an enormous mahogany wardrobe. I thought for a while we were going to have to smash it up. But we got it downstairs in the end, with a bit of manoeuvring.'

'I think I heard you,' said Cooper.

'What, even through these solid walls?'

Thomson laughed as he thumped the adjoining wall, disturbing a thin trickle of plaster from one of the cracks.

'Is that a new car outside, by the way?' he said. 'I don't recognise it. Got rid of the old one, have you?'

'Yes, I've just bought it,' said Cooper.

'Toyota RAV4, isn't it? Nice.'

'Thank you.'

Thomson threw him a shrewd sidelong glance.

'You must have come into a bit of money, then?'

'I got a promotion.'

'Ah. Shall we have a look upstairs?'

Cooper had never been upstairs at number six Welbeck Street before. In fact, he'd hardly ever gone up to the first floor of number eight next door, even though he lived there. He'd always met the various tenants in the first-floor flat, but there had been quite a number of them over the years. They'd come and gone pretty quickly, and he'd never got to know any of them properly. He'd been told that was just the way it was in rented accommodation. Now he was beginning to feel like an oddity for having stayed so long.

He wondered if the neighbours in Welbeck Street regarded him as strange, a single man who lived on his own and kept himself to himself. Perhaps they'd all forgotten by now that he'd almost reached the altar, that he'd been ready to walk up the aisle and start a perfectly normal married life.

But nothing was normal now. Not any more. He might have begun to look a little odd and solitary to his neighbours – but they'd begun to look strange to him too. He no longer felt he understood some of these people, the ones living in comfortable domesticity on the side streets of Edendale, with their curtains closed against the world. Somehow his curtains didn't keep the world out, the way theirs did.

It was ridiculous, he knew – but he was starting to feel that he was too far into his thirties to start all over again. He'd convinced himself that he'd be a father by now, settled down with a home of his own. It felt too late to think about planning a family with someone else.

Cooper followed Guy Thomson up the narrow stairs to the first-floor landing, listening to him rattling off the patter as if he was a born estate agent.

'Well, I'm sure I don't need to tell you about how convenient the location is,' Thomson was saying. 'Since you've already lived here for a few years.'

'No.'

'How many years is it exactly?'

'I can't really remember,' said Cooper, though he knew to the day how long he'd lived in Welbeck Street. Moving into the flat had been a major event in his life, a step into freedom from his upbringing at Bridge End Farm.

'It's quite a while, though,' said Thomson. 'I remember my aunt talking about it – how she'd just let the flat to a nice policeman. She was thrilled.'

'She was very nice to me.'

'Good old Aunt Dorothy.'

Guy was the oldest of his former landlady's nephews and nieces. Since Dorothy Shelley's death, the distribution of her estate had been complicated by the absence of a will and no doubt a certain amount of the usual in-fighting between potential beneficiaries.

Cooper couldn't imagine that she had much to leave, apart from these two adjoining terraced houses. But it meant both houses had to be sold to enable the proceeds to be shared.

'It's the condition of the property that concerns me mostly,' he said.

'Oh, they were built to last, these houses. Not like the modern stuff.'

'They need a lot of maintenance, though. Modernisation. This place would need some money spending on it to get it up to scratch.'

Thomson was still looking at him curiously, his face creased in effort as if he was trying to remember something.

'You knew Lawrence, didn't you?' he said eventually.

'Yes, that's how I came to hear about the flat in the first place.'

'That was very sad about Lawrence.'

'He was your cousin, of course,' said Cooper.

'Yes. It's a long time ago now. But still . . .'

Mrs Shelley had never mentioned Lawrence Daley to him, at least not after the funeral had taken place and Cooper had moved into the flat at number eight. She'd probably kept quiet out of a sense of propriety, a feeling that it wouldn't be quite nice to talk about such a tragedy. Or perhaps she'd been considerate of Cooper's feelings, given his own involvement in what had happened to Lawrence.

He remembered Mrs Shelley now, as she'd stood waiting in the hallway of number eight that first day to look him over. He could even recall the cashmere cardigan she'd been wearing, with another slung over her shoulders. The cardigans looked a bit frayed round the edges, giving her an air of decayed gentility. She took to him straight away, perhaps because he was the right sort of person and met her requirements for a tenant. *Reliable and trustworthy professional people only.* Or perhaps it was because he was willing to take on the lazy cat that came with the flat. Yes, that was probably the clincher for Mrs Shelley.

'My Uncle Gerald had plans to knock these two places together,' said Thomson. 'Unfortunately, he never got round to it.'

'I remember Lawrence telling me that. But there were only ever the two of them living here, weren't there? Your aunt and uncle, I mean? No children?'

Thomson eyed him suspiciously, as if Cooper had just cast doubt on his right to inherit the property as a mere nephew.

'No, there were no children,' he said. 'None.'

'Shame. She must have been quite lonely in her later years.'

Cooper felt a sudden wave of guilt at his own words. The old girl had been very good to him, but he hadn't been paying much attention to her when she became seriously ill. She'd treated him pretty much as a grandson and he was sure his rent ought to have gone up substantially in the past few years, but for her indulgence. He should have returned the consideration by keeping a closer eye on her as she got increasingly frail and confused.

He certainly ought to have been there the night she needed him. She could have just banged on the wall and he would have gone straight round. But Mrs Shelley's stroke had been a serious one. She'd looked more than just frail as she lay in her bed in the intensive care unit. She looked so thin that her fragile bones protruded from the sunken skin on her shoulders. One stroke was followed by another and the last one was fatal.

It was shocking how much that had changed things. Even when she was living next door, he'd hardly been aware of Dorothy Shelley's presence most of the time. But when she was dead, it made all the difference. From that moment, living at number eight no longer seemed the same. Death had crept a little bit too close to his walls, reminding him once again that there was no escape.

Thomson had moved into one of the bedrooms and was waiting for him with an impatient cough, while Cooper made a pretence of studying the walls, tapping the plaster with his knuckles. He'd never liked this man. He'd never had any interest in his aunt until she was dying. The prospect of inheriting her two properties in Welbeck Street had brought him to her hospital bed. If Cooper didn't buy one of these houses himself, he had no doubt they would be sold off to the first property developer who came along.

He could afford the house now – or at least, he could afford the monthly mortgage repayments. What he hadn't decided was whether he wanted to stay in Edendale. On the one hand, it was a great place to live and work. But did he really want to continue living in Welbeck Street, with all the memories and living in these walls? It was a question he kept asking himself. And he still didn't know the answer.

Cooper took a surreptitious glance at his watch as Guy Thomson continued his sales pitch. He had plans for this evening. And tomorrow was Tuesday, the start of a new working week after his rest day.

He wondered what would be waiting for him in his office at Edendale CID. Whatever it was, it would involve blood. There would always be blood. It was one of the facts of his life.

Chapter Three

THE NOISE WAS Mac Kelsey's first warning. It was like the scrape of claws against metal, a screech echoing inside his cab, loud enough to set his teeth on edge.

Kelsey could see the road was already too narrow. The undergrowth on the banking reached out onto the road and made it seem even tighter, branches scratching their way along the curtain sides of his DAF, leaves slapping his windscreen, the thump of what sounded like a stone but was probably just a conker from one of the chestnut trees.

It wasn't the first time Mac Kelsey had been lost when he was delivering for Windmill Feed Solutions. Even with a satnav, he often seemed to find himself straying off the route into some unmarked back road. In fact, today it was *because* of the blasted satnav.

That last turning had been wrong, he was sure of it. He'd known it as soon he squeezed the truck into a narrow gap between two dry-stone walls. In parts this lane was barely wider than single track. He hadn't met any cars coming the other way yet – but if he did, they'd have to back up to a gateway to let him pass.

So Mac wasn't happy. He was running late with a delivery already and he had no idea where this road would bring him out. He jabbed at the screen angrily for an alternative route. The smug voice told him: 'Perform a u-turn as soon as possible'. He gazed at the walls closing in on either side of the cab. Some chance of a u-turn. This was the last time he was going to follow instructions without question. Definitely the last time he was going to get lost in the Peak District.

He could only hope that when he reached his destination, there'd be plenty of room to turn the truck. If he ever did reach his destination. But these little hill farms were notorious for their difficult access. They were built on steep slopes and had narrow entrances, usually on a blind bend. They were designed for use by horse-drawn carts. The twenty-first century hadn't reached some of these places yet.

Kelsey checked his delivery docket. Bankside Farm. He'd delivered to places called Bankside Farm before. The name told you everything you needed to know about them.

He stamped his foot on the hydraulic brake. Where had all these sheep come from? There was no sign of a farmer, or shepherd, or whoever was supposed to look after these things. And there were hundreds of them, milling about aimlessly, not going anywhere in particular, just standing there blocking the road from wall to wall, bleating their silly heads off. Mac revved the engine, hoping the sudden noise would scare them off.

'Roast lamb for dinner tonight, then?' he yelled through the windscreen.

But the sheep just rolled their eyes and gaped at him. They didn't care. He could see they couldn't give a damn. He'd heard that sheep had a suicidal instinct, and this lot were practising to be roadkill. If he ran over a few of them, the others would probably just stand and wait for their turn to go under the wheels.

'Blasted woolly buggers! Get out of the way!'

The light seemed to have gone from the valley suddenly. Kelsey leaned forward on his steering wheel and looked up at the sky. A mass of dark cloud was surging in from the west. The few patches of blue he'd been looking at previously were rapidly disappearing.

'Damnation,' he cursed under his breath. 'Hell *and* damnation.'

A mate of his who knew this area had once told him the weather was so unpredictable in the Peak District that you could get all four seasons in one day. Kelsey had thought he was exaggerating. But now, from sweating in his cab half an hour ago, he found himself shivering and squinting into the sky for the first drops of rain. A gust of wind rattled the tarpaulin sides of his truck. It was like being trapped in a tunnel, a live specimen for nature to experiment on.

He glanced at the satnav again. This section of the route wasn't at all clear. In fact, the screen seemed to be showing that he was on a non-existent road a few hundred yards to the north. The blasted satellite must be out of alignment or something. Either that, or the earth had shifted suddenly under his wheels and he'd driven into a parallel universe. In another minute he might emerge from a bank of supernatural mist into an impossible world, like an unsuspecting tourist in a creepy horror film.

Kelsey had been checking his satnav when he passed the diversion sign. He'd reacted too slowly, though he was sure the arrows had pointed down this side road. He was already a couple of miles along it before he started to think it might be wrong. Too late to reverse his way out.

He winced as he passed into darkness under the first section of a bridge. He wound down the window. But all he could hear was the slow rumble of his own engine, the chug of the diesel exhaust echoing back at him from the arched stone walls. Fumes swirled into the cab, unable to disperse in the confined space. Kelsey coughed as he slid the window shut again.

He was down to first gear now, the transmission grumbling as he edged the truck forward. He cursed as something thumped against the chassis, a tree stump or a loose rock falling from the banking.

His scalp was itching under his baseball cap. He was supposed to wear it all the time when he was working, because it carried the company logo on the front, that stupid windmill. But the caps were cheaply made and they didn't let enough air to his head. Something was giving him an itch all over the back of his neck too, a painful prickling that made him shift uneasily in his seat. Perhaps he was allergic to cattle feed. Or windmills.

Kelsey jumped as the anguished screeching echoed through his cab. It was so loud that it nearly split his ear drums. He looked up, half expecting to see a creature with red eyes and bared fangs staring through his windscreen, a monster leaping out of the mist. But instead he saw that his truck had rolled slowly under the railway tunnel. Though the arch was high enough in the middle, the frame of the truck body was scraping along the edge of the brickwork. He braked to a halt, feeling the bridge already squeezing his front wings like a giant pincer.

'Double damnation.'

So that was it. He was wedged in solid. What should he do next? Well, he ought to call the office and tell them he was stuck.

But that recent incident had got him a dressing down from the manager and the other drivers had been talking the piss out of him about it ever since. His reputation was already at rock bottom and Kelsey knew he was on the brink of losing his job. He couldn't go through that again. Not after the last time.

Eight years ago his whole world had almost shattered. Every time he thought about it, he felt sick with despair, terrified by a glimpse of that black pit he'd fallen into for a while. The guilt had eaten at him so badly – far worse than anything that had happened to him, the police and the courts and the newspapers, and the split with his wife. He could put some of those things behind him. But one thing he could never escape was the guilt.

Something thumped onto his cab roof and scrabbled on the surface. An animal of some kind? Kelsey had done enough driving around remote areas of the countryside to know that there was more wildlife out here than people in towns cared to think about. He'd hit deer, badgers, foxes – and once a wallaby while he was driving over the Roaches into Staffordshire. From time to time, in the dusk, he'd glimpsed what he'd convinced himself was one of those mysterious big cats. A panther or a puma. Something that shouldn't be lurking in the English countryside, but was definitely out there.

Kelsey picked up his phone and gave a deep sigh. There was going be so much fuss. But he couldn't sit under this bridge for ever, like a peak-capped troll. It was already starting to get dark and he was blocking the road. If he didn't act now, he'd be here all night. There was nothing for it but to bite the bullet and take what was coming to him.

But he didn't complete the phone call, didn't manage to call for assistance. Mac Kelsey never locked his cab doors when he was driving. He had never seen the need. But he still turned in surprise when he heard the *clunk* of a handle and saw the passenger door begin to open.

AMANDA HIBBERT WAS late getting home to Shawhead that afternoon. She'd been helping out backstage at the Arts Theatre in New Mills, where the Amateur Operatic and Dramatic Society were holding a casting read-through for *Blood Brothers*. When rehearsals started they would continue three nights a week for six weeks. She was just realising what a commitment she'd signed up to. And she was anticipating what her husband might have to say about it when he found out.

When her headlights picked out the tail of the truck under the bridge, she frowned with irritation. Yet another hold-up. Cloughpit Lane was so narrow that anything could block it. A branch, a rock, a badly parked car. Even, once, a dead sheep that no one wanted to touch. The last thing they needed in this area was people just stopping in the middle of the road.

Amanda pulled up in her car a few yards short of the bridge and sounded her horn. The lorry had no lights on, which was ridiculous. Somebody could be seriously injured if they drove round the corner a bit too fast and went into the back of it. She hit her horn again, more angrily. When the driver appeared, she would give him a piece of her mind.

But there was no sign of a driver. Was he asleep, or what? She could see the name of the company on the rear door, over one of those little forklift trucks mounted on the back. Windmill Feed Solutions. She would be phoning them to make a complaint tomorrow.

She looked at her watch. Ian would already be jumping up and down with impatience wondering where she was. At this rate she wasn't going to get home for a while yet, even though she lived only a few hundred yards past the bridge.

She dialled her husband's number and he answered almost immediately. She could hear the dog barking in the background, its claws rattling on the kitchen floor. And wasn't that their youngest boy, Adam, shouting petulantly from somewhere in the house? Ian had probably lost control by now. She hoped he hadn't lost his temper, either with the children or the dog.

'Where the hell are you?' he snapped.

'Can you believe I'm stuck at the railway bridge?' she said, trying to sound breezy. 'Some idiot is blocking the road with a feed lorry.'

'What, delivering to Higher Fold? Have a word with the bloody Swindells.'

'No, before that,' she said. 'He's just stopped in the road. No lights or anything. I haven't a hope of getting past.'

'I'll come down there and give him a piece of my mind.'

As so often when she talked to her husband, Amanda found her annoyance being replaced by anxiety about what he might do if she didn't stop him. He was so easily provoked that she had to be careful what she said all the time.

'Don't do anything silly, Ian,' she said. 'It's nothing for you to worry about. He must have lost his way, that's all.'

'He'll lose his head if I get hold of him.'

'You just stay there. I'm sure we'll sort it out soon.'

He was silent for a moment. 'No, I'm coming down,' he said.

Amanda ended the call. 'Oh, Lord,' she said.

Quickly, she turned off the engine of the Ka, released her seat belt and climbed out. She hesitated over whether to leave the headlights on. They would drain her battery without the engine running and Ian would be furious with her if that happened. But it was much too dark up there by the bridge.

She had a sudden rush of unease. She'd felt reasonably secure while she was sitting in her vehicle. But now apprehension began to overwhelm her. The night was so dark, the road so quiet, the undergrowth so close as it crowded above her. There were no street lights within half a mile, so this was proper darkness. Without those headlights she would be plunged into intolerable blackness, with no idea who was waiting for her up there at the bridge.

Perhaps she should wait for Ian to come down from the house after all. It would certainly be safer. But she didn't want to give him the satisfaction of seeing her cowering in her car while she depended on him to sort out a problem. And it was something and nothing, really. She could deal with it herself.

Amanda walked up to the lorry and banged on the side. She caught sight of something strange on the ground. Flakes of something green lying around her feet. It was only then that she realised the problem. The roof of the truck was stuck under the bridge. In the glare of the headlights from her car, she could just make out the marks gouged into the arch above her. The flakes were green paint that had been scraped off by the stone.

Cloughpit Lane Bridge had a double arch. It looked as though the cab had passed through the first arch, but the body of the truck had jammed fast behind it. With a sinking heart, Amanda realised that she wasn't going to get past this obstruction any time soon. It was going to need a very large tow truck to release the thing. And if the bridge was damaged, that would create a whole new nightmare for the residents of Shawhead.

She felt her way along the side of the truck, cringing at the feel of the cold, damp stone on her back. She could taste the diesel exhaust fumes that the lorry must have been pumping out until the engine was switched off. She was starting to feel foolhardy now, but decided to press on rather than going back. The cab was just ahead of her, in the open section between the two arches.

Feeling breathless with tension, she thumped on the driver's door. But it was obvious by now that the driver wasn't with his lorry. She tried the handle and was surprised to find that it wasn't locked. Cautiously, Amanda peered into the cab, half expecting someone to jump out at her. But all she saw was an empty driver's seat and a clipboard full of paperwork.

What should she do next? Well, it would help if she knew where the driver was supposed to be delivering to. He'd probably gone on foot to warn them, so the chances were that he was either at Higher Fold Farm with the Swindells, or the Lawsons' place further up. It was odd that he'd left the lorry unlocked, though. Surely he couldn't have been fooled by the quietness of Shawhead into thinking there was no possibility of crime.

She pulled herself up onto the metal step. She could see a sleeping compartment curtained off behind the seats. Anything or anyone could be behind that curtain. Nervously, she reached into the cab. It was a long stretch for her and she was balanced precariously on the step. When she drew her hand back suddenly, she lost her balance and slipped back onto the road, twisting her ankle on the tarmac as she fell.

Amanda Hibbert stared up at the lorry, wondering whether she'd really seen what she thought. When she lifted the clipboard, a thin red trickle of blood had run across the paper like an insect. She could still see it in her imagination, as the blood dripped slowly onto the floor of the cab.

Chapter Four

Tuesday 10 February

IT WASN'T THE sort of surprise you wanted first thing on a Tuesday morning. Or at any time, come to think of it.

Not for the first time, Ben Cooper was driving back from Nottingham when he took the call. It was a long trip, nothing like the distance to West Street from his flat in Edendale, which he could walk in a few minutes if necessary. So he'd set off bright and early. He didn't feel too bright when he first climbed into his new RAV4 Icon to face the traffic. But on the start of his journey he passed a sign telling him it was four miles to Gotham, which always made him smile.

It was a cold, wet February after a cold, wet winter. Christmas had glistened, but not with snow. The New Year had come in with a downpour. Ben Cooper wondered if it was a sign of approaching middle age that he could remember winters when snow lay on the ground for weeks. Kids used to build snowmen and go sledging. They had snowball fights and never went out except in scarves and gloves. Perhaps it was just his imagination. An idealised picture of winter had implanted itself in his mind from all those Christmas cards with scenes of Victorian carol singers. Had it ever been like that really?

He'd been told by a counsellor that it could be one of the symptoms of a post-traumatic condition, the inability to distinguish clearly between real memories and imagined ones. It could make it difficult to recall exactly what happened during the incident that had caused the trauma in the first place.

Of course, that might be a blessing for some people. His idealised memories of Christmas were definitely just age.

Cooper was about to start his week's work after his rest day. But back in Edendale his boss was already at her desk. Detective Superintendent Branagh must have his number on speed dial. Since his promotion to DI, he had barely been able to escape her attention. Hazel Branagh loved to communicate with her junior staff. Perhaps she'd done a course on it at some time. The longer you worked for Derbyshire Constabulary, the more courses you'd done. By the time you completed your thirty years' service, you were trained for everything but no longer wanted for anything.

'You'll have a new team member arriving this week,' said Branagh. 'It seems like a good match. I hope you'll agree.'

Cooper detected a familiar firmness in her tone on the last few words. She was indicating that it was more than a hope. It was an expectation. In fact, there were currently two vacancies in his CID team at E Division. Since his own promotion to inspector rank, there was an opening for a new detective sergeant. And his old-school DC, Gavin Murfin, had finally retired and was off to pastures new as some kind of private enquiry agent.

Cooper reminded himself that it was Murfin's retirement party tonight and he mustn't miss it. Gavin was long past his sell-by date as a serving police officer. He'd never adjusted to the modern approach to policing and could never hope to pass a fitness test. Worse, he was often guilty of that most heinous of twenty-first-century crimes – being 'inappropriate'.

But Cooper had been his supervising officer for some time now, and there was such a thing as loyalty. Besides, he had a sneaking liking for Murfin that was risky to acknowledge too openly.

There had been a presentation to Murfin in the office on his last day. Superintendent Branagh made the presentation herself and even the Divisional Commander had come along for a few minutes. It was the end of an era, after all. Or 'the end of an error', as his youngest DC, Becky Hurst, kept calling it.

Murfin had provoked exasperation and disapproval from the command structure, because he was the type of detective who no longer fitted in with the modern ethos. His chances of promotion had long since disappeared down the plughole, leaving him cynical and embittered in his last few years, with an ingrained disregard for authority and procedure.

But Murfin was viewed with great affection by his colleagues, despite all his foibles and failings. Becky Hurst had done her best to change him and shape him into a modern man. She'd tried, but failed – and she was in no doubt it was Murfin's fault. He was a lost cause, she said. He was an idle, sexist, politically incorrect anachronism who should have been kicked out years ago. But even Hurst wiped away a tear as he walked out of the door for the last time.

'So you're getting a new DS,' Branagh was saying.

'Where from, ma'am? Is it an internal promotion?'

'A transfer from D Division.'

'Derby?' said Cooper.

'I know what you're going to say, Ben. Another city cop, eh?'

Cooper had pulled up at traffic lights on Middleton Boulevard, indicating to turn right into Wollaton Road, which was already solid with cars backing up into the junction. He had the sudden feeling of a weight sinking to the bottom of his stomach. Superintendent Branagh only called him 'Ben' when she was trying to soften him up for something.

'No, I wasn't going to say that . . .'

'Mmm. You're a bit too easy to read sometimes.'

He could hear Branagh smiling. It was a rare enough occasion. In fact, it was really only noticeable on the phone, since her voice changed slightly but her face hardly moved.

And she was right, of course. He couldn't deny that sinking feeling. He was already dreading the task of coaching someone in the very different conditions of policing in E Division. Police officers in Derby referred to their rural colleagues in a variety of disparaging terms. The 'E' was said to stand for 'Easy Street'. Cooper knew that was far from the truth. But who had he been sent and why were they being transferred from the city?

'I was rather hoping . . .' he began.

Branagh was slow to respond, as if she was doing some other task at the same time, perhaps talking to someone else in her office.

'I know, Ben,' she said. 'But sometimes we just have to accept things as they are. We can talk about it when you get in.'

'Yes, ma'am.'

Cooper owed a lot to Superintendent Branagh and she knew it. Obligations tended to eat at him until he felt he'd repaid them in full. Sometimes, he thought, it would better not to feel obligated to anyone. It would make life much simpler.

The lights had changed to green, but the traffic still wasn't moving. The roads around Nottingham city centre were always choked in the morning. For Cooper, the urban rush hour was one of those horrific experiences that he'd happily avoided most of his life by living in a rural area like the Eden Valley. The town of Edendale could be busy, but only at peak tourist times. You could usually rely on being able to get to and from work without sitting for hours in a queue with hundreds of others, impatiently going nowhere.

When he finally got moving towards the A610, his phone signal began to break up. He could hear Branagh speaking, but he couldn't make out the words and wasn't even sure whether she was talking to him any more.

'Ma'am,' he said, 'who is it we're getting? Do we have a name?'

But his superintendent was no longer there. Cooper ended the call and concentrated on driving. There was no point in worrying about it now. Well, was there?

SOMETIMES BLOOD WAS exactly what Detective Sergeant Diane Fry wanted. There were cases that were so difficult to deal with that her personal feelings welled up in outrage.

Fry had already reached her desk before Ben Cooper made it across the border into Derbyshire. She didn't have as far to travel. Fry was a city girl and she was back in the city now, though it was one she wasn't familiar with. Nottingham. Robin Hood and lace making. And a terrible reputation for gun crime. But so far it was looking better than she expected.

She was working for Major Crime at the East Midlands Special Operations Unit, based at EMSOU's Northern Command at St Ann's police station in Nottingham. The remit for Northern Command covered the whole of Nottinghamshire and Derbyshire. But it was events in the neighbouring city of Derby that had caused ripples throughout the region.

Fry's head was full of the details from the intensive briefings she'd sat through during the past week. Some of the specifics she would prefer to forget, if she had the choice. The unrelenting descriptions of multiple offences described in victim statements. The sheer number of victims and the one characteristic they all had in common – their vulnerability. And of course there were the photographs. The endless parade of desperate eyes. Those eyes were the hardest thing to look at, the most difficult to forget.

The first prosecutions for child sexual exploitation in Derby had taken place a few years previously. Operation Retriever involved thirteen defendants who had worked together. Over the course of three separate trials, nine of them had been convicted of systematically grooming and sexually abusing vulnerable teenage girls. They were jailed for up to twenty-two years for a total of seventy offences.

Almost all those perpetrators were Asian. They were considered devout Muslims and family-orientated men, but away from their homes they would cruise around the streets of Derby in a BMW, wearing designer clothes and targeting young girls.

After the jailing of two of the sexual predators, a Home Secretary at the time had suggested that some men of Pakistani origin saw white girls as 'easy meat'. A serious case review found agencies had missed opportunities to help the victims.

The details were harrowing. The men would pick out girls at train stations, or walking home from school. The gang would first befriend them, inviting them out for a drive in a flash car, plying them with alcohol and drugs. The grooming process would then intensify. The girls were invited to parties and met more men. Witness statements had described how victims were sometimes driven to secluded areas, where they were sexually abused and raped. But the abuse also took place in houses and hotels across the Midlands, and even the victims' own homes. CCTV images had even captured some of the men driving around Derby, stopping girls on the street.

It was only a chance arrest that halted the Derby gang. Staffordshire police stopped a car in nearby Burton-on-Trent which was carrying three men and two young girls. They were suspected of shoplifting. The girls were taken back to Derby, where they told officers what was going on.

It was the start of a huge undercover operation involving a team of a hundred detectives. Even now it was believed that not all the girls ensnared by the gang had been found.

A later inquiry, Operation Kern, secured the successful prosecution of another eight men, who had operated independently of each other. But this time seven of the men were white. The multi-agency task force had been forced to confront two facts. Many of the sexual predators in Derby weren't Asian, but white middle-aged men. On the other hand, briefings said there was now a specific problem of Muslim men targeting Sikh and Hindu girls.

Proof, if ever they needed it, that there was no way of creating a typical profile of an offender. No simple causes and no easy answers.

Fry considered her role in the multi-agency team that had been set up to identify and bring to justice the remaining offenders. There were men still believed to be grooming vulnerable girls in the region, but they were now operating much more covertly after the high-profile court cases. No blatant activities on the street for CCTV cameras to catch.

She hadn't for a moment considered trying to refuse the job, but she did wonder why she'd been chosen. A reputation for toughness and a lack of emotion had probably followed her from her previous posting in Derbyshire Constabulary's E Division. She could imagine what some of her ex-colleagues might have said about her.

But she wasn't as cold as everyone thought. Occasionally, someone had the rare ability to find that out about her. But only occasionally.

St Ann's was a modern police station, unlike the building she'd worked in at Edendale, with its leaking roof and drafty corners. Fry glanced at the small window, screened by blue louvre blinds, which was all she had in this office. It was hardly worth looking out, of course, since all she would see was a road and a sprawling housing estate, with perhaps a glimpse of the office blocks in the city centre, or the old cinema that was now a cash and carry warehouse.

Fry wondered how far away Ben Cooper had got from her by now, whether he'd reached Derbyshire yet and was back in the hills he loved so much.

She wondered, too, whether he would come back again. She questioned that every time. And she wasn't used to being in doubt.

There was one other issue on her mind. Her sister Angie was due to have a baby soon. Somehow the idea of a baby threatened to change everything for Fry, even though it wasn't hers. It meant there was a future, something to look ahead for that she hadn't planned herself. There were different, unexpected possibilities in the world. Life didn't have to stay the way it was now. And perhaps things could be put behind her so she could concentrate on what came next.

But what did come next? Fry was aware of a swirl of mixed emotions when she thought about the subject. Some of those feelings were negative, bitter reactions that she tried to shy away from but was forced to acknowledge.

Of course, she loved her sister. But Fry was conscious of a small stab of resentment, perhaps even envy, whenever she thought about the baby. Angie hadn't made many good choices in life, not since the day she ran away from their foster home in the Black Country. Why should Angie's future be the one they always talked about on the phone? Why wasn't Diane's future considered? What *was* her future?

Well, one thing was certain. It was up to her to take her life into her own hands and make the best decisions.

Chapter Five

BEFORE HE COULD reach Edendale, Ben Cooper's route was diverted. Instead of descending into the town he could already see lying below him, he found himself turning and heading west towards the A623 and out of the Eden Valley.

His duty DC, Carol Villiers, had been called to a scene outside New Mills, a town way over in the north-west of the county. She'd been there since the early hours of the morning, attending an incident that had gradually been escalated and was causing local complications.

Cooper had known Villiers for years. They'd grown up in the same area and had gone to school together. She'd been through an entire career and marriage since then, spending nine years with the RAF Police, and gaining and losing a husband, before she came back home and was recruited into Derbyshire Constabulary. He'd come to rely on Villiers a lot, valuing her experience and maturity to balance the young DCs in his team. The trouble was, he had something to tell her now that she wouldn't want to hear.

'Does it look bad, Carol?' he said.

'There's an awful lot of blood. A lot more than the woman who called it in noticed. She said she thought the lorry driver must have cut himself. If so, it was one hell of a cut.'

'And no sign of the driver?'

'Not a whisper. Our problem is that the lorry is jammed under this bridge and it's completely blocking the road. I'm talking about a tractor unit with forty-foot trailer. Nobody's getting past this thing, in or out. It might just be an accident, but we don't want to call out a recovery vehicle to shift the lorry if it might turn out to be a crime scene. No one here wants to take that responsibility, so . . .'

'So that's my job,' said Cooper.

'You're the DI.'

'Don't I know it. I'm on my way.'

'How long will you be?' asked Villiers.

'Twenty minutes maybe. Why?'

'It's just that we're dealing with a bunch of irate residents here.'

'What's the problem?'

'Like I said, no one is getting past. Well, you'll have to see it for yourself, Ben. Just don't take too long getting here, please.'

'I'll do my best.' Cooper paused. 'But what does your instinct say, Carol?'

He could hear Villiers breathing, the distant murmur of voices in the background, the cackle of a rook overhead. He pictured her standing on a road somewhere in the middle of nowhere, members of the public and uniformed officers alike looking to her for a quick judgement. It was a position that came with additional responsibility. Villiers could do that. He'd always had confidence that she could.

'I wouldn't move this lorry,' she said at last. 'And, Ben – I think time might be running out for the driver too.'

'Thanks, Carol.'

Cooper put his foot on the accelerator and climbed out of the Eden Valley. As always when he crossed Tideswell Moor, the landscape opened up and the sky became bigger than anything he was used to in the valley. Today clouds streamed in from the western horizon, tinted in shades of blue and grey like a vast watercolour painting. He could see all the way ahead, over the limestone quarries in Doveholes Dale to the slopes of Black Edge and Combs Moss.

He hit the A623 near Peak Forest and swung onto the main A6 at Higher Hallsteads. New Mills was about eight miles north from here, past Chapel-en-le-Frith and Chinley. At Whaley Bridge the road overlooked a stretch of the Peak Forest Canal where it diverged into basins at Bugsworth and Whaley.

As he crossed over Charley Lane, he could see over Chinley towards the distinctive shapes of Chinley Churn and Mount Famine. One was cut into ridges by the quarrying on Cracken Edge, the other a prominent flat-topped mound at the end of South Head.

But by the time he reached Furness Vale, the character of the area had changed and was looking much more built-up. Of course, New Mills was close to the borders of Cheshire and Greater Manchester, and that made a big difference. This part of the county was rapidly becoming a commuter belt for workers in the urban sprawl beyond the Pennines. People here knew very little about Derby or Chesterfield. They looked to Manchester for their allegiances. They did their shopping at Trafford Park rather than at Westfield or Meadowhall. They followed United, instead of County or Wednesday.

Only a few fields in this area actually fell within the Peak District national park. When the boundaries were drawn in the

1950s, planners made a dramatic sweep around New Mills and the neighbouring towns of Whaley Bridge, Hayfield and Chapel-en-le-Frith. They were too built-up and too industrial to be subject to the stricter planning regulations. That deliberate gash on the maps ran all the way south past Buxton and the quarries along the A616.

The resulting outline of the national park resembled a leaping salmon, its head pointing into Yorkshire, its tail sweeping across the Staffordshire moorlands as it surged northwards. New Mills lay just off the tip of the salmon's tail, a semi-urban fragment that might have broken away from the dark mass of Greater Manchester and drifted into the Peak District to escape.

CLOUGHPIT LANE LED off away from the A6 towards the foothills around the vast, dark plateau of Kinder Scout. Cooper drew his car as far into the side as he could when he saw the collection of vehicles up ahead. And there was the railway bridge Carol Villiers had mentioned. The rear end of an HGV protruded from the arch like an animal that had failed to make it all the way into its burrow and had died there.

There was barely enough room for a normal-sized person to squeeze through the gap between the lorry and the stone wall of the bridge. Cooper had to get up onto the banking and push his way through the branches of elder saplings and clumps of bracken to reach the cab, supporting himself with one hand against the side of the truck. He noticed that some of the straps holding down the curtain sides were unfastened along one section, creating just enough space for someone to crawl inside. It might just be carelessness by the driver.

When Cooper reached the cab, he found himself staring at a giant cartoon windmill painted in bright green. It was obviously the company's logo. Windmill Feed Solutions. He didn't recognise the name. Back at Bridge End Farm, his brother Matt used a company based in the Eden Valley for his animal feed deliveries.

The lorry was a typical cab-over-engine design, with a driver's position above the front axle and access to the cab via a couple of steps. That flat-nosed look had become almost universal since HGV lengths were strictly regulated. Its extra turning ability made it better suited to delivery conditions in areas like this with narrow, winding roads. The only problem was getting access to the engine, which required the whole cab being tilted forward.

He knew Carol Villiers was already at the scene and he could see Luke Irvine had just arrived too. Irvine followed him along the side of the truck.

Cooper wondered how he was going break the bad news to Villiers. She would be disappointed, though not perhaps as much as he was himself. He'd been through the same experience a few years ago, when someone else got the promotion he'd been hoping for – had been depending on too much, in fact. But things came right in the end, didn't they?

It wasn't too late for Villiers, though her previous career in the RAF Police meant she was already of an age when promotion came, if it was ever going to. For some it never did, of course. But it was hard to imagine Carol Villiers becoming another Gavin Murfin. It just didn't add up.

Villiers looked remarkably alert considering how long she'd already been here. She never seemed to mind early mornings. Even when she wasn't on an early shift she was usually out for a run at the crack of dawn. Perhaps it was a leftover habit from the military routine she'd lived with for eight years. It seemed to suit her anyway. She still had that fit, sporty look that he'd always associated her with. Villiers was brisk and businesslike at work, but able to relax outside the job. He liked that ability.

'The missing driver's name is Malcolm Kelsey,' said Villiers, flipping open her notebook. 'And the lorry is a DAF twenty-six-ton curtainsider with a tail-mounted forklift,'

Cooper was immediately impressed. 'That's good, Carol.'

'I phoned the company,' she admitted.

'Windmill Feed Solutions.'

'That's them. The body of the truck seems to be about a quarter full with bags of animal feed stacked on pallets. There are quite a few empty pallets.'

'He'd already done most of his deliveries for the day,' said Cooper.

'Looks like it. We don't know exactly when the lorry got stuck under the bridge. It wasn't reported until six o'clock in the evening, when a local resident couldn't get past it on her way home.'

'That's late to be doing deliveries. Not impossible, I suppose, if it was an emergency. But we'll need to interview everyone who uses the road regularly, and try to pin down a time.'

Cooper stood back and looked at the jammed lorry. The curtain-sided body was about forty feet long and green overall, apart from the company's name and windmill logo picked out in gold. The driving position was high above the engine and there looked to be a sleeping compartment for overnight journeys.

'He hadn't driven long distance, had he?' said Cooper.

'No, the company is based near Stockport. He picked up the truck from their depot early yesterday morning. I checked his dockets. All his addresses for today are within a thirty-mile radius.'

'All local deliveries, then.'

'Yes. But apparently, this wasn't his usual patch,' said Villiers. 'He didn't normally deliver here. Not in Derbyshire at all, in fact. He was a complete stranger to the area.'

'Do we have a description of Mr Kelsey?'

'Better than that. I got them to send a photo to my phone.'

The image on Villiers' phone showed two men in brown fleeces and matching baseball caps standing in front of a pair of lorries similar to the one jammed under the bridge. One of them might have been the identical lorry, but the registration numbers were obscured.

'He's the one on the right,' said Villiers.

She increased the size of the picture to show his face. Mac Kelsey was looking directly at the camera with dark, rather brooding eyes. A curl of black hair showed under his cap and his mouth fell naturally into a confident smile. He was heavy shouldered, with the first signs of middle age in the softening contours of his face. He was aged in his late thirties, forty at the most.

'Send it to the rest of the team,' Cooper said, 'so we can use it for identification.'

'No problem.'

Cooper turned his attention to the bridge. A warning sign attached to the stonework at its apex gave its height as eleven feet three inches. On top of the cab was a roof air deflector, which seemed to rear like an animal's crest. It looked high, but presumably wasn't as high as the body of the truck, since it had made it through the first arch of the bridge.

And that was the most unusual aspect. There were two arches, almost as if there were two separate bridges joined together. It wasn't obvious when he'd entered, but Cooper had been surprised to find himself standing in daylight in the middle.

'Have you ever seen a bridge like this before, Carol?' he asked.

'No, not me. It's strange the way there's a gap in the middle, where the cab is.'

'Yes, two separate arches. Between them it's open to the sky. The driver himself wasn't under the bridge when the truck jammed. He was probably concentrating on the next arch he was about to go under, when—'

'Bang,' said Villiers.

'Well, something like that.'

'Would it have made a difference?'

'From his position, the driver would have been in daylight, but looking into the darkness of the bridge.'

Cooper pulled on a pair of latex gloves before opening the door of the cab, which was unlocked. He could see the keys still in the ignition.

'We should also ask if anyone heard bleeping noises,' he said.

'Bleeping?'

'There's a reverse bleeper on the truck. If anyone heard it, that would indicate whether the driver tried to reverse out from under the bridge, or just stayed where he was when he got stuck.'

'I see.'

Cooper clambered onto the first step and pulled himself up to the level of the passenger seat, careful to avoid actually stepping into the cab. He could see the blood drying on the floor. It had run backwards in runnels on the rubber matting and pooled behind the seats. Some of it had splattered onto the clipboard lying on the passenger seat and he could see a clear thumb print in the blood on a docket. A bottle of Buxton spring water had fallen onto the floor, but lay just clear of the blood.

'When the Traffic officers arrived at the scene, they reported that there had been some kind of altercation with the driver,' said Villiers, peering up at him from road level.

'That's an understatement, Carol, judging by the amount of blood. But who would be that angry with him?'

'Everyone, if the residents I've met are anything to go by.'

With a stretch, Cooper reached over to the ignition and turned the key. The engine started instantly. The radio burst into life too: 102 Capital FM. The driver had been listening to a commercial music station based in Stockport. Drivetime traffic news was always useful when you were on the road all day.

Cooper shut off the engine and climbed back down. He felt his shoes sticking to the road surface. When he looked down, he found squashed sheep droppings. Most of them had been trampled into the tarmac by all the boots passing over them, police officers and members of the public alike. But some of them were still intact – small black pellets that glittered in the drizzle.

AMANDA HIBBERT WAS trying to work. She had a new client to develop a website for and all the graphic design concepts to work on from scratch. She was trying to get an idea of the company she was working with. Their ethos had to be reflected in the designs she came up with. Did they want wild and contemporary, with bright colours and fun graphics? Or were they classic and stylish, preferring navy blue and black? Discovering a client's needs was the crucial start to a fruitful long-term relationship.

But she was finding she could hardly concentrate. For once she wasn't worrying about one of the children, or even about Ian.

Lord knew, there were enough drawbacks to working from home. They all expected her to be at their beck and call, just because she was there.

No, today she was worrying about what was going on down at the bridge. She felt quite stupid now that she hadn't realised how serious the situation was right away. When she found there was no driver in the cab of the trapped lorry, she'd made the emergency call sound less urgent than it should have been, whingeing on about not being able to get her car past an obstruction in the road. The first police officers who arrived had treated her as if she was a batty old woman.

'Didn't you notice the blood, luv?' one of them had said. And the other had laughed. She felt like making a complaint about it, but she was too embarrassed.

And of course she *had* noticed the blood. Amanda shuddered now as she remembered it, the thin trickle spilling off the delivery docket she'd picked up. But for some reason she'd tried to pretend it wasn't there, or it didn't mean anything, or it wasn't blood at all. She'd just imagined it, and the police would ridicule her if she mentioned it.

But they'd ridiculed her anyway. Well, that was the way it went in her life. She was wrong whatever she did.

When Ian arrived at the bridge last night, he'd bombarded her with questions. He'd been really angry, though she had no idea what about. Probably nothing. More likely, it was just the whisky she could smell on his breath. There was no mistaking what he'd been doing while she was out at the theatre in New Mills. The drinking didn't do his temper any good. She hardly dared to suggest to him that drinking on your own was a sign you had a problem.

But he'd made it sound as though it was all her fault, as he usually did. If she didn't get this proposal right for the new client, that would be her fault too.

Sighing with exasperation, Amanda got up from the computer, where she'd left a piece of artwork half finished on the screen.

Her little home office looked out onto the back garden. Beyond that was the small turnout paddock and the stable block they'd built. Not that she got much chance to ride any more. Zoe spent most time with the horse when she was home.

With an expanse of hills beyond, the view from the office was usually quite peaceful. She could watch the trees swaying in the wind and the clouds moving across the sky, and the birds clustering round the feeder she stocked up every morning. It looked a bit bleak at this time of year. It was too cold and there was too much damp in the air. The ground was muddy and the branches were bare, still waiting for the first signs of spring. But she didn't mind that. It made her feel momentarily at peace, being unable to see anyone or hear any intrusive voices.

But today it was wrong. Her window was facing in the wrong direction.

Amanda left her shoes on the floor of the office and walked through the hallway into the kitchen. A large asparagus and goats' cheese flan stood ready to go in the roasting oven of the Aga for tonight's supper. The Golden Retriever had been fed and was sleeping in his basket. She walked to the sink and peered out into the road. She could barely see past the end of Top Barn from here.

A movement caught her eye and she ducked back quickly as she saw Donna Schofield pass a first-floor window. Shouldn't it be one of her days teaching? Perhaps she'd taken a day off, told them she couldn't get out because of the blocked road.

But that was the answer, of course. Amanda went back through the hall and crept quietly upstairs. Ian was in the sitting room, still holding a long phone conversation with a disgruntled customer he was supposed to be working with today. It had been going on for some time now and Ian's voice was beginning to rise with impatience. Soon he would be shouting. When he lost it completely and started swearing, he would lose another account for his company. That would be her fault too.

But at least it meant he couldn't hear her as she padded up the stairs. Zoe's bedroom was the only one that faced the right way. She would never know her mother had been in her room. In fact, she wouldn't have left anything she didn't want her parents to see when she went off to university, and she would assume that her mother would want to keep it clean. So Amanda wasn't really intruding.

Now, if she stood on tiptoe, she could see down Cloughpit Lane to the bridge. The police were still there and the lorry was still stuck under the bridge. She could see men in uniform searching in the undergrowth along the edge of the road and clambering over the walls. No doubt they were still trying to find some trace of the missing driver.

How long was all this going to continue? Ian had threatened to go down and instruct them to move the lorry if the road wasn't clear by the afternoon. Well, he knew how that would end – with him losing his temper again. She almost hoped he would do it, then perhaps he would get arrested and spend a night in the cells. It would teach him a lesson.

Amanda watched for a few minutes, saw a tall, dark-haired man arrive – another detective, she presumed, since he was in plain clothes. The others seemed to cluster round him as he emerged from the bridge. A more senior police officer? Perhaps now something would get done.

She bit her lip sharply at the thought. That also meant they would find out what had happened to the driver of the lorry, why there were blood stains in his cab. And as sure as night followed day, they would work out who had attacked him.

Her heart stopped for a moment when she looked back at the bridge again. A female detective was pointing this way and the tall man had turned to look. She had the impression that he was looking right at her and reading her thoughts. There were some things in her mind that she didn't want anyone to know about.

Chapter Six

'APPARENTLY, THE RATHER random collection of buildings you can see up the road there is a place called Shawhead,' Carol Villiers was saying as Ben Cooper peeled off his gloves. 'There isn't very much to it. Just a couple of farms and a few houses.'

'Shawhead,' said Cooper. 'Just one road in and one road out.'

'You know it?'

He wasn't sure whether he'd actually been here before or he'd just heard someone use that phrase about Shawhead. It certainly looked familiar, but there were dozens of similar hamlets scattered around the Peak District in forgotten corners, so far off the beaten track that they barely appeared on the map.

And to reach Shawhead you had to pass under this bridge. An arched railway bridge with just over eleven feet of headroom. You'd have to judge it precisely to the inch – and not just the height, but the width of the truck. The arch was eleven feet only at its apex. At the sides it was a good deal less. Well, that was the nature of an arch.

'Network Rail are sending a team of engineers,' said Villiers. 'They have to check the safety of the structure after a bridge bash.'

'There have already been half a dozen trains over the bridge since I've been here,' said Irvine. 'Most of them didn't even slow down.'

There was a sign on the bridge with instructions what do in the case of a collision. A number to call and the number of the bridge to identify it.

'Who called it in to Network Rail?' asked Cooper.

'One of the FOAs.'

The first officers to arrive. Two yellow jackets from a Traffic unit. Understandably, a call handler in the control room had allocated it as a road policing issue.

'And Kelsey, the driver?' asked Cooper.

'Malcolm Kelsey, known as "Mac". We've got all his details from his employers, including a mobile phone number. We've tried calling the number several times, but it's just going to voicemail.'

'Do we think he's got his phone with him?'

'All we know is that it's not in the cab and it's not lying around near the scene.'

'Any witnesses?'

'The lady who called it in – a Mrs Hibbert, who lives nearby at Shawhead Cottages. Oh, and there's another gentleman around somewhere. A farmer. He's being a bit, well . . .'

'Awkward?' said Cooper.

'That's putting it mildly.'

'I'll speak to him.'

'You'll soon get the chance,' said Villiers quietly, swivelling her eyes to the side of the road.

Cooper could hear him before he saw. He was breathing heavily and grunting with effort as he clambered over a gate. He was red-faced and overweight, his face swollen under his tweed cap like a cartoon image of a farmer. He wore a padded jacket over a checked shirt and carried a stout stick as if he was out herding a flock of sheep on the mountainside. His boots crushed the stems of nettles as he covered the last few yards towards them, and Cooper could hear him clearing his throat ready to launch into a verbal assault.

'Well, this is a proper mess,' said the farmer, emerging from the undergrowth near the front wing of the lorry as Cooper scrambled back down the banking and turned to face him.

'Ah. Mr . . . ?'

'Swindells. Higher Fold Farm. Our place is just along the road a bit. I've told everyone that information so far, but I don't suppose anyone has bothered to write it down.'

'Are these your fields, sir?'

'Yes, along this side of the road, but only as far as the railway. Are you in charge?'

'For now, sir.'

'You're not in uniform. Are you a proper policeman?'

Cooper showed his ID. 'Detective Inspector Cooper, Edendale CID.'

Swindells looked at the ID sourly and pulled down his cap. 'Well, anyway. You take your time, you lot.'

'We have to do things properly, Mr Swindells. There's a protocol.'

The farmer snorted. 'Protocol. Why should protocol stop honest people from going about their business?'

'What business have you got that's so urgent?'

'I've got to get these fields ploughed before the weather changes.'

'Not at this time of year you don't,' said Cooper. 'Not if you call yourself a proper farmer.'

Swindells glowered at him, then turned and glared at Villiers, as if suspecting she might be laughing. Cooper thought she probably was, but she was good at hiding it. It wasn't appropriate for a police officer to let members of the public know you found them hilarious.

'Do you have any idea why the lorry was in this area?'

'It belongs to the feed company, doesn't it?' said Swindells. 'I recognise the windmill. They're based near Stockport somewhere.'

'According to the delivery docket in his cab, the driver was heading for Bankside Farm,' said Cooper.

Swindells shook his head and sucked at his teeth. 'That's the Elliotts' place,' he said with a vague gesture at the surrounding fields. 'Over yonder. It's not even on this road.'

'I see.'

'He was in the wrong place then,' said Swindells.

'I think that's a safe assumption.'

'He ought to have known the bridge was too low in any case,' pointed out Swindells.

Cooper nodded. 'Yes, he ought.'

Gingerly, Cooper squeezed his way back along the side of the truck until he emerged on the far side of the bridge and walked back to where his car was parked. Then he turned and stood in the middle of the road, trying to put himself in the position of the lorry driver as he came round this bend. In a vehicle that size, and on a lane this tight, he would probably be looking out of his side window and watching his wing mirrors to check for clearance on either side.

But when Cooper did look at the bridge, he realised something was wrong. From this direction the height warning was missing. There ought to be a triangular sign like the one on the east side, giving the exact height of the arch. When he came closer to the bridge, he could even make out the marks on the stonework where it had been attached. So where had it gone?

For a few minutes Cooper hunted around on the verge on either side of the road until he found the sign thrown into a patch of brambles. Eleven feet three inches. If Mac Kelsey had seen that, he would never have come this far. But clearly, he had stood no chance of seeing it.

COOPER NOTICED A young Asian man approaching the outer cordon. He was stopped by the uniformed officer on duty and showed some identification. He was allowed through the tape.

'Who is that?' asked Cooper.

Villiers threw a casual glance at the newcomer. 'Ah. I heard he might want to show his face at the scene and introduce himself.'

'Who?'

'That's our new DS.'

Cooper nodded slowly. No more need to worry about how he was going to break the news to Carol Villiers then.

The newcomer came forward, holding out his hand. He was a few inches shorter than Cooper, with brown eyes and an intense gaze.

'Detective Sergeant Devdan Sharma. Were you expecting me?'

'In a way,' said Cooper.

Sharma nodded unsmilingly, as if it was nothing he hadn't heard before many times. 'I'm sorry. I expected to be able to introduce myself properly, in your office at West Street. But it seems we're at work already.'

'That's all right. We'll catch up later,' said Cooper.

'I'm sorry if my arrival has been sprung on you,' he said. 'It isn't the way I would have wanted it to happen.'

'It's not a problem,' said Cooper.

But Sharma just gazed at him, his dark brown eyes unblinking. 'I believe it is, though. Somehow it causes a difficulty for you.'

Cooper felt flustered by his gaze, as if he'd just been accused of something politically incorrect. The feeling made him fall back on phrases that seemed to come straight from a training manual and sounded artificial even as he spoke them. 'It's not a problem with you, DS Sharma. I'm sure you're an excellent officer and I'm looking forward to working with you. You're very welcome to the team.'

'Something else, then.'

Cooper couldn't help but look away, throwing a glance towards Carol Villiers, who had started talking to one of the uniformed officers. He was conscious of Sharma following his gaze.

'Ah. I see,' he said.

'I can't imagine that you do.'

But Sharma only smiled. 'It helps to know the situation from the start. Now what would you like me to do?'

Cooper turned to find the rest of the team watching him.

'Well, first of all, what's inside the lorry?' he said. 'What was Mac Kelsey carrying?'

Villiers looked at Irvine now.

'Animal feed, presumably,' she said.

'Have you checked?'

She shook her head. 'Not yet.'

'Have you noticed the open section of the curtain side? Somebody could have got in or out of the trailer.'

'I didn't see that,' said Villiers.

'Better get on with it, then. It's a big lorry. But luckily DS Sharma is here to assist us.'

'We need to get a few more bodies together for a proper search, don't we?'

'There's too much ground to cover in a short space of time. We have to find some way of focusing on a narrower search area,' said Cooper.

'Someone crashed their way through the undergrowth here,' called Irvine. 'There's a drop of blood, I think.'

'Mark it.'

The crime scene examiners would follow on behind when the scene was sealed off. Cooper tried not to look at the crime scene team these days, at least not from a distance. Closer to, it was obvious who each of them was. The Crime Scene Manager, Wayne Abbott, couldn't be mistaken for anyone else, even in his scene suit, hood and mask. But from a distance those baggy white suits and face coverings made them all look the same. They could be anybody. That was what bothered Cooper. Each figure could be the person he most wanted to see, but knew he never could.

'So where do you think the driver went?' asked Irvine.

'Where *could* he have gone?' said Villiers. 'There isn't exactly a lot of choice, is there?'

'I've got a list of the properties in Shawhead,' said Villiers. 'It's from the electoral register, but it should be pretty well up to date. There are only five addresses. Ten adults in all. Here, I've made a couple of extra copies.'

Cooper took a copy of the list. 'I don't know what I'd do without you, Carol,' he said.

Villiers looked at him with sudden directness. 'I think you'd manage, Ben. You'd manage perfectly well.'

'I hope I won't have to then,' said Cooper, trying to lighten the tone.

But Villiers bustled away. She was always busy, constantly with some other job to organise, something else to check on. He really did appreciate her efficiency. Carol had come into the job from a military background and yet she'd slotted right in, picked up the reins when things fell apart, supported him when he'd been out of action himself. What price could you put on that ability? Why did senior officers above him not appreciate it more?

Cooper stood by the front of the lorry and looked around. Whatever had happened to Mac Kelsey in his cab, the first thought in his mind would surely have been to seek help. And from the driver's seat up there, Kelsey would have focused on just one thing – the cluster of houses he could see up ahead. The signs of civilisation, a place to find help. He would have gone to Shawhead.

THREE MILES AWAY, in the town of New Mills, Scott Brooks was spending the last day of his life. Everything he saw and heard meant something important to Scott, because he knew it would be his last day. He'd made that decision himself.

Scott had first come to New Mills when he caught a folk train on a Saturday morning one summer. He'd joined the crowds of folk music fans in the packed carriages when the train left Piccadilly Station in Manchester on one of its monthly runs. As he listened to the live band entertaining passengers, he'd gazed out of the window at each stop on the way to the Derbyshire town for the carnival, noticing the change in the landscape with each new station.

He couldn't remember who the musicians were on that trip. Crimson Moon, the Galley Canters, Treebeard? It didn't matter. There had been other folk trains since. But he remembered that they'd performed a set at the Pride of the Peaks in town before the return journey to Manchester. And it was in that pub that he'd first met Ashley and found out where she worked.

In a sudden flood of memory, Scott was overwhelmed by the recollection of a sweet smell, a sugary fog through which he still seemed to see Ashley. It made him stumble to a halt, almost staggering to his knees on the pavement at the saccharine taste on his tongue.

But he'd already made his preparations for the day and had everything he needed in a plastic carrier bag. It wasn't heavy.

On Union Road he passed the headquarters of the Plain English Campaign, housed in a brick building with a stone façade. There was probably something symbolic about that, but he couldn't think what it was today. He approved of their attempts to improve the standards of English. He'd tried to do his bit as a teacher, when he still had a job. He hoped the Plain English Campaign would survive and weren't a victim of cuts.

Scott shifted his carrier bag from one hand to another, glancing around him at the faces of people passing, in case he saw anyone he knew. The last thing he wanted to do was stop and chat to some casual acquaintance today, making meaningless small talk for valuable minutes before he could make an excuse to escape. He had too many memories to get through and not enough time. His last few hours were on a schedule, the way things should be if they were done properly.

He walked up to the top of Union Road and past the Pride of the Peaks. He'd already been inside the pub and said his silent goodbyes.

There were a lot of pubs and takeaways in the town. People in New Mills ate plenty and drank even more. At night the place was full of knuckle-dragging muppets who thought they were hard men with their fake Manchester twang. They'd never been anywhere near Manchester and didn't know what the city was like. They still thought you had to pay a toll to leave New Mills. Yet some of their expressions were stolen directly from Manchester dialect. They talked about 'scran' and 'having a buzz', about going to someone's 'gaff' and being 'safe'. Everything was 'dead good' unless it was 'sound'.

He heard the familiar sound of children in a group. At lunch-time school kids gathered below Torr Top car park with their fish and chips. All the teenagers spoke with that flat Manchester accent too, as if they'd been brought up on an inner city housing estate, instead of in a small Derbyshire mill town.

But the main trouble with the town was that everybody knew your business. The rumour mill got going, the Chinese whispers started. The crowds got whipped up and were ready for a lynching, or a burning at the stake.

The pubs in New Mills mostly stocked Robinsons, the beer made up the road in Stockport. Saturday night was for fighting in some of those pubs. Any customers who looked too respectable, or had too short a haircut, would be asked if they were police officers. Sometimes they were, of course.

There were parts of the town he hadn't been to for a long time. He hadn't been up Dye House Lane since the Pineapple closed. He'd tried another pub in that area, but it had turned out to be karaoke night. The place was full of depressed alcoholics singing 'All by Myself'. Scott couldn't stand that.

Tomorrow people would probably be saying that he was depressed himself. But it wasn't true. He didn't feel miserable or desperate, not any more. He'd made his plans and now he felt calm. That was the benefit of being properly organised. You knew exactly what was going to happen and when. You had nothing left to worry about. A lot of people couldn't grasp that. Their lives were a chaotic mess. They certainly wouldn't understand what he was about to do next.

At the corner he turned into Market Street. The Simply Indian had been a pub too, years ago. There had been a raid on it once, heaps of cash stolen from the fruit machines. When the Millennium Walkway was opened in the Torrs, they found money scattered all the way down the slope. The thieves had tried to hide it somewhere safe, no doubt planning to return for their haul. But they'd never made it. What happened to them? Did they go to prison for something else in the meantime? Or was it just bad planning?

The town continued to rise up Market Street to the town hall and an old Carnegie library on a steep street to the side of it. A few houses in New Mills were built on such steeply sloping ground that they rose to two storeys on one side but three or four storeys high on the other. Even today you might find one family living in the upper half while another occupied the 'underliving'. There were some houses on Meal Street just like that.

The old police station opposite the library had the one word 'Constabulary' still picked out in the stonework over the front door. A brown plaque on the wall commemorated the fact that six ramblers had been held here for trial after the mass trespass on Kinder Scout in April 1932, the protest that had brought about the national park.

Below him was the football ground at Church Lane, the home of New Mills Football Club. They were doing well in the Northern

Premier League Division One North, which wasn't bad in a town of ten thousand people. Scott had seen the Millers play Accrington Stanley once in a pre-season friendly. He was glad of that memory.

Scott turned uphill and entered High Lea Park, passing the human sundial near High Lea House and on into the community orchard. There were plans to organise group fruit-picking sessions in the orchard one day, when the fruit crops were ready. He wouldn't see it, though – which was a pity. New Mills was being transformed, but not quickly enough for him.

High Lea Park was one place that changed in character through the year. In June it was the venue for the One World Festival, when it was full of drummers in multicoloured costumes and stalls manned by Quakers and members of the Green Party. At other times it was where half the population of New Mills were conceived. Many local girls seemed to think it would be fun to lose their virginity in a bush.

And that was part of the trouble. The locals seemed stuck in a continuous cycle of small town syndrome. The same families, the same bullshit, a different decade. Despite recent incomers on the new housing developments, it remained at heart an insular town, where everyone was related, or knew one another. It was a dangerous place to be a stranger. Scott hadn't felt safe since he lost Ashley.

But now he was experiencing negative thoughts and that wasn't in the plan. Scott made the descent towards the central railway station. The view was extensive from here. At the bottom end he could see the huge Swizzels Matlow confectionery factory, one of New Mills' biggest employers. The workers carried the smell of that factory around with them on their clothes all the time, completely unaware of the fact. If he stood too close to a Swizzels worker, the sweet aroma was enough to make him feel queasy.

And there, nearly a hundred feet below the town, he could see the half-empty Torr Vale Mill, sitting in the Torrs gorge. He'd been to a concert at Torr Vale once. It was held on the events floor of the mill during the festival, just after the lantern parade. Mart Rodger's Manchester Jazz. They were pretty good too. People had been coming into New Mills on the train from Manchester for the evening.

But they'd all gone home after the concert was over. Most people did. It was Scott who had moved in the other direction. But that was because of Ashley. She was a New Mills girl. Marrying her and coming to live here had been very much part of his plan.

For a moment Scott Brooks paused on the bridge overlooking the Torrs. He was almost at his final destination.

There were lots of things he would miss. But there were others he'd be glad that he was finally free from. He could think of three straight away. The sense of loss since Ashley was killed – that was one of those things. Another was the alienation he'd felt while living on his own in New Mills. With Ashley gone and his job over, he'd begun to realise how little he belonged, how little anyone here would care if he no longer existed.

And a third? Yes, there was a third thing he would be very glad to be rid of. It was the sickly, overpowering smell of sweets from that blasted factory.

Chapter Seven

HIGHER FOLD FARM was the first property in Shawhead. The walk up Cloughpit Lane from the bridge took Ben Cooper and his team past a cobbled entrance to the farm, with a stream running through a stone culvert and an ancient well set into the wall, with a muddy trickle of water escaping from a trough. A box of free range eggs sat by the gate, as if expecting passers-by to buy them.

From here a track running down into the valley past a row of chestnut trees to another railway bridge. At the bottom a pony and a couple of pygmy goats grazed in a field near a horse box and an abandoned Range Rover.

Beyond Higher Fold lay Shawhead Cottages. They had probably been farmworkers' cottages originally. But, despite the name, they probably weren't cottages any more. It looked as though two or three small homes had been converted into one larger property, internal walls demolished and doors blocked up.

The same thing had happened all over the country. There were far fewer farmworkers than there used to be and most of these small hill farms were purely family-run enterprises now. So the old, unused cottages had become desirable residences for thousands of people seeking the rural idyll.

'Is this it?' asked Irvine.

'There's a bit more,' pointed out Villiers. 'Round the bend.'

'The bend?'

Villiers pointed ahead. 'There, look. Can't you see it?'

Cooper himself had almost missed it. For some inexplicable reason the narrow lane took a sharp turn in the middle of Shawhead. It was a complete right angle, a blind bend that would be impossible to negotiate without slowing almost to a halt. Anything coming round that corner at speed would be a hazard to animals, pedestrians, vehicles and property alike.

The situation wasn't made any better by residents' cars drawn up on the narrow strips in front of their houses and black wheelie bins protruding into the road at awkward angles. It was as if they didn't expect any traffic at all here, except for the occasional horse rider or hiker. A driver lost in this area might well want to turn back and try a different road if he wandered this far.

Cooper understood Luke Irvine's bafflement. Until you got right up to it, the turning was concealed by the corner of a converted barn. There were no road signs, none of the usual chevrons indicating a bend, which appeared on every other road in the Peak District that Cooper had travelled on, even where the bend was much less sharp than this one. Presumably, even the highways authority didn't expect anyone to be driving past this point who didn't already know about the bend. The wall of the property facing him gave the impression of a dead end. You would only take this turning if you knew where you were going. Otherwise it was a leap into the unknown and a risky one at that.

Cooper stood on the bend and looked at the houses, wondering whether any of the residents were inside, looking back at him. He watched for the twitch of a curtain, or a shadow moving against the light behind a window. But he saw nothing. He could hear no sounds either, except the faint murmur of voices from the officers working down at the bridge. The hamlet itself was eerily silent, as if he'd already stepped into that unknown world. A breeze blew downhill and whistled round the corner, making him shiver suddenly.

So this was Shawhead. Only one road in and one road out. And they really didn't want you coming here in the first place.

Cooper turned as he heard the distinctive sound of a helicopter approaching. He was relieved to see it was G-NMID, the air support unit from Ripley. They would sweep the area around the bridge and out into the fields around Shawhead. The helicopter represented his best hope of locating the missing driver quickly. But only if he was out there in the open.

'We need to make sure no one has seen the driver, Malcolm Kelsey,' said Cooper. 'Ask the residents to check their property – all those outbuildings, look. We can't do that ourselves. We don't have the manpower.'

'So we're relying on the help of the public?' said Sharma.

'Don't we always?'

Sharma looked as though he might have a contradictory opinion, but he kept his mouth closed.

'Don't forget to ask if anyone heard bleeping noises,' he said. 'The reversing bleeper on the truck. If anyone heard it, that would indicate whether the driver tried to reverse out from under the bridge, or just stayed where he was when he got stuck.'

'Okay,' said Irvine.

Cooper took a deep breath. He would have to put his new detective sergeant in charge of a team. He knew nothing about Sharma, but that was part of a DS's job and he had to be trusted from the outset. Sharma must be sufficiently experienced to have reached his rank and he couldn't be treated like a trainee.

Instead Cooper decided to take Carol Villiers with him in Shawhead. He didn't know what he was going to say to her, but he owed her an explanation of some kind.

'DS Sharma, if you and DC Irvine could visit these properties. We'll . . .'

He looked at Villiers hesitantly.

'What will we do?' she said.

'We'll see what's further up the road. We'll go round the bend.'

'I can't wait.'

'Oh, and the sheep,' said Cooper as the team began to disperse. 'Ask them about the sheep.'

LEFT ALONE WITH Sharma, Luke Irvine studied his new DS, not sure how to proceed. A sergeant ought to be taking the lead, giving instructions. But Irvine felt as though he should make the first move.

'Higher Fold Farm,' he said, pointing at a sign on the wall.

'Yes, I can see it,' said Sharma.

Irvine felt himself flush, wondering if he'd already started out on the wrong foot.

'I'm sorry.'

'Luke, isn't it? Would you like to do the talking?'

Well, that sounded genuine enough.

'Fine, if you like.'

They were welcomed into the farmhouse by an elderly lady with white hair, who introduced herself as Mrs Swindells. Irvine assumed she must be the mother of the farmer who'd been glowering at them near the scene at the bridge. She was just as broad as he was, but not as tall. She was wrapped in a thick woollen cardigan over a padded body warmer, which made her look as though she was wearing a life jacket and was about to jump off a sinking ship.

'Can I ask your first name, Mrs Swindells?' said Irvine.

To his surprise, she almost simpered at him as she replied. 'Doris. And what about you, young man?'

'Oh. Luke,' he said.

'That's a nice name. Biblical, isn't it?'

'Yes.'

The old lady looked closely at Dev Sharma, narrowing her eyes slightly. Irvine wondered what she was thinking. He couldn't read her expression, but he knew there was a good chance she might say something inappropriate at any moment. It was what old people did. They'd been brought up in a different era, when you could say those things and no one batted an eyelid.

But she made no comment, instead ushering them into an old-fashioned sitting room and shuffling off into the kitchen. Irvine and Sharma sat awkwardly on an uncomfortable settee for a few minutes until she returned, bringing tea and a plate of cake. Irvine's interest perked up. The cake looked home-made. Without Gavin Murfin here, he might get some to himself.

'I see it all from here,' said Mrs Swindells when she'd settled into a well-used armchair. 'Not that there's much to see in this place. I'd rather be living in New Mills. Or better still, somewhere nice in Manchester. Didsbury or Chorlton perhaps.'

'Didn't you grow up living in the country?' asked Irvine.

'Yes, of course I did. But there comes a point in your life when you want something different. It was all right when I was busy all the time, helping to keep the farm running. You don't have time to stop and think about anything then. But now . . . well, I have nothing to do now, except die of boredom.'

'Your son,' said Irvine.

'Grant. He has to do everything himself now, so I hardly see him. He comes in for a meal at night, then he falls asleep.'

'Has he never married?'

The old lady smiled a small, bitter smile. Suddenly, she didn't look quite so benign and unthreatening to Irvine.

'Oh, yes,' she said. 'He was married all right. A big wedding, it was too. Her parents weren't around, so we ended up paying for most of it.'

'We?'

'Me and my husband Bill. He was alive then. He died of a heart attack eighteen months later. It was a blessing really. It would have broken his heart to see what happened.'

Irvine glanced at Sharma, but they both knew it was the wrong moment to interrupt or ask any questions. The old lady was going to tell them anyway.

'She divorced him,' said Mrs Swindells. 'Two years after they were married. Two years. What sort of marriage is that? She said she couldn't cope with being a farmer's wife. But she must have known what she was letting herself in for when she agreed to wed him. I reckon she just wanted the wedding, not the marriage. That's the way girls are these days. They dream of being the centre of attention for a day, with the dress and the flowers, and the bridesmaids and all that. When it's all over the rest is a big disappointment. They can't deal with real life. Grant was devastated, of course. I don't think he's ever got over it. He probably never will.'

She paused and Irvine allowed her a second or two of silence before he asked the next question.

'And children?'

Mrs Swindells shook her head. 'Children would have been nice. But there was never any sign of her getting pregnant. And there's no hope of that now. Have you seen him, my son? He's hardly anyone's idea of a catch any more.'

'Well—'

She ignored him as if he hadn't spoken.

'So I sit here,' she said, 'and I watch the empty road most of the day, hoping for something to happen. And when it goes dark, I turn on the telly and I watch repeats of *Midsomer Murders*.'

AROUND THE CORNER at Shaw Farm, Ben Cooper and Carol Villiers had disturbed a young man who was tinkering inside the engine of a John Deere tractor. He was wearing green overalls and a radio was playing in the workshop. He didn't hear them coming until they were halfway across the yard.

'Oh. Are you looking for someone?' he said, wiping his hands on a rag.

Cooper identified himself and the young man stared at his warrant card.

'I'm Nick,' he said.

'You live here?'

'Yes.'

The young man looked a bit nervous, or hesitant.

Cooper was about to ask him if his parents were home, but an older man was already coming round the side of the farmhouse.

Perhaps he'd heard voices in the yard. Unfamiliar voices, which meant visitors. A rarity in Shawhead probably.

'Jack Lawson. You've met Nick,' he said when he found out who they were. 'I'm glad you're taking this business seriously. It could cause us a real headache if it goes on much longer.'

Lawson was a tall, slender man with a full beard, greying to match his slightly unkempt hair. He had that angular look of a man who might have been bigger once but had lost weight dramatically. An illness perhaps. It must certainly have been something to do with his health. He didn't look like a man who would be too concerned about his appearance. His eyes were green and had a tendency to stare as if he was short-sighted but couldn't be bothered wearing glasses. When he walked, he showed signs of a slight limp.

Cooper glanced round at the buildings, wondering what they produced here. Arable or livestock? It was difficult to tell.

For a start the yard was full of vehicles. A Range Rover, a grey Fiat Panda, the tractor Nick had been working on. But there were several other vehicles, crammed in so tightly together that it would take hours to move them out. Not that most of them would be moving ever again. A couple of classic American cars had sunk on to their hubs, their rusted wings flaking into the grass. A white Transit van had been partially dismantled and its side panels removed. Its interior struts lay exposed like the skeleton of a beached whale.

'How's the farming business?' he asked casually.

'Difficult,' said Lawson.

He didn't bother to expand. Cooper expected the usual complaints about feed prices and the weather, but they didn't come. Jack Lawson was clearly a man of few words if he could resist the opportunity to grumble.

'We're into sheep mostly,' he said when Cooper waited for more. 'And a small suckler herd.'

Cooper nodded. Lawson stood with his hands on his hips, his legs planted firmly in a pair of ill-fitting blue jeans. The denim was stained with oil and streaked with something bright green – raddle perhaps, or the dye used for marking sheep. It was obvious from his stance that they weren't going to be invited in to the house. Any conversation would take place out here in the yard. It might not be deliberately rude and Cooper knew he shouldn't take it personally. It probably came naturally to Mr Lawson, the way it did to a lot of other people in this area.

Villiers took her cue from Cooper's discreet nod. She had a print-out of the residents in Shawhead and their addresses, ready to be ticked off when they'd been spoken to.

'When did you become aware of the lorry that got stuck under the bridge, Mr Lawson?' she asked.

'Only this morning,' he said. 'With all the activity down there. We're a bit out of the way here, but I saw the flashing lights when I went out to feed the sheep early on. I could see something was up. Then I noticed the lorry under the bridge. Driver missing, is he? That's a bit of a turn-up.'

'Who told you he was missing?' asked Villiers.

Lawson jerked his head towards the lower part of Shawhead. 'Grant Swindells, down there. Of course, he'd been nosing about and found out whatever he could. Making a nuisance of himself, I suppose?'

'Have you spoken to anyone else here about it?'

'We don't really talk to people here much. I know it's a really small place, but it's not one of those tight-knit communities you hear about.'

'What about your neighbours across the road?' Villiers consulted her list. 'The Durkins?'

'The ones with the goats and pigs? They're a bit hippy for us.'

'Do you happen to know the driver of the lorry?' asked Villiers.

Lawson frowned. 'Why would I?'

'He was delivering animal feed.'

'What firm?'

'Windmill Feed Solutions.'

'Never heard of them.'

'The driver's name is Malcolm Kelsey.'

Lawson shook his head. 'Sorry.'

'And we're asking everyone to check their outbuildings,' said Cooper. 'If you could please look in every nook and cranny where someone might be hiding.'

'Hiding? Aren't you looking for a lorry driver? Why should he be hiding somewhere?'

Cooper didn't know why he'd said 'hiding'. It was just a word that had popped into his mouth, an image in his head of an injured man sheltering in a dark corner. He had no idea where it came from. It didn't really make sense in the circumstances, did it?

'Perhaps I should have said "might be sheltering",' he said.

Lawson looked at him curiously. 'Is there more to this than meets the eye?' he asked.

Cooper smiled, but didn't answer. In his experience there was usually more to everything than met the eye.

'I'll mention it to Mum too,' said Nick.

Lawson nodded. 'Yes, Sarah is the one who remembers things around here.'

'Thank you.'

They left a card and turned to leave. But Cooper stopped just before they reached the gate.

'Oh, Nick,' he said.

The young man straightened up in surprise. 'Yes?'

'Can I ask how old you are?'

'Eighteen. I'll be nineteen in March. I left school last summer.'

'Are you registered to vote?'

Nick's mouth fell open.

'No,' he said. 'I haven't bothered. Not yet anyway.'

'Not interested in using your right to vote?'

'It hardly seems worth the bother,' said Nick. 'Politics is such a turn-off.'

A lot of young people seemed to feel like that. You had no real voice, your vote didn't make any difference, politicians were all the same. It was a shame. If they all registered and voted, young people could actually make a difference together.

'Why do you ask?' said Nick.

'Oh, I just noticed that you weren't on the electoral register,' said Cooper, waving his copy of the list Villiers had given him. 'Do you know the electoral register? It lists the names of all the adults registered to vote and their addresses. I can see you're not on it.'

'Right.' Nick wiped his hands on the rag again, though he hadn't touched anything yet. 'Well, I might get round to it one day.'

'It's up to you,' said Cooper. 'See you later.'

He could feel Jack Lawson's eyes on him as they walked back to the road. Lawson had tensed when he asked the question about the electoral register, which was interesting. His list was hardly a threatening document, on the face of it.

'What was all that about registering to vote?' asked Villiers when they were out of earshot.

'Just an innocent question,' said Cooper. 'Don't you agree that young people ought to be interested in voting when they reach eighteen.'

'That wasn't it. I know you, Ben – and you're looking smug about something.'

Cooper laughed. 'You produced the list yourself, Carol. As you said, there are ten adults on it. One of them is Zoe Hibbert at Shaw-head Cottages, who's nineteen years old. She's on the electoral register here in Shawhead, even though she's away at university in Birmingham. I'm guessing her parents automatically entered her on the registration form when it came round. She could vote here if she's home during an election, or she could register in Birmingham as well and vote there.'

'So?'

'Well, the rest is just counting,' said Cooper. 'Do the maths.'

'Ten adults,' said Villiers. 'Three at the Hibberts, the two Scho-fields, Mr Swindells and his mother, the two Durkins, and—'

'Just one at the Lawsons,' said Cooper. 'Jack Lawson is on the list on his own. The electoral register shows only one resident at Shaw Farm.'

Chapter Eight

LUKE IRVINE OPENED a gate and walked up a path through a neat garden to knock on the next front door. After a visit to the Hibberts at Shawhead Cottages, the remaining address in Shawhead was Top Barn and the people were called Schofield.

He didn't need to read the name to guess that it was a barn conversion. You could tell by the shape of the house. It was a long building and new windows had been inserted into the walls, which probably had no windows at all at one time, or just holes for ventilation.

It puzzled Irvine that people were so keen to live in a property like this. It was the same in the village he lived in. There was always pressure for disused farm buildings to be converted into residential use. There were plenty of perfectly nice houses to live in available without creating something like this. It must be very expensive, and inconvenient.

'A barn conversion,' said Sharma.

'Yes, I can see that.'

Irvine rang the bell, then rapped on the imitation brass knocker. It was a stable-type front door. And that didn't make any sense either, since it had been a barn, not a stable.

'No one's home,' said Irvine.

He peered through a window into an enormously long sitting room, which ran right into a dining area and a kitchen at the far end. Most of the light came from French windows looking southwards into the back garden.

'If no one's at home, we need to check their garden and outbuildings ourselves,' said Sharma.

'Fine.'

Irvine and Sharma walked round outside of the house together. All the doors and windows were secure and there were no signs of a forced entry. Why anyone should have broken into Top Barn recently, Irvine couldn't imagine, but Sharma seemed insistent on checking. Did his new DS think the missing lorry driver had decided to turn burglar while he was in Shawhead?

A double garage built on to the side of the house was solidly locked too. In a paddock was an old farm building with tiles missing from the roof. Irvine walked down and peered through the door. It had probably been an old cow byre, he guessed. Some building work had been going on here – there was a pile of breeze blocks, some bags of cement and several neat stacks of new roofing tiles. Another conversion, then. But no sign of anyone taking shelter here.

And that seemed to be it for outbuildings at this address, apart from a wood store piled high with split logs. It was open at the front and there was no room for anyone to conceal themselves among the stacks of wood.

Irvine gazed about him. A small water feature tinkled in the garden, a fountain in the shape of leaping fish, spouting water from its mouth into an ornamental pond. There were plenty of other outbuildings in sight, but they were on the other side of a fence. They looked as though they belonged to Higher Fold Farm – which Top Barn probably did once too. There was a much bigger and more modern barn now, a giant steel structure that overshadowed the original and was built right up to the boundary.

And that was another reason not to live in a barn conversion. You were still pretty much on the farm.

Irvine twisted round, thinking he'd seen a movement out of the corner of his eye. But it must only have been his own reflection in one of the windows of the house. He peered through the French windows and saw himself in a large mirror on the wall of the sitting room.

'Go back to the Hibberts and ask them if they know where their neighbours are,' said Sharma.

Immediately, Irvine felt himself bridling at being given instructions by someone he'd only just met.

'Me?'

But Sharma barely glanced at him. 'Who else?'

Reluctantly, Irvine did as he was told. This situation was going to take some getting used to.

THE ROAD THROUGH Shawhead ended in the yard of a property called Cloughpit House. Beyond were fields and rough grazing, which Cooper assumed must belong to Shaw Farm.

Higher Fold Farm had looked in excellent condition compared to these two holdings round the bend. The yard of Shaw Farm had been bad enough with all its half-dismantled vehicles. But Cloughpit House had been converted to a smallholding, with a series of sheds and outbuildings sprouting from the original house like fungus and spreading down the slope of the field.

Most of the house crouched low in a hollow of ground, with ancient stone walls that wavered and bulged. At the rear the roof line changed dramatically, forming a taller section that you would almost call a tower, three storeys high at least.

When they entered the yard, a young woman came towards them from a shed. She was dressed in old jeans and a baggy sweater, and her feet were shoved into black wellies that were a size too large for her. But she also had studs through her nose and eyebrows. Her hair was dyed magenta and pulled into tangled clumps.

Villiers checked her list, as if she couldn't quite believe she was in the right place.

'Tania Durkin?' she said.

'Yes, that's me. Are you the cops?'

Cooper and Villiers introduced themselves. Tania didn't seem interested in their identification, but studied them with open curiosity, looking from one to the other and back again. Perhaps she too couldn't believe she was having this encounter. She'd never expected to be chatting to the police in her own yard.

'No one comes up this far,' she said when they explained the reason for their visit and enquired for sightings of Malcolm Kelsey. 'It's a feed lorry, is it? One of those big ones? He'd never get it round that bend, even if he made it under the bridge.'

'Haven't you seen the lorry?' said Cooper, surprised.

'No. When did it get stuck?'

'Late yesterday afternoon, it seems.'

Tania shook her head. 'We haven't been out today. We've been busy on the smallholding. There are always jobs to do with the animals.'

She pulled a small knife from her pocket. It had a wooden handle and a tightly curved end. She cackled when Cooper and Villiers both took a step backwards.

'I've been trimming hooves,' she said. 'Look, it's just a hoof trimming knife.'

Cooper relaxed, recognising that what she said was true.

'Is Vincent Durkin at home?' he asked.

'Vinnie is down the field somewhere,' she said. 'Do you really need to talk to him? I'd call him, but he's probably not in any fit state to speak to.'

'I'm sorry?'

'He's mucking out the pigs.'

'Right.'

'We only have two sows here. And there are the goats, of course, and the hens. We're not proper farmers like the Swindells. We don't have the land for it. We really just want to be self-sufficient, but you've no idea how difficult that is. We still have to pay bills and the council won't take payment in cabbages or pints of goat's milk.'

'So how do you manage?'

'Vinnie has to work part-time at a garage in New Mills. He's a good mechanic. Better with his hands than he is with words. But at least it's a proper job. You want to ask that bloke Hibbert what he does.'

'Mr Hibbert at Shawhead Cottages? What does he do?'

'He says he works for a marketing consultancy in Manchester. Something to do with financial planning. That sounds like nothing to me. A made-up job. Another useless sod who doesn't produce anything.'

Two pygmy goats ran into the yard, their tiny hooves clattering on the concrete like tap dancers. They scampered round Villiers' feet and began chewing at her coat.

'They're quite cute, aren't they?' she said. 'I've always liked goats.'

'They're great, but they're little buggers for escaping,' said Tania.

One of the goats drew back its head, backed up a couple of feet and gave Villiers a friendly butt on her leg with its stubby horns.

'Ouch,' said Villiers.

'That'll probably bruise,' said Tania, without a trace of sympathy.

'Not so cute, after all.'

'Here's Vinnie now anyway,' said Tania.

Vincent Durkin had dark, spiky hair and tattoos on both sides of his neck, the blue lines snaking round his ears to disappear into his hair-line. His face was gaunt, his cheek bones prominent. But he looked to have a wiry strength, and the fingers of his hands were long and bony where he clutched a steel fork encrusted with soiled straw.

Tania told him who they were, and he gave them a non-committal nod and a grunt that might have been a monosyllabic version of 'hello'.

'I gather you don't have much land of your own, then?' said Cooper.

'No,' said Tania. 'We've tried to get a bit of grazing off Grant Swindells, but he won't part with a single acre. It's a shame, because he obviously can't manage it on his own. He has to get contractors in for all the big jobs and that's got to be costing him a fortune. And there are bits of land just going to waste, full of bracken and weeds. Odd corners we could make use of. But he's a stubborn old bugger.'

'I take it you don't get on with your neighbours?' said Villiers.

'We don't fit in really. That's the top and bottom of it. I wish people would take us as we are. But you know what it's like – you end up living in a barn conversion and suddenly you think you're someone special.'

'Top Barn?' said Cooper, checking Villiers' list. 'That would be Mr and Mrs Schofield.'

'I didn't mention any names.'

'But there are no other barn conversions in Shawhead.'

'Maybe not.'

There was no sign of a car in the Durkins' yard, but a Yamaha motorbike was parked under a length of corrugated iron roofing and the back doors of an old VW van were visible in a wooden garage. It wasn't clear whether it was a viable vehicle or just another metal carcass slowly rotting away like the classic models at Shaw Farm.

'Do you want a brew or anything?' she said. 'I'm just going in the house anyway. You look a bit cold out there, not doing very much.'

Tania Durkin was taking her boots off in a porch, or perhaps more accurately a conservatory. It had a glass roof, but the glass was green with mould and hardly let any light in.

'I don't think we have time, thank you,' said Cooper, moving to the door so that he could see inside.

Tools were piled here and there, and Vincent Durkin added his fork to the stack after wiping it on a patch of grass. Dark brown compost spilled onto the floor from half-open bags of compost.

A bale of straw sat next to a teetering stack of plastic bread trays marked with the name of a well-known supermarket chain.

Near the door into the house a dozen bulging black bin liners were lined up against the wall. Cooper got a distinct whiff from them of, well . . . bins. It was the smell from the bottom of his wheelie bin after the council refuse men had emptied it. Did the Durkins not believe in putting their rubbish out for collection like everyone else? Or didn't the council bin lorries manage to get this far up Cloughpit Lane either? One of the disadvantages of living in Shawhead perhaps.

Villiers was still being pursued by the pygmy goats, which had now been joined by two others. They danced around her, trying to tempt her into chasing them.

'They're so small,' she said. 'Surely you don't get much milk from them, do you?'

Tania laughed. 'No, not from them. We have some bigger goats for that.'

'So what are these for?' said Villiers. 'Pets?'

Cooper noticed Tania and Vincent exchange a glance. He was familiar with that look. He saw it often from farmers and from people who worked as butchers or had jobs in slaughterhouses. They didn't know how much of the gory truth they could tell people without upsetting them. The reactions they expected made them keep their mouths shut.

'Pygmy goats were originally bred in Africa,' said Cooper. 'They were developed to provide a small carcass instead of having too much meat that would go off in a hot climate.'

Villiers looked as though she didn't really believe him, but Tania Durkin laughed. Even Vincent grunted in agreement.

'What chance would we have of being self-sufficient if we didn't eat everything we raised?' said Tania.

But Cooper's eye had been drawn to a stone structure on the other side of the yard from the house. When he approached it, he realised it was a sealed well. An iron grille had been cemented across the opening.

Cooper peered through the grille into the blackness. It was much too dark down there to see any water in the bottom, but he could sense it. He could almost taste its acidity and feel its chill. He wouldn't fancy drawing it up and trying to drink it – though people must surely have done that at one time.

'They call that the Boggart Well,' said Tania, coming to stand next to him.

She was wearing soft-soled shoes now and he hadn't heard her cross the yard. When he turned he could smell the odour of animals on her clothes, the sour whiff of half-decayed muck that was scraped out of overgrown hooves. Her face was pink from the cold and the physical exertion, and the stud in her eyebrow glinted from a bead of sweat.

'That's the name it's marked with on the old maps,' she said. 'The Boggart Well. You know what some folk are like around here. Very superstitious.'

'Yes, I know.'

Cooper wondered what sinister presence the well was supposed to contain. In local folklore a boggart might be a spirit or a ghost, but it might equally be an embodiment of some evil that had been perpetrated here. Memories of dreadful incidents were sometimes dealt with by creating a physical symbol to focus or contain them, putting them away safely where people could point at them as something from the past, no longer representing any threat.

'This business with the delivery – it's just another satnav mess-up, isn't it?' said Tania. 'It happens all the time round here. They don't usually ram their lorries into that bridge, though.'

'That might be the case. We can't say yet.'

'Well, he wasn't following a diversion sign, that's for sure,' she said. 'They wouldn't divert traffic up Cloughpit Lane, no matter what. It goes nowhere.'

'Well, it goes to Shawhead,' said Cooper.

'That's what I mean. Nowhere.'

'THAT BACK PART of the Durkins' house is an odd shape,' said Villiers as they left. 'It must be a conversion from some old farm building, I suppose. A windmill, do you think?'

'It's possible.'

Villiers tilted her head sideways and squinted her eyes. 'Mmm. I'm not sure. It doesn't look quite right for a windmill.'

But Cooper had lost interest in vernacular architecture. He was gaining an overall impression of Shawhead and it wasn't positive. The word 'community' seemed alien to the residents here. They seemed to live in a state of mutual unhelpfulness and suspicion.

Was this really the idyll that people converting that barn and those old farmworkers' cottages had dreamed of?

WHEN COOPER AND Villiers walked back round the corner, Irvine was still talking to a slightly frazzled-looking woman with short blond hair, while Sharma chatted to an old lady leaning on her gate across the road.

'Oh, this is Mrs Hibbert,' said Irvine. 'My boss, Detective Inspector Cooper.'

Cooper hadn't yet got used to anyone calling him 'boss'. But he could see that it made the woman look at him with a bit more respect than he normally expected from members of the public. So perhaps it could be a good thing.

'I'm Amanda Hibbert,' she said.

'Ah, the lady who reported the incident.'

'Yes, that was me, for my sins,' she said, laughing rather nervously.

'I'm sorry that we're not able to clear the road for a while yet,' said Cooper. 'I appreciate it must be very inconvenient.'

'Oh, we're used to getting cut off here,' she said. 'Snow, floods, fallen trees. We even had a sinkhole open up once. It took us days to get that filled in. You realise, if this road gets closed, there's no other way in or out. We're completely trapped.'

Cooper nodded, wondering why she was stressing that.

'Do you know this company the lorry belongs to?' he asked.

'Yes, we get our horse feed from them sometimes,' said Mrs Hibbert. 'But not today. We're weren't expecting anything.'

'I'm going to have to send someone to take your fingerprints, Mrs Hibbert.'

'Mine? For heaven's sake, why?'

'For elimination purposes, that's all. You must have touched parts of the lorry.'

'Well, yes – the door handle, I suppose. And the papers on the seat, you know . . .'

'Of course. So if we find prints around the cab, we need to be able tell whether they're yours. I'm sure you understand that.'

'I suppose so.'

'But don't worry. They'll be destroyed afterwards. We don't keep them on file.'

She didn't look entirely convinced. Cooper didn't think he would find her prints on record in the database. But some members of the public just hated the principle of the police having possession of their fingerprints or DNA. They saw it as a kind of violation of their privacy.

Suddenly, Cooper realised that stopping had been a mistake. He should have headed straight back to the bridge. A small crowd was starting to gather in the road between Higher Fold Farm and Top Barn. Grant Swindells had come out, Ian Hibbert had emerged from Shawhead Cottages and even the Durkins were slouching at the corner with a lurcher on a lead, as if they were taking the dog for a walk. Only the Lawsons from Shaw Farm were missing. And of course Mr and Mrs Schofield from Top Barn. Where were they?

'Have you spoken to the Schofields, Luke?' Cooper said quietly.

'There's no one home,' said Irvine. 'No sign of them. We did a check round the property while we were there.'

'If you're looking for the Schofields, I think they're away,' said Ian Hibbert. 'Last time I spoke to him, he said they were thinking of going on holiday to Thailand.'

His wife looked as though she was about to correct him, perhaps to point out it was Turkey, not Thailand. But he scowled at her, and she shrugged and stayed quiet. It was a fairly normal exchange between a married couple, in Cooper's experience. And with a crowd gathering round him, it was hardly the time to pursue it anyway.

'Ladies and gentlemen, I'm afraid we're going to have to ask everyone to stay in their homes until we've processed the scene,' he said.

'What does that mean?' asked Ian Hibbert.

'We have to examine it thoroughly for evidence before we can move the lorry. I'm sorry, that means the road will remain closed for a while yet. If you're due to go to work, please phone in and explain to your employers.'

'Stay at home?'

'Yes, sir.'

'Are we going to miss another day tomorrow, or what?'

'We don't have much choice, do we?' said Mrs Hibbert. 'We can't get out.'

'If we lose business because of this, there'll be compensation claims.'

Cooper threw his hands out. 'That's up to you, sir. We're doing our best to expedite things.'

When he heard himself say that, Cooper realised that he'd never used the word 'expedite' out loud before. He'd only written it in reports laden with other jargon and buzz words.

'I can tell you, my employers aren't going to be happy,' said Hibbert.

For the first time Cooper looked at him properly. He'd hardly taken notice of Ian Hibbert so far. He'd been spoken to by Irvine and Sharma. Wasn't he the one who worked for a marketing consultancy in Manchester? Something to do with financial planning. It didn't sound too exciting. Not a job where his absence for a day would be life threatening.

'You could always walk across the fields and get a taxi to pick you up.'

That was the old lady, Doris Swindells, leaning on her gate with an old coat around her shoulder against the drizzle. Her son gave her a surprised glance, but said nothing.

'You must be joking,' said Hibbert, a bit too loudly to sound natural. 'I couldn't walk all that way through all that wet grass and mud, and . . . well, cow pats and heavens knows what. Think of the state my clothes and shoes would be in. How could I go into the office like that?'

'Yes, it's ridiculous,' said Amanda, glaring at Mrs Swindells. 'I had some appointments scheduled for today, but I've cancelled them. We all have to make the best of it, in the circumstances.'

'Besides,' said Hibbert. 'I've missed the train into Manchester.' He looked back at Cooper. 'I have a season ticket for the Newtown to Piccadilly service. So that's paid for in advance, you see. I can't get that money back.'

'I understand,' said Cooper.

It was all he *could* say. He couldn't blurt out what he was actually thinking. He was wondering whether some of these people had actually met each other before. They were behaving like a bunch of complete strangers who'd been thrown together just a few minutes ago as a result of a crisis, like a cast of ill-mixed characters in a disaster movie, who immediately set about arguing with each other while the world fell apart around them. There wasn't one of them who didn't have the knack of infuriating the others.

But then his eyes were drawn to the back of the group. Over the heads of Amanda Hibbert and Mrs Swindells, he saw the Durkins. Vinnie and Tania.

Mr Lawson had referred to them as 'a bit hippy for us'. But Cooper had met proper hippies. They flocked to ancient sites like the Nine Ladies stone circle on Stanton Moor every year in June to celebrate the midsummer solstice. The Durkins didn't look like hippies. Yes, they were quiet and inoffensive. They kept hens and goats, and they seemed to be trying to revive the old self-sufficiency ethos that had once been called 'the good life'. But they didn't dress like hippies, or talk like them. They didn't seem to have any belief system they lived by. His impression was that they were entirely practical and down to earth. Much like small-scale farmers, in fact.

But the Durkins kept themselves to themselves, which wasn't necessarily a sign that they were harmless. Now they were observing their neighbours with a kind of impatient contempt, faintly mocking expressions on their faces below the hoods of their jackets, fidgeting as if they couldn't wait to get away from these awful people and back to their goats. And probably they would have a good laugh at their fellow residents of Shawhead when they got back to Cloughpit House.

'It's wheelie bin day today,' said Ian Hibbert.

'I'm sorry?'

'We have our bin collection on Tuesday. It's black general waste bins this week. They only collect them once a fortnight, so we can't miss it.'

'I'm afraid we turned the refuse collection vehicle back at the bottom of Cloughpit Lane,' said Cooper.

The news was met with a chorus of groans and protests. Cooper knew that reaction. Not having your bin collected on wheelie bin day was one of the worst things that could happen to a law-abiding household. And deliberately turning the binmen away? Now that *was* a crime. Much worse than a bloody murder on your doorstep.

'And no post allowed through?' said Hibbert. 'We're running a business, you know.'

'I'm really sorry, sir. It will only be a short inconvenience.'

'Inconvenience?' repeated Hibbert, the pitch of his voice rising as if he was going to throw a tantrum.

'Oh, shut up,' said Grant Swindells.

He said it casually through the side of his mouth, as if he was speaking to an awkward beast. It hardly sounded like a threat. Yet Hibbert went quiet.

In a way Cooper would have liked to stand here all day listening to these people. In a group they told him far more about themselves than they did when they were being interviewed individually or in couples. Most interesting were the relationships between them, or the lack of relationships. You would think a community so small would develop a neighbourly spirit. But that was probably an idealistic fantasy too. Cooper had seen far more small communities where living cheek by jowl engendered not neighbourliness, but enmity.

Chapter Nine

FINALLY, SOME SUPPORT had arrived, a minibus full of officers wearing overalls and baseball caps, their trousers tucked into their boots for a tramp through the countryside. The air support unit had reported a negative result from their sweep of the area. That meant no warm bodies out there, except livestock. There was no option left but a long slog across the ground on foot.

But it would be getting dark soon and it was already too late to mount a full-scale search tonight. They would only be able to touch the edges of the scene – the verges, the undergrowth and a few yards of field beyond the stone walls.

As the light began to change in the late afternoon, the area beyond the immediate environs of the bridge was becoming a grey emptiness, an indistinct jumble of walls and hedges, rough grazing and clumps of trees, slopes and ditches. If Mac Kelsey wasn't at Shawhead, he must be out there somewhere.

Cooper was concerned that it had taken much too long to get the search started. But it was always a question of available

resources and priorities. No doubt his request had been competing with other demands.

But he'd taken all the initial actions he could at the scene.
He would have to wait to deal with any forensic issues Scenes of
Crime came up with.

'I think it's fair to say the residents aren't happy,' said Villiers.

'Yes, you were right about that,' said Cooper.

'We've just had to turn the postman away too. He's been up
Cloughpit Lane in his van. He didn't get as far as the bridge,
though. One of the uniforms turned him back.'

Dev Sharma looked puzzled.

'The postman?' he said. 'At this time of day? It's nearly dark.'

'Lots of rural areas don't get their post delivered until this time
of day. In December it may always be after dark.'

Luke Irvine worked his way back along the edge of the road
from liaising with the officer in charge of the search team.

'It's funny that the residents of Shawhead haven't been flocking
to volunteer their help with a search,' he said.

Villiers nodded. 'Yes, it's gone very quiet up there suddenly.'

'Actually, I think it's probably always this quiet,' said Cooper.
'Even when the road's open.'

'As Mrs Hibbert said – no other way in or out.'

'It's not true, though, is it?' said Cooper.

'What isn't?'

'That there's no other way out of Shawhead. We're all focusing
too much on the road. Cars aren't the only means of transport.
You could walk across the fields, for a start.'

'You're right. And I bet some of these people have quad bikes.
Or what about a tractor? It's the ultimate off-road vehicle.'

'Fine, but you could only get so far on a tractor or quad bike,' said Cooper.

'How do you mean?'

'Well, you need access from one field to the next. You need a gate to get through. There are only gates between fields belonging to the same farm. Once you reach someone else's property, there's no gate. Just stone walls.'

'A footpath, then. A bridleway?'

'There's another possibility. One of these farms could have a field entrance from another road.'

'Of course, but what other road is there?'

'Let's have a look at the map.'

Villiers laughed. 'Always the map.'

'It tells you a lot you can't see on the ground.'

'I know. Just joking.'

DS Sharma leaned in to look as Cooper extracted an Ordnance Survey Explorer map for the Dark Peak area from his glove compartment. At two and a half inches to the mile, it was an extraordinarily detailed map and so big that it almost filled his car when it was completely opened up. It covered both sides too, so required turning over and a lot of folding to get it to the right area.

Someone like Luke Irvine would probably opt automatically for an iPhone app to show Google Maps. The satellite image might be useful, but the screen of a smartphone couldn't show anything like the detail and the context. From his OS map, Cooper could judge the height of the surrounding hills, the steepness of the contours, the relationship of one place to another in the landscape, all the things that weren't obvious on the ground.

Higher Fold Farm was an extensive holding. It looked to have fields bordering a lane that meandered through the Low Leighton area of New Mills, struck out into the countryside, then petered out on the lower slopes of Chinley Churn.

But the map showed a network of tracks or bridleways branching out from the point where it ended.

Cooper tapped the map. 'There's certainly a public right of way going in the right direction. It starts near Higher Fold Farm and comes out on the road further down, about a hundred yards before the turning into Cloughpit Lane. There's also a branch heading off towards the canal.'

'It must go under the railway line.'

'Yes, it looks as though there's another bridge there. It's difficult to tell whether the path would take a horse, or even a trail bike.'

'If it's a bridleway, they're often wide enough for an off-road vehicle to use.'

'Let's take a look later.'

'Here's someone who could help,' said Villiers.

Before he looked round, Cooper could guess who it was. Grant Swindells loomed over a gate with a Border collie panting at his heels. Mr Swindells' face was a picture of placid curiosity.

'Mr Swindells,' said Cooper.

'Can I help?' said the farmer.

'We were wondering about the footpath that runs across the fields from your farm. A public right of way?'

'Aye, there's a path right enough. It's a bit muddy until you get down to the bottom where it goes under the railway.'

'Could you get a vehicle down it?'

Swindells shook his head vigorously. 'No, no. I wouldn't even want to try it in a tractor. It's too steep and slippery on the slope. You'd turn over before you got a few yards down.'

'Mmm,' said Cooper. 'Thank you.'

Not a road, then. But what about a waterway? Or of course a railway?

'Why is this a double bridge?' he said, almost to himself.

'No idea,' said Villiers. 'Two railway lines, I suppose?'

Cooper nodded doubtfully. It was true that New Mills was served by two railway stations. Here the Sheffield to Manchester express trains and a local service into New Mills Central shared the same track until they separated at a junction further to the north. The other line was way over to the west of the Peak Forest Canal. It ran alongside the A6 as it headed up from Whaley Bridge, and served Newtown station. What other line could there be?

He looked over the landscape. Rolling fields, stretches of woodland, a scattering of farms. This wasn't mining or quarrying country, surely?

'Well, you're going back a bit,' said Grant Swindells when Cooper tentatively asked him the question.

'Back how far?'

'More than a hundred years, I reckon. In my grandfather or great-grandfather's day. It's hard to believe now, isn't it?'

'Yes, it is.'

'Well, there were lots of coal mines in this area. The biggest pits were at Ladypit and Pingot. But there were more. Maybe a dozen or so. The coal was poor quality and in the end they couldn't compete with cheaper stuff from Lancashire and Yorkshire. They'd all pretty much closed by the First World War, so my dad told me.'

'And there were railway lines to carry the coal away?'

'Yes, of course. But they're long gone too.'

'Perhaps not entirely,' said Cooper.

Swindells looked puzzled. But Cooper didn't try to explain. It was strange how you could live in a place all your life and see only the things that were relevant to you on a day-to-day basis, without seeing the whole picture. For Grant Swindells this was just a railway embankment dividing his fields from someone else's. He only ever saw the bridge from underneath as he was driving through it.

'They say there used to be a tunnel leading from the pit to the loading wharf on the river,' said Swindells. 'I don't know if that's true. I've never seen any signs of it.'

A road, a railway line, a river, a canal. And perhaps even a tunnel somewhere. That was getting too complicated.

Cooper turned. 'Luke, can you scramble up that banking? Then tell us what you can see at the top.'

Irvine went to a locked gate in the wall below the bridge. It provided access to the banking, which was covered with a mass of bracken, a dense patch of brambles and a few elder saplings near the top. There was a warning sign on the gate, which Irvine stopped to read first.

'There are forensic traps in use,' he said. '*Deployed by British Transport Police to deter thefts of equipment and materials from the trackside.*'

The warning sign was illustrated by a 'green man' picture, a photo of a suspect whose face was splattered with fluorescent green, the tell-tale signs of Smart Water. The Transport Police claimed a 100 per cent conviction rate for thefts from sites like this. Derbyshire Constabulary should be so lucky. Their detection rate for crime in the county barely touched 35 per cent.

'It's only Smart Water,' said Cooper. 'Just don't touch anything. Above all, don't try to remove any sleepers or copper cable and you'll be fine.'

'Okay.'

Irvine climbed the gate, carefully avoided the barbed wire.

'Hell's bells,' he said.

'What have you found?'

'Only this. It looks like a scythe or something.'

The implement had been left propped against the inside of the gate. And Irvine was right – the steel blade looked freshly sharpened. Perhaps it was waiting for someone to find the time to cut down the bracken. But it might be here for another purpose altogether.

'It's a long-handled slasher,' said Cooper.

'Whatever. The blade is sharp enough to do some damage.'

'It looks clean, but we'll bag it anyway.'

A moment later Irvine had disappeared into the undergrowth. All that could be heard of his progress was a faint rustling.

'What do you see?' called Cooper. 'Is there a railway line on this side of the bridge?'

'No, the tracks have gone and the line is overgrown,' came Irvine's reply. 'It looks as though it hasn't been used for decades. There are tracks on the other side of the bridge, though.'

'That's what I thought. Anything else?'

'Just horses.'

'Horses?'

'Three of them grazing near the lines, just this side of a fence.'

'I'm coming up,' said Cooper.

The opening between the bridges was protected by a wall of blackened stone, spotted with lichen. The parapet was no more than four feet high. Cooper leaned over and gazed down at the road. Yes, a reasonably fit person could drop down onto the roof of a stationary lorry if it was trapped between the bridges. It was a bit of a jump, though, and you might risk serious injury if the roof was slippery. It would have taken someone pretty determined. Or desperate.

But there, growing out of the brickwork, was a handy sapling, sturdy enough to provide a foothold. He could see that the leaves had been torn and a couple of branches were snapped, the breaks on them fresh.

'We need forensics on the roof of the lorry,' he said. 'Though God knows how they're going to get to it, until the recovery vehicle pulls it free from the bridge.'

Cooper hadn't stood quite so close to railway lines for a long time. The sight of the shiny rails, the massive sleepers, the heaps of stone ballast, took him back to his childhood, when he and his friends would take the chance to sneak up to the track and listen for that singing in the lines that told you a train was coming long before it appeared in the distance.

'If a train went past at the time of the incident, the driver or passengers might have seen something,' said Cooper.

'If it went past at exactly the right moment.'

'There are both express trains and local services using this part of the line. They must come through every few minutes. We'll get someone to check.'

The old mineral line ran between avenues of brambles and birch, easily wide enough to drive a vehicle along. The ground was firm, probably still lying on a bed of stone chippings laid as ballast for the tracks. In fact, there had been vehicles using this route from time to time. It was obvious from the two channels worn on either side of a central grassy strip. But not recently. There seemed to be no fresh tyre marks, even on the muddier sections.

In any case, how would you get access to the old line?

The answer lay five hundred yards along at the next bridge. It was a single bridge at the bottom of an unsurfaced track reached from the footpath across Mr Swindells' fields by a worn set of steps. Here the route of the old railway track didn't go over a bridge but stopped at a padlocked gate.

And there, in a field just off Cloughpit Lane, was the only surviving remnant of the mining industry that had once thrived in this area – a small stone shaft sitting in isolation, dwarfed by an electricity pylon. It was held together by iron mesh and cement, crowned by a rim of barbed wire, in case you felt like climbing into it. And no doubt someone had done exactly that at some time.

'Could someone have come this way?' asked Irvine.

Cooper took hold of his shoulder to hold him back from walking any further.

'Yes, look at the tyre marks on the ground here,' he said. 'They're quite fresh. Made since the last heavy rainfall, anyway. We had quite a downpour on Saturday, which would have washed these away. But they've hardened in the mud.'

'Can we get impressions from them?'

'Let's hope so.'

A few hundred yards away a recovery truck was backing slowly up Cloughpit Lane to begin the task of removing the obstruction. The beep of the reversing alarm came loud and clear through the air. They would surely be able to hear it from the houses at Shawhead.

Cooper looked up at the sky. 'We'd better get forensics up here straight away, before the rain comes again.'

AT THE END of the afternoon, as dusk was falling, Ben Cooper left the forensics team still working at the scene, lit by the harsh glare of their mobile lighting.

They'd finished their examination on the cab of the lorry and the recovery vehicle had edged it carefully free from the bridge.

The sight of the tow truck had been a relief. They might soon be able to open the road for the residents of Shawhead to get through. But he was anxious that he didn't allow the scene to be contaminated too soon. The forensic evidence was minimal already. He would hate to find that he'd lost something vital because of his decision.

After the lorry had been freed, Network Rail engineers had declared the structure of the bridge safe. Mac Kelsey had left only a few superficial scrapes along the stonework to show that he'd ever been there.

So the trains had started running over the bridge again. Cooper didn't feel at all happy about hundreds of members of the public peering out of their carriage windows at the police activity below the embankment, lit by those arc lights like a film set. Some of them would be taking photographs on their mobile phones, no doubt. It went against all the instincts to have people passing over an active crime scene, if not actually through it.

He could imagine what Wayne Abbott would have to say about it. Circumstances beyond his control at a scene were intolerable. But that was part of the job – competing demands had to be balanced. The transport system couldn't be disrupted for ever.

The search team had turned up nothing yet, but they'd barely touched the surrounding fields by the time the light failed. Tomorrow would be different.

Before he headed home, Cooper called in at West Street in Edendale. He drove through the barrier into the staff car park behind E Division headquarters, parked in one of the bays behind the station. He hung his police-issue blue lanyard round his neck, with his identity card on a quick release clip. He couldn't walk around the corridors at West Street without one. Then he keyed in the access code to enter the building.

He had his own office now, a room that had changed little since it was occupied by his old DI, Paul Hitchens. On his desk he found a file waiting for him. His new detective sergeant had arrived in Edendale without any advance warning and he was wondering why. The situation was unusual. He needed to spend a few minutes discovering exactly who this person was that he was expected to work with.

Chapter Ten

THE STREETS OF Edendale were quiet tonight. Apart from a few people waiting at the bus stops at the end of Clappergate, Cooper could see only a young couple sitting on the steps of the war memorial in the Market Square and a man using the cash machine at Barclays Bank, close to the front door of the Red Lion.

It was one of the reasons Gavin Murfin's farewell party had been arranged for a Tuesday. There wasn't as much demand on police time as there was on a Friday or Saturday, when the town's pubs were heaving with drinkers and the pavements were littered with drunks. Then it was all hands on deck for the uniformed section to keep the worst of the disorder off the streets and deposit the most belligerent of the revellers in the cells at the custody suite in West Street.

The upstairs function room at the Red Lion had been booked for the party to celebrate Murfin's retirement. It was one of the largest and most convenient venues in the centre of town, and the pub manager was glad to have the business during the quietest time of the week. Well, he would certainly have plenty of business.

Off-duty police officers didn't hold back when they came in sight of a bar.

As Cooper entered the Market Square, he was aware of figures emerging in ones and twos from the surrounding streets, where they'd been dropped off by spouses or paid off a taxi. He recognised an officer he knew from B Division in Buxton, who was standing in the light spilling from the window of Ferris's the butchers. A cloud of smoke rose into the damp air and Cooper realised he was having a cigarette before going into the pub and facing the smoking ban.

There would be quite a few smokers hanging around outside the doors of the Red Lion later on. Before the end of the evening, when they'd had too much to drink, they might become the sort of anti-social mob that the police would normally want to move on.

Cooper pushed open the doors of the pub and looked around. Even the bar of the lounge downstairs was lined with short haircuts and thick waistlines, warming up for the main part of the evening. He walked through to the stairs and suddenly found himself part of a purposeful crowd, all heading in the same direction. They barged into the room like the drugs squad executing a tactical entry.

And the place was already packed. Every old-school copper in Derbyshire was here tonight, along with many who'd retired in the last few years and were now working as pub landlords or driving instructors. They were all busy catching up on the station gossip, laughing at the latest example of insanity from the senior management team. The noise level generated by a room full of old bobbies was deafening.

Cooper got himself a beer from the bar. He turned at a tap on his shoulder and found Gavin Murfin himself swaying unsteadily in front of him, a silly grin on his pink face. He'd obviously started the celebrations a bit earlier in the afternoon.

'Ben. How the hell are you? Well, you look great.'

'Thanks, Gavin.'

Murfin threw his arms wide, spraying liquid from a bottle dangling from one hand.

'And what about me?'

Gavin had never really made much effort towards sartorial elegance in all the years that Cooper had known him. But now he was in danger of letting go completely. His wife had probably stuffed him into his clean shirt and freshly pressed suit for the evening. But the shirt was already hanging over his waistband and the bottom button had popped, exposing the occasional glimpse of wobbling stomach. The jacket had been slung over the back of a chair and there was a dark stain on the leg of the trousers. It was only beer. Probably.

'Are you having a good time?' said Cooper, avoiding the question.

'Brilliant,' said Murfin. And he repeated twice, with more emphasis. 'Brilliant. Just brilliant.'

'Everybody's here, I see.'

'Everybody. Just everybody. It's brilliant.'

Cooper looked around the room. Here and there senior officers stood uncomfortably clutching their drinks, looking round for an escape route as if they'd found themselves trapped in a den of villains and their cover was about to be blown. Perhaps they were afraid a fight might break out any time and put them in a compromising position. Given the character of some of Murfin's acquaintances, it wasn't impossible.

Some of those senior officers had passed briefly through Edendale CID on their way up the ladder, before going on to better things. A few months at a desk job in force headquarters at Ripley made you forget what front-line police officers were actually like. It wasn't always pretty.

'Diane Fry is here,' said Murfin.

'Yes, I know.'

'Of course you do.' Murfin grinned. 'She gave me a hug earlier, can you believe it?'

'You never liked her, Gavin.'

'True, true. I suppose I might have passed a derogatory comment now and then. But only when she deserved it. Which, let's face it, is most of the time.'

Murfin looked at Cooper, noting his silence with a smile of satisfaction.

'And your new DS, then. What's his name? I must have missed it.'

Cooper was glad that he'd gleaned a few facts from Sharma's personnel file. He was likely to be asked about Sharma again tonight and he would look an idiot if he knew nothing about him at all.

'Devdan Sharma,' he said. 'He's transferred from D Division. He has several commendations on file.'

Murfin nodded. 'He's a Muslim, like.'

'No, he's a Hindu, not a Muslim,' said Cooper.

'He doesn't wear a turban.'

'No, he's a Hindu, not a Sikh.'

He waited for Murfin to say something like 'same difference', but he didn't. From the bleary gleam in his eye, Gavin was probably just trying to wind him up anyway.

Cooper looked across the room at Sharma. He was conscious of his own ignorance of other cultures, though it wasn't as abysmal as Murfin's. Well, an insight into the Asian community was probably too much to expect in rural Derbyshire. He knew there were almost as many Hindus in the East Midlands as Muslims, though they lived mostly in the cities. He wondered how they felt about being constantly mistaken for members of a different religion. Perhaps he could ask Dev Sharma one day, if he ever got to know him well enough. And if it wasn't considered an offensive question.

'I bet he hates being mistaken for a Muslim,' said Murfin. 'I reckon I could wind him up about it, for a bit of fun. Shall I?'

'No,' said Cooper.

Murfin chortled into his beer. 'Just kidding.'

'It's not funny, Gavin.'

'Well, he won't be here long anyway,' said Murfin.

'Why?'

'Come off it. He's in E Division as part of his progress up the ladder. He's just learning what it's like out here in the sticks. He's getting his diversity training.'

Cooper didn't know what to say to that. He ought to argue. But deep down he had a suspicion that Murfin might be right.

'So what case have you been working on today?' asked Murfin.

'You know I can't tell you that, Gavin. Not any more.'

Murfin didn't bat an eyelid. 'Luke says you've been in New Mills, though.'

'Well, yes. That much is true.'

'Inbredonia,' said Murfin.

'What?'

'Inbredonia. You can tell the outsiders when they take their shoes off. If they only have five toes on each foot, they're not really from New Mills.'

'You can't say that, Gavin.'

'I just did.'

'But—'

Murfin waved a hand. 'I'm not a slave to the tsar of political correctness. Not any more. And thank God for it. I'm leaving all that to you, mate.'

Cooper was overcome with a surge of pity for Murfin. He was trying too hard, going way over the top with the non-PC attitude, as if trying to recapture the old DC Gavin Murfin for one last time before he disappeared for ever. But he was failing. This wasn't the Gavin that Cooper had known. He was almost a caricature of himself. Desperation oozed from him in every word. It was very sad. But there was nothing he could do. Like everyone else, Murfin had to adjust to reality.

'Gavin – you're not sorry to be going, are you?' he said.

'What do you think?' said Murfin. 'There are no jobs for the likes of me any more. You've got to admit that, Ben. I've heard they're looking to recruit more and more volunteers.'

'Yes, that's true.'

'Somebody will be doing my old job for less than a handful of peanuts soon, then. They're getting rid of the monkeys and replacing us with donkeys.'

Cooper didn't reply. He couldn't disagree, so it was best to say nothing.

But Murfin was right. A lot of vacancies had been advertised for what they called police support volunteers. After a year-long trial of the volunteer scheme in the High Peak and Derbyshire Dales, it was being rolled out across the force.

Support volunteers were being recruited to maintain equipment for operational police officers, to clean vehicles and stock them with first aid kits and police tape, to support Farm Watch or the Licensing Team, or to help keep response officers out on patrol longer by doing their routine photocopying, inputting data and writing reports. CCTV monitoring had turned out to be such a popular activity that there were far more volunteers than the system needed.

But why were volunteers so willing to give their time for free? What did they get out of it? According to the recruitment adverts, it helped their professional development, boosted their CV and gave an insight into policing in Derbyshire. It also saved the force money, of course. So a win-win all round.

'You youngsters will be the ones to lose out in the end,' said Murfin. 'Eventually it will dawn on some clever bugger at Ripley. Why should they pay police officers proper wages when folk are falling over themselves to do the job for nothing?'

Cooper didn't think of himself as a youngster any more. There were much younger officers here. Two of them were in his own CID team, DCs Luke Irvine and Becky Hurst. No one knew what might be in the future for them when they were ready to move up the promotion ladder.

He could see Irvine and Hurst now, in the middle of a densely packed dance floor, where a DJ was belting out rock classics from the 1970s, Gavin Murfin's era. Irvine and Hurst weren't actually dancing together – that would be too much to expect. He was surprised that they would even respond to the same music, since they seemed to agree on so little.

Carol Villiers was here too, though he'd caught only a glimpse of her. He would have liked to have bought her a drink, but he couldn't avoid the impression that she was avoiding him. He might have some work to do there. He couldn't do without Carol's support.

And, as Murfin said, Diane Fry was here too. She'd made the trip from Nottingham for the occasion, despite the fact that Murfin had infuriated her beyond measure when they were forced to work together. Had she come to help soften her image? A Diane Fry who was supportive of her colleagues was quite a new phenomenon to most of the officers here.

Fry was talking to a female inspector from the uniformed section. But now and then Cooper could feel her eyes on him across the room. It was a physical tingle on the back of his neck, a burning sensation on the skin of his ears. His whole body was aware of her gaze.

For a while he tried hard not to look at her, but he couldn't help himself. Fry's presence was drawing his attention like a powerful magnet. When their eyes finally met, it was as if everyone else in the room ceased to exist for a second. The roar of drunken voices fell away and the crowd of faces blurred into an indistinct background. He felt as though he existed for that fleeting moment in an entirely different place, one where the unexpected could happen – and had happened.

Cooper felt a smile forming automatically as he looked at her. Fry didn't smile back. But she tilted her head, lifted her glass and gave him a look across its rim. Her eyes said it all, with a subtle glint that transformed her normally severe expression, sending out a suggestion of something private and intimate. Cooper felt himself almost blushing as their thought waves met in a hot embrace in the middle of the room.

The inspector Fry was talking to noticed her gesture and turned to follow her gaze. Cooper quickly looked away, though he knew it was too late. Police officers were a suspicious lot by nature and they loved a bit of station gossip more than anything.

Questions would be asked, rumours would spread, jokes would be made behind his back.

But perhaps that was happening already. It was difficult to keep anything secret in this job. Cooper knew he had better be careful.

Gradually, he became aware that Gavin Murfin was still talking. He seemed to have been to the bar in the last couple of minutes, since he was clutching a fresh drink. Or more likely some passing acquaintance had shoved it into his hand without him even noticing.

'And that will probably be my first assignment,' Murfin was saying, 'when I start work next Monday.'

'Assignment?' said Cooper.

'At the agency. You know – Eden Valley Enquiries, my new employers? Pay attention, Ben. You're not old enough to have a senior moment. That's my privilege.'

Cooper shook himself. 'Sorry. You were talking about your new job with EVE. You need a licence now, don't you? From the Security Industry Authority?'

'Yes, but don't worry,' said Murfin. 'I've been through all the checks, filled out all the forms. And my licence has come through. So I'm legal.'

'You've still got as much paperwork to do, then?'

Murfin sighed. 'Almost. What was it someone once said? Nothing is certain in life except death and paperwork.'

'Benjamin Franklin,' said Cooper. 'And it was taxes.'

'What?'

'Taxes. It was taxes he said were certain in life.'

'Well, plenty of folk have proved that isn't true recently,' said Murfin sourly. 'I think he must have meant paperwork.'

Cooper didn't have much experience of private enquiry agents. But he knew that business had changed dramatically for them over the last few decades. At one time their bread and butter would have been earned from work on divorce cases. They would have spent the whole of their time conducting surveillance on straying spouses, following them from home to assignation and back, or sneaking surreptitious photographs of their adulterous encounters.

But adultery no longer held the same legal significance and courts no longer required the same level of proof. Suspicious husbands and wives had abandoned the employment of enquiry agents as an unnecessary evil. The slightly seedy, anonymous little man in the mac had disappeared from the profession.

Cooper took another glance at Gavin Murfin. Well, he supposed there was always room for a few of the old school, just as there was in the police service. Murfin had merely switched from one to the other in a seamless conversion. But his new employers had diversified now, taking on a bit of crime, some corporate clients, the occasional missing persons case the police weren't interested in.

And Cooper remembered his last conversation with an employee of Eden Valley Enquiries – a man called Daniel Grady, who had described himself as a property enquiry agent. He had the job of checking up on the prospective neighbours for house purchasers. That was a new line of business, but Cooper could see the potential. Anyone who'd thought of buying a property must have wondered who they might find themselves living next door to.

Murfin glanced around him surreptitiously before speaking again.

'If you want any help some time – you know, with anything that I can do. I'd like to keep in touch with things.'

Cooper raised an eyebrow. 'What sort of help, Gavin?'

'There are things,' said Murfin. 'I know there are. Things that I might be able to do that none of your lot can.'

'Are you talking about something illegal?'

'Of course not. Perish the thought. Just a bit of casual assistance.'

'I don't know, Gavin.'

'Well, think about. Bear it in mind for the future. Now let's have another drink.'

'To old times?' said Cooper.

'And to the future.'

MURFIN GRADUALLY BECAME the centre of a growing knot of laughing well-wishers. A steady stream of senior officers began to filter their way. After greeting Murfin with a few words and a hearty handshake, they moved on and tended to cluster together in little groups for safety.

Before long Cooper found himself being drawn reluctantly into their orbit. He was a detective inspector now, after all. In this environment there was 'us' and 'them', but there was also 'us' and 'not quite us'. Cooper didn't feel that he'd quite moved from one to the other yet and didn't know if he really wanted to.

He was conscious of the eyes on him, watching for which way he moved. But when the inspectors and chief inspectors began to make their excuses and drift away into the night, Cooper stayed. There was such a thing as loyalty, after all.

He looked around the slowly emptying room, seeking Gavin Murfin's familiar figure, hoping he was still upright and not causing too much trouble. He located Murfin finally, sitting in a corner at a table covered with empty glasses and half-full bottles. He was deep in eager conversation with Devdan Sharma.

TYLER SMITH HATED growing up in New Mills. Like everyone else, he would be off to Manchester as soon as he could escape. In fact, he liked only one thing about his home town. And that was the Millennium Walkway.

Late that night he ran down the steps from Union Road between Lloyds Bank and the Masonic Hall, which led into the Torrs. They called this the 'park under the town'. Two rivers came together under the Union Road bridge, and there were ruins of old mills and cottages scattered along their banks.

Loads of people were down in the Torrs during the day. There were rock climbers, old folk walking their dogs or just sitting by the water; hikers who were on the trail that came right through the valley from the nature reserve just outside town.

There was still one big mill, Torr Vale, standing across the river, towering over the weirs like a ruined castle. Part of it had been burned down a few years ago, but someone had bought it and was trying to restore bits of it. There were lights on in the windows of one of the upper floors and he could see a van parked in the yard with some workmen moving stuff around. But soon they would all go home and the mill would be empty.

The walkway was amazing. It had been built for the celebration of the new millennium in 2000. He'd been very small then, but he remembered his parents bringing him to see it because it was such a big deal for New Mills.

A steel rail and a few strands of wire cable formed the sides. Weeds sprouted out of the high wall of the railway embankment way above. And the walkway swung right out over the water where it cascaded over the weirs. You could stand on the curve of the walkway and be alone with the water, where no one could see you.

A train passed overhead on the embankment as he stepped onto the walkway. He was planning to head up towards the old-fashioned signal box near the station. There would be some lads up there to hang out with. The ticket office was only open in the morning for people travelling to Manchester, so they just had to dodge the CCTV cameras on the gates.

At the quietest end of the walkway, a footbridge crossed to the mill if they wanted to go and mess about in the woods.

He broke into a trot, making the deck of the walkway vibrate underfoot. The roar of the weir drowned out everything else, even his own footsteps. Unless they were peering over the wall outside the heritage centre, no one could see him here. He was overlooked only by the broken windows and rusted girders of the mill.

Tyler stumbled to a halt, his breathing suddenly harsher than it ought to be. Something was lying on the deck of the walkway a few yards ahead. A pile of clothes, maybe just a coat and a pair of shoes. There was an old dosser with long hair and a beard who slept in the Torrs sometimes. Tyler had seen him sheltering under the rock face below the back of the buildings in Union Road. Had something happened to him here?

He found the idea strangely exciting. More slowly now, he moved forward, glancing over his shoulder to make sure no one else was around. When he looked more closely at the coat, he could see it didn't belong to the homeless man. It was too clean and too new. Could a tourist just have taken it off and forgotten it? There might be something in it to take, then. A wallet or a phone. You never knew. People could be really stupid like that.

But would someone have left their shoes too. Now that didn't make sense at all.

Tyler straightened up. It was only then that he noticed the rope tied to the steel rail. It was a thick nylon rope, the kind he'd seen some of the rock climbers using. So that was it. Some nutcase had lowered himself down to the river – though what for, he couldn't imagine.

The rope squeaked as it moved slightly on the rail. Some weight below was making it swing. Tyler leaned over the rail, expecting to see a face looking back up at him. They must have heard him, or seen him coming onto the walkway.

But there was no face. He could see only the top of a head. Thin, wet hair plastered to the skull. A glimpse of purple, bloated skin. The body of a man, without a coat or shoes, just hanging from the rope. Not holding the rope in his hands, but hanging. Hanging by the neck.

Chapter Eleven

Wednesday 11 February

NEXT MORNING AT West Street, Cooper walked into a subdued atmosphere. He could almost sense the headaches around the station from those who'd been at the leaving party last night. The officers who hadn't attended because they were on duty walked around looking virtuous and laughing at their colleagues.

In the CID room Gavin Murfin's place was still empty. There was no replacement for him yet and might not be for some time. Murfin had left behind a few mementoes of his presence, though – just in case his former colleagues were missing him too much. There was a Derby County fixture list for last season, a plastic policeman's helmet he'd worn at the Christmas party and which still had a dent in it where Becky Hurst had hit him with the matching plastic truncheon, and a drawer bursting with Snickers wrappers and empty doughnut boxes, every corner and crevice full of crumbs and glinting with powdered sugar.

The state of Murfin's desk could explain why the office had been infested with ants during the summer. Maintenance staff had been driven to distraction with complaints about them. Columns of ants seemed to turn up out of nowhere and crawl over computer keyboards, or creep inside a monitor and die in the middle of the screen.

It could have been worse, though. They might have been overrun with mice instead. Cooper wondered if they could be there now, inside the walls, waiting patiently for Gavin Murfin to come back from the pie shop.

He could see that Detective Sergeant Dev Sharma had settled at his new desk anyway. It was the one that had been Cooper's own until recently. But now he had this cubby hole to work in, with a wall half made of glass so he could see into the CID room, and everyone in there could see him – at least if he stood up.

It was an odd feeling being cut off from his old working environment yet still able to see what was happening. It was like watching a story taking place on a TV screen instead of being involved in it himself. Cooper suspected it would take him a while to get used to this.

He sat in his new chair and swivelled backwards and forwards for a while, listening for a faint squeak he'd detected in the wheels. He looked at the reports and messages in his in-tray, but he couldn't concentrate on them. He felt too restless. His natural instinct was to be out there talking to people, not sitting in an office.

That was one thing he hadn't quite got used to yet about being a DI. He couldn't interview everyone himself. He had to reply on feedback from members of his team and try to get an impression of the people he was dealing with at second hand. It made him feel oddly detached from the job. He really wanted to be out there seeing these people for himself, figuring out who everyone was and what their relationships were.

But he knew he mustn't try to do that. He'd probably already gone too far by visiting Shaw Farm and Cloughpit House with Villiers. He wondered if Dev Sharma had been watching him disapprovingly, comparing him with the last detective inspector he'd worked with back in Derby.

He reminded himself of the job description he'd somehow met the criteria for. *The ability to motivate others, delegate tasks and maintain a general overview of cases. Strong people skills and the ability to communicate with people at all levels are also crucial.*

He also recalled that warning that the role of a detective inspector might involve working longer than average hours. So not everything had changed.

Cooper got up and went out into the CID room. Everyone stopped what they were doing and looked up, as if he was a visiting member of royalty. He perched on the edge of Murfin's old desk, regardless of the crumbs.

'I need to brief Superintendent Branagh this morning,' he said. 'So help me – who has any thoughts on where we stand with the Shawhead inquiry? What decent leads do we have? Anyone?'

As he expected, Luke Irvine was the first to chip in. Always eager, that was Luke. Not necessarily right in his assessments, but keen.

'If Gavin was here, he would have the old lady in the frame for something,' said Irvine. 'Mrs Swindells at Higher Fold Farm.'

'Oh yes. She's the mother of the farmer, Grant Swindells,' said Cooper.

'Right. She wanted to give us a cup of tea and a chocolate biscuit before we'd even got through the door. She talked non-stop, so we could hardly get away from the house. Bombarded us with questions, too. In fact, she was a bit too friendly, if you ask me.'

'So you made another conquest, Luke,' said Hurst.

'She's eighty if she's a day,' protested Irvine.

'Just your type, then.'

Dev Sharma had turned slowly to look at Irvine when he began to speak about the old lady. Cooper couldn't read the expression on his face. Was he disapproving of Irvine's levity?

Irvine shook his head. 'Well, I'm just saying. All those questions . . . What did we think had happened? Who were we going to talk to next? Had we spoken to the Durkins at Cloughpit House?'

'She was just being inquisitive,' said Cooper. 'She's probably lonely living out there, doesn't get many visitors.'

'Well, there's no one else in the household. Just the old lady and her son.'

'There you are, then. He'll be out all day on the farm and Mrs Swindells doesn't see a soul to talk to. Then a couple of nice policemen knock on the door.'

Hurst laughed sarcastically. But Sharma turned back to Cooper.

'Mrs Swindells did tell us some useful details,' he said.

'Oh?'

Irvine frowned at his notebook, as if he'd just been accused of missing something. Which perhaps he had.

'The old lady watches from her window. She sits in the same place most of the day. She calls it "the room". It looks out onto the road and she can see two of her neighbours' houses.'

'Which ones, Dev?'

'There's Top Barn, where Mr and Mrs Schofield live. They only moved in recently. Mr Michael Schofield is a chemical engineer. Mrs Schofield runs some kind of internet business. She sells hand-made soap and candles, that sort of thing. She also teaches creative arts and crafts at a local adult education centre two days a week. And there's Shawhead Cottages, owned by Mrs and Mrs Hibbert. Ian Hibbert travels into Manchester every day for his job at a marketing consultancy. His wife Amanda is a graphic designer and website developer, working mostly from home. They have three children. There's a daughter Zoe, who is nineteen and away at university. She's studying sociology in Birmingham. And there are two sons – the youngest, Adam, is eleven, while Leo is sixteen and attends New Mills School, which is a Business and Enterprise College. He's in Year 12, studying for his A-levels. He's a very polite and helpful young man.'

'And how did you find all this out?'

'From Mrs Swindells of course,' said Sharma.

It didn't go unnoticed around the room that Sharma hadn't referred to his notebook at all. Luke Irvine glowered at him. Hurst had a quiet smile to herself. Carol Villiers looked reluctantly impressed.

'And seventy-five,' added Sharma suddenly.

'What is?'

'Mrs Swindells. She isn't eighty, she's seventy-five years old.'

'How do you know that?' asked Irvine.

'She told me as she was showing us out of her house. I stopped to say goodbye while you walked to the gate.'

'You just went right in there and asked the old lady her age?'

'It came out in conversation.'

'Yeah, right.'

Sharma shrugged. 'Can I help it if people tell me things?'

'Hold on – the Hibberts have two children of school age?' said Cooper.

'Leo, aged sixteen, and the youngest Adam—' began Irvine.

'I know, I know. They both attend New Mills School. But where are they? Did they get into school yesterday? If so, how?'

'Oh, you're kidding,' said Villiers. 'Two young boys found their way from Shawhead, while everyone else was telling us there was no way in our out?'

But Dev Sharma was smiling as he listened to the conversation. He shook his head.

'No,' he said. 'It's half-term.'

Cooper relaxed. 'Of course it is.'

He could almost kick himself for having reacted the way he did. And Villiers looked embarrassed too. It was one of the weaknesses of his team, he supposed. Neither he, nor any of his DCs, had children of their own. But he did have his two nieces, Matt's daughters. They were teenagers, but they were still at school in Edendale. If he'd been keeping in touch with his family as much as he used to, he would have known perfectly well it was half-term. He used to take them for trips out on his rest days when it was school holidays. When had they drifted away from each other so much? Or was it just him who'd drifted?

'How did you know that, Dev?' he said.

'I have older brothers and sisters,' said Sharma. 'We're a close family.'

'Oh, and the sheep,' said Villiers. 'You wanted to know about the sheep.'

Cooper turned to her. 'Yes? Whose were they?'

'They belonged to Mr Swindells. It took him an hour to round them all up and get them back into their field.'

'Did he manage it on his own? Sheep aren't usually so cooperative.'

'No, the Durkins came down to help him from Cloughpit House.'

'Interesting.'

'Mr Swindells claims that someone must have opened the gate and deliberately let his sheep out onto the road. But they always say that, don't they?'

Cooper nodded. 'You're right. But it might be true in this case.'

COOPER HAD TO brief Detective Superintendent Branagh. She was a good listener, always very attentive. She made brief notes and asked all the right questions. Well, sometimes they were the most difficult questions. But Cooper appreciated that. It made him think hard about the answers.

After a few minutes Branagh put her pen down, with an air of finality. Cooper felt able to relax.

'Did DC Murfin's send-off go well?' asked Branagh.

Her tone suggested that she was really asking for an assurance that he definitely wasn't coming back again.

'Yes, it was a lively occasion.'

'Everyone was there, I imagine?'

'Yes, pretty much everyone.'

'Did Detective Sergeant Sharma come along? I suggested he might want to show his face.'

'Yes, he was there, ma'am.'

'Excellent. It's good for him to fit in with the team straight away. You haven't had much chance to get to know him yourself yet, have you?'

Was that a hint of criticism? Cooper felt himself bridling with resentment.

'Not with the inquiry we got under way yesterday at Shawhead.'

Branagh nodded. 'Of course, of course. But don't leave it too long. Have a conversation. I'm hoping you two will work well together, Ben.'

'Yes, ma'am. But you know there's also a vacancy for another DC? Since Gavin Murfin's retirement, we're one short on the team.'

'Ah, that's a bit more difficult. For the time being you'll have to cover the shortfall with extractions from other sections when necessary.'

'But they're short-staffed too,' protested Cooper.

His superintendent didn't blink. 'Aren't we all?' she said.

WHEN HE RETURNED to the CID room, Cooper called Dev Sharma into his office. There was one chair available for a visitor to sit on, though it was crammed in between the door and a filing cabinet.

'I gather you've transferred from D Division,' said Cooper. 'Where were you stationed?'

'Derby West. Peartree.'

'Really?'

Cooper had visited Peartree police station once. It was part of Derby South policing section, and he remembered it being sandwiched between the clinic and the library on Pear Tree Road, right in the heart of one of the most culturally mixed areas in the whole of the county.

But Peartree was also well known around the force for a recent example of successful twenty-first-century policing – the rescue of a Slovakian man who had been forced to live in subhuman conditions by a slave labour gang. The man was a victim of human trafficking, shipped to the UK as a sixteen-year-old after being dumped by his own family on the doorstep of a children's home, aged ten. He'd been forced into jobs like car washing and labouring on a chicken farm. His passport and wages were taken from him, he was forced to sleep in a room with ten other people and he'd been beaten up when he tried to escape from his captors. When the police first made contact with him, he'd been reduced to skin and bone after working up to twenty hours a day for food and cigarettes.

'Did you work on the slave labour case?' asked Cooper.

But Sharma shook his head. 'Some of our officers at Peartree were responsible for arranging for him to be flown home to Slovakia safely. But the gang masters weren't operating in our area. We had to pass the inquiry to West Midlands.'

'Interesting case, though,' said Cooper.

'It has raised some issues for the force to consider.'

That was true. In fact, it was a case that had brought home very graphically the existence of modern-day slavery. Cooper had a briefing on his desk from the Modern Slavery Helpline, which listed all the signs to watch out for. People who looked malnourished or unkempt, who seemed unfamiliar with their surroundings, who avoided eye contact and appeared frightened of strangers, who had no identification and few personal possessions, or who travelled at odd times, being collected and dropped off for work on a regular basis late at night or early in the morning.

And this wasn't just another briefing that had no relevance to E Division. Some of the isolated farmsteads out here in the hills of the Peak District were exactly the sort of places where trafficked slave labour might be employed, and no one would have any idea what was going on.

He supposed it was one of the issues Diane Fry's unit would be concerned with at EMSOU. They would aim to bring the traffickers and slave masters to court as part of their remit to tackle organised crime.

'Dev, it was good of you to come to Gavin Murfin's leaving party last night,' said Cooper. 'I'm sorry if Gavin was a nuisance at all.'

'A nuisance?'

'Well, he can say the wrong thing at times, especially when he's had a few drinks.'

Sharma shrugged. 'There was no problem between us.'

'According to your record, you've served in Peartree and Normanton, and some of the other inner city areas of Derby,' said Cooper. 'All very culturally diverse.'

'Yes, there's a much higher percentage of the population who belong to the Asian communities. Much higher than in this division, I mean.'

'Hindus are in a minority, though, even in the Asian communities.'

'My family are from the Punjab,' said Sharma, 'where Hindus are also a minority.'

'Really? You mean there's a majority of Muslims?'

'No, all the Muslims left the area after Partition and went to Pakistan. The population of Indian Punjab is majority Sikh. About 60 per cent.'

'I didn't know that.'

Sharma shrugged. 'It was a convenient place for my grandparents to come from. It's not too remote or isolated. It's near enough to the National Capital Region and New Delhi. My family were lucky to have access to the best opportunities. Including the chance to make a life here in Britain, without starting out as illegal immigrants or asylum seekers. We have never been poor.'

'Why the police, then?'

Sharma didn't answer at first, and Cooper wondered if he had gone too far and was being too intrusive. Perhaps the management of human resources wasn't one of his greatest talents.

'Do you mind me asking these questions?' he said.

'No,' said Sharma. 'I understand. You need to know your team.'

The detective sergeant's face remained expressionless. And despite his words, Cooper began to feel even more uncomfortable. Someone else might have politely told him to mind his own business by now. But Dev Sharma was being excessively amenable and polite. Coldly polite.

'I wanted to serve my community,' he said.

And that made Cooper relax a little. He was reassured by the familiar phrase. Serving the community. It was a phrase that appeared in much of Derbyshire Constabulary's public relations material, was mentioned in almost every quote from a senior officer in a newspaper report. It was the force's unofficial slogan. The badge said, '*Vis Unita Fortior*': 'United Strength is Stronger'.

'There was a programme in Derby to reach out to the Asian community,' said Sharma. 'Police officers came to my school and talked to us. I don't know why, but the job appealed to me. My parents didn't approve, but they came to terms with my decision.'

That was more like it. Cooper could empathise with the rather conflicted urge.

'Have you experienced any problems at all during your service?' he asked.

'Racist attitudes, you mean?'

'Yes.'

'From the public, or my fellow officers?'

Cooper hesitated, worried that he was on delicate ground again. But he was aware of some recent incidents in the area. Racist graffiti had been sprayed on the wall of a cave in Dovedale, one of the Peak District's busiest tourist hot spots. And just this winter someone had drawn a swastika in the snow on the bonnet of a car in New Mills.

'Well, either,' he said.

'Very little, to be honest,' said Sharma. 'And I don't suppose you've experienced many problems here in the past? I haven't seen any other officers or civilian staff from ethnic minorities since I've been in E Division.'

'No, that's true.'

Cooper winced as he recalled stories told by some of the older officers who remembered serving with a black officer decades ago. From all accounts, he'd been treated very badly. But times had changed, even in Edendale.

'Well, as far as the public are concerned, it won't be a problem,' said Sharma. 'The further away from the front line you work, the less racism you encounter. When you're dealing with a serious incident, people want your help whatever your colour.'

'One last question,' said Cooper.

'Yes?'

'Are you a vegetarian?'

Sharma shook his head. 'In my form of Hinduism we can eat fish and even chicken. No cows, obviously. They're sacred.'

'Of course.'

For a moment Cooper had a mad idea of taking Sharma to Bridge End Farm to meet his brother. Matt worshipped cows too, in his own way. Not just because they helped to earn him a living, but because of their personalities, so he said. Cooper wondered how the two of them would get on. It was actually quite hard to imagine.

But then he looked at Sharma and thought he detected a suggestion of a twinkle in his brown eyes. Cooper relaxed a little. Like Gavin Murfin, he was probably trying too hard.

'There's a restaurant in Edendale where they specialise in fish dishes,' he said. 'The Mussel and Crab in Hollowgate. We should go for a meal one night. You and me.'

'Bonding?' said Sharma

'If you like.'

Sharma nodded. 'I'd be happy to do that.'

Cooper watched him, hoping for a bit more response, but not getting it. Dev Sharma was about as impenetrable as anybody he'd met. This was hard work.

He looked at Sharma's personnel file again.

'I see you live in the Normanton area of Derby too,' he said. 'Isn't that a bit of a journey to get here in the morning?'

There was silence for a moment, which made Cooper look up. Sharma's face was impassive, but the silence began to grow uncomfortable.

'It can be a problem to have someone living so far out of the area,' said Cooper, feeling some explanation was necessary. 'If traffic is bad around Derby, you may be delayed getting to work.'

'I know,' said Sharma. 'But I suppose I might say that it isn't as far as travelling in from Nottingham.'

That gave Cooper a jolt. He felt himself flushing with anger at the softly spoken jibe. But Sharma's face was still calm. There was no smirk or disrespectful stare to accompany the comment. He was just making use of a bit of information he'd gathered. And letting his new DI know that he was aware of his relationship with a member of the East Midlands Special Operations Unit. Most junior officers would just have kept it to themselves, or gossiped about it behind his back. But Sharma had come straight out with it.

In a way it was impressive. Not least because it demonstrated that Sharma had found out more personal detail about Cooper than the other way round, even in his short time in E Division. And Cooper felt he might actually have deserved the remark. His questions had perhaps become too intrusive, out of a genuine curiosity. Handling people could be so difficult to get right.

'Look, I know you're probably not going to be here in Edendale for very long,' he said.

Sharma raised an eyebrow. 'Why do say that?'

'I imagine you're destined for higher things. You'll be moving on. Promotion.'

'Eventually perhaps. But . . .'

'What?'

Then Sharma smiled a genuine smile for the first time. 'I think I'm going to enjoy working with you as long as I'm here.'

Chapter Twelve

WINDMILL FEED SOLUTIONS was based on a modern industrial estate on the outskirts of Stockport. The company's surroundings contradicted the bucolic image on their trucks. There wasn't a windmill in sight – only a vast DIY distribution centre, some smaller factory units and a slip road onto the M67.

Cooper drove past the giant hoppers for raw materials and parked his Toyota near the mill. Through enormous double doors, he could see workers filling storage bins and stacking pallets of feed. Some of them wore masks against the dust swirling in the air from the milling process.

Inside the offices he was met by the transport manager – a man called Bateman, middle-aged and tired-looking, with black-rimmed glasses he kept taking off to rub at his eyes.

'Thank you for taking the time to talk to me, Mr Bateman,' said Cooper.

'I can only spare a few minutes, I'm afraid. This a very busy operation.' He looked out of a window onto the yard, where a lorry was backing up to one of the loading bays. 'We have a fast turn-around. We deliver Monday to Friday, with a one-to-three-day delivery service from point of order. Even when we're not delivering, the mill is still in production. It never stops out there.'

'Your driver, Malcom Kelsey,' said Cooper. 'What can you tell me about him?'

'Yes, Malcom Kelsey,' said Bateman. 'Everyone calls him Mac. He's been with us for nearly ten years. Started off driving vans, then did his HGV training and got his Category C licence. One of our best drivers.'

'Really? No problems with him in the past?'

'Not much. Well, not really.'

'Could I see his personnel file, please?'

Bateman looked uncomfortable. He replaced his glasses and opened a manilla folder, then closed it again.

'These are confidential details, of course. I willingly gave one of your officers a copy of Mac Kelsey's schedule of deliveries for Monday. But personal information is rather a different matter, I believe.'

'Mr Kelsey is missing, sir. Given the evidence, we're treating his disappearance as suspicious.'

'I heard he was assaulted in his cab. Is it true, detective inspector?'

'We'll know for certain when we've completed our inquiries. In the meantime we really need your cooperation. I need to inquire into Mr Kelsey's background circumstances.'

Bateman sighed. 'I can't see that it's relevant.'

'Deciding the relevance of any facts isn't really your job, sir. It's what I'm here for.'

'Questions of confidentiality still apply,' said Bateman. 'I can't let you have the file, but I can share with you some of the less personal details perhaps.'

He opened the file again and stared at the first page, as if he hadn't seen it before. But Cooper felt sure he'd studied it carefully as soon as he got the first phone call.

'Well, it's true to say there have been a few minor incidents.'

'I would be very interested to hear about them.'

Still Bateman hesitated. 'Our drivers are all fully trained to industry guidelines of course.'

'No doubt.'

'But we have an extensive range of vehicles in our fleet. We use curtain-sided vehicles to deliver bagged feed and they require more headroom than a bulk vehicle. Normally, we check with a customer whether there any access restrictions, or obstructions such as overhead power lines.'

'Whose job is that?'

'Well . . . mine.'

'I see.'

Nervously, Bateman fiddled with his glasses before he continued. 'Obviously, we have to be able to accommodate any access restrictions. So some vehicles have mechanical off-load where required. Our drivers are always available to stack products, as long as it's safe.'

'Safe?'

'Ideally, we need an area off the public highway with sufficient space for unloading. But sometimes vehicles have to be unloaded at the roadside. It can mean drivers working where they're in the way of other road users. Safety can be a major issue. You know what some of those farms are like out there, particularly in the hillier areas.'

'Yes, I do know. So . . . ?'

'Well, all right.' Bateman cleared his throat. 'Mac Kelsey had an incident near Marple, where he was alleged to have caused an accident by forcing a car to swerve when he reversed his fork-lift into the road. The car ended up in a ditch and the driver was slightly injured.'

'How slightly?'

'Only a few bruises, I believe. Perhaps a bit of whiplash. Our insurance covered it, but anything like that affects our annual premium, of course. A business like ours can't afford too many extra overheads, especially if it can be attributed to our employees' negligence.'

'Was there a court case? Was Kelsey charged with anything?'

'No charges were brought.'

'Was Mac Kelsey ever accompanied?' asked Cooper. 'A driver's mate. A trainee perhaps?'

Bateman shook his head firmly. 'No, our drivers work alone. They're not allowed to let anyone else in the cab. No lifts or hitch-hikers, anything like that.'

'But it might happen, mightn't it?'

'I'm sure it wouldn't. But if I found out, they would be in trouble.'

'But if one of your drivers picked someone up, how would you know?'

'Unless someone actually saw them and reported it,' admitted Bateman, 'the chances are I would never find out.'

Cooper made a note. 'Anything else?'

'And then there was the equipment damage,' said Bateman.

'What kind of equipment?'

'The type of truck that Mac Kelsey drives has a Palfinger Crayler mounted on the tailgate.'

'A what?'

'Its own forklift. You see, we service a lot of farmers who still prefer the small twenty-kilo bags. They're easier for manual

handling. But they have to be delivered in pallet loads, so we oper-
ate a truck-mounted forklift. The trouble is, operating a forklift
truck on uneven ground can cause an overturn. Kelsey had the
appropriate training, but he overturned a forklift on a delivery
one day. Another insurance job.'

'So has Mr Kelsey been the subject of disciplinary proceedings?'

'He's had a couple of warnings.'

'Recently?'

Bateman referred to the file again. 'The forklift incident was
two months ago.'

'Who reported that?'

'The customer did.'

'A local farmer?'

'Yes.'

'It's a bit different from getting his lorry trapped under a bridge,
though,' said Cooper.

'And that's not the first time either,' said Bateman.

'What isn't?'

'Mac Kelsey getting stuck. He was suspended for a while
when he got a vehicle trapped in a lane that was too narrow
and couldn't reverse out because he was on a steep hill. He
nearly burned out that clutch trying to extricate himself. On
that occasion we discovered that his satnav setting had been
changed from HGV to car mode. We couldn't accept that as
an excuse, of course. An experienced driver should use some
common sense.'

'I see.'

'Was that the case here?'

'I don't know,' said Cooper. 'Until just now it hadn't occurred
to me.'

'Well, I'm glad to have helped a bit, then. Will you let me know the outcome? It might help us to avoid this kind of incident in the future.'

'Yes, I'm sure we can do that.'

Bateman hesitated again, aware that something else was expected of him before he showed Cooper the door.

'You should talk to Mr Kelsey's wife,' said Cooper. 'I'm sure she would appreciate some support.'

Bateman jumped up. 'Certainly, certainly. You're quite right – that's what we should do. I'll get straight on to it, and see what we can do for her. A valued member of staff and all that. I'll get her address from the file. You don't need that, do you?'

'No, we have that already,' said Cooper, watching Bateman's sudden enthusiasm for action.

'Naturally you have. So, er . . .' Bateman tilted his head on one side as he looked at Cooper expectantly. 'Was there anything else I can help you with, inspector?'

'Yes. Did Mac Kelsey have any enemies? Anyone you can think of who might have wished to do him harm?'

'Well, no one here, that's for certain,' said Bateman. 'The drivers all get on well, so far as they ever see each other. It's a solitary job by its nature, of course. I've never heard any complaints about him from members of staff, or anything like that.'

'Nothing you've heard about his home life, his relationship with his wife.'

Bateman shook his head. 'Nothing at all, I'm afraid. Perhaps I haven't been so much help, after all.'

Cooper stood up to leave. 'No, you've been very helpful. I wish everyone was so forthcoming.'

Hesitantly, Bateman shook his hand. 'I wouldn't want you to go away thinking this company isn't concerned about the possibility of injury and damage during deliveries. We always carry out risk assessments, you know. It's part of our responsibility under health and safety regulations.'

'Of course you do,' said Cooper. 'But I don't think your risk assessment would have covered this case.'

MAC KELSEY'S WIFE had been contacted by phone, but a personal visit was essential. Anne and Malcolm Kelsey lived in a dormer bungalow in the Heysbank area of Disley, one of the first villages over the border in Cheshire. It was an easy call on the way back from Windmill Feed Solutions.

Cooper parked his car at the kerb and walked through a dense box hedge to reach the steps to the front door. He saw a blurred figure appear through the frosted glass panes before he even rang the bell.

Inside, the house was neat and bright, and smelled of pine air freshener. Anne Kelsey looked as though she might have dressed for his arrival, her hair brushed and a fresh touch of make-up.

'I don't understand what's happened to Malcolm,' she said. 'Someone tried to explain it to me when they called, but it just didn't sink in. I mean, Mac has gone missing or something? Don't his firm know where he is? If you ask them at the office . . .'

'No,' said Cooper as gently as he could. 'They have no idea, any more than we do. We've found his lorry, but not your husband.'

'He wouldn't just leave it,' she said. 'He must be ill, don't you think?'

'Or injured, I'm afraid.'

'Oh?'

She hesitated, seemed to be about to ask the obvious question, but then decided not to. Sometimes it was better not to know too much detail. It could send the imagination off in the wrong direction.

And Cooper was thankful not to have to explain about the blood in her husband's cab. She must surely know by his very presence in her house how seriously the police were taking Malcolm's disappearance.

'He'll turn up somewhere,' she said.

'What can you tell me about his routine on Monday?' asked Cooper.

'Well, not much. He left for work at the usual time, so far as I know. He sets off early, before I'm up.'

'I see.'

'And I was out on Monday night,' said Anne. 'Malcolm knew I was going to be out. Mondays are the nights for my creative writing class.'

'Creative writing?'

'Yes. It's a change, you know. And I enjoy it. Afterwards we tend to go to the pub for a chat. So he would have to fend for himself, instead of me having a meal ready for him. But Malcolm was used to that on a Monday night. Not that it meant anything more than him calling at a takeaway.'

'Has your husband had any problems recently?' asked Cooper.

'Problems?'

'Money troubles? Debt? An argument with anyone?'

'Not that I know of.'

'Would you know if he did, Mrs Kelsey?'

'I'm his wife,' she said simply. 'I would know if there was something wrong. He wouldn't be able to hide it from me. I would get it out of him in the end.'

'But you hadn't noticed anything recently?'

'No,' she said.

'Does he have any brothers or sisters? Or close friends?'

'You mean people he might have talked to, because he couldn't talk to me?' she said.

'I didn't mean that,' said Cooper, though it was very close to what he did mean.

'Malcolm has an older sister who lives in Manchester with her husband. They have two grown-up children, and grandchildren. We don't see very much of them. They're always too busy.'

Cooper wondered if the slightly aggrieved tone indicated envy of Mrs Kelsey's sister-in-law. Was it her children, or her grand-children? Or perhaps even her husband, who she was too busy to spare time away from to visit her brother down the road in Disley.

'There are some people we know in the village, of course,' said Anne. 'People we socialise with. They're friends of both of us, though. I can't think who Malcolm might have confided in, unless it was one of his colleagues at work. One of the other drivers?'

'Has he always driven a lorry?'

'Well, he worked up to it, you might say. He started off driving vans for a courier company. He liked being on the road. Then he got a job at Windmill and took the training to get his HGV licence. He's always said they're a good company to work for.'

'No trouble at work, then?'

'Nothing much,' she said, loyally. 'Nothing that was worrying him.'

Cooper hesitated before the next question, wondering whether she could anticipate it. Some spouses did – perhaps because they already had their own suspicions, or they'd run through all the scenarios in their minds and eventually arrived at this one.

'And what about any problems in your marriage?' he said.

From her expression, Mrs Kelsey seemed to be genuinely shocked.

'Seriously?' she said. 'You're asking me that?'

'I'm sorry. But I'm afraid it's a possibility we always have to take into account. You'd be surprised how often it comes down to something like that. So I'm obliged to ask. It saves us a lot of time if we know from the beginning, one way or the other.'

Mrs Kelsey was quiet for a moment and Cooper could see her thinking about what he'd said. He didn't tell her that even if she assured him there were no problems, he still wouldn't discount it as a possibility. Yes, it did happen often that a relationship problem was at the root of a disappearance or a violent incident. And in many of those cases the spouse had no idea there was a problem.

'No,' she said finally. 'I couldn't say there was a problem. Oh, Malcolm used to have a bit of a roving eye, but that was years ago. I never asked too many questions at the time, because I didn't want to know. And he settled down. He lost interest, I think. It happens with age, I suppose. No, there are no problems.'

Cooper nodded. It was only half an answer she'd given. There didn't have to be anyone else involved for him to want to disappear. If things were bad enough at home, that was enough of a motive. And age didn't make any difference, in his experience.

'Thank you, Mrs Kelsey. I'm sorry to have to ask these questions.'

'I understand.'

He wasn't sure that she did. But at least he'd escaped an angry outburst. Some situations he hated – they made him feel so intrusive. He'd been telling her the truth, though. The questions were necessary.

'And does your husband have any interests outside work?' he asked.

'Interests?' she said vaguely.

'Any hobbies, or sports he's involved in?'

Mrs Kelsey rallied now, grateful to be on safer ground. This was a subject she felt much happier talking about.

'Oh, I see,' she said. 'Well, Malcolm isn't very sporty. Not when it comes to participating anyway. He likes to watch football and rugby on TV. He has a drink occasionally. We went to see *The Meat Loaf Story* at Manchester Opera House. That was probably the last time we went anywhere together.'

'*The Meat Loaf Story*? That's a new one on me.'

'It's a tribute act,' she said.

'Oh, one of those.'

There were so many successful tribute acts now that there were whole 'fake festivals' dedicated to them. Everybody was watching New2, Oasish, the Antarctic Monkeys.

But Cooper was more interested in the tension that had been immediately evident in Anne Kelsey's manner when he asked that innocuous question about her husband's interests outside work. What interests had she been thinking of, if not hobbies and sports?

'Where's Malcolm's car?' said Anne suddenly.

'I'm sorry?' said Cooper. 'Mr Kelsey was driving a DAF lorry.'

'No, I mean his car. The Megane. The one he drives to work in.'

Kelsey owned a car, of course. It was strange that it hadn't occurred to Cooper much earlier. He'd got so fixated on the image of Kelsey sitting in the driver's seat of a large HGV that it hadn't struck him straight away that he would also be a normal motorist.

'Can you give me the details?'

'A silver-grey Renault Megane. I'll have to find the registration number if you want it.'

'Yes, please.'

That was an oversight. No doubt Mac Kelsey's silver-grey Megane was still standing in the staff parking area at Windmill Feeds. If it wasn't, he wouldn't know how to explain the circumstance.

'I'm quite sure Malcolm will turn up somewhere,' Anne Kelsey said again when she came back with the registration number. 'There'll be a logical explanation.'

THE SEARCH FOR Mac Kelsey had resumed at first daylight and was making better progress. A team had started out from the Cloughpit Lane bridge, with a line of officers slowly moving across the ground, heads down in concentration, alert for any traces of evidence. A spot of blood, a discarded item, a patch of crushed vegetation.

Two dog units had been called in to help the search. A four-year-old German Shepherd called Max, who had come direct from Germany for his training with the Derbyshire dog unit, responded mostly to commands in his native language. But he was the first across a field between two dry-stone walls, nose down as he followed a trail through coarse grass and dead bracken to a stack of old straw bales slowly rotting near a gateway.

Max stopped at the corner of the stack, dwarfed by the giant round bales, and indicated for his handler. The officer hurried up to see what he'd located. A few minutes later it was obvious to everyone.

The body of Mac Kelsey had been hastily buried in a shallow pit under the loose stones of a collapsed wall. When officers lifted some of the debris clear, the imprint of the heavier stones was still visible on the softening skin of his corpse.

Chapter Thirteen

AN HOUR LATER Ben Cooper stood with the Crime Scene Manager Wayne Abbott as officers in scene suits photographed the heap of stones and uncovered the body inch by inch, setting each stone carefully aside to be labelled and bagged. Every rock might carry vital traces that could be used as evidence.

'We should get the tents up quickly before any more trains come over the bridge,' said Cooper. 'We don't want gawpers and gongoozlers seeing all this.'

'We'll only be a couple of minutes,' said Abbott. 'They shouldn't have moved so many stones before we got here.'

'From your perspective, perhaps,' said Cooper. 'But they had to be sure the victim wasn't still alive. That's the first priority.'

Mac Kelsey was still wearing his brown fleece with the green Windmill logo on the breast pocket and a yellow high-vis jacket, the reflective strips glowing garishly in the powerful crime scene lighting. His matching baseball cap had been found lying at his feet, thrown in with the body and covered up. On his feet were heavy black safety boots with steel toe caps. The maker's name on the side said, 'Himalayan'.

Kelsey was a big man, but in death his torso looked deflated and squashed. In time he might have become flattened by the weight on top of him, as the soft tissues decayed and the bones gave way under the pressure.

As Cooper approached, the forensic medical examiner stood up and brushed himself off.

'The post-mortem examination may find other injuries,' he said. 'But it looks as though the fatal one was a stab wound to the left side of the neck. I'd say it punctured his jugular vein. There's a great deal of blood on his left hand and the sleeve of his jacket on that side.'

'He was holding his neck to try to suppress the bleeding?' said Cooper.

'That would be my guess.'

Mac Kelsey had been trying to get away from whatever had happened. He'd tried to make it to safety, but hadn't known where he was heading. Looking at him lying in his shallow makeshift grave, Cooper wasn't sure how fast he could have run in his high-vis jacket and Himalayan safety boots.

Cooper remembered Carol Villiers' first call to him about the incident in Shawhead. *'There's an awful lot of blood. A lot more than the woman who called it in noticed. She said she thought the lorry driver must have cut himself. If so, it was one hell of a cut.'*

Well, there had certainly been a lot of blood. Kelsey's fleece was soaked in it. It had turned the brown fabric to a dark magenta mantle around his shoulders, and there were flecks of it on his arms and back.

When they turned the body over, Cooper could see that the blood had begun to pool in the shallow depression, clotting into sticky wads on the grass. Kelsey's hair was stiff with it and his face was partially obscured. Against that background, the green windmill logo on his breast pocket stood out in a garish mockery.

'Whoever did this, they certainly meant it,' said Carol Villiers.

Cooper jumped. For a moment he'd forgotten she was even there. But that was Villiers – quietly efficient, capable of being unobtrusive when necessary.

'What do you mean, Carol?' he said.

'Look at the extent of the injuries. This wasn't the result of a few bruises sustained in a struggle. Someone intended him to die and wanted to make sure of it.'

'It's always difficult to understand how anyone could beat a person to death like this. How could you physically do it? What would be going through your mind?'

'I have no idea.'

Cooper wondered how he would react if a colleague said he or she could imagine exactly what it felt like to beat someone to death. Luckily, no one ever had.

'It's been quite a few hours now since he first went missing.' Villiers looked at her watch. 'Forty hours since we got the original call. Maybe a bit longer.'

'It's far too long,' said Cooper. 'But I don't know what we could have done any better, given the circumstances.'

'I think I know that song.'

Cooper sighed. 'If we can get a time of death, it will help,' he said. 'I don't suppose they buried him until he was dead.'

Villiers winced. 'Good point. But I'm not sure how we'll get that. If he died on Monday night, we're well past the point of rigor mortis or body temperature being any use.'

'We'll see what the post-mortem can tell us.'

'I've alerted the mortuary. Dr van Doon is on call.'

'Good. I don't suppose there's any sign of a weapon?'

Cooper turned to the Crime Scene Manager, who was supervising the collection and recording of evidence. So far there looked to be nothing in the evidence bags that would constitute a weapon.

'Unless it was one of these stones,' said Abbott. 'There's blood on some of them. If one was used as a weapon, there may be traces of hair and skin from the victim's scalp. We'll know when we can get them to the lab.'

'It would be useful to know if all the stones were from the same place,' said Cooper.

'I'm not sure what you mean.'

'If a stone was used to attack Mr Kelsey, it's more likely to have been one that was picked up by the roadside, not one from this wall. It's a good three hundred yards from the scene of the assault.'

'I see,' said Abbott. 'Well, I'm not sure how we'll tell the difference, but I'll make a note of it for the lab.'

'Is there anything else of interest?' asked Cooper.

'Just general rubbish here. Nothing immediately suggestive. Unless you're interested in the two other bodies we found.'

'*What?*'

Abbott smiled. 'When I say "we", I'm taking credit for someone else's achievement. They were found by the search team, buried a few yards from the road.'

It was the nature of the smile that tipped Cooper off. He'd been about to explode, but of course Abbott was joking. It was just the sort of wind-up that SOCOs delighted in. They loved to take the

mickey out of innocent coppers. But this one seemed a particularly juvenile and meaningless joke.

'Yes, very funny,' said Cooper.

'I'm serious,' protested Abbott. 'They dug up two corpses from
shallow graves. Recently deceased too. We've bagged them, just in
case. It's a bit late for the mint sauce, though.'

'They're sheep,' said Cooper.

Abbott laughed. 'Ewe got it.'

Cooper and Villiers left the forensic team to their work and
walked back towards Cloughpit Lane, following a carefully
marked-out approach and ducking under the tape at the outer
cordon.

'It's a long way from the bridge,' said Cooper. 'I wonder if Mac
Kelsey made it that far under his own steam.'

'If he did, he was probably running away from someone,' said
Villiers. 'Trying to escape his attackers?'

'Exactly.'

Cooper looked back towards the hamlet. If that was the case,
it surely couldn't have happened until well after dark had fallen.
Even in Shawhead, someone would have been likely to notice
an injured man being pursued across open fields, murdered,
then buried under a makeshift cairn. It didn't seem credible
otherwise.

Villiers had managed to persuade Grant Swindells to unlock a
field gate so that they could get police vehicles off the road. Cooper was intending to ask her how she'd done it, but of course it was
in Swindells' own interests to have the road clear. Nevertheless,
he could imagine the farmer grumbling about the damage all the
vehicles were doing to his field. No doubt he'd be muttering the
word 'compensation' to anyone who'd listen.

'Where had Mac Kelsey been delivering earlier in the day?' asked Cooper thoughtfully.

'We've got his schedule from Mr Bateman at Windmill Feed Solutions.'

'I know. But I'd like someone to check the completed dockets to make sure he made all his deliveries. Then phone the customers and ask them whether they noticed anything unusual, if he seemed nervous or was behaving oddly. You know the routine. And I'd like to be sure that he was on his own, that he hadn't picked someone up in his cab at any point during the day.'

'Anything else?'

'Yes, one crucial thing: what route would he have taken on his way to his last delivery?'

'According to the schedule, his previous call was at a farm the other side of Dove Holes. He was almost in Buxton.'

Cooper nodded. 'He would have driven up the A6 then. No doubt about that.'

'Well, no satnav would convince you that you weren't on the A6,' said Villiers.

'No,' said Cooper. 'It was after he left the A6 that he went astray somehow.'

Cooper remembered something one of the Shawhead residents had said the previous day. Who was it now? Yes, Tania Durkin. She'd talked about Shawhead being 'nowhere'.

'Well, he wasn't following a diversion sign, that's for sure. They wouldn't divert traffic up Cloughpit Lane, no matter what. It goes nowhere.'

Well, this might be the road to nowhere. But Cooper recalled seeing roadworks near Chinley when he drove past it on the A6. A section of road was closed near the PVC factory at Whitehough for resurfacing or repairs to a collapsed stretch. He felt sure there had been a diversion, probably through the centre of Chinley village to Leadenknowle.

He despatched a couple of uniformed officers back down to the corner where Cloughpit Lane turned off the road between Furness Vale and New Mills. They had instructions to search the verges and undergrowth, and to check behind stone walls. Whatever they could find that shouldn't be there. You never knew your luck, as long as you tested every possibility.

The two dead sheep that had been found during the search lay over the wall in one of Grant Swindells' fields, close to the railway embankment. Among the firmest evidence Cooper had from the scene at the bridge was the presence of sheep on the road. Had Mac Kelsey run into the stray flock milling about on Cloughpit Lane?

Some drivers got very impatient with sheep on the road and tried to push them out of the way with their vehicles. But sheep didn't react in predictable ways. They tended to panic. Might Kelsey have driven over a couple of ewes in his irritation? Did these sheep die under the wheels of his curtainsider? That would have angered Grant Swindells, no doubt. Perhaps Kelsey's death was the result of a violent argument with the farmer over the damage to his stock.

It was certain that at some point both Kelsey's body and those of the sheep had been removed from the scene. It seemed reasonable to conclude that the same person or person had moved both. And Swindells had been hanging about at the scene too, not just Amanda Hibbert. Cooper had encountered him almost straight away when he arrived on Tuesday morning.

It was behaviour typical of an individual who was implicated in the crime. When you'd killed someone and buried their body under a heap of stones, most people couldn't just sit still at home not knowing whether it was about to be found or not. There was an irresistible impulse to see what was happening and what the police were doing. And whether they were looking in the wrong direction.

Cooper's thoughts went back to the scene in Shawhead when the crowd of residents had gathered in the road. There was one moment that had struck him. Hadn't Ian Hibbert seemed a little frightened of Swindells? Why would that be?

Yesterday a Scenes of Crime officer had visited Shawhead Cottages and taken Amanda Hibbert's fingerprints for elimination purposes. It would have been with the old ink pad and paper technique. He could picture her expression of horror at the black stains covering her hands. The ink washed off easily, though he'd known SOCOs tell people it would 'wear off in a few weeks' just for a joke. Even SOCOs were human, after all. But if an officer had told Mrs Hibbert that, no doubt he'd soon be hearing about it. She would be down here at the bridge bashing his ear with her complaints.

Now he was wondering whether he was going to have to take prints from everyone at Shawhead.

Cooper turned to Villiers. He didn't need a map to guess the answer to his question, but he asked it anyway.

'The site where Mac Kelsey was buried,' he said. 'How near is that footpath we identified on the map?'

'It's just on the other side of the wall,' said Villiers.

'I thought so.'

Cooper walked under the Cloughpit Lane bridge. The underside of the nearest arch was streaked white where salt had leaked out of the damp stone. Within a few yards, he was standing in the gap between the two arches, looking up into daylight. He could see the stone parapet and the broken branches of the elder sapling growing out of it.

In his imagination he saw figures appearing up there, their heads peering over the parapet before they scrambled down onto the roof of the lorry. Sitting here in his cab, Mac Kelsey would already be confused and distracted. He ought to have been reaching for his phone to call somebody for help, surely? That would be the first thing that anyone would do. But Kelsey hadn't made that call. He'd been interrupted.

Unfortunately, Cooper's imagination couldn't manage to fill in the details of the faces he pictured above him on the parapet. They were just grey blurs, anonymous and of indeterminate gender.

Why was he picturing two people? Because it seemed like a crime committed by more than one. Kelsey was a big man. Not fit perhaps – he had a sedentary job, after all. But he must have been heavy, and strong. Overpowering was a job for more than one person.

And Cooper felt sure this had been an ambush, planned and executed well. True, whoever did it had relied on some measure of luck. But there was one other thing they seemed to have relied on. They had depended on no one coming along the road while they were carrying out their assault. Otherwise there would have been witnesses.

Standing there, in the middle of the Cloughpit Lane bridge, Cooper concluded that it meant someone who was familiar with Shawhead. Someone who knew the habits of the residents and could predict what times they came in and out, and when it would be quiet. They'd banked on being unobserved, and it had worked.

AN HOUR LATER, when the black van had been and collected the body bag from the field, Cooper went back to his car to return to Edendale.

One of his jobs was to meet Anne Kelsey when she was brought to the mortuary at the Edendale District General Hospital.

He had to wait with her for a few minutes before they were allowed into the viewing area. It gave the mortuary staff enough time to clean up the features of the corpse sufficiently.

When they finally went in, Anne Kelsey seemed prepared.

'Is this your husband, Mrs Kelsey?' asked Cooper.

She took just one ragged breath.

'Yes, of course it—' she said. And then a pause as she took in the obvious signs of his injuries. 'But who would do *that* to him? And why? For heaven's sake, *why*?'

Who and why. They were always the questions that bereaved relatives asked when faced with the brutal truth. Once they found themselves in the viewing room at the mortuary for a formal identification there was no point any more in trying to deny the reality. It was too late then to pretend it was all a mistake, that it was someone else's husband or wife on the slab. The last shreds of hope died at that moment. And only the questions remained.

'Why?' she said again, turning her contorted face up to Cooper's in an angry snarl, as if he was personally guilty, the culprit for her spouse's murder standing right before her eyes.

Cooper flinched at her expression. 'I'm sorry, we don't know that. Not yet.'

'But you'll find out. You'll catch the person who did it.'

And now they were no longer questions, but statements. Instructions. Her husband had been killed and it was someone's job to deal with it, to bring her all the answers she demanded, all the explanations she needed to know.

And it wasn't just anyone's job. It was Detective Inspector Ben Cooper's job.

'We'll do our best, Mrs Kelsey,' he said. 'I promise you that.'

COOPER HAD HIS phone turned to silent while he was in the mortuary. So it was as he left and went back to sit in his Toyota that he checked his messages and returned a call to Becky Hurst.

Hurst had been called to an incident in New Mills. She was only three miles away from the site of Mac Kelsey's murder at Shawhead. And she had another dead body on her hands.

'It definitely looks like a suicide,' she said. 'He was found hanging from a walkway over the river here.'

Cooper started the car. 'The Millennium Walkway?' he said.

Hurst laughed. 'Is there anywhere in this area you don't know?'

'You wouldn't be calling me if it was just a suicide,' said Cooper. 'There must be something else.'

He could hear noises in the background of the call. A rushing sound. The roaring of water over a weir. The sound had a strange, echoey quality as if the water was flowing in a confined space. The Torrs, of course. A one-hundred-foot gorge below the town of New Mills. That was where Becky Hurst was standing.

'Obviously,' she said. 'I think there may be a connection with the murder inquiry at Shawhead. I'd like you to tell me whether I'm right or wrong.'

Chapter Fourteen

O<small>N HIS WAY</small> into New Mills, Ben Cooper had reached the uncomfortably sharp right-hand turn from the lights at the foot of Albion Road and dropped down the hill past Newtown railway station and the big Swizzels Matlow sweet factory to the bridge over the Torrs gorge.

Cooper hadn't been to New Mills for a while. Not since his CID team had helped to execute search warrants in the Hague Bar area as part of a major drugs operation in the town. When you'd only visited properties where drug dealers were operating, or a house that had been converted into a cannabis farm, you could get quite a negative impression of a place. It tended to reinforce the stereotypes.

He thought about what Gavin Murfin had said about New Mills. It was nothing he hadn't heard before, of course. The town sat in a sort of no man's land. It wasn't really part of Derbyshire and it didn't belong to Manchester either. That could give a community like this a sort of pariah status.

Modern New Mills looked like a typical mill town, owing more to similar places in Lancashire than to Derbyshire, with a warren of narrow streets and stone-built cottages. The typical air of post-industrial decline had been compensated for by its growth as a home for Manchester commuters, and a lot of new houses had been built.

Cooper remembered a detail he ought to have asked for a check on and he phoned Carol Villiers, who was still at the bridge scene.

'Carol, can you make sure Scenes of Crime examine the satnav in the cab of the lorry?' he said. 'Any faults on it, what settings it was on.'

'No problem.'

'Thanks.'

'How was the widow, by the way?' she said.

'The usual. In denial.'

'Did she hold together for the identification?'

'Yes, I think she'll be fine.'

Cooper ended the call. Had he really just said Anne Kelsey would be 'fine'? What sort of word was that to use in the circumstances? No one whose husband had just been murdered was 'fine'.

Below New Mills in a gorge one hundred feet deep was Riverside Park, extending for two miles along the River Goyt. It started at the Goytside Meadows nature reserve to the south, ran under the Union Road bridge, and snaked through the gorge known as the Torrs and past Torr Vale Mill, where it was linked by the Millennium Walkway.

Until the nineteenth century New Mills was virtually cut in two by the deep gorge of the River Goyt, known as the Torrs. The only crossing involved a tortuous descent to a bridge just above river level, followed by an equally tough ascent on the other side. The problem wasn't fully solved until the construction of the Union Road bridge, ninety-five feet high, built over the centre of the gorge and constructed out of rock from the Torrs. Viewed from the level of the river, it looked impressive.

With difficulty, Cooper found a space to park his car on the approach to the gorge, tucking as far in as he could behind a marked police car.

A series of arched bridges now crossed the gorge at the Union Road end. Two rivers met here. The Sett rose way up near Edale Cross on Kinder Scout, while the Goyt flowed from the Axe Edge moors through Whaley Bridge to reach New Mills. At Furness Vale they said that the colour of the River Goyt had once run red, its colour depending on discharges from the calico print mills in the valley. From these two rivers, millions of litres of water must pour over the Torrs weir every day – perhaps billions of litres during a wet winter.

There had been at least two other mills down here. The site of one had been restored as a hydro power project, with a twelve-ton reverse Archimedes screw nicknamed Archie. It was owned by the community and generated enough electricity to supply the Co-op supermarket off Church Road and fed some surplus energy into the national grid.

It had been big news for New Mills for a while, the local papers full of pictures of the massive screw being lowered two hundred feet from the Union Road bridge for installation. The other major event for the town had been the construction of the Millennium Walkway.

The walkway was part cantilevered from the railway embankment and part raised on pillars set into the river bed. It consisted of a steel rail, a few strands of wire cable forming the sides. Willowherb sprouted out of the high retaining wall of the railway embankment. A train passed overhead as he approached the scene of the hanging.

Cooper stepped onto the walkway and was immediately bombarded by a host of sensations. The reverberation of footsteps on the walkway, the slight vibration of the deck underfoot, the roar of the weir drowning out all other sounds. He was very conscious of the only surviving mill in the gorge, Torr Vale, located on its wooded peninsula in a dramatic curve of the Goyt. He leaned on the rail and gazed down at the weir and the sluice gate of the old mill.

DC Becky Hurst met him on the walkway. The remains of the suicide victim had been lowered to the level of the river and were now lying in a black body bag on a concrete platform that had once been the site of some ruined mill buildings.

'According to the driving licence and credit cards in his wallet, this man is Scott Brooks. He lives at an address on Peak Road, New Mills.'

'Are there any suspicious circumstances?' asked Cooper.

'No signs of foul play,' admitted Hurst. 'He left a bag the rope had been in and he fastened a scarf round his neck to protect him from getting cut.'

Cooper stood at the steel rail and looked down.

'How long was the rope?' he asked.

'Six or seven feet.'

'A long drop hanging,' said Cooper. 'It's quite unusual.'

Everyone knew that hanging wasn't a 100 per cent certain way of killing yourself. Top of the list was a shotgun to the head. You couldn't miss with a shotgun at close range. Unlike many farmers in the rural parts of the Peak District, Scott Brooks perhaps didn't have access to a firearm.

But suicides by hanging were usually of the short drop type. A simple noose from the ceiling and a chair kicked away. A short drop caused death by asphyxiation. It was the method of choice for prisoners who had no other means of killing themselves in their cells.

The long drop was a different matter. It was the old means of judicial execution until capital punishment was abolished in the 1960s. It was designed to fracture the cervical vertebrae and produce immediate unconsciousness and almost instant death. A drop of five to nine feet was said to be the optimum, depending on the height and weight of the victim. Too long a drop and you risked complete decapitation.

'It's a very public way to kill yourself too,' said Cooper. 'Most people who really want to do away with themselves get on with it quietly at home. When it happens so publicly, it's usually a cry for help rather than a serious suicide attempt. Individuals who climb up onto bridges or window ledges – they're really hoping to get lots of attention. They want someone to talk them down at the last minute.'

'It isn't as public as you might think,' said Hurst. 'Not at the time Mr Brooks chose to come here.'

She pointed up at Torr Vale Mill, which was the only building overlooking the scene.

'According to local officers, the mill has been semi-derelict for about fifteen years since it was closed,' she said. 'There is some usage now. The company that took it over are converting part of the mill into office spaces and there's one floor where they hold events sometimes. Concerts, even weddings.'

Cooper looked at the five-storey main building. Lights were on in some of the third-floor windows. But on the tip of the curve, where the river roared round a bend and disappeared, there was a gaping hole in the mill complex, the ruins of former buildings with exposed beams and piles of rubble.

'About fifteen years ago there was a major fire caused by trespassers,' said Hurst. 'It destroyed one entire building. Because the fire exposed asbestos that had been used in the boiler house, they had to demolish that too. The old cotton mill is still there, plus the weaving shed, the chimney stack, the foreman's house and some other buildings.'

On this side of the river the elegant curve of the walkway clung to the high retaining wall of the railway line until it disappeared beyond the mill. At the far end a path led up to the railway bridge and the entrance to New Mills Central station. The walkway itself continued into the woods along the bank of the river and became the Goyt Way, while a separate path crossed a footbridge to the mill.

'Did nobody see anything?' said Cooper, already guessing the answer.

'As far as we can establish, there was no one else on the walkway, or in this part of the Torrs. So to see anything, you'd either have to be looking out of one of the upper windows at the old mill, or watching from the viewpoint at the heritage centre. No one has reported seeing a man committing suicide by hanging himself. But that doesn't prove anything.'

Cooper nodded. The fact that no one had reported seeing Scott Brooks hanging himself from the walkway didn't necessarily mean that no one had seen him do it. Some individuals were as likely to have stood filming it on their mobile phones, rather than dialling 999 or trying to help. They might be uploading their footage to Facebook or YouTube right now.

'So what makes you think this is more than just a suicide, Becky?'

'Well, I'm not saying that exactly. But I do think there's a connection with the Shawhead murder inquiry. It may mean nothing, of course . . .'

'Don't doubt yourself so much,' said Cooper. 'Your instincts are good.'

Hurst smiled. 'Thanks.'

'So . . . ?'

'Mr Brooks left a note.'

She handed Cooper a plastic evidence bag. It contained a single sheet of white A4 paper, folded in half. There were only a few lines printed on it.

I didn't intend anyone to die. It was all a misunderstanding. Don't blame them. For Ashley's sake.

Cooper read it through a second time. It was hardly very informative.

'Who's Ashley?' he said.

'It looks as though she's his wife, or girlfriend at least. There's a photo in his wallet. See, it says, "Ashley and Scott" on the back.'

It looked like a holiday snap, two young people smiling in bright sunlight against a backdrop of deep blue sky and a glint of sea. The woman was very striking – not what he would have called beautiful, or even pretty, but eye-catching. Her face seemed full of life and personality. Her eyes glowed with a warmth and a glitter of amusement that would have caught any eye.

'It's quite an old photo,' said Hurst. 'He looks ten years younger there.'

Cooper hadn't seen the face of the suicide. He could go down and ask for the body bag to be unzipped, but it didn't seem necessary. There would be pictures later and Hurst had already experienced the unpleasant task of viewing the corpse. But she was doing very well to see past the bloated features, bulging eyes and discoloured flesh of the typical hanging victim.

'How can you tell, Becky?' he said.

'He's much slimmer in the photo,' said Hurst. 'I'd say he's put on a stone or two since then. And he had more hair in those days too. The man who's just hanged himself looks unkempt. I'd say he wasn't in the best of conditions, even when he was alive.'

Cooper nodded, still studying the woman in the photograph.

'A memory of a happier time, perhaps,' said Hurst.

'Yes. I'm sure you're right.'

Cooper couldn't look at her. Hurst had made the remark so casually that she must be completely unaware of how deeply it had pierced him. Cooper had a similar photograph in his own wallet, taken when Liz was alive, on the day they'd got engaged. He understood the need to keep a memento of a happier time close to your heart.

He wondered if his photograph with Liz would get as old as the one Scott Brooks had carried. He hoped so. And it would probably start to look as dated too. He would age and he would no longer look the same. In time he might become unrecognisable as the happy young man in the picture. Only Liz would stay preserved, the same for ever.

'She would be his next of kin then,' he said.

'If she's still alive,' said Hurst.

And that struck even deeper. For a moment Cooper felt dizzy, as if he was falling towards the river. But he shook himself to clear his head and forced himself to focus on the facts he was being presented with.

Two bodies within three miles of each other on the same day – that was certainly out of the ordinary in this area, even if one of them was a suicide. He couldn't ignore the potential significance, the possibility of a connection. A murder, followed by a suicide? It was an old, familiar pattern in criminal investigation. And the note suggested guilt as a motive for Scott Brooks taking his own life. But Cooper knew he needed more. A lot more. If he was going to get anything concrete, he would have to let Becky Hurst follow those instincts of hers and see what she came up with.

'Get someone on to tracing Mr Brooks' movements,' he said. 'He must have been seen around town, and probably recognised if he lived in New Mills. Shops he might have called at. Pubs nearby. People often need a few drinks before they have the courage to do something like this. And he might have a car parked not far away.'

Slowly, Cooper and Hurst walked back to the steps leading up to Union Road. Here the Torrs were overlooked by the balconies of some flats behind a vegetarian café. One of the flats was available to let – Cooper could see a board for the estate agents whose offices stood directly opposite on Union Road.

'And we'll need to speak to the residents of those flats,' said Hurst, without being told.

Cooper nodded, though he held out little hope of getting an account of what had happened. The story was probably very simple anyway. Yet one more desperate person who couldn't take living any more. It was so common that it was hardly worth commenting on, barely something to notice as you went about your daily routine.

SCOTT BROOKS HAD lived in a terraced house in the Peak Road area of New Mills, with just enough space to get a car off the road if you didn't care about having a front garden. Nearby, several vehicles were parked half on the road and half on the pavement. Their wheels had churned a thin strip of grass into mud and potholes. All along the street a row of satellite dishes pointed east, as if they were all praying to Mecca.

A fancy letterbox on a line of decorative brickwork was the only ornamentation on the frontage of Mr Brooks' house. Vertical blinds were drawn shut on all the windows. And the front door stood open.

'A break-in?' said Hurst quietly.

'I don't think so,' said Cooper. 'But we'd better check there's no one in the house first.'

But the house was empty. And it seemed tidy too. No signs of intruders ransacking the place after finding the door unlocked. In fact, it was tidier than Cooper's flat. Unusual, for a man living on his own.

'So why was the door open?' said Hurst, puzzled.

'I think he knew someone would be coming,' said Cooper. 'I'll be okay here for a while, Becky. Go round and speak to any neighbours you can find.'

'I'm on it.'

Scott Brooks' home was a typical council house, part of a terraced row of identical properties, with two bedrooms upstairs and a small patch of garden at the back.

Displayed on the window ledge in the sitting room were photos of Ashley and a few of Scott and Ashley together, some obviously taken on their wedding day. The usual poses loved by wedding photographers. To Cooper's eye, Ashley had a hard look, a coldness in her eyes that belied the smile she'd put on for the photographer and didn't suit the white veil and the flowers and the scattering of confetti. It looked like a perfect day. But he sensed that Ashley had never been the perfect bride.

The smallest of the bedrooms had been in use as a study or library. Brooks had put a desk in there with a computer that looked well past its best days. Cooper didn't bother trying to switch it on. It was probably password-protected. And he could guess what its owner might have been doing on it anyway.

Many individuals who planned to kill themselves now used the internet to research the best methods. Scott Brooks had been very organised. It was likely that he'd taken advice from some websites when he planned his death. He'd used that thin scarf as padding to prevent the rope cutting into his neck. And he'd known that it was important to avoid interruption. If someone intervened during a hanging, it might save the victim, but was likely to result in permanent brain damage.

And Mr Brooks might even have calculated the optimum length of the rope. Too short and he would strangle himself, a long and painful death. But too long a drop could result in instant decapitation. Scott Brooks had got it pretty much right.

The walls of the study were covered in bookshelves. Cooper ran his eye over row on row of classic novels in old editions dating back several decades at least. Charles Dickens, Thomas Hardy, Anthony Trollope. They were the sort of books many people only saw when they had to study them at school. The pages were dogeared and the spines were cracked from frequent use. Scott must have picked them up for a few pence at second-hand bookshops. As a result the room was full of the distinctive aroma of old books, the smell caused by chemicals breaking down in the ink and paper, and in the glue used for the bindings. That scent was like the headiest of perfumes to a book collector.

In the sitting room Cooper picked up a small square of pink paper pulled from a notepad. It had a line of adhesive on the back and had been stuck to the table. Just two words were written on the front in an ornate but slightly unsteady hand: *For Ever.*

The hairs on the back of his neck prickled, as if he could sense a presence in the room. It was almost as though someone had spoken those words out loud. Cooper glanced over his shoulder. But Becky Hurst had gone to talk to the neighbours and there was no one else in the house. It was just his imagination.

As he walked round the house, Cooper collected more messages. There were dozens of them. The words varied, but they had the same theme. *My Angel, Only You, Sweet Heart, I Want U, Ever Yours, Find Me, For Keeps, You and I, You're Mine, Come Back To Me.*

It began to feel relentless, as though the voice of Scott Brooks was pursuing him through the rooms, addressing him personally. But surely not *him*. Not Ben Cooper, or even some random police officer who'd come to Mr Brooks' house after his suicide. These were addressed to someone else entirely. Someone who wasn't here.

He was reading a final note when Hurst returned. *Luv U 24/7.* That looked like a text message.

'I was right about the wife,' said Hurst when she met Cooper at the door. 'The neighbours say Mr Brooks was a widower. He lived on his own and didn't talk to anyone. Some complained he was a bit snooty and thought he was too good for them. You know the sort of thing.'

'Yes. That's explains the graffiti on his fence. He wasn't welcome here. A loner always attracts rumours and suspicion.'

'One neighbour says he often saw Mr Brooks drinking around town. He went into lots of pubs, apparently.'

'So that he wasn't a regular anywhere. It sounds as though he was deliberately trying not to belong.'

'But there is a sister living locally,' said Hurst. 'She's probably next of kin.'

'Can we get an address for her?'

'That's my next job,' said Hurst.

'Good. And if you find anything else significant, let DS Sharma know. I'll be on my way back to Shawhead.'

'Okay.'

'What do you make of these, Becky?' asked Cooper.

Hurst studied the messages, picking them up one by one and putting them down with an expression of slight distaste.

'To be honest, they seem a bit creepy.'

'Not romantic?' said Cooper.

'Perhaps, if he wasn't living on his own. But the neighbours say his wife has been dead for eight years.'

'Yes, in that case it does look a bit obsessive.'

'*Ever Yours, For Ever, You and I.* That's one thing,' said Hurst. 'But *Come Back To Me*? That's weird.'

'I suppose he was thinking that they'd meet again,' said Cooper. 'When he was dead, I mean.'

'So perhaps he'd been planning it for some time. I'll keep trying neighbours to see if I can find out more.'

Cooper picked up the note that said *Come Back to Me*. 'But why leave the messages here? It was hardly as if she was going to walk through the door and see them.'

'And they're certainly not meant for us,' said Hurst.

But Cooper frowned, repeating Hurst's phrase to himself. He didn't know why, but it sounded like one of those casual statements that seemed obvious at the time, but turned out to be completely opposite to the truth.

Chapter Fifteen

As he arrived back at the bridge scene in Shawhead, Cooper saw the Lawsons' Range Rover go past, taking advantage of the road finally being open. Young Nick was in the passenger seat, with a dark-haired woman driving, presumably his mother. What was her name – Sarah?

At the same time a train approached the bridge. Even during his brief periods at the scene, Cooper was learning to distinguish between the Manchester express trains and the smaller local units, which had a distinctive rattle as they approached the bridge, rather than the whine of the express.

Carol Villiers had the scene well organised – the tape at the outer cordon securely attached instead of flapping in the breeze and trailing in the mud, and the line of vehicles neatly parked instead of stuck in at random angles. It was always Villiers sorting things out. That should be his sergeant's job. But it just came naturally to Carol.

As he approached the cordon, Cooper spotted a figure lurking on the other side of the wall.

'Mr Swindells?'

The farmer straightened up and stared at Cooper, as if he'd just happened to be passing and hadn't realised anyone else was there.

'Yes. What's up now?'

'I assume those are your sheep that we found buried in the field near the bridge?'

'Well, that's probably a good assumption. I mean, what are the chances of someone else sneaking in at night with a couple of dead sheep and burying them on my land? We get poachers round here sometimes, but they're usually interested in taking animals away, not bringing them in.'

'What happened to the sheep?' said Cooper patiently. 'How did they die?'

Swindells stared at him. 'What interest is it to you?'

'If you could just answer the question, sir.'

'A fox got them, or maybe somebody's dog. It happens. They even die of old age sometimes. Sheep are like that.'

'It wasn't anything to do with the incident at the bridge?'

Swindells frowned. He looked genuinely surprised and puzzled at the suggestion. 'Some of the flock got onto the road,' he said. 'I reckon someone left a gate open. It might have been deliberate. It might just have been ramblers. I put the sheep back in the field. That's all. The two ewes were dead before that.'

'So was it you who buried them?' asked Cooper.

'Who else?'

'When did you do it?'

The farmer shook his head. 'I can't remember. Sunday probably.'

'You didn't bury them very deeply, Mr Swindells.'

'I didn't have time. I'd normally get the tractor down to a dig a decent hole, but I was too busy that day. I just got them out of the way to keep the scavengers off. Dead animals attract all kinds of things you don't want. What do you want with my dead sheep anyway?'

'We might get a vet to take a look at them, to establish the cause of death.'

'Help yourself,' said Swindells with a shrug.

'You mentioned poachers,' said Cooper. 'Have you had trouble recently?'

'Not me. There was a bloke over Mellor way who lost some stock a month or two back. They come out from Manchester with a truck, you know. Sometimes they don't even bother taking the sheep away. They just slaughter them in the field and leave the heads and innards.'

Swindells looked across the field at where the crime scene tents were up around Mac Kelsey's shallow grave.

'I kept meaning to repair that wall,' he said.

'How long has it been collapsed?'

'About five years.'

Cooper laughed. 'You could hire a dry-stone waller, you know. There are plenty of them around. You could get someone who'd do a proper, permanent job of the repairs.'

'Wallers cost money,' said Swindells. 'Money I haven't got. The best quote I could get is about forty pounds a square metre. That's why I have to do everything myself round here.'

'Thank you for letting us use your land for our vehicles,' said Cooper. 'We won't be here any longer than necessary.'

Swindells pulled a face. 'And that will be too long.'

DS DEV SHARMA was gesturing from the collection of police vehicles and Cooper walked over to join him.

'Have you got something?' he said.

'Yes, DC Hurst called in with this. She's got a bit more on the suicide, Scott Brooks.'

'She works fast,' said Cooper. 'I only left her a few minutes ago.'

'Well, it turns out Mr Brooks lost his wife in tragic circumstances,' said Sharma.'

'What happened?'

'She was killed in a serious road traffic collision, when her car was hit by an HGV. The lorry driver was convicted of causing death by dangerous driving.'

'A fatal accident?' said Cooper. 'Where did this take place?'

'Well, nowhere near here. It was on a dual carriageway section of the A6, near the Bridgemont Roundabout.'

Cooper hunched his shoulders for a moment, his face creasing in pain, as if he'd been punched in the ribs. Then he relaxed again. But slowly.

'Come with me.'

'Sir?'

'This way. Watch out for the brambles.'

They scrambled back up the slope, walked over the line of the old mineral track and reached the railway line.

'DI Cooper, are you sure it's safe?'

'As long as you don't hang about on the line. But you can go back and put on a high-vis jacket, if you feel it's necessary.'

Sharma didn't hesitate any longer. 'No, all right. I'm coming.'

They crossed the rail line and crunched over a few feet of crushed stone, the bed of the track. Cooper leaned against the far parapet of the bridge and motioned Sharma to join him.

Below, the valleys of Black Brook and the River Goyt met a few hundred yards north of Whaley Bridge. Between this point and the opposite hills lay two rivers, a canal and another railway line. And, just visible among the trees in the bottom of the valley, streams of traffic moving in both directions on a major road, an articulated lorry painted in dark green on the inside lane, a red car coasting past it on the outside. A BMW or a Mercedes, paintwork catching a gleam of light.

'Is that . . . ?' asked Sharma.

'Yes,' said Cooper. 'The A6.'

'I had no idea. It's all the hills, I suppose. And the way these little back roads twist and turn so much.'

Cooper sighed. He'd been so conscious of the continuous hum and swish of traffic in the background that he'd made the mistake of thinking it would be obvious to everyone. When you'd grown up in a place where that sort of noise was an alien intrusion, you couldn't help but be aware of its presence, like the buzz of a fly intruding on the silence of your bedroom.

But it was different for those like Devdan Sharma and Diane Fry, who'd spent their formative years in cities, brought up in the heart of the urban sprawl. For them the dull roar of traffic became the soundtrack to their lives, so familiar that it was below the level of awareness. It was their equivalent of birdsong. They heard it growling and thundering in the morning as rush hour grew to a dawn chorus. They heard it swelling again at the end of the day. In between they were never completely without that swish and murmur. It was so familiar that it must become a kind of reassurance to them, in the end.

Cooper had seen townies panicking at the sound of proper silence in the countryside, the way that tourists did in the show caves beneath Castleton when they encountered true darkness for the first time. It was so alien to them that it was terrifying. It made him feel very sad that the natural world had become so unfamiliar to so many people. It was a great loss.

But that was the way society was heading. More and more people lived in towns and cities, and fewer in the countryside. Eighty per cent of the population was urban now and they spent most of their time staring at concrete and brick. Driving on urban roads, they could easily get into the idea that the ribbon of grey tarmac they saw reflected the landscape for miles around. It was only when they looked out of a plane window as they came in to land at Heathrow or Manchester airport from a Mediterranean holiday that they realised how green the British countryside was.

Cooper recalled an early science fiction story by E. M. Forster, 'The Machine Stops'. He described a future in which people lived out their lives inside a giant machine with no idea there even was an outside. Not until the machine stopped.

He turned to look at Sharma.

'If you're going to work in this area,' he said, 'you need to learn how to listen. What you hear can tell you a lot.'

'I couldn't have known the traffic noise was the A6,' protested Sharma.

'But you would have asked,' said Cooper, 'if you'd noticed.'

Sharma nodded. Cooper was pleased to see that he took the advice on board, instead of reacting defensively, as he might have done. As some other individuals certainly would have done.

Sharma pointed to the north, where traffic was slowing for a junction.

'And is that . . . ?'

'Yes,' said Cooper. 'That's Bridgemont Roundabout.'

As THEY SCRAMBLED back down the banking, Cooper reflected that Sharma was right in a way. Despite its proximity to the A6, Shawhead felt very isolated. It was part of the atmosphere here, a feeling that you'd taken a step outside the everyday world that was passing close by. A dead end in more than just the usual sense.

One road in and one road out? Well, if that was true, he would have a very limited field of suspects. Just the residents of Shawhead, in fact. But it wasn't true, was it?

So why had Amanda Hibbert tried to plant the idea in their minds that there was no other way out than the blocked road? Was she trying to cast suspicion on one of her Shawhead neighbours by suggesting that no one could have got away after killing Mac Kelsey? It was very subtle, if so. It had soon become obvious that it wasn't true, from a quick glance at the surrounding landscape. But she might have taken Cooper and his team for a bunch of city cops who wouldn't know any better. She'd almost been right.

And then there was the fact that Mrs Hibbert had been at the scene herself. In murder cases many detectives made it a firm rule to suspect the person who reported finding the body. Anyone with the least bit of forensic knowledge, even if it was gained from reading crime novels or watching TV, would know that it created an explanation for the presence of their fingerprints, a trace of their DNA, or a smear of the victim's blood on their clothes. It was those who claimed to have been nowhere near the scene of the crime who were faced with difficulty in explaining the evidence away. But Amanda Hibbert herself had described how she'd opened the door of the cab, picked up the delivery dockets, reacted in shock at a trickle of blood.

Yet what connection could there be between Mrs Hibbert and Mac Kelsey? None that he knew of. Or none that he'd discovered yet.

Cooper looked around at his team. Dev Sharma, Carol Villiers and Luke Irvine. This was all he had to follow up the immediate lines of enquiry.

'We need to know where everyone from Shawhead was at the time of this incident,' he said. 'Let's see what we can dig up. Even if they weren't involved, how could they not have seen or heard something? Dev, what about your old lady, Mrs Swindells? Everyone must pass her window.'

'She could see comings and goings, but only on the road,' said Sharma.

'Get her to be specific then, pin her down on details. I don't care how long you spend talking to her, or how many cups of tea you have to drink. She could be a good source of information. And Luke . . .'

'Yes?'

'I want you to check on Amanda Hibbert's story. Was she really working backstage at the theatre? We'll start with those two, then move on to the rest of the residents until we get a clear picture of their exact movements.'

'Do you think the answers we need are here in Shawhead?' asked Sharma.

'I hope so,' said Cooper. 'Otherwise the answers may have died on the Millennium Walkway with Scott Brooks.'

Chapter Sixteen

BECKY HURST HAD certainly been busy. Her ability to gather information made everyone else look as though they'd taken the day off.

From what she had to tell Cooper on the way into New Mills, it seemed as though Scott Brooks had planned his afternoon very carefully. At about eleven o'clock he'd left his house in Peak Road and driven into the centre of the town, where he found a parking space on Rock Mill Lane, just behind the bus terminus. His Vauxhall was still there when it was located by the police next day.

There was free parking on Rock Mill Lane, but only half a dozen spaces, so he was lucky to have found an empty spot. But parking was limited to thirty minutes until 6 p.m. At three twenty-four he'd been issued with a parking ticket for overstaying the specified period.

It was the one thing he'd failed to plan properly. He hadn't managed to time his actions to avoid a parking fine, which someone would have to deal with.

From Rock Mill Lane, Brooks had called first at the heritage centre, which was only a few yards away. The staff had noticed him particularly, because he'd spent a long time browsing the local history books and nostalgic scenes of New Mills, but had left without buying anything. He'd walked through the exhibition and out onto the viewing platform, with its vertiginous outlook onto the gorge and Torr Vale Mill, and the Millennium Walkway directly below.

Then he went for lunch. He'd eaten a hot roast beef and onion barm at the Pride of the Peaks on the corner of Market Street, followed by a Jammie Dodger cheesecake. Then he'd washed it down with a bottle of Guinness. The condemned man's last meal. He'd stopped at one drink, though. Unlike so many suicides, he'd wanted to be sober for what he did next.

And what was it he did next? He crossed the road to Barton's hardware shop, where he bought a length of rope.

Cooper met Hurst outside the heritage centre overlooking the Torrs gorge.

'There must be a gap in that time line,' he said. 'People would have been on the walkway or down in the Torrs, at least until dusk fell. That would be around five o'clock, I suppose. Where did Mr Brooks spend his time between visiting the hardware shop and his final moments on the walkway?'

'What about here at the heritage centre?' said Hurst. 'That's the best vantage point.'

'It closes at four o'clock in winter.'

Cooper looked over the wall into the gorge. From this viewpoint he had a dramatic view of Torr Vale Mill and the water foaming over the weir below the walkway. Inexplicably, visitors standing here had dumped their rubbish over the iron railing.

On the slope below, he saw a shower of drinks cans. Emerge, Rubicon, Strongbow. There was also a faint smell of urine. Probably not your average tourist then. Perhaps this was a spot for the homeless to hang out, or for youths to congregate at night. Every town had those, even Edendale. It was one of those essential modern facilities, like a bus station and a Tesco.

A couple of High Peak buses were drawn up at the terminus. Cooper stopped for a moment to look at some strange sculptures on the wall. They appeared to be the imprints of feet, painted blue.

It must be satisfying to be an artist, to know that you could leave a mark on the world that people would want to look at for decades to come. Some individuals didn't have that option and could see no value in their presence.

Scott Brooks was one of those. When he stood on that walkway, he'd decided to leave no mark on the world at all.

SCOTT BROOKS' OLDER sister was called Pat Turner. Becky Hurst had come up with her address. She lived not far away, off Godward Road on the northern outskirts of New Mills. Cooper took Hurst with him to break the bad news.

Housing developments had spread up the hillsides to the north and west of New Mills during the last few decades. Executive estates sprouted off both sides of Eaves Knoll Road towards a golf course just outside town. Of course, there were no 'streets' on these developments, only crescents, drives, ways and views. Anything to suggest they weren't part of an urban environment. There was even a Heather Falls, which didn't seem to mean anything at all.

They found the Turners' address on the furthest edge of the current housing line. It was a new build of pale brick, one of a

cluster of modern detached properties at the end of a cul-de-sac
lined with semis. All the houses here had panoramic views over
the town towards Brown Knoll, with probably a glimpse of Kinder
Scout itself on a good day. No doubt the view added a few thousand pounds to the property prices.

A little Ford Ka and a two-year-old Subaru stood on a
paved driveway in front of the Turners' house. The woman who
answered the door was cold-eyed, middle-aged and suspicious.
She gave Cooper and Hurst that stare with raised eyebrows that
many members of the public adopted when they found the police
on their doorstep. Wild conjectures would be going through her
head. What had she done wrong? Who was in trouble? Or who
had died?

At least she looked like a woman who was strong enough to
bear most things. And Cooper had the impression that the suicide
of her brother wasn't the biggest shock she'd ever had in her life.
But it was a few minutes before they were able to sit her down and
ask some questions.

'Do you know of any reason why your brother would want to
kill himself, Mrs Turner?' he said.

'No, of course I don't. It's unimaginable. Scott would never do
something like that to himself.'

It was the usual first response. Suicide was still regarded
as something shameful, a sin not to be acknowledged within
the family, like bankruptcy or incest. Coroners often recorded
open verdicts to avoid writing 'took his own life' on the inquest
report. Like unlawful killing, a verdict of suicide required proof
beyond reasonable doubt. It was more than just a question of
the balance of probabilities that coroners weighed up in other
verdicts.

'There must be some mistake,' she said, a pleading tone entering her voice. 'It was an accident, wasn't it?'

'We're fairly sure it wasn't,' said Cooper.

She started to ask how he knew that, but she seemed to read the expression on his face, and her voice faded away. Cooper was glad of that. He would much rather avoid having to explain the details just at the moment. He particularly didn't want to mention the rope.

'There was a note,' he said instead.

'Oh? Was there?'

Becky Hurst showed her a copy of the note Scott Brooks had left. She looked at it for a long time, though it was very short.

'Ashley?' said Hurst. 'His wife, wasn't she?'

'Yes.'

'And you still can't think of any reason your brother might have killed himself?' asked Cooper.

She sobbed suddenly and pulled out a tissue to wipe a tear from each eye.

'It broke him when Ashley was killed,' she said. 'Broke him completely. He doted on that girl, you know. But if you ask me, she was never good enough for him. A bad family.'

'What happened?'

'It was eight years ago. She was killed in a road accident. It was very sad. Very shocking. The car was completely crushed by a lorry.'

'Was your brother with her in the car at the time?'

'No, she was on her own. That made it worse, I think. Scott once said that he wished they'd been together and died at the same time. So they'd still be together.'

'*For Ever*,' said Cooper.

She looked at him curiously. 'Well, yes. Why do you say that?'

'We went to his house,' said Cooper. 'There were messages everywhere. Notes he'd left.'

'Oh, that,' said Mrs Turner. 'It was one of his odd ways. Scott would probably have called himself an eccentric. We tried to persuade him to get some sort of psychiatric help, but he wouldn't hear of it. So everybody thought he was a bit strange. His neighbours wouldn't have anything to do with him. The kids on that estate used to shout things at him in the street sometimes.'

'We noticed a bit of graffiti too,' said Cooper.

'Nasty stuff, I suppose.' She gave a deep sigh. 'Scott grew to hate living in New Mills, you know. He only moved here for Ashley's sake. It was different for us – when we came, the town had changed. There are lots of nice houses to choose from now and it's only half an hour or so into Manchester on the train, so it's convenient for John. It's a good place to live for us. But not for Scott. After Ashley died he could have gone somewhere else, but he said there was no point. Everywhere would be just as bad. And at least he was still close to her here, in a way.'

'So he blamed himself for Ashley's death?'

'I suppose he did. He felt responsible because he wasn't there. And the lorry driver was to blame too, of course. But he went to prison. He was punished for it. I think that was the difference for Scott.'

'What was he charged with? Causing death by dangerous driving?'

'That was it. The police said he was texting on his phone when his lorry drifted off the road and hit Ashley's car. He got sent down for eight years. It hardly seems enough for taking a life, does it?'

'That would mean he's out of prison now,' said Cooper.

Mrs Turner shook her head. 'I don't know. We've tried to forget about that time in our lives. Talking about it seemed to make Scott worse, so we didn't mention it at all, if we could avoid it.'

'Your brother might have known when the driver was due out, though.'

'Possibly. If he did, he kept it to himself. He became very secretive in the last few years.'

Cooper wasn't surprised at that. If even your family made it clear they didn't want to hear about the subject closest to your heart, you were bound to start keeping it to yourself.

'Does the name Malcolm or Mac Kelsey mean anything to you?' he asked.

Pat Turner looked at him blankly. 'Not a thing.'

'Nothing in connection with Ashley's death?'

'I'm sorry, no. I can't remember any of the names now. It's all in the past as far as I'm concerned, and I'm happy for it to stay that way. You can look up all the details of the crash for yourself, if you want to. But I can't see how it's relevant.' She sighed deeply. 'Scott was just a very unhappy man, I suppose. That's obvious now, isn't it?'

Cooper held up the note again.

'So who did he mean when he wrote "*Don't blame them*"?' he said.

'I have absolutely no idea,' said Mrs Turner.

She was starting to become edgy and defensive now. That was another stage of reaction after a suicide. It was perfectly normal.

'What did Scott do for a job?' asked Hurst, instinctively taking a different approach.

'Nothing. He was living on benefits.'

'Really?' said Cooper. 'He seems to have been quite an educated man.'

'Unemployment can happen to anyone these days,' she said sharply.

'True.'

Then Mrs Turner looked at Cooper and made a decision.

'Oh, well. You'll find out soon enough. Scott used to be a teacher, but he lost his job. I wouldn't want to drag all that up again. It was a very long time ago and it was all rather painful.'

'I'm sorry.'

'Well, after that he held down a few manual jobs for a while. Work that was below the level of his abilities, of course. He was always intending to find something more suitable. And he probably would have done, except for what happened to Ashley. In the end he wasn't in any condition to make any employer interested in taking him on.'

She'd recovered herself now. The tears had come at the memory of the road accident, the death of Scott's wife. That had been a more traumatic event in her life, perhaps. A more sudden and unexpected one anyway.

Cooper remembered the two cars parked outside on the drive.

'Is your husband home, Mrs Turner?' he asked

'John? No, he's at work.'

She explained that her husband commuted into Manchester every day, taking the train from New Mills Central. Cooper thought that was probably true of many of the neighbours in these housing developments on the edge of New Mills. He could imagine them sharing a carriage on the way to the office, and when they came home again at night, then never seeing each other for the rest of the time, even though they might live next door.

'I drove him to the station this morning,' said Mrs Turner. 'It's better if we can do it that way. There isn't much room for parking down there.'

'I was wondering if there's anyone you can call,' said Cooper. 'Someone who can come and be with you. It's best not to be alone when something upsetting happens like this.'

Pat Turner didn't look all that upset by her brother's suicide, but the principle was the same. She might feel it as a relief now, an inevitable end to the problems of the last few years. But it could hit her badly later. And he wouldn't be here by then, or anyone else from his team. There would be no family liaison officer allocated to Mrs Turner, as there would be in a murder case.

'John wouldn't be able to come home from work. He's much too busy,' she said.

'A neighbour perhaps?'

'I don't know them that well.'

'There must be someone.'

'I do have a friend who lives nearby. Should I phone her?'

Cooper noted her voice already faltering uncertainly. Who knew how she might feel in an hour or two?

'Yes, I think that would be best,' he said.

THAT EVENING, WHEN he went off duty, Ben Cooper called at Bridge End Farm to see his brother and his family. He didn't get to Bridge End as often as he used to, though his memories of growing up here hadn't faded at all.

Every visit to his old home was comforting yet strangely distancing at the same time, as if each occasion he came here was one more step away from his past. Perhaps there was only so much nostalgia to draw from and soon the well would be dry. Then the farm would no longer be recognisable as the place he saw in his memories.

The mind was perfectly capable of such tricks. It created false recollections layer by layer, until your remembrance had drifted well beyond reality. Sometimes that was a good thing.

Driving down the track to Bridge End still felt the same, though. He had to twist the steering wheel at all the same points along the way to avoid the potholes, though tonight he was conscious of the jarring on the suspension of his new car. No matter how often Matt carried out repairs to the track with hardcore and compacted earth, the first heavy rain of the winter washed it all away again. Water that came rushing down from the hillside turned it into a river, sometimes overwhelming the field drains and flooding the yard.

Just like at Higher Fold Farm, some stretches of dry-stone wall were beginning to bulge and would collapse within a season or two. It was an endless task keeping those miles and miles of wall in good condition. More repairs were inevitable. Like death and paperwork. Other things were changing, of course. His nieces, Amy and Josie, were growing up fast – and the trials of their teenage years weren't making Matt's temper any better. Well, that was unavoidable too.

Soon he'd left the Toyota in the yard, wincing at the mud and fresh cow manure coating its tyres and splashed onto the paintwork. Inside, the farmhouse was warm and cosy, as always. Matt relaxed with him in the sitting room. This rare hour when they sat down together was good for both of them. They'd been so close as boys that it was vital to take the opportunity to talk when they could.

Ben had always thought he and Matt had little in common physically, except perhaps a look of their late father around the eyes and nose. It was Matt who'd inherited their father's size, the wide shoulders, the enormous hands – and the uncertain temper. But spending time with his younger brother seemed to provide an outlet.

After catching up on the latest family news, Matt had begun to grumble. He was talking about a farmer further down the valley who'd decided to move with the times and was now selling mature ewes and wethers for mutton in the halal market. There was a rapidly growing demand, apparently. Mutton had gone out of fashion in England more than a century ago, when consumers switched to lamb. Sheep were slaughtered at a younger age to suit the change in tastes, and an endless supply of refrigerated meat from New Zealand made lamb available all the year round.

Ben remembered reading *The Diary of Samuel Pepys* and novels by Dickens as a child and wondering why everyone in London ate mutton, when it no longer seemed to exist in the world he lived in. But mutton was making a comeback now, thanks to a changing ethnicity.

'Shetlands are the breed he wants,' said Matt. 'Shetlands in Derbyshire? It seems all wrong to me.'

'Perhaps it will work out okay for him.'

'Maybe.'

Ben smiled. Every change in farming seemed wrong to Matt. If he'd been born a generation or two earlier, he'd have been shaking his head in disbelief at those new-fangled tractors.

If Shawhead had been nearer to Bridge End, he might have asked Matt about the farmers there, Grant Swindells and Jack Lawson. But Matt's world ended at Bakewell Agricultural Centre in the south and Buxton Market in the west. Anyone beyond that was a foreigner. New Mills was outside the edges of the known universe.

His sister-in-law Kate was busy somewhere else in the house. Probably in the kitchen, judging from the enticing smells. In the past Amy and Josie would have been thrilled to see him. He missed the days when they would have run to meet him as soon as they heard his car and would throw their arms round him shouting with delight. Now it was different. The girls came to say hello, but without any great enthusiasm, then went back to their rooms as soon as they could, to do whatever teenage girls did in their rooms. He didn't know and he felt sure Matt had never even dared to ask. Maybe they were texting their friends, or skyping, or updating their Facebook profiles, or playing *Angry Birds*.

'We were in town on Monday night,' said Matt. 'We called at Welbeck Street to see how you'd got on with the house viewing. But you weren't at home.'

'No, I was down at Diane's place in Nottingham,' said Ben.

Immediately, Matt narrowed his eyes at the mention of Diane Fry's name. It was the closest he'd ever come to warning his brother off.

Matt had met Fry a couple of times. And he wasn't impressed, to say the least. Though he couldn't have been described as the most sensitive of people, or the best judge of character, he'd made his reaction clear in this case. Ben could recall his brother looking at Fry with the same expression on his face that he used when he found a ewe suffering from advanced foot rot. It was a mixture of disgust at the noxious smell, irritation at the work involved in dealing with a problem – and a hint of pity for a suffering animal.

Since Matt had become aware that there was more between Ben and his old colleague than a working relationship, he'd developed a version of that expression for every mention of her. He would probably never say anything, would shy away from speaking his mind out loud. But then, he didn't need to. The Cooper brothers had always been able to communicate their feelings without the need for words.

Ben smiled as he saw his brother's expression. Would he bring himself to say something one day? Perhaps he would have to. Even if it was only a reluctant 'congratulations'.

He made a bit more small talk with Matt, telling him about the house viewing, but sensing all the while that the predictable question was coming. His brother was more interested in things than in people. Preferably mechanical things with engines.

'And how's the new car, by the way?' he said.

Ben sighed. 'Right now,' he said, 'it's covered in mud.'

Chapter Seventeen

Thursday 12 February

BEN COOPER HAD found it difficult to sleep. He felt so restless that he was up and out of the flat well before daylight. The roads out of Edendale were empty, the moors black and forbidding against a heavy blanket of cloud.

Because it was so quiet and free of tourists, he decided to head through Castleton and drive over the Winnats Pass. The limestone crags loomed towards the sky on either side of him as he climbed the narrow road, his headlights picking out the reflection from sheep's eyes as they clustered close to the unfenced tarmac.

This was another road completely unsuitable for heavy goods vehicles. But since the land slips from Mam Tor had permanently closed the old A625 in the 1970s, there was no alternative route westwards out of Castleton.

It took him less than half an hour to reach New Mills. The town was just stirring into life, commuters setting off on their journeys into Stockport or Manchester, or perhaps even further afield. Some of these motorists would be joining rush hour congestion on the M60. He didn't envy them at all.

It was just before 7 a.m. when he parked on Union Road near the headquarters of the Plain English Campaign. The first hint of dawn was starting to show in the sky to the east, but the sun wouldn't rise for another half hour or so.

He found the steps down into the Torrs and descended carefully, hanging on to the handrail as he left the street lights of the town behind him and headed into the darkness of the gorge. As his eyes adjusted, he could see the river foaming over the weir and the high arches of the Union Road bridge, with the lights of traffic passing over it.

But Cooper turned away from the bridge and the hydro project and stepped onto the walkway. He followed its course as it swung towards the bend in the river, with the burned-out shell of the wrecked mill building on his left and the water rushing underneath. The roar of the weir echoing off the sides of the gorge filled his ears and drove out any thoughts of the town and the traffic.

He leaned over the rail for a moment, but felt uncomfortably disorientated by the awareness of the drop into the darkness below his feet and drew back again. He'd reached the point in the cantilevered section where Scott Brooks had been found hanging.

Cooper could see the appeal of the walkway. Down here it felt completely remote from the town just starting to come awake above his head. Scott had chosen the location with care, the way he'd done everything else. The plan had been fully worked out. Even the messages left around the house were part of it. Cooper felt sure of that now. They hadn't really been meant for the dead Ashley. They were intended to be read by whoever came to the house when his suicide was discovered. The door had stood open so they would have no problems getting in. Scott had set the scene for them to find.

What a pity, then, that his suicide note was so vague. A bit more information would have helped tremendously. Had Scott deliberately decided to be ambiguous at that point? Or had he lost confidence as he stood here on the walkway, with the rope in his hand and the drop to the river in front of him?

Cooper could imagine how Scott Brooks had felt, but only up to this moment. The act of calmly and deliberately taking your own life was beyond his comprehension. Some people said it was the easy way out. But, as he stared at the foaming water in the darkness below, Cooper knew it must have taken an awful lot of courage.

Perhaps Scott genuinely believed that he would be joining Ashley somewhere in death. That would be the only justification. Had that belief carried him along in his carefully laid-out plan, even in the face of the reality of this final moment? Cooper hadn't gained a picture of Scott Brooks as a particularly spiritual man. But who really knew what went on in people's minds in these circumstances?

With an effort, Cooper pulled himself away from his contemplation of the drop from the walkway. The noise and movement of the water down there had started to seem too hypnotic, even enticing.

He continued along the walkway, accompanied only by the sound of his own footsteps, passing round the sweeping bend to the other side of the mill and climbing the slope from the walkway up towards the signal box.

He found himself standing on Station Road at the entrance to New Mills Central. There was traffic here, cars crawling over the narrow bridge in the hope of finding a parking spot near the station. It was only a few minutes to sunrise now, but it was still gloomy. The commuters looked miserable as they passed through the gate into the station, shoulders hunched in their coats. No one gave the impression that they were looking forward to their journey into Manchester. But it must be their own choice to do this every day.

Then Cooper saw someone he recognised. Unsure at first, he crossed Station Road and watched the figure join the crowd on the platform. Like train users everywhere, they were all staring anxiously up the line, watching for the first glimpse of an approaching train.

Yes, it was definitely Ian Hibbert from Shawhead Cottages. Cooper recollected that Hibbert was the one who worked for a marketing consultancy. Something to do with financial planning? He had been most worried about the blocked road at Shawhead, because of his important job. But this morning he looked so miserable as he waited for a Manchester train that he ought to have been glad of an excuse for a day off, surely?

Well, everyone was different. Maybe Mr Hibbert thought his work was vital and his presence at the marketing consultancy indispensable.

Cooper saw a flurry of movement on the platform and a second later he heard a train arriving. The track passed along the high retaining wall over the walkway and the train was soon pulling into the station. Doors slammed and the platform rapidly emptied.

Cooper looked at his watch as the train drew out again. It was seven thirty-nine. The sun was just coming up.

But he needed to stop off somewhere for a coffee before he headed back into Edendale for a day's work. There were some things he'd found he couldn't manage without. A full night's sleep wasn't always necessary. But coffee was.

AS A RESULT Cooper barely had time to prepare for Thursday morning's briefing at West Street. He wanted to tell Detective Superintendent Branagh that he had some useful leads to follow. But right now he'd be struggling to explain where they led.

So far the forensic haul from the bridge scene had been pitiful. Amanda Hibbert's fingerprints were on the door handle of the lorry's cab and on the bloodstained delivery docket. Some of the prints on the bodywork could be hers too. They were too smudged to be definite, but there were a number of comparison points.

And what else did he have? Well, he had a mass of circumstantial details. There were tyre impressions on the track of the old mineral line that passed over the disused part of the bridge, and broken branches on the sapling growing out of the stonework in the gap between the two arches.

Those details, taken with the scuffed shoe marks on the roof of the trapped lorry, gave him a picture of someone dropping onto the cab from above. It was a possibility to consider, but it wasn't hard evidence.

Then he had the height sign that had fallen, or been removed, from the arch on the approach to the bridge. He read through the forensic report again. He couldn't see any reference to an examination of the screw holes where the sign had originally been positioned. It would be helpful to know whether the sign had been ripped off deliberately. Scenes of Crime would have to get their ladders out again.

And then there was the diversion sign. The two uniformed officers he'd sent to do a search had come up with the goods. The yellow sign had been thrown over a wall at the corner of Cloughpit Lane. Its arrow pointed to the left.

No viable prints had been recovered from either of the two signs, which was a shame. It meant they would have to be discounted as firm indications of a planned ambush. They might just be a result of coincidental vandalism or mischief. But as a whole they were definitely suggestive.

He went into the briefing hoping for some more positive news from the forensic examination. For that he had to reply on the Crime Scene Manager, Wayne Abbott.

'First of all there's the site where the body was concealed,' said Abbott when everyone had gathered together. 'The makeshift grave, if you want to call it that. We've lifted some prints off the smoother stones. The ones at the bottom of the pile were dry and protected, so the prints were clear enough.'

'Did you get a match on the database?'

'No such luck. But then, you probably didn't expect that.'

'It was a long shot,' admitted Cooper.

Abbott shook his head. 'You're just going to have to find a suspect we can compare prints from.'

'Easier said than done.'

'Well, fortunately, that's *your* job,' said Abbott, with a smile. 'We do hope to get a DNA profile from the unidentified fingerprints in the cab. Whoever left them was sweating. There's enough residue for the lab to work on.'

'That would be great.'

'It takes time, of course.'

'Anything else?'

'Yes, the satnav. You asked us to examine it. It was in car mode.'

'It was? That's interesting.'

'Yes, but . . .'

'What?'

'Well, this wasn't specifically asked for, but we did a full examination of the satnav device. We recovered a number of fingerprints from the casing. Many of them were Mr Kelsey's, of course. But they were overlaid by a set of partials. As far as we can tell, they match the prints taken from the door handle of the cab.'

'Raising the possibility that whoever was in Kelsey's cab changed the settings on his satnav. Perhaps with the intention of making it look as though it had led him onto the wrong road. Whereas in fact he'd learned from his previous incident not to rely on his satnav too much, but to use his common sense.'

Cooper made a note. So the satnav settings had been changed, but it was impossible to tell when it had been done. That was of limited help too.

'We've analysed the victim's mobile phone records,' said Abbott. 'There were no calls within the last hour before the estimated time of his collision with the bridge. Or afterwards, which is perhaps more surprising.'

'We know that his depot didn't get a call from him when he got trapped,' said Carol Villiers. 'And whatever happened, he didn't have the chance to phone for help.'

Cooper turned to Abbott again. 'What about earlier calls?'

'There's nothing of any interest in Malcolm Kelsey's phone records. A fairly normal number of calls home and to his employer's number. Nothing that stands out at all.'

'His wife has no helpful information either, unfortunately,' said Cooper. 'We need to get the names of some close friends we can interview. They might well have a different perspective. There might be somebody he talked to in the pub. And did we recover Mr Kelsey's car from Windmill Feed Solutions?'

'Yes, a silver-grey Renault Megane,' said Villiers. 'There's nothing of any interest, so far as we can see.'

Wayne Abbott was waiting patiently. Cooper checked his notes again. There was another vital question.

'Did you find any sign of a weapon?' he said.

'Well now,' said Abbott. He had that smile on his face again, the one Cooper was learning to distrust. 'There was nothing near the body. Some of the stones had traces of blood on them, but none we could say with any certainty were used as a weapon. However . . .'

Abbott pinned a set of photographs onto the board. Cooper leaned closer to make out what he was seeing.

'The item on the left,' said Abbott, 'is a retractable shark knife. It's a fairly common DIY tool used for carpet fitting, but also by delivery drivers for cutting nylon twine and packing tape, that sort of thing. The other two items are more unusual for a driver to possess. The middle one is a baseball bat. I don't suppose Mr Kelsey played baseball in his spare time?'

'I doubt it,' said Cooper.

'Perhaps it was kept for protection, then. The bat was stored under the sleeping compartment behind the driver's seat. Now, on the right, you might recognise the third item . . . ?'

'It's a Taser,' said Irvine.

'Indeed. More accurately, a conducted electrical weapon made by Taser International. These items were all found concealed in the cab of the DAF when we conducted a thorough search in the garage.'

'A Taser is classified as a prohibited weapon under the Firearms Act,' said Sharma. 'The maximum sentence for unauthorised possession is ten years in prison.'

Abbott nodded. 'Nevertheless – it seems your murder victim was in possession of one in the cab of his lorry.'

A PRESS CONFERENCE was being held that morning. Ben Cooper was asked to sit at the table alongside Superintendent Branagh. He took his seat praying that he wouldn't be called on to answer any questions. This was one part of the job that most coppers hated. But it was a necessary evil sometimes. The media had to be kept on side, in case they were needed at some point. Press appeals to the public could produce useful results, if all else failed.

The death of Malcolm Kelsey wasn't a high-profile case as far as the press were concerned, so there was only a small turnout. Cooper recognised Erin Byrne, chief reporter of the *Eden Valley Times*. From what he'd heard about the staff cuts they were going through, she might be the only senior reporter left now. But Edendale was lucky that it still had a local paper at all. Many other towns of a similar size had lost theirs already.

When the opportunity came to ask questions, Byrne was the first one to raise her hand. Hazel Branagh nodded at her.

'How certain are you that this is a murder inquiry, Superintendent?' she asked.

Branagh gave her a hard stare for a moment – not out of any anger probably, but simply because it was her usual expression.

'While we don't yet have a specific cause of death, the circumstances are clearly suspicious,' she said. 'I can tell you, for example, that significant efforts were made to conceal the body. Certain unidentified persons were involved in this incident, and we intend to find them and get an explanation of what happened to Malcolm Kelsey.'

WHEN THE PRESS had gone, Detective Superintendent Branagh sat down with Ben Cooper and asked him if there really was some possibility of getting answers.

'I think we're making real progress now,' said Cooper. 'Some active lines of enquiry to follow at least.'

'That's good to hear. But what connection could there be between the death of Malcom Kelsey and this suicide, Scott Brooks?'

'At this moment we don't know. We're following up as many leads as we can. But all we can do is carry on asking questions everywhere until we turn something up. And keep our fingers crossed.'

'At least let's hope that Mr Kelsey's death wasn't a random killing,' said Branagh, echoing the nagging worry that had been at the back of Cooper's mind for two days.

'Yes, let's hope so. It might mean we have some chance of success.'

Branagh frowned at a form on her desk.

'I've been asked to sign something to do with deceased sheep,' she said. 'A post-mortem examination. Really?'

Hesitantly, Cooper explained the possible significance of the sheep.

'The owner, Mr Swindells, says the sheep were already dead. I asked for a vet to take a look at them, to see if we can get a cause of death.'

'Is that necessary, Ben?'

'It will confirm whether Mr Swindells is telling the truth. It eliminates a potential motive.'

Branagh seemed happier with that.

'Ah, motive,' she said. 'Yes. Money, jealousy, revenge? We can count out money, can't we? There was no robbery in this case.'

'It seems not,' said Cooper.

'But we always keep an open mind, don't we?'

'Of course we do.'

'And Detective Sergeant Sharma?' said Branagh.

'Yes, ma'am?'

'Fitting in, is he?'

Cooper was at least beginning to feel that he knew Sharma a little bit better. He'd learned that his wife's name was Asha, that they had no children yet, that they attended the Geeta Bhawan Temple on Pear Tree Road in Derby. It was information. But he still didn't feel that he knew the man. He had a surface impression, but nothing deeper. Perhaps it would just take time. That didn't mean it wouldn't happen. Everyone had to be given a chance.

'Oh yes,' he said. 'DS Sharma is fitting in just fine.'

BACK IN HIS own office, Cooper immediately began to have doubts. As he sat at his desk he found himself turning over in his mind the names of officers he might know well enough to ask for a discreet bit of information.

There was a detective sergeant he'd been on a course with once, when he was still hoping for promotion to DI. Marston, was that his name? Yes, Phil Marston. Cooper remembered him as the sociable type, much happier leaning on a bar counter with a few mates than sitting in a classroom being lectured about the identification and management of operational resources.

Marston had been aiming for inspector himself, but hadn't made it yet. Perhaps he'd just been unlucky that no suitable vacancy had arisen. Instead he'd been put back into uniform for a while to get more experience and was now in charge of a response team in D Division.

Cooper knew if he phoned Marston, he would have to put up with half an hour of grumbling about the pressure he was under, the shortage of staff, the impossible targets he was being given. But he would know Devdan Sharma.

Yes, D Division might be bigger – it covered the city and some of the larger towns in the south of the county. But coppers were the same everywhere. They wanted to know who was getting promotion, who'd applied for a transfer, which officers had been commended by their divisional commander, or had been summoned for 'words of advice' after a complaint. It was amazing how fast speculation and rumour could be firmed up into positive intelligence. That applied to fellow officers as much as to members of the criminal community.

Cooper looked up Marston's number and found he was based at St Mary's Wharf, just to the north of Derby city centre. He put in a call and left a message. Within a few minutes Marston rang him back.

'A DI, then?' he said straight away. 'Do I have to call you "sir" now?'

'You know you don't.'

It had been said lightly, but Cooper thought he detected more than a hint of resentment in the tone. It was understandable. Everyone wondered why someone else got promotion ahead of them. It was only human to conclude that there was some hidden reason for it. Influence in the right places, perhaps. But it might do no harm if Marston thought he had that sort of influence. The ability to put in a good word.

'Devdan Sharma,' said Cooper when he tentatively got around to the question after the obligatory small talk.

'Sharma? Yes, he's pretty well known in D Division.'

'Is that a good thing?'

'It's good for your prospects. If the bosses are already aware of you, it's an advantage when it comes to promotion time.'

'You'll make it soon,' said Cooper.

'Thanks. I'll tell them you'll give me a good reference, then.' Marston laughed. 'Sharma won't have this trouble, though. All he has to do is keep his nose clean. Funny thing is, though . . .'

'What, Phil?'

'Well, I'm not sure he *has* kept his nose clean. There was a bit of talk about his connections with the wrong type of people in the Asian community here in Derby. Nothing too major. Low-level organised crime. The story was that one of his DCs had gone to Professional Standards with a complaint about Sharma's conduct.'

'He didn't go straight to his line manager?'

'Apparently not.'

Cooper thought about that for a moment. An officer who failed to report suspicions about a colleague's unprofessional conduct could face disciplinary action himself these days. But bypassing the management structure suggested a lack of confidence in the normal procedures.

'And what happened?' he asked.

'Nothing,' said Marston. 'Well, that's not quite true. The DC was shipped off to C Division shortly afterwards and he's working in some out of the way place over there now. Staveley or Shire-brook, somewhere like that. Junkies mugging old ladies, retired coal miners having their whippets stolen. As for Sharma . . . well, you know all about that. You've got him.'

Chapter Eighteen

In the CID room Cooper found Luke Irvine not doing very much. He was used to finding Gavin Murfin doing that, or less. But he couldn't accept it from Irvine.

'Luke, have you confirmed Ian Hibbert's movements on Monday?' he said. 'What time he arrived home, where he was when Mac Kelsey was killed?'

'That's my next job', said Irvine defensively.

Cooper could see he knew it was something he ought to have done by now.

'And did you check on the theatre production Amanda Hibbert says she was involved in?' he said.

'No. But I could Google it.'

Cooper stared at Irvine. Was he joking? But perhaps not. The internet was an essential tool for police officers now. Even social media had become obligatory. Public alerts were sent out by email and all the Safer Neighbourhood Teams had Twitter accounts. One of the PCSOs had recently been tweeting pictures of a family of pigeons nesting on a ledge in a corner of the garage at West Street.

'I'd prefer it if you went yourself and spoke to someone,' said Cooper. 'Or phone them at least, if you're too busy to spare the time. It's always better. You pick up things you would never know in any other way.'

Irvine shrugged, his expression suggesting that he would do it, but only to humour an out of touch Luddite.

Cooper was about to expand on his view when he heard the phone ringing in his office. He dashed to answer it. A missed call was often a missed opportunity, or a bit of information that went overlooked.

'Detective Inspector Cooper.'

It was Mr Bateman, the transport manager at Windmill Feed Solutions. And he'd called to have a grumble.

'I don't suppose you've any idea when we're going to get our vehicle back?' he said, when Cooper answered.

'No. I'm sorry, sir. Not until it's been fully examined.'

'It's a bit of a nuisance, you know.'

'I thought you had an extensive fleet.'

'We do, but it's a busy time for us. I've got customer orders stacking up on the system.'

'I'm sorry, Mr Bateman, there's nothing I can do. It will take however long it takes.'

'You do realise there are dozens of bags of cattle feed in the back of that vehicle? That's a valuable asset. Our company has a lot of money tied up in that vehicle you've impounded. Not to mention that we've had the customer on the phone playing merry hell with us.'

'Which customer?' said Cooper quickly.

'Mr Elliott at Bankside Farm, of course.'

The name meant nothing to Cooper at first. His brain tried to relate it to the people of Shawhead, but failed to make a match.

Then he remembered standing by the lorry while it was still stuck under the bridge and talking to Grant Swindells. Bankside Farm was the address where Mac Kelsey should have been delivering to when he took the wrong road and ended up near Shawhead. Mr Elliott must have waited all evening for his animal feed to arrive. It was one of those unconsidered consequences that rippled out from a serious crime. A lot of people were affected.

Cooper apologised to Bateman a third time and put his phone down. Before he could move, it rang again.

'It's Erin Byrne,' said the voice at the other end of the line.

'Hello, Erin,' said Cooper cautiously. 'What can I do for the *Eden Valley Times*? Due warning – it may not be very much.'

'Actually, I thought I might do something for you,' she said.

'Really?'

'Well, unless you've already made the connection yourself.'

'What connection.'

'There was a suicide case in New Mills yesterday. I've just heard that the man has been identified as Scott Brooks.'

'That's right,' said Cooper, confident that the information was already general knowledge after a force press release.

'I knew him,' said Byrne. 'I did a story about him, nearly eight years ago now. A sad case really. I thought he must have got over it by now. But obviously not.'

'Over what?' said Cooper.

'So you haven't enquired into his background very much.'

'I can't comment. You know we have an active murder inquiry on our hands at the moment.'

'Well, exactly.'

Cooper began to get impatient. 'Spit it out, Erin. Why are you trying to say?'

'The story I did about Scott Brooks followed a tragic accident on the A6. A serious crash involving a couple of HGVs. A woman died in her car, which was parked in a lay-by. The woman was Ashley Brooks, Scott's wife. He was devastated, of course. After the driver was convicted of causing death by dangerous driving I did a long interview with him. He poured his heart out, and it was very moving. A terrific human interest piece. Even better, we got it as an exclusive. He didn't talk to anyone else.'

'Congratulations. But what does this have to do—'

'I'm getting there,' said Byrne. 'Hold your horses.'

'I am quite busy.'

'With your murder inquiry. I know. But that's exactly what I'm telling you. Scott Brooks made some very bitter statements about his wife's family in our interview. Flynn, they're called. There was quite a bit of fallout from that. A real family feud. Both sides were as bad, but some of the Flynns even threatened to sue us for libel. That was touch and go for a while, but it was settled out of court.'

'And?' said Cooper, ready to put the phone down if she didn't get to the point.

'Well, one of the most outspoken members on the Flynn side was an aunt of Ashley's. We had her shouting the odds in the office a few times and I remember her well. We couldn't calm her down. She kept swearing that she would do anything for her family. The thing is – and this is what made me phone – she lives in that little hamlet, Shawhead. She moved there not long ago.'

Cooper found he was gripping the handset a bit more tightly, no longer thinking of putting it down.

'I take it she's married and her name isn't Flynn any more.'

'No. Her married name is Schofield. Donna Schofield.'

'Thank you, Erin,' said Cooper.

'Do you owe me one now?' said Byrne brightly.

'Within reason.'

She sighed. 'That's always the way.'

Great. Everyone had complaints to make today.

'But I'm grateful,' said Cooper. 'Truly. That's very helpful.'

'I suppose that will have to do, then,' said Byrne. 'And, Ben – if you happen to be speaking to dear old Donna, give her my love. Not.'

When she'd rung off, Cooper banged the phone down a bit too hard. Donna Schofield. That was definitely a priority job for today. He needed to locate Mrs Schofield and her husband, whether they were in Thailand or wherever.

But he had another important job to do this morning. He was due at the mortuary for the results of the post-mortem on Malcolm Kelsey. Cooper looked at his watch. He'd better get moving, in fact.

He stood in the door of the CID room as he pulled his jacket on and addressed the sparse team of detectives at his disposal.

'DS Sharma,' he said, 'I want you to pull out everything you can find for me about the fatal crash on the A6 in which Ashley Brooks was killed.'

Sharma sat upright and stared at him, as if startled by his tone. 'Yes?'

'It was about eight years ago,' said Cooper. 'Find me court reports, witness statements, everything. I want an in-depth briefing when I get back.'

'Right.'

Sharma looked around uncertainly and Cooper had a moment of sympathy for him as a newcomer.

'DC Villiers will assist you,' he said. 'And DC Irvine . . .'

'Yes?'

'You'll be back at Shawhead. You've still got the Hibberts' movements to check on. And I want a current location for the Schofields of Top Barn urgently. Not just hearsay from the neighbours that they might be in Thailand. Pin them down. Produce them for me, if you can.'

'Okay, boss.'

'And Luke?'

'What?'

'Make sure you go there. In person.'

THE MORTUARY AT Edendale District General Hospital wasn't Ben Cooper's favourite place in the world. He only came here when death had entered his life. There were only so many times you could do that without being affected by it. You either became hardened and immune to the underlying humanity of the victim, or it all became too much and you couldn't stand it any more.

Today he was here for the results of the initial post-mortem on Malcolm Kelsey. And that meant dealing with the forensic pathologist, Dr Juliana van Doon.

Dr van Doon had worked in Edendale for some time now. That was the one thing Cooper had in common with her. He didn't know what the usual professional development for a forensic pathologist was, but she hadn't moved on and pursued other opportunities. Perhaps she'd tried for other jobs, but failed. Or perhaps she just enjoyed meeting the dead residents of Derbyshire.

Looking at the pathologist, Cooper found he still couldn't decide which it was. And he certainly couldn't ask her. He'd been slightly afraid of her ever since he first encountered her when he was a fresh young detective constable. She was one of the few people who'd been willing to put Diane Fry in her place too. The frostiness in the atmosphere when Fry was present owed more to the nature of their relationship than to the chill of the coolers where the bodies were preserved. Cooper had felt the shiver of hostility more than once.

But Diane Fry wasn't here today and Cooper felt able to smile at the pathologist, hoping for a reciprocal response. But it didn't come.

'It's difficult to tell whether some of these injuries were caused pre-mortem or post-mortem,' she said. 'I think this individual was freshly deceased when he was buried.'

'His body was covered with large stones to conceal it,' said Cooper.

'Yes, that's what I mean. If he'd been dead for some time, I would have expected the stones to have left impressions in the soft tissue. Some of them have. But there are also contusions which look from their shape to be due to an object like a stone. Bruising like that only occurs before, during, or immediately after death.'

'Do you think he might still have been alive when they piled the stones on him?' asked Cooper.

The pathologist waggled a hand in an uncharacteristically indecisive gesture. 'All I can say is that it was a close run thing. They didn't wait to be sure he was dead.'

'And perhaps they didn't care,' said Cooper.

Dr van Doon didn't comment. It wasn't her concern. Her job wasn't to consider who committed this act of violence, or what they were thinking at the time. Perhaps that was how she coped with the job, why she felt comfortable in the mortuary. She only had to deal with the physical evidence, which could be analysed and explained. Dealing with living people and their emotions was much more difficult and messy.

'This individual is overweight, of course,' said Dr van Doon wearily. 'It's rare to see anyone coming in here who isn't these days. We used to record whether an individual was well nourished, or not. Now I prefer to put "over nourished". What was his occupation?'

'He was a lorry driver,' said Cooper.

'Ah yes. I'm immediately picturing burgers and chips. Sausage, egg and beans. Deep-fried cholesterol with a bucket of carbohydrates on the side.'

Cooper's thoughts wandered for a moment. 'Sally's Snack Box,' he said.

The pathologist looked up sharply from her notes. 'I beg your pardon?'

'Did I just say "Sally's Snack Box"?' asked Cooper.

'I believe you did. Why did you say that?'

'Because it's what I was thinking.'

Dr van Doon stared at him. Then, inexplicably, she smiled. Cooper had never seen her smile before – not a genuine smile of amusement like that, instead of her usual sarcastic grimace.

'Is there anything else I can tell you, DI Cooper?' she said. 'You know about the fatal injuries. There were a series of contusions to the head and body, but the fatal injury was a wound to the neck from a sharp blade. Two wounds, in fact. Very close together, the result of two separate stabbing actions.'

'The weapon?'

'It wouldn't have to be anything unusual. A sixteen-centimetre bladed kitchen knife – that would do the job. Unfortunately for this individual, the blade severed his external jugular vein. That causes rapid blood loss, due to the relatively large size of the jugular and the reflux of blood flowing back the other way. I'd put cause of death down to shock and haemorrhage as a result of the severed jugular vein.'

'I suppose he would have bled out fairly quickly?' said Cooper.

'Significant blood loss leads to haemorrhagic shock and subsequently death. Loss of consciousness undoubtedly occurred within, say, five minutes or so. It was a survivable injury, if he'd received medical attention quickly. But left untreated, he wouldn't have got far before he became unconscious.'

'A couple of hundred yards?'

'With an injury like that?' said Dr van Doon. 'Well, he'd be in serious difficulties. But you never know with the human body. It can get a long way on adrenalin.'

Cooper nodded. Five minutes would have been enough for Mac Kelsey to struggle from his cab and set out across the fields to the point by the dry-stone wall where he eventually collapsed and died. Of course, it didn't explain why he ran across the fields instead of towards the houses in Shawhead. But he would hardly have been thinking straight in the circumstances and he might not have realised where he was heading in his panic.

The best thing for Kelsey to have done was to try to reduce the loss of blood and phone for help before he lost consciousness. But he didn't do that. He was afraid of something and he'd tried to run away, to escape.

And he'd been quite right. There was definitely something to be afraid of near Shawhead. Or someone.

Chapter Nineteen

WHEN COOPER RETURNED to West Street, he was relieved to see that Luke Irvine was out of the office – though there was no news yet from Shawhead on the whereabouts of Michael and Donna Schofield.

As the hours passed, Cooper was getting more and more anxious to speak to Mrs Schofield. It was too much of a coincidence that she should be living in such a small place as Shawhead. He needed to hear what she had to say. Cooper called Irvine's number and left a voicemail asking him to check in.

At least Carol Villiers and Dev Sharma had followed up Becky Hurst's enquiries in New Mills and collected a mass of information on the fatal crash that had occurred on the A6 eight years previously. Villiers and Sharma crowded into Cooper's office, bringing another chair. With three of them inside and the door closed, the space felt extremely cramped.

'We think it's all here,' said Sharma, 'though we haven't had chance to study it. Given a little more time ...'

'It'll do,' said Cooper. 'Time is a luxury we don't have much of.'

'I understand.'

Cooper looked at Villiers. She was unnaturally quiet and developed a fixed expression that he couldn't read. He wasn't sure whether it was for his benefit, or Sharma's. One thing he hadn't asked was how they got on together when he wasn't there.

'Carol?' he said.

'I agree with DS Sharma,' she said. 'In fact, we don't really know what we're looking for. Some kind of connection with the Shawhead murder inquiry?'

'That's what I'm hoping,' said Cooper.

'Well, the lorry driver's name was James Allsop. He was thirty-six years old. Married, but no children. He lived at Whaley Bridge.'

'Local, then,' said Cooper. 'Interesting.'

First he read through a press report of the court hearing. It didn't tell the whole story – and like most press reports, it left a lot of questions unanswered and probably unasked. But it was a useful summary without having to wade through endless transcriptions of witness statements and expert evidence.

James Allsop had been a long-distance driver making overnight runs from his depot to distribution centres around the region. He ought to have been resting during the day, but his trial heard evidence that Allsop had been getting too little sleep because he was working on vehicle maintenance for his firm during the day to earn extra money.

But the immediate cause of the crash wasn't just his tiredness. He was said to have been in the habit of using his iPhone to send text messages and check email while carrying out deliveries.

The court was told that Ashley Brooks had died instantly in the crash on the A6 near Bridgemont Roundabout. Allsop had pleaded guilty to a charge of causing death by dangerous driving. And the trial judge hadn't minced his words when he sentenced Allsop.

'At the time when this accident occurred, you were travelling too fast in wet and dangerous road conditions,' the judge said in his summing up. 'You were also in a state of fatigue that made you unable to concentrate fully on the task of driving. You should not have been driving at all at the time, as you had failed to take sufficient rest. All the indications are that long before the fatal collision you must or should have been aware of your condition.

'It is equally obvious that you were disregarding the rules of the road by texting continuously. At the time you were illegally using your mobile phone and this was the primary cause of the accident. People who use a handheld phone while driving are a major risk to other road users. Your conduct involved a flagrant disregard for the rules of the road and an apparent disregard for the danger caused to others.'

The prosecution told the court the fatal crash had happened at just after 11 p.m. a few miles after Allsop had left his depot in a white articulated Iveco Stralis. He was planning to drive overnight to deliver his load to a distribution centre in the West Midlands.

Statements were heard from drivers who had noticed his erratic driving on the A6. They described his lorry weaving from side to side on the dual carriageway and running over the rumble strip on the hard shoulder. The prosecutor said that when the collision happened another motorist driving behind Allsop did not see him apply his brakes or take any evasive action.

Police investigations found that at the time of the crash Allsop was travelling at fifty-five miles per hour but had previously been doing over sixty in a forty miles per hour zone. He had apparently been driving as fast as the vehicle's speed limiter would allow him.

After the crash Allsop told police that having finished a similar shift the previous night he had gone home and slept until 6.30 p.m. But subsequent investigations proved this was a lie. In fact, he had been working on maintenance jobs at the depot until three o'clock before returning home for just a few hours' sleep. He had habitually been working an extra day shift in the yard to earn extra money. During the thirty-six-hour period before the fatal collision, it was clear he had failed to take sufficient rest.

Investigations also found that he'd been sending messages while driving his lorry at fifty-five miles per hour. One message had been sent just seconds before the crash. In one text exchange about his lack of sleep, he said: *I've survived so far.*

'James Allsop was an experienced driver working for a local haulage company,' said Villiers, seeing Cooper pause. 'It seems he was heading for a distribution centre near Wolverhampton.'

'Did he have any previous convictions?'

'None.'

Cooper nodded and continued to read.

At the end of a trial at Derby Crown Court, Allsop had been sentenced to eight years in prison after being convicted of causing death by dangerous driving and had been disqualified for eight years. With an early release on licence, that meant his driving ban would have lasted longer than his prison sentence. After the end of his ban he was supposed to take an extended driving test before he could consider getting behind the wheel again.

'Who was he sending text messages to?' asked Cooper, picking out the first unanswered question.

'The way he was going at it, you might think he was having an affair or something,' said Villiers a bit too cheerfully. 'Exchanging secret messages with his lover. But no – he was texting his wife. It wasn't mentioned in court, but Allsop's wife told the investigating team that they had a row that day, just before Allsop set off to work.'

'So they hadn't resolved the argument.'

'No. Allsop was texting her because they hadn't spoken to each other before he left to start his overnight run down to Wolverhampton.'

'Was he apologising? Trying to resolve the argument?'

'It seems so, at first.'

'At first?'

'Well, if you read through the transcript of all his texts that day, you'll see that he starts off sounding contrite, but the tone changes later on. His wife wanted to carry on the argument. Allsop begins to sound more and more angry, and his texts get longer.'

Villiers glanced through the transcripts.

'And more badly spelled,' she added. 'The last few texts are full of counter-accusations and attempts to justify himself.'

'What was the argument about?'

Villiers shrugged. 'The usual.'

'But if he wasn't having an affair . . . ?'

'No. And she wasn't either, by the way. So far as we know.'

'And neither of them had suspicions, unfounded or not?'

'No.'

'Money, then,' said Sharma confidently.

Villiers laughed. 'The voice of the married man. But yes – you're right, it was money. She was asking him where it had all gone.'

'And where *had* it gone?' asked Cooper.

'We don't know.'

Another unanswered question, then.

'He must have needed it for something,' he said. 'He was working maintenance shifts during the day to earn extra money. That was why he was so tired. You don't do that unless you've got a pressing need for cash.'

'I don't think it was gone into,' said Villiers. 'They probably thought it wasn't relevant.'

'Just the facts,' said Cooper.

'I suppose it didn't really seem necessary to support the prosecution. They had Allsop's own statement and his wife's. They had independent witness reports of the crash. And of course they had the forensic evidence – including the mobile phone data. It was a sound case.'

'Of course it was. It was cut and dried, more than enough to obtain conviction for causing death by dangerous driving. Unfortunately, it doesn't give us many leads on the subsequent murder of Mac Kelsey.'

As usual Cooper felt a nagging sense of dissatisfaction that he hadn't been there to ask the questions that came into his head, which others might have considered irrelevant. It left him with an incomplete picture.

Villiers handed him another cutting. James Allsop was pictured entering court with his head bowed and a manilla folder full of papers held over his face to shield him from the photographers. He was accompanied by his lawyer and a slightly brassy blonde woman with a hard, pinched face. The caption said she was the defendant's wife, Mrs Vicky Allsop, who had sat behind her husband in court throughout the trial.

Cooper wondered whether this woman stayed loyal after seeing Allsop sentenced to eight years in prison. Many wives weren't able to deal with that. After a year or two of waiting, they reached a point where they decided they wanted to get on with their own lives. It was a common experience for prisoners to receive the *Dear John* letter in their cells. It made their rehabilitation back into society at the end of their sentence so much more difficult.

But what could the criminal justice system do about that? People made their own decisions. They formed relationships for their own inexplicable reasons and tore them apart again just as easily. It was beyond the scope of legislation.

The newspaper photos of James Allsop were useless, so Cooper turned to the police file compiled when Allsop was processed through the custody suite on his arrest. There was the usual mugshot, the glowering stare of an apprehensive suspect, trying to look defiant but failing. He'd been treated for his injuries first, but they were minor – some bruising around the cheekbone, a slightly swollen eye and a cut near the right temple. He looked very tired too, his eyes bloodshot and his face puffy, even where it wasn't bruised.

In the custody record he was described as a Caucasian male, thirty-eight years old, five feet ten inches tall, weighing fifteen stone and two pounds. That was just creeping into the obese range for his height. From the photos in the papers, he didn't look as though that weight was muscle either. Cooper supposed it was a long-distance lorry driver's occupational hazard. Too much time spent with his backside in the driving seat and not enough exercise, apart from lifting his elbow in the pub.

'What's happened to James Allsop since then?'

'We don't know.'

'Find out, then.'

Cooper pulled out a newspaper report published after the end of the trial. In the usual way of newspapers, it concentrated on the human interest angle instead of any useful information about the evidence given at the hearing. This often meant a long, emotional outpouring from the bereaved family, a release of all the pent-up grief and frustration they'd been unable to express during the court proceedings. Sometimes a statement was read out after sentencing by a family member, sometimes by a lawyer or even a police officer.

This one was a cutting from the *Buxton Advertiser*. It was accompanied by a photo of Ashley Brooks that was familiar to Cooper. He'd seen a copy of it in Scott's house in New Mills.

A6 crash victim family's 'nightmare'

The family of a woman killed in a horrific crash on the A6 caused by a lorry driver texting at the wheel have told of the nightmare of losing her. Twenty-six-year-old Ashley Brooks died after her car, which was parked in a lay-by, was hit by a heavy goods vehicle being driven by James Allsop. He had been composing text messages while driving at fifty-five miles per hour.

Ashley's father Mr Edward Flynn said: 'Losing a child is the worst nightmare any parent could be forced to live through. Our grief is so overwhelming that we are struggling to cope with this loss. We think about Ashley every minute of every day. There has not been one moment since that terrible night that we have not experienced the sorrow.'

The crash happened on the A6 near New Mills in September last year when Allsop's Iveco lorry hit the Honda Civic owned by Ashley Brooks, causing her horrific injuries. After being hit by the truck, her Honda collided with another lorry parked in the same lay-by. She was trapped in her vehicle by a resulting fire and was later pronounced dead at the scene. The dual carriageway was closed for six hours after the pile-up.

Standing with other members of Ashley's family outside the court, Mr Flynn said: 'The sentence passed on James Allsop today will not bring Ashley back and does not ease the pain and grief that we will always feel. In this situation it is the family of the victim who have been given a life sentence. We didn't have the opportunity to say goodbye to our daughter and that is something we will have to deal with for the rest of our lives.

'Ashley was a bright and intelligent young woman, full of personality. She was a loving person, who brought joy to everyone who knew her. We have lost a daughter who might *well have gone on to be a loving mother herself. Our family will never be the same again, and nothing that has been said in court today can change that.'*

He added: 'We will always miss hearing Ashley's voice and seeing her smile. We will always live with the sorrow of knowing that her life was ended much too soon. Our daughter has been stolen from us by a driver who behaved with no regard for other road users.'

'The usual stuff,' said Villiers, shuffling her notes impatiently.

Cooper was looking at the photograph accompanying the piece. It showed the family in front of a cluster of cameras and microphones as they left court. Clutching the sheet of paper he'd read his statement from was a tall middle-aged man with grey hair. He was staring defiantly out at the reader. Next to him was a tearful woman, presumably the mother. Behind stood a group including an obvious lawyer and a couple of young men in their twenties or thirties, squeezed into suits and ties for the occasion, as if they were attending a funeral. Of course, in a way they were doing exactly that.

'What about her husband?' said Cooper. 'Scott Brooks. He isn't mentioned at all.'

'No, he doesn't seem to have got much of a look-in. The father did all the talking. Do you think the family pushed him out? It happens sometimes, especially if he was a fairly recent husband. On the other hand, he could have been too broken up by grief. Not everyone can stand up and make a statement in front of the media.'

Cooper looked at the picture again.

'Not everyone would want to,' he said.

'And some people go way over the top when they see the cameras and microphones. They start to think they're on *The X Factor* or something, and they have to win the public over with a sob story.'

'That's a bit cynical for you, Carol,' said Cooper. 'What's wrong?'

Villiers gazed back with a straight face. 'Nothing.'

Cooper made a mental to ask her later, when they could get a few minutes alone. He expected the cynical comments from Luke Irvine or Becky Hurst, not from Villiers. But now obviously wasn't the right time to pursue it.

'These news reports aren't enough,' he said. 'Have you got the witness statements there?'

Villiers looked at Sharma, waiting for him to speak.

'Yes, we do have them,' he said. 'But they're extensive. Is it really necessary?'

'Humour me,' said Cooper.

'Well, the driver of the other lorry involved was Polish, a man by the name of Artus Borzuczek.'

He pronounced the name badly, sliding over the 'z' sounds as if he was 'shushing' a noisy child. Was that why he'd been reluctant? It was nothing to be ashamed of. East European names caused problems for many people.

'And ah, let's see ...' Sharma murmured to himself as he flicked through the pages. 'Yes, here's the gist of it. According to his statement, Mr Borzuczek was asleep at the time of the crash. He was interviewed of course, but they didn't get much out of him, even with the help of a translator. He said he couldn't remember anything about the crash, except a loud bang. He thought a bomb had gone off, he said. But his memory must only have been of a split second, because he was knocked unconscious when he hit the windscreen of his cab. He never saw Ashley Brooks' Honda Civic. It wasn't there when he stopped.'

'Was he injured?' asked Cooper.

'Yes. As a result of the collision, he suffered a broken collarbone, scalp lacerations and facial injuries. He spent some time in hospital, then went back to Poland. His statement was given to the court in writing.'

'Who else have we got?'

Sharma was beginning to look flustered. Cooper watched him closely as he fumbled at the file. Did he have a problem responding under pressure?

'The owner of a roadside cafe on the opposite carriageway,' he said. 'She didn't see the collision, but witnessed the aftermath. She was the first to call the emergency services. And a number of drivers were traced who'd been travelling behind Allsop's lorry on the southbound carriageway of the A6.'

'What did they say?'

'They testified that they'd seen the lorry being driven erratically and swerving off the road. They said Allsop made no attempt to brake until it was too late. None of the drivers was local, though. One was from Burton-on-Trent, one from Birmingham—'

'Is that it?' interrupted Cooper.

'Not quite. There were two people looking down from a bridge over the road. Two of the drivers mentioned seeing them at the time of the collision.'

'A bridge?'

For a moment Cooper pictured the Cloughpit Lane bridge, but he knew he must be wrong. There was no railway bridge like that over the A6. Then a different image came into his mind. A small road bridge built to cross the dual carriageway connecting the outskirts of Whaley Bridge to . . .

'Bugsworth Basin,' he said.

Both Villiers and Sharma looked at him in surprise.

'The canal basin,' said Cooper. 'It's the terminus of the Peak Forest Canal. It used to be a busy industrial area, full of lime kilns. It was derelict and disused for decades, then there was a restoration project. It's in water again and they've turned it into a visitor attraction. A road runs through the basin and it crosses the A6 on a bridge near there.'

'Yes, I think that's the one,' said Sharma. 'Should I have known that?'

'No,' admitted Cooper. 'It takes a bit of local knowledge. People park their cars on that bridge sometimes if they're visiting Bugsworth Basin. Uniforms have dealt with a couple of complaints of youths throwing objects off the bridge into the traffic. Nothing serious, but that's only by luck.'

'If not kids, why would anyone else be standing on the bridge at that time of night?' said Villiers.

'It's anyone's guess. It's an isolated spot, in its own way. If you don't count four lanes of traffic passing underneath you.'

Cooper turned back to the original newspaper report. '*Travelling too fast in wet and dangerous road conditions*'. That was what the trial judge had said.

'It was raining too,' he said.

'Yes, heavily,' said Villiers. 'It had been raining for hours.'

'Did these people come forward as witnesses?'

Sharma shook his head. 'No. Efforts were made to find them, of course. Appeals in the papers, signs out by the road. Officers even went to the pub at Bugsworth to talk to the staff and customers, to see if they could identify them. But no luck. They were never traced.'

'So we have two people standing on a bridge in the rain, at night, just watching the traffic,' said Cooper.

'It sounds odd enough, doesn't it?' said Villiers. 'But people do strange things.'

'And they watched a fatal collision happen right in front of their eyes, but did nothing.'

Sharma frowned. 'We don't know for certain that they did nothing.'

'What do you mean, Dev?'

'For all we can tell, they might have come down from the bridge to see if they could help.'

'There were several 999 calls made in a short space of time by other road users,' added Villiers. 'They might have come down, then realised there was nothing they could do.'

'So why weren't they there when the first emergency vehicles arrived at the scene?'

Sharma shrugged. 'Witnesses leave the scene of an accident all the time, even when they've stopped to help. People don't want to get involved. They have somewhere to go, or—'

'Or something to hide?' suggested Cooper.

'Or that too.'

His last comment must have had a sound of finality. Both Villiers and Sharma began to gather the scattered papers together as if they were about to leave his office. They felt they'd given him all the information they'd gathered. Now it was up to him what he did with it. He was the DI. He had to make those assessments.

But Cooper held up a hand to stop them leaving. There was always one more small detail that was important to complete the picture. He didn't know what that detail was, but he knew that it was still missing. What he'd been presented with was a jigsaw that someone had dropped and vital pieces were lost, leaving a hole where a figure should be, a small scene that would change the whole meaning of the picture.

Villiers and Sharma sat back down and waited uncertainly while Cooper grasped for the elusive question. For a long moment it slipped away from him like a dream that vanished the instant he woke up.

Then it came to him.

'There was a van involved,' he said. 'A van parked in the lay-by. Wasn't there?'

'Yes,' said Villiers. 'Hold on.'

Sharma was holding the witness reports. He spread them out on the desk – a great sheaf of them. Post-mortem examination, forensic reports, expert witnesses, phone records. There was far too much for anyone to grasp.

Villiers leaned over and pulled the relevant statement out of the pile, as if she was picking a card for a magician's trick. She glanced at it and nodded.

'Here it is.'

Then she stopped. Cooper watched her, puzzled by her sudden silence. The colour had drained from her face. She looked shocked. And guilty too, as if she'd committed some fatal over-sight. She could hardly meet Cooper's eye.

'What is it, Carol?' he said.

Villiers shook her head in despair.

'I can't believe this,' she said. 'The van driver who was parked in that lay-by on the A6. His name was Malcolm Kelsey.'

Chapter Twenty

THE STRETCH OF road between the two roundabouts on the A6 was a distance of about three and a half miles, according to his dashboard trip meter. It felt longer.

This section of dual carriageway had been built to bypass both Chapel-en-le-Frith and Whaley Bridge, which the old A6 had gone straight through. Well, perhaps not straight through, given the traffic congestion that had been suffered in those two small towns for many years. Further on the stretch towards Stockport was slow and always very busy.

Bridgemont Roundabout was the junction between the A6 and the A5004 road into Whaley Bridge. On the map it became obvious that the roundabout was right at the centre of a transport network. As well as the main roads, three arms of the Peak Forest Canal ran under it. The River Goyt passed below too, squeezed into a narrow corridor by two railway lines. In between all these transport links lay the Bugsworth canal basin, though by car it could only be reached by a twisting back road through.

Opposite each other between the Charley Lane underpass and the Whitehough Head bridge were two lay-bys. Both were full of massive HGVs: there was a Hovis lorry, a few trucks from the big haulage companies and a flatbed loaded with gas cylinders; between them a scatter of vans and pick-ups, like minnows round a school of whales.

But there was another pull-in just before the canal basin at Bugsworth, close to a length of steep banking and a few yards past a small road bridge over the A6. This was the lay-by where the fatal crash had taken place eight years previously. It was the spot where Ashley Brooks' life had ended.

Cooper drew in by a sign warning him of a £100 fine for littering. Almost concealed by the trees next to it was a fingerpost for a public footpath. It didn't look as though the path was used very much. He opened his OS map and located his position. The path led to a back road that skirted the hill, Eccles Pike, with another branch leading off towards the canal basin.

He'd sent Dev Sharma on to Shawhead to join Luke Irvine, with instructions to make Irvine pull his finger out. He felt more comfortable with Carol Villiers alongside him. Should he feel guilty about that too?

Cooper stood in the lay-by and looked back at the road bridge, trying to picture the two people who'd been reported by drivers to be standing in the rain watching the traffic that night. He could see a couple cars up there now, parked half on the kerb by visitors to the canal basin. There was no sign of anyone interested in watching the traffic on the A6. But then, why would you?

He supposed Villiers was right in her guess that those two people could have come down from the bridge when they saw the crash.

It was just about possible for someone to clamber over the parapet, slide down the banking, push their way through the trees and scale a fence. Difficult, though not impossible. But what about going back up? That did look really tricky. It was too steep to scramble up the banking to the bridge. It had been raining for hours at the time and that slope would have been lethally slippery with mud. And the angle to reach the parapet from below was surely unfeasible.

Villiers came to stand next to him and read his thoughts as she followed his gaze.

'They would have been the closest witnesses, wouldn't they?' she said. 'Whoever they were.'

'Male or female?' asked Cooper. 'Or one of each?'

'Impossible to say. One of the motorists said he thought they were wearing dark clothing with hoods. As you would, since it was raining hard.'

'Yes. So was there a car on the bridge too?'

'We don't know.'

Further down the A6, on the opposite carriageway, was another lay-by where the roadside cafe was sited. It was housed in a couple of converted shipping containers by the look of it. And according to the lettering painted on the side, it was called Sally's Snack Box. An illuminated sign over the cafe said, 'Open'. There were several potential customers parked up in the lay-by. Mostly vans and a few HGVs.

But roadside cafes were closed at night, weren't they? That would normally discount Sally as a witness. But she'd been the first to dial 999 and report the collision that killed Ashley Brooks.

'Ben, have you seen this?' called Villiers.

He turned to see that Villiers had moved away and was standing by the fence, bending over something on the ground.

'What have you found, Carol?'

'Come and look for yourself.'

It was one of those twenty-first-century roadside shrines – an informal memorial for the dead. They sprang up spontaneously after any fatal road accident, a tribute that had come to be expected now from those who knew the victim, but often added to by complete strangers, especially if the death was that of a child.

Most of the memorials by the side of roads in Derbyshire seemed like a random accumulation of items scattered among a sea of dying flowers. Balloons, crosses, football scarves, teddy bears. Sometimes, if it was a car driver who'd been killed, their number plate would be displayed close to the crash site.

The remains of this one in the A6 lay-by were badly stained and faded after surviving several Peak District winters. There were no football scarves, but a couple of small teddy bears lay mouldering in the long grass. Some of the floral tributes had been arranged on crosses, but that didn't necessarily suggest any religious significance these days.

There was one fairly fresh set of flowers, a wreath of yellow roses tied to the fence with a twist of wire. Next to it a handwritten dedication had been pinned to the wood. It consisted of a single sheet of A4 paper, protected against the rain by one of those plastic wallets punched with holes for use in a box file or binder.

Cooper picked his way carefully through the debris. There were conflicting opinions on these roadside memorials. Some local authorities disapproved of them and would order the flowers to be removed after a certain length of time. People would often get upset by this and simply create a new memorial. But the council were usually acting on the advice of the police, who feared that drivers would be distracted by these displays. On an already dangerous stretch of road, it would be ironic if they caused further accidents. It was a difficult balance to strike, one of those situations where it was impossible to satisfy everyone.

There were cards still lying on the ground in their cellophane covers, now crumpled and grubby. *Miss You Already, Rest in Peace, Always in Our Hearts.*

Near the ground he found a partially inflated foil balloon, its helium almost leaked away. The message on it read, *You're Special.* Beneath it lay a remnant of red foil, what was left of another balloon. He prised it open and stretched the wrinkled surface. *Together Forever.* He wondered who that one was from. *Together Forever* seemed an odd sentiment to express to someone who'd died. The only way you could be together for ever was if you were dead too.

But he'd seen similar messages in Scott Brooks' house in New Mills. Cooper continued to search among the debris, feeling like a scavenger. He finally discovered the remains of a wreath with a message formed at the centre. *Ever Yours, Come Back to Me.*

They got back into Cooper's car and he pulled out into the traffic. He drove just over three miles southwards to the Chapel-en-le-Frith exit at Bowden, went all the way around the roundabout and headed back north again.

'Where are we going?' said Villiers.

But Cooper just pointed at a sign board by the side of the road. It was placed to give drivers enough time to slow down and pull in. It said, 'Good food next lay-by'.

OF COURSE, SALLY's Snack Box was one of those semi-permanent roadside cafes that looked as though it had been there for ever, like a Neolithic henge. He could imagine Roman legionnaires calling

in for salted bread and a bowl of porridge en route to Aquae Arne-
metiae, or Bonnie Prince Charlie's Jacobite rebels stopping off for
a consoling tankard of ale on their way home from Derby. The fact
that the Snack Box was housed in an old shipping container didn't
seem to make any difference. From the outside it looked ageless.

An English flag flew over the cafe. Not a Union Jack, but the
cross of St George. A lorry driver with tattooed forearms sat on
the front bumper of his truck smoking a cigarette. He eyed them
suspiciously when they drew into the lay-by, correctly judging
them to be out of place.

'Perhaps I'd better go in alone,' said Cooper.

'Suits me,' said Villiers. 'I can feel my arteries hardening from
here.'

Cooper nodded at the lorry driver as he passed, but got no
response except for a disdainful puff of cigarette smoke.

Fortunately, the facilities inside the cafe had kept up with modern hygiene standards, at least according to a sticker in the window claiming a five-star rating. Cooper looked a bit closer. The
rating was actually for 'hygeine'. It probably went with the stickers
advertising 'tasty snax's' and 'tea in a mug or takaway'.

The original doors of the shipping container had been replaced
and windows added. The interior had been clad in plywood and
finished with melamine. The near end of the container had been
fitted out as a catering kitchen with griddles, a microwave, a small
oven and grill, and a serving counter with a till. There was even
a chilled display cabinet containing canned drinks and chocolate
bars. Coca-Cola and Tango, Picnics and Snickers. A pair of refrig-
erators stood side by side behind the counter. Raw meats kept
separate from salad vegetables and dairy produce. Essential for
that five-star rating.

Tables in the cafe would probably seat about twenty-four people, with a few tables outside on the grass when the weather was better. From the loud hum as he passed it, the other unit must house a generator, though there would be lots of space left over for storage.

Sally herself wore a white cotton apron with the slogan 'The Full English'. She looked Cooper up and down, instantly assessing him. He wasn't one of her normal customers. Not a typical trucker or van driver, or even a salesman spending his time on the road.

Cooper stood at the counter and studied a scrawled menu. A starred item was the Special Burger. There was no indication what was special about it. It was probably best to give it a miss, just in case. The aroma that had hit him as he opened the door was an ingrained odour of old cooking fat and fried onions. He'd made the right decision coming in here alone. Villiers would have been horrified.

'What can I do you for, luv?' said Sally.

'Just a cup of tea, please.'

'In a mug, or to take away?'

'Oh, a mug.'

'Can't I tempt you to a bacon and egg butty while I'm at it?'

'No, just the tea, thanks.'

'Coming up in a jiffy.'

For some reason Cooper had imagined a large woman with big forearms. But she was slim, in her mid-forties, with dyed blonde hair pulled back behind her ears. Under the apron she was wearing denim jeans and a T-shirt. Her face and arms were tanned, as if she'd spent most of the winter on the Mediterranean. She had an egg and a couple of sausages cooking on the grill.

A worker in a reflective vest sat at a table eating scrambled eggs and bacon on toast with a mug of tea and a copy of the *Daily*

Mirror. The bacon was very well done. It was so dark that it was hardly recognisable as meat.

Two younger men were sitting at the table nearest to the counter. One of them was just about to start on a cheeseburger with onions and a good squirt of tomato sauce. The other was waiting for the sausages, which Sally whipped off the griddle with a pair of tongs just before they turned black.

The two men had turned and stared at Cooper when he entered. He'd experienced that reaction many times. Usually in a pub, or anywhere they knew how to recognise a police officer when they saw one.

Cooper had a feeling he might know these two. It wasn't an unusual feeling and it might explain the awkward silence. He'd encountered many criminals in his career. He couldn't remember all of them. Often it was a slight familiarity of the features or the voice. A name might jog his memory better. But there was little doubt that these two had a pretty good idea about who, or what, he was.

Their faces were angular and brooding, with dark stubble to their cheekbones and curly black hair onto their collars. They were wearing sweatshirts and dirt-streaked denim jeans, and the older one had a tool belt strapped round his waist. They said nothing as they ate, only now and then looking up with a quick stare from their intense, dark eyes.

The generator was buzzing too loudly for a proper conversation in any case. HGVs were constantly passing on the nearby road, with the occasional air horn honking a few yards away, greeting a fellow trucker parked in the lay-by, or perhaps sending a friendly signal to Sally herself.

He'd given the right answer to the question anyway. His tea came in a giant mug, branded with the logo of a local tyre business.

It was hot too – so hot that he had to put it down straight away on the counter. Better than a polystyrene cup, though.

The location of truck stops like this figured in the route planning of many lorry drivers. For a long-distance driver, the proprietor of a lay-by transport cafe might be the only person they saw for hours at a time.

Some of the owners had been working in the same spot for twenty years or more, while others might have invested their redundancy money in a roadside pitch. They were there come rain or snow, because their regular customers relied on them. Five or six days a week, from early morning to late afternoon. Reliability was everything.

'So how's business?' said Cooper.

'Very busy. We opened as a cafe for lorry and van drivers. But with the economic climate as it is, we're getting a lot more suits. Some blokes put up with squirrel-food breakfasts at home, then stop off here for something more interesting. Home-made burgers, toasted sarnies, toasted teacakes, probably with a squirt of brown sauce. They like their all-day English breakfasts. Good grub and a bit of banter.'

'Suits?'

Sally threw back her head and laughed. She had a loud laugh that filled the cafe, echoing off the plywood walls of the container. With the door standing open, he could probably have heard it from the other side of the A6, even above the roar of traffic.

'That would be people like you, luv,' she said. 'People stopping in cars. We got some families too, especially at weekends. You meet all sorts.'

'I'm not sure about "suits".'

'It's a term of endearment, honest.'

'Is it?'

'I wouldn't disrespect my customers. You've got to be friendly. People who come through the door, they don't expect you to be miserable. They want to come in and see a smiling face. Some drivers want to talk. Some have had a bad day and don't want to talk to anybody. You just go with the flow. The long and short of it is, I'm happy to talk to anybody, if they want to talk to me.'

'You'll be happy to talk to me, then,' said Cooper, showing his ID card. 'Detective Inspector Cooper, Edendale CID.'

'Ooh, are you going to arrest me?' said Sally. 'Can you just wait until I've got this egg off the grill? Then I'll let you get the hand-cuffs on.'

'I told you your prices were daylight robbery, Sally!' called the truck driver sitting at the back of the cafe.

No one laughed, though. Cooper could sense the silence behind him, the tense atmosphere that made the back of his neck prickle. He knew the two men at the nearest table were listening to his conversation. When he produced his ID, it had only confirmed their suspicions.

'I'm all legal and above board,' said Sally. 'I'm a bona fide busi-nesswoman. I own this place outright. I had to get a loan from the bank, of course. But it's a good business venture – it came with all the equipment, generator and everything. I reckon it's worth about ten grand now. That's not to be sneezed at these days. So I keep my nose clean and I don't let my customers cause any trouble.'

'I wasn't suggesting you did,' said Cooper, sighing inwardly at the predictably defensive reaction to the sight of his ID card.

'This is my livelihood for the foreseeable future,' said Sally. 'I wouldn't think of selling up until I get too old for the hours.'

'You'd miss us all, Sally,' called the lorry driver.

'Like a boil on my arse.'

Everyone laughed then, except Cooper. So Sally's regular customers could be disrespected as much as she liked. They probably loved to exchange a few insults with her. Around here that was a sign of genuine affection. Its effect was to make him feel even more excluded.

'The only thing is, I wish they would extend the lay-by,' said Sally. 'I'd like to be able to pack in a few more forty-foot rigs and still leave room for the vans and cars. As it is, I can see drivers slowing down, then going on past when they see the lay-by is full.'

Cooper drank his tea. That it was hot was about all that could be said for it. He glanced at the clock prominently displayed on the wall of the cafe, no doubt for the benefit of drivers working to a tight schedule. He seemed to have been in here too long already. But it felt rude to leave the tea undrunk when he'd ordered it, and refused the bacon and egg butty too.

'What are the hours like for you?' he asked.

'It's a dawn start from Monday to Friday,' said Sally. 'I get up at 5 a.m. and I'm here for 6.45. The first job is to get the sausages on – they need twenty minutes and have to be ready for regulars when they arrive just after seven.'

'So what time do you close in the evening?'

'Around six. But I'm here later cleaning up and restocking for the next day.'

Sally eyed him with a guarded expression. He could see she was wondering what it was all about. No amount of small talk would fool her into thinking he wasn't here about something quite different. The longer he delayed the real questions, the more suspicious she would become.

'Do you remember a fatal collision in the lay-by opposite here?' he said.

'Oh, that?' said Sally. 'You're asking about *that*. It was years ago.'

'About eight years,' said Cooper.

'Well, eight years is a long time. Besides, the bloke who caused it got sent down, didn't he?'

'Yes, he was convicted of causing death by dangerous driving.'

Sally sniffed. 'Well. So what does it have to do with you, then?'

'You were a witness, weren't you?'

'Not really. I didn't see the crash, I just heard it. Everything else was just talk.'

'What do you mean "everything else"?'

She looked around the cafe. Although Cooper had his back to the tables, he knew she was exchanging glances with her customers, who sat silent over their food, taking everything in.

'Only that it was talked about in here for a long time afterwards,' said Sally. 'People who come in here like to have something to talk about. They have their own opinions. I can't blame them for that.'

Her lips tightened into a thin line and she turned away to fuss about the sink, turning the tap on at full force to create a gush of running water and a cloud of steam.

Cooper could have cursed with frustration. He knew he was close to something. If Sally was more willing to talk, she could tell him something useful. But he wasn't going to get any more out of her right now. It was the wrong time and place. Or perhaps he was the wrong person.

'Thank you anyway,' he said, draining the last of his tea.

Before he left Sally's Snack Box, Cooper paused in the doorway and glanced at the tables. The tide of hostility rolling towards him was almost overwhelming.

It was a relief to step outside into the cold February air. The smell of diesel fumes from the traffic on the A6 was like a waft of perfume after those mingled aromas of cooking fat and fried onions.

Chapter Twenty-one

LUKE IRVINE WAS sweating, despite the chilly air and the threat of more drizzle. He seemed to be doing everything wrong and he wasn't sure how it had happened. There was one thing he definitely understood. Ben Cooper wasn't happy with him. Maybe he'd just been unlucky and his DI was taking some other frustration out on him. But he'd better keep his head down for a while, just in case.

Now here he was in Shawhead and DS Sharma had been sent to keep an eye on him. What did Cooper think he would get up to if he was left on his own? It hadn't escaped Irvine's notice that Becky Hurst was being given her independence and the opportunity to use her initiative.

'DC Irvine, have you located the Schofields?' asked Sharma, without even a 'hello', as soon as he got out of his car.

'I've got Mrs Schofield,' said Irvine. He indicated Top Barn. 'She's at home now. Claimed to be surprised that we were looking for her. She's never been near Thailand.'

'What about her husband?'

'He's at a conference in Germany.' Irvine looked at Sharma, expecting some kind of acknowledgement.

'Who told us the Schofields were away on holiday?' said Sharma.

'I don't think they did really. The Hibberts didn't know where they were, but said they often went on holiday. Last time Mr Hibbert spoke to them, they'd talked about going to Thailand.'

'Not according to Mrs Swindells.'

'Oh, well. Your girlfriend would know.'

Sharma stared at him. 'There's no need for that tone. What other tasks were you given?'

'I followed up on the Hibberts' movements on Monday.'

'Do they check out?'

'Yes. Well, Mr Hibbert was at home, but taking part in a conference call. And his wife was working at the theatre, as she said.'

Irvine recalled his visit to New Mills Art Theatre earlier that day. It was located down an unprepossessing side street just past the Swizzels Matlow factory. It looked like a former cinema, probably built at the beginning of the previous century. But it had been converted into a five-hundred-seat theatre, the bulk of its auditorium stretching back down Wood Street.

Irvine hadn't realised places like that existed in the Peak District. Beyond the theatre lay streets of terraced, back-to-back houses, like something out of *Coronation Street*. From the alleys between the houses, he could see that some of them still had the old privies in their back yards, now converted into tool sheds or shelters for wheelie bins.

At the end of a street, perched close to the edge of the Torrs, he saw a Robinsons pub, the Rock Tavern. At one time he would have called in for a quick beer. But since Ben Cooper had become his DI, he no longer felt able to do that. Cooper would know immediately.

'DI Cooper is on his way here soon,' said Sharma.

'Good,' said Irvine, though he wasn't sure it was a good thing at all.

As BEN COOPER arrived at the Cloughpit Lane bridge with Carol Villiers, a little Fiat Panda went past, the one that he'd seen in the yard at Shaw Farm. Sarah was driving this time, but she was on her own. Her husband would have looked odd crammed into the passenger seat of such a small car anyway.

'It's interesting to watch people coming and going, isn't it?' said Sharma, appearing at Cooper's side as he got out of the Toyota. 'You get a feel for the life of the village. You start to notice the times they come in and out, who drives which car, who never goes out at all.'

'Good observation.'

Sharma and Irvine joined him and Villiers in a tight little knot around the car, as if they were concerned about being overheard by the inhabitants of Shawhead. There was no one to be seen, though Grant Swindells for one had been to known to lurk within earshot.

'First of all, what have we gleaned about the residents here?' said Cooper. 'Where were they on the evening Malcolm Kelsey was killed? Do they have viable alibis? Luke, this was your task, wasn't it?'

'Well, Mrs Hibbert's story checks out for a start,' said Irvine. 'She was at the art theatre, preparing for the next production.'

'What are they doing?'

'*Blood Brothers*.'

Irvine passed him a flyer.

Coming to New Mills: a stage version of the powerful West End hit Blood Brothers, *performed by New Mills Amateur Operatic and Dramatic Society. Written by Willy Russell, it tells the story of twin brothers, separated at birth. Their contrasting upbringing and the hand fate deals them provides a fast-moving, perceptive and ultimately tragic ending.*

'They're only on casting read-through at the moment. Rehearsals start soon. They take place on Tuesdays, Wednesdays and Thursdays for six weeks.'

'Amanda Hibbert is playing a part in *Blood Brothers*?'

Irvine shook his head. 'No, she's backstage, on set design.'

'And her husband?'

'I've established that Ian Hibbert commuted into Manchester on Monday, as he does every day,' said Irvine, with a hint of pride in his voice at the amount of detail he'd obtained. 'He drives into New Mills and catches the 7.47 a.m. train from Newtown every morning. It arrives in Manchester Piccadilly by 8.25 a.m. He walks the rest of the way from Piccadilly. He works in one of those high-rise 1960s office blocks on Portland Street. His employers share it with the Polish Consulate and a radio station serving Manchester's gay community.'

'That's not right,' said Cooper.

Irvine looked stricken. 'It is. He has a season ticket for that train.'

Cooper remembered Hibbert saying that too. But it wasn't true that he took the train from Newtown every morning.

'This morning he was at New Mills Central,' said Cooper. 'He took the 7.39 train.'

'How do you know that?'

'I saw him.'

'You did?' said Irvine.

'Yes, I did. So why?'

'What do you mean "why"?'

'Why did Mr Hibbert take that train on this particular morning? I wonder.'

'He always takes the train to work,' protested Irvine.

'But why *that* train? On every other day he took the 7.47 a.m. from Newtown. As you say, he had a season ticket. But this morning he switched to New Mills Central. It wasn't just a different train, but a different station. Why would he do that, when it must have cost him extra?'

'But that was this morning,' protested Irvine. 'Surely it's incidental. His movements on Monday are what's important – the day of the murder.'

'But it's inconsistent,' said Cooper. 'It casts doubt on Mr Hibbert's statement. That *is* important, Luke. We should be asking the question.'

'Well, perhaps he missed the train from Newtown and knew he was going to be late for work, so he decided to dash back into town to get the alternative service.'

'But he wasn't, though,' said Cooper.

'Wasn't what?'

'Late for work. Since he took the 7.39 from New Mills Central, he would have arrived ahead of his usual time. It was an *earlier* train, not a later one. He hadn't missed the 7.47.'

Irvine waved a hand in despair. 'I don't know, then. Apart from the extra cost, the only thing that would be different was the route.'

'Yes, that's right,' said Cooper. 'A different route.'

He could see from Irvine's face that he'd made the point. It was time to move on.

'What else?' said Cooper.

Irvine mumbled uncertainly now, as if he was expecting to be proved wrong about everything. Cooper regretted making him feel that way, but it was a good lesson. 'Mr Hibbert got home early on Monday,' said Irvine. 'His company let some of their staff leave to avoid the worst of the rush hour and do some work from home.'

'So he was back in Shawhead before his wife?'

'Yes, and before the lorry got stuck under the bridge.'

'But he told you he was working, I suppose.'

'It was true,' said Irvine. 'I checked. He was taking part in a conference call via Skype with some clients in New York.'

Cooper nodded. That was better.

'The Swindells say they were at home too,' said Irvine. 'Mrs S was watching TV. Grant came in when it went dark and fell asleep in an armchair after his dinner. The Lawsons were in their workshop, trying to get a tractor fixed. And I've discovered that Michael Schofield is away in Germany. He's a chemical engineer and he's been attending a symposium in Frankfurt, so he's out of the picture completely. But Mrs Donna Schofield is at home.'

'That just leaves the Durkins.'

Irvine shook his head. 'Vincent Durkin works part-time at a garage, but he was at home that day. Mucking out the pigs.'

'Oh, yes.'

'And Tania has to be around to feed and milk the goats. I think they're sound anyway.'

'Sound?' said Cooper.

'They're okay. Clean.'

'Well, thanks for that, Luke.'

'There is one other thing,' said Sharma.

Cooper turned to him.

'Yes, Dev?'

'Mrs Swindells told me that she saw one of the Shawhead residents walking back home in the dark that night.'

'The night Malcolm Kelsey was killed?'

'Yes. About nine o'clock, she said. And not along the road either. She thinks he crossed a field by one of the footpaths and climbed over a stile near Higher Fold Farm. She'd been watching TV, but she happened to pull back the curtain and look out of the window. It was dark, of course, but she saw him clearly.'

'Excellent. That's a promising lead. Which of them was it?'

'Ian Hibbert from Shawhead Cottages. The trouble is . . .'

'What? Don't spoil it now, Dev.'

'Well, she has no idea where he'd been, or where he was coming back from. Though she did ask him.'

'She *asked* him?'

'When she saw him climbing the stile, she went to her front door and spoke to him as he passed. She's a very inquisitive lady.'

'And a brave one,' said Cooper. 'Did she actually ask him where he'd been?'

'Yes. But she says he seemed vague and disorientated. He jumped right out of his skin when she spoke to him. She says she couldn't get any sense out of him. He just muttered that he'd been to visit Anne-Marie.'

'Who on earth is Anne-Marie?'

'I have no idea. Nor does Mrs Swindells.'

'I'm surprised she hasn't figured out where he went,' said Cooper. 'Or is she just not telling?'

Sharma shrugged. 'I couldn't say for certain. But I think she was being as helpful as she could.'

'Mr Hibbert didn't mention this when we spoke to him, did he?'

'Not a word.'

'That doesn't look good for him,' said Cooper. 'If Mrs Swindells' account is accurate, it puts him very near to the scene where Malcolm Kelsey's body was found. He must have come via the footpath that runs just on the other side of the wall. If Ian Hibbert wasn't involved in the crime himself, he might well have seen something. Yet he hasn't even admitted to being in the area. If there's an innocent explanation, he would have come forward with it by now.'

'Shall we confront him with it?' asked Sharma.

Cooper considered it. 'I'd like to have some corroboration. Where could he have been if he came from that direction?'

'It's only a short walk across those fields to the railway line,' said Villiers, 'and then under the railway to the canal. You could reach Bugsworth Basin within a few minutes. And if he was down at the canal basin, he might have been meeting someone there. Some of the boat people might have noticed him.'

'Let's ask them when we've finished here.'

'Boat people?' said Irvine.

'Waterway users,' explained Cooper. 'There are a number of boats moored at Bugsworth Basin and more along the canal towards New Mills.'

'There's a marina at New Mills,' said Villiers. 'It's just off Albion Road, near the Swizzels factory.'

'So there is. When we've finished here in Shawhead, we'll head down there and split the boat people between us. DS Sharma, you and DC Irvine can take the lower stretch and we'll meet up at New Mills. Okay?'

'We could do with a photograph of him to show people,' said Villiers.

Cooper nodded. 'That would be very helpful. But how are we going to manage that?'

Irvine had his smartphone out. 'He works for a marketing consultancy, doesn't he?'

'Yes.'

'Well, he's bound to be on LinkedIn or one of the other networking sites.' Irvine looked up at Cooper with a smile. 'This is where Google comes in handy.'

'I'll be impressed if it works,' said Cooper.

But it took Irvine only a few seconds before he found Ian Hibbert's profile and downloaded a picture.

'There you go. I'm sending you a copy.'

'Pretty good, Luke.'

'Thanks.'

When the others dispersed, Sharma didn't move away.

'Was there something else, Dev?' said Cooper.

'Why do you partner me with Detective Constable Irvine?' asked Sharma. 'I should be working with you.'

'No,' said Cooper. 'You have the rank of sergeant. You should be capable of taking a supervisory role.'

Sharma nodded, then turned to go.

'Wait a minute,' said Cooper. 'There's something I've been meaning to ask you.'

'Yes?'

'Dev – did you apply for a transfer to EMSOU? When you were in D Division, I mean?'

Sharma was surprised now. 'Yes, I did. Major Crime. I didn't get it, though.'

'Do you happen to know DS Diane Fry?'

'I know *of* her,' said Sharma cautiously.

Cooper wondered what Dev Sharma had been told before he came to Edendale and who had briefed him. Someone had been talking to him, but Cooper felt it was probably futile trying to get anything out of him. Not until they knew each better, anyway.

'So back to the subject,' said Cooper. 'The Schofields?'

'Mrs Schofield is expecting us.'

'Well, we'd better not keep her waiting, then. At least, not as long as she's made us wait.'

Chapter Twenty-two

BEN COOPER AND Dev Sharma walked up Cloughpit Lane into Shawhead. Cooper could see the black wheelie bins still standing hopefully on the side of the road. There had probably been phone calls made to the refuse department at High Peak District Council. Pleading or threatening, depending on the nature of the individual resident.

He imagined that Shawhead wouldn't be the favourite call for the refuse collection crew anyway. They must have to reverse all the way up that hill and under the bridge, just to reach five properties. It was amazing the residents hadn't already been asked to transport their own bins to the bottom of the road for collection. It did happen in some isolated areas.

As Cooper and Sharma approached, the old lady tottered down the path from Higher Fold Farm. Grant's mother, Mrs Swindells. She didn't notice them at first, but stepped out into the road and went up to the nearest wheelie bin. Cooper noticed she was wearing pink slippers. They would be damp by the time she got back in the house. He started to feel concerned for her as she lifted the lid of the bin, peered in and slammed it shut again.

'Is everything all right, Mrs Swindells?' he called.

She jumped, startled, and clutched a hand to the front of her cardigan as if afraid for her heart. Cooper had forgotten how unusual it must be for strangers to be walking up the road into Shawhead.

'You gave me a fright,' she said. 'Creeping up on me like that.'

'I'm very sorry.'

She looked at Sharma and smiled.

'Hello, Doris,' he said. 'How are you?'

Cooper blinked. *Doris?* It sounded disrespectful. Many an old lady he knew would have given Dev Sharma a piece of her mind for having the cheek to use her first name. Some would have used language that made his ears bleed. But Mrs Swindells practically simpered.

'I was just checking to see whether the binmen had been yet,' she said. 'But the lazy devils haven't been near. The bin is still full. If they don't come tomorrow, I'm going to have to take it back in for another fortnight.'

Cooper looked down at her slippers, slowly changing colour as the dampness rose up from the surface of the road.

'The bin must be heavy for you when it's full,' he said. 'Your son should do it for you.'

She laughed. 'Grant is useless for jobs like that,' she said. 'He's always out in the fields with his sheep, or driving trailers of straw around. That nice young Leo Hibbert comes across and does it for me, but he's away at his grandma's for half-term. So there are no other young men available. I have to do it for myself.'

'There's Mr Lawson's son,' said Cooper. 'Wouldn't he come down and help you out?'

'Who do you mean?'

'Nick Lawson. Jack and Sarah's son.'

Mrs Swindells shook her head and gave him a sly smile.

'They're not married, you know. She calls herself Wyatt.'

'It's not uncommon these days.'

'And young Nick isn't his son either.'

'He isn't?'

'No, he's a Wyatt too. Jack Lawson doesn't have any children of his own, so far as I know.'

'Interesting.'

Mrs Swindells scuffed her way back towards her front door.

'He's been in a bad mood recently,' she said.

'Who?'

'*Him*. Grant. This morning I said to him, "What's upset you? Have you been reading the newspapers again?"'

She laughed again and shut the door. A moment later Cooper saw the curtain in the front room move. Mrs Swindells was watching to see what they did next.

LUKE IRVINE WAS waiting outside the gate of Top Barn, standing almost at attention as if he'd been posted on guard in case Mrs Schofield tried to escape.

'Luke,' said Cooper, 'while we're talking to Mrs Schofield, would you walk round the corner and do a DVLA check on the registrations of the cars in the yard at Shaw Farm.'

'All of them?' asked Irvine.

'No. Just the usable ones.'

Donna Schofield didn't look anything like her niece, Ashley Brooks. She was in her fifties, a large woman in a loose dress with baggy sleeves and a long scarf wrapped round her neck and draped across her shoulders, though it was hardly necessary indoors, even in February.

Top Barn was warm – a bit too overheated for Cooper's comfort. He'd been brought up at Bridge End Farm, where the wind howled round the walls and the heating never quite reached some parts of the house.

As soon as Mrs Schofield opened the door, he was also aware of the scent. Not just a hint of perfume, but something much stronger. In a way it reminded him of Sally's Snack Box, the smell of something cooking – though fortunately it was much more aromatic than chip fat and fried onions.

'I'm terribly sorry,' said Mrs Schofield. 'I understand you may have been trying to speak to me. I don't always answer the door, you see. I get *so* involved when I'm working. I play music to get me in the mood. Sometimes rather loudly.'

'On headphones presumably?' said Cooper.

'Oh, er . . . yes.'

He could almost see her thought processes taking place before she answered. Anyone at the front door would have heard loud music and know someone was at home. So the answer to his question had to be yes, whatever the truth.

Of course, Donna Schofield had been given plenty of time to work out her excuses. She ought to be word perfect by now. But people rarely thought through all the answers. Suspects who made up a date of birth neglected to calculate what star sign they would be. An individual who gave a false address never seemed to know who lived next door.

'We only moved in two months ago,' said Mrs Schofield, as if that was relevant. 'The conversion work had been done when we bought it, but we spent a lot of money getting it just right. We're still not finished actually. There are a few small improvement projects we have in mind.'

'It's a nice house,' said Cooper. 'It must have been expensive.'

'Michael has a very good job. He does have to travel quite a bit, though. He's in Germany at the moment. Frankfurt.'

'Yes, for a conference, I believe.'

'He'll be back next week. I can't imagine how he puts up with those things. They must be deadly dull.'

'And you, Mrs Schofield?'

'Me?' she said, with an exaggerated gesture of surprise.

'What do you do?'

'Oh, I run a little online business. Just a sideline.'

'Scented candles and handmade soaps?' he said.

'And various other crafts too.'

'And you teach sometimes.'

'You know all about me already,' she said with an unnervingly flirtatious little smile. 'Yes, I teach creative arts and crafts at a local adult education centre. I only commit myself to two days a week. I don't do it for the money or anything. It's just to give something back, you know.'

Cooper watched her flounce around the room. It was odd seeing her performance. If he hadn't been told, he would have guessed that Donna Schofield was the resident involved in the amateur dramatic society. Except that she was a very bad actress. She was overdoing the role terribly.

'What days do you teach at the adult education centre?' asked Cooper.

'Tuesdays and Thursdays.'

'But this week you've stayed at home.'

'It's half-term,' she said promptly, with a smug smile.

'So where would you have been on Monday evening?'

She looked taken aback at the direct question, and its inference.

'I was here, of course. In the house.'

'But alone, obviously.'

'Yes.'

Cooper gazed out of the window in the sitting room. Hardly anything had been done in the garden. It was pretty much a wasteland, with a stretch of recently laid concrete and a small conifer in a tub. But if the Schofields had moved in a couple of months ago, they'd hardly been able to do very much. The middle of winter was the wrong time for that sort of job. In this area it was a wonder that it hadn't been covered in snow.

'What work are you still having done?' he asked.

'There's an old farm building on the property. A byre. It wasn't part of the original conversion, but we decided to turn it into something useful. A garden office, or storage.'

Cooper turned back quickly into the room. He caught Donna Schofield in a pose. She'd taken up a position in the centre of the carpet and was checking herself in the mirror, making sure her expression was appropriate.

She flushed briefly when she saw Cooper watching her. Then she tried the flirtatious smile again.

'Is there anything else I can help you with, Inspector?' she said. 'I want to be as cooperative as I can. Your officers have already asked me about the lorry driver. I told them, I didn't know him and I certainly didn't see him here in Shawhead. It must have been some terrible, terrible accident, I suppose.'

'I may have some bad news for you,' said Cooper, 'unless you've already heard?'

That surprised her. He could see possibilities going through her mind, the expression on her face changing from mild concern to horror. Yet even the horrified lift of the eyebrows and widening of the eyes looked exaggerated. Her feelings seemed to be as artificial as her voice. Underneath her pretentions she had traces of that flat, Manchester-style accent Cooper heard elsewhere in New Mills.

'Not Michael?' she said. 'It can't be something that's happened to my husband? No, you would have said so straight away. You wouldn't have kept me talking like this. You—'

Cooper suspected she'd been about to call him some crude name. But she restrained herself in time. It wouldn't have fitted the image.

'No,' he said calmly. 'It's nothing to do with Mr Schofield. It's your late niece's husband.'

Mrs Schofield frowned, as if she was having difficulty figuring out who he meant.

'My late . . . ? Oh, you mean Ashley. It's Scott Brooks, then.'

'Yes.'

She relaxed considerably. Relief hardly covered this emotion. She looked almost pleased.

'No, I hadn't heard,' she said. 'What happened?'

'He took his own life.'

'I can't say I'm surprised. He was never terribly stable. Not after—'

'After the accident? When Ashley was killed?'

She put a hand to her mouth and twisted her face into a tragic mask.

'It was a very bad time,' she said. 'Poor Ashley. I was very, very upset by what happened to her. She was family, you see. And for me there's nothing so important as family. But I suppose justice was done in the end.'

'Do you think so?' asked Cooper.

It was a question he genuinely wanted to know the answer to. And for the first time since he'd been in her house, Donna Schofield seemed to reply honestly.

'Nothing could have been bad enough for *him*,' she said, with a tight grimace that changed her face altogether. 'He should never be released.'

Cooper left the house, glad to step out into the fresh air. He was reflecting how ironic it was that a woman who was prepared to put on such an act had waited so long before she made her appearance on the stage. Perhaps she liked to keep her audience in anticipation and make a dramatic entrance. Only a leading part suited Donna Schofield.

He found Luke Irvine waiting for him in the road.

'Did you do a DVLA check?'

'Yes, the Range Rover is registered to Sarah Wyatt and the Panda to Nick Wyatt,' said Irvine.

'Thanks, Luke.'

Irvine looked puzzled. 'Is that useful?'

'Very,' said Cooper. 'It may lead us into the next act.'

Chapter Twenty-three

BUGSWORTH BASIN WAS the southern terminus of the Peak Forest Canal. It lay in a natural valley cut through by a small brook and had been the centre of burnt lime production for over a hundred years, with nineteen kilns operating here and six miles of tramway bringing limestone to the basin.

It looked very different now as Cooper drove down into the complex. The site had been closed back in the 1920s and lay abandoned and derelict for more than forty years. As a result it had suffered the fate of medieval castles and ruined abbeys, and many other abandoned sites. Local people had regarded it as an open invitation to help themselves to stone for the construction of their homes or repairs to farm buildings.

Cooper had seen the effect of that at locations around the Peak District. Stone robbing could destroy a site completely within a few decades. Original bits of Bugsworth Basin were probably scattered all over this corner of Derbyshire by the time a restoration project had begun in the late sixties. Without a bunch of enthusiasts, the complex would have been lost for ever. They'd faced massive leakage problems, when water was found to be seeping away into the underlying rock from dozens of places. But here the basin was now, protected by law as an ancient monument, fully in water and open to use by narrowboats for the past ten years.

Above the basin stood the village. Many local people still called it 'Buggy', despite the fact that villagers had voted to change its name to Buxworth years ago. They thought 'Bux' sounded better than 'Bug'.

When he and Villiers got out of the car, Cooper could hear the continuous rush of traffic on the A6. When it was built, the bypass had been rerouted slightly to the west to avoid the canal basin. But it was very close. An inn that had once been on the opposite side had disappeared under the southbound carriageway.

So there was just one pub left now. The Navigation Inn. A banner on the wall was advertising a steam rally, while a hazard sign warned motorists of toads crossing the road.

'Perhaps the pub first?' said Villiers.

From the car park they walked down a set of steps into the beer garden past an old gas lamp. A millstone rested against the outside wall, the familiar symbol of the Peak District National Park.

Inside the pub people were sitting on cushioned wooden settles eating pasta and garlic bread. Around them were bits of canal paraphernalia – painted cans, a model of a narrowboat. Adverts for local businesses kept flashing up on a large screen. It seemed incongruous, until he noticed that the backs of the settles had adverts painted on them. WH Cowburn and Cowpar Ltd of Manchester. A company that used to transport its products by boat on the canal.

The staff shook their heads when they were shown the photo of Ian Hibbert. He hadn't been in the pub, as far as they could remember. And there was no one called Anne-Marie, either on the staff or among the customers.

'The boat people, then,' said Cooper. 'Let's see who's home.'

The Upper Basin had originally been covered by a lime transfer shed. But it had been one of the main targets of stone robbing, and now all that remained was a set of steps down to water level and an inner arch like a lonely fragment of ancient bridge over a stagnant bed of rushes. Collapses had destroyed the drawing tunnels to the Gnat Hole lime kilns and exposed the brickwork of the combustion chambers. The mouths of the tunnels were still visible in the stone banking by the side of the canal, black little caves that tempted the curious to crouch and duck inside.

The water here was brown and slick with patches of oil where each arm of the canal ended. Here the stagnant surface was cluttered with dead branches and empty plastic bottles. The wind pushed the water sluggishly towards the end of the basin.

Cooper stopped on its edge. A road cut through the canal complex over Silk Hill bridge, then crossed the A6 a few yards from the lay-by where Ashley Brooks had died. That road crossing was where two people had been seen on the night of the collision, standing in the rain watching the traffic. It was so close to the scene of the fatal crash here. Yet you would know it from the noise of the road.

They crossed the narrow road and stepped through a gate. They descended a grassy slope to a stubby arm of the canal where one boat was moored, tucked away from the rest of the basin. A bearded man was leaning on the boat. When they stopped to speak to him, he was willing to talk, but unable to help them with their enquiry.

They carried on, under an echoey stone bridge and emerging into the Middle Basin, where two lines of boats were moored.

Cooper heard the dull rumble of a diesel engine as a boat started up. From the footbridge he looked along a row of narrowboats with orange life belts and boat hooks on their roofs. As he walked along the towpath, he noticed the names of the boats. *Top Dog, Mollie, Clarice, Leanne.*

'What are the chances?' said Villiers. 'Realistically?'

'Better here than in Shawhead,' said Cooper. 'People are more observant here. They know what's going on around them.'

'If you say so, Ben.'

Cooper felt sure it was true. There were said to be thirty-five thousand boats on Britain's inland waterways. And about fifteen thousand people lived permanently on their boats. Yet there was still an element of mystery about life on the waterways. Those people known as 'live-aboards' had taken a step outside society. They avoided not only the daily commute, but the whole concept of roads. They spent their time down here on the canal, below the level of the traffic and largely unnoticed by the rest of the world.

So their lives were inevitably slower. Even when they were on the move, the speed limit on the canal system was four miles an hour. It was a life lived at walking pace. Surely it meant they were more likely to notice things – the smallest changes in their environment, the least bit of unusual activity? They weren't rushing past in one of those insulated metal bubbles, oblivious to their surroundings.

The next two boat owners they spoke to were apologetic but said they had only been moored in the basin a day or two and would be moving on soon. They only had leisure or visitor moorings.

'There are no residential moorings here at Bugsworth,' one of them said. 'So no permanent live-aboards.'

'What does that mean?' asked Villiers as they moved on to the next boat.

'If you want to live on a static boat for any length of time and list it as your home, you have to find a residential mooring where you can stay long-term,' said Cooper. 'The only official alternative is to be a continuous cruiser – always travelling the waterways, never staying in one spot for longer than fourteen days.'

'The only "official" alternative?'

'There are always unofficial ways,' said Cooper. 'There are plenty of moorings available for a boat over the winter, where owners aren't supposed to stay on board. But if you look carefully for signs of live-aboards, you can see them. Possessions stored on the roof, well-tended plants around the boat. Mooring owners might not openly accept live-aboards, but they can turn a blind eye if you talk to them nicely.'

'And pay them enough?' suggested Villiers.

'I couldn't possibly comment.'

They tried two more boats and turned under another bridge in the Lower Basin, where more boats were moored by the remains of the old crushing house, where lime had been produced. Mallard ducks climbed onto the bank and clustered at their feet, hoping for tidbits of food. A school party straggled by and visitors stood around a scale model of the basin.

'I don't know what the appeal is about a place like this,' said Villiers. 'It's basically just a flooded car park, isn't it?'

'Perhaps when you look at it from the outside,' said Cooper. 'But we're trying to see things through other people's eyes.'

They were heading towards the horse bridges, where it was possible to cross to either side of the basin. A couple of volunteer workers were manning a small shop selling guides near the gauging point, the narrowest part of the canal. The garden of the old Wharfinger's House was full of pigs, goats and hens, fenced off from the vegetable beds.

Cooper and Villiers had to step back as a Royal Mail van drove along the towpath to deliver to a terrace of canalside cottages known as Teapot Row. The cottages looked quaint in this setting and probably featured in many photographs taken by visitors.

Just past the last cottage was an entrance to Bugsworth Mill. It was another ruin. But around the shell of the burned-out mill an industrial estate had sprung up. Steel fabrication, motorcycle repairs, a stonemasons.

They found more narrowboats moored against the bank on this stretch of the canal. And it was here that they had their first success.

'Yes, we've seen him,' said the boater, handing back the photo of Ian Hibbert. 'He visits someone on a boat here.'

'A person by the name of Anne-Marie?'

'I don't know that.'

'Which boat?'

'It's not here now. They move around.'

'Do you know the name of the boat, then?'

'There's no name on the side. If you see it, it's the black one with a diamond pattern on the bow.'

Cooper studied the boater. He was wearing a life jacket, essential for single-handed boating, especially in the winter when the banks could be slippery.

'Do you think anyone else might know who they are?'

'There are the people on the working boat.'

Of course, there weren't only leisure boats on the Peak Forest Canal. Cooper recalled hearing of a restaurant boat that ran from

Whaley Bridge. In its glory days it claimed to have had Princess Diana on board, enjoying a dinner cruise while chugging up and down the canal.

'There's a couple who run a working boat,' said the man. 'They carry supplies for boaters and canalside properties. You know the sort of thing – they sell diesel, logs and kindling, and keep a stock of rope fenders, mooring pins, windlasses, guide books . . . We're on their regular route here and they know everyone.'

'Have they been through recently?'

'They've just gone back down the canal, as a matter of fact. I think they were topping up someone's water supply in the basin, or pumping out the toilet tank. You only missed them by a few minutes.'

'Thanks very much.'

'A pleasure.'

By the time they'd got half a mile from the basin, Cooper and Villiers found themselves close to the point where the River Goyt passed under the canal.

Cooper looked around. An interpretation board with a map of Bugsworth Basin. A dog waste bin overflowing with plastic bags, their handles knotted tightly together. Above him was the A6 on its approach to the Bridgemont Roundabout.

To his surprise an unlocked gate provided access from the canal towpath directly onto the side of the A6. Within a few seconds Cooper found himself standing almost on the road markings designed to slow vehicles down as they got close to the roundabout.

He looked south towards the lay-by and saw lorries thundering round the bend towards him. Even as they slowed, the draft of their passing swept his hair across his forehead and tugged at his clothes, as if they were trying to blow him right off the road and back down to the canal.

IN NEW MILLS the marina was being refurbished. Pontoons were being replaced and new bollards installed to supply water and electricity. A new toilet and shower block had been built, and the site surrounded by security fencing.

They met up with Sharma and Irvine on the canalside.

'Any luck?' said Sharma.

'We're looking for a black narrowboat with no name on the side but a diamond pattern on the prow. Have you seen any sign of it?'

'No, nothing like that.'

'Whoever it was, they've moved on then,' said Cooper. 'Did you notice a working boat go through, selling diesel and logs?'

'Yes, I saw that,' said Irvine. 'It stood out from the other boats. But it disappeared that way.'

He waved his hand towards the north, where the Swizzels factory looked over the canal on the other side of Albion Road.

'You're certainly a man for details,' said Sharma. 'Are these things important?'

'Yes, they help to form an overall picture. Details reveal the connections. In this case there has to be some connection between the suicide of Scott Brooks, the people in Shawhead and what happened to Malcolm Kelsey that night.'

Cooper remembered the notes left around Brooks' house. Scott had definitely been sending a message, but he was failing to grasp the significance of it.

A narrowboat nosed under the Albion Road bridge towards the marina and one of the boaters called out to a man walking his dog along the towpath.

'What is that big factory we've just passed?' she asked. 'Do you know?'

'Swizzels Matlow,' called the man in return.

'What do they make there?'

'Confectionery,' he said. 'Sweets.'

'Ah, I thought I could smell something.'

Cooper watched the narrowboat chug slowly away up the canal and turned to the dog walker.

'Swizzels Matlow,' he said.

'Yes?'

'What sort of sweets do they make?'

'Oh, all kinds of stuff. Parma Violets, Refreshers. And of course the old favourite – Love Hearts.'

Love Hearts? Cooper suddenly realised the significance of the messages left around Scott Brooks' house. They may have meant nothing to Becky Hurst, because she was from a different background and generation. But he ought to have known. And now he owed it to Hurst to get her in on this.

Cooper turned to Dev Sharma, who just smiled.

'I thought I could smell something myself,' he said. 'And of course I was just going to ask.'

SWIZZELS MATLOW WERE still based in the same Victorian wick factory they'd moved into in 1940 to escape the Blitz. From here they shipped their confectionery all across Europe. Not only Love Hearts and Parma Violets, but Fruity Pops, Drumstick Lollies and Refreshers. All the fizzy tastes of childhood. They also happened to be one of the area's largest employers.

The Swizzels factory was down in Newtown, between the River Goyt and the Peak Forest Canal. A large packaging and export facility stood at the end of a road skirting the Newtown recreation ground. But the bulk of the factory consisted of an old stone mill backing onto the canal, close to the Albion Road bridge.

It was a typically no-nonsense, solid slab of a building, four storeys high with long rows of huge windows and a tall chimney. A more modern concrete and brick extension had been built along the canalside. Despite its size, it was really only visible from the bridge or the towpath. Narrowboats chugged past it each day, some of the boaters unaware that they were passing a real-life Willie Wonka's Chocolate Factory.

To Cooper's eye, it didn't look much like its media nickname. They called it the Factory of Love.

And that was only partly because Love Hearts were their most famous product. Everyone knew those tablet-shaped sweets with short, pithy love messages printed on one side. Cooper could taste them, from his childhood. The yellow lemony ones, the sweet orange, or the purple, perfumed berry flavour. When you sucked them, they disintegrated into a starchy powder in your mouth.

When he drew into the visitors' car park, a twenty-ton tanker full of sugar was just arriving at the gate. Blue Swizzels Matlow lorries were heading out in the other direction, no doubt laden with sweets. As soon as he got out of the car, he became aware of a high-pitched hum and a powerful smell like burned sugar.

Becky Hurst was already there ahead of him. After a wait in the reception area, they were directed to the staff canteen. Inside the factory the panes of the windows were coated with sugar. Staff were everywhere, in white overalls, gloves and hair-nets. Conveyor belts were running continuously. Cooper glimpsed a warehouse full of colours and flavours. Through a window he could see a hot, thick syrup pouring from taps and running along steel belts as it cooled and hardened. Plastic containers of it were being squeezed into shape, cut into blocks and packed at the end of a production line.

Rotating brushes swept the sherbet dust off Fizzers, giant rollers squeezed slabs of brightly coloured goo into thin snakes, trays packed with jelly sweets queued to be baked in an oven. In one room he saw huge, gurgling cauldrons and pieces of puffed rice popped out of silver machines. It was impossible to escape a vision of that real-life Willie Wonka's.

A tall man in his forties entered the canteen. He was wearing a white coat with the Swizzels logo on the breast pocket, a white hair-net and a blue beard cover.

'I'm Duncan Kime,' he said. 'They sent me down from the powder room to talk to you.'

'Thank you, sir. We're sorry to take up your time.'

Cooper introduced himself and Hurst, then asked Kime about Scott Brooks and Ashley Flynn. He pulled off his hair-net and beard cover, revealing dark hair pushed into untidy strands as if he'd just got out of bed.

'Yes, I worked with them both,' he said. 'I remember them becoming a couple.'

Like so many other couples, Scott and Ashley met in the factory. There must be something about working in a building where the window panes were covered in sugar, with pink chewy goo spilling from taps, puffed rice popping out of machines and millions of Love Hearts being stamped out with cute messages. *Hug Me, For Keeps.*

Ashley had worked at Swizzels since she was sixteen, leaving school to start on the Double Dip machines, then becoming a machine operator in the jelly room. Her parents had both worked here in the old Bettabars section making sweets of puffed rice and caramel. Her uncle worked in lolly wrapping and other members of the family had done spells in the factory at various times. In the summer, when extra staff were needed, the management encouraged the children, grandchildren, nieces and nephews of existing employees to come in and work, rather than hiring temporary employees through agencies.

'It's family friendly here,' said Kime.

He explained that the factory had complicated shift patterns to accommodate staff and the need for a twenty-four-hour production schedule. One of his colleagues took a two-hour lunch break so that she could go home to look after her elderly mother, a retired employee who used to work in the chew department.

Scott and Ashley had met when they both worked in the powder room on the fourth floor, where Love Hearts were made. At times, said Kime, you could barely see each other through a thick fog of powdered sugar. He described workers adding colour and flavouring before vast oceans of sugar were poured into a hopper. Down below, a clanking machine pounded it into tablets and stamped in the messages. *My Girl*, *It's Love*, *For Keeps*.

Those tiny Love Hearts were produced under eight tons of pressure, Kime said. Cooper repeated the information. Eight tons? Far more pressure than real-life love could survive.

Scott and Ashley had started passing Love Hearts down the production line to each other, then got chatting in the canteen.

Was it the constant sugary love messages, or was there something in the air? According to the media hype, the Swizzels Matlow factory claimed to be the most lovestruck workplace in Britain. A quarter of its five hundred workers were said to be in a relationship with another employee.

Cooper looked at Hurst and caught the sceptical look on her face. There was a cynical version of the story. Some would say it was nothing to do with the factory, just with the nature of New Mills. After all, the local people here were often referred to as 'in-breds', and not just by Gavin Murfin.

'It's a very close-knit place.'

Duncan Kime told them his mother had worked here on Love Hearts too. She could remember messages from the fifties and sixties that had long since disappeared. *Hey Daddio* and *Far Out, Man*. Recently, the factory had produced a special edition of Love Hearts dedicated to the boy band One Direction. The messages read *Harry 4 U, I Love Louis, Always Niall*.

'We get customers to suggest new messages from time to time. I don't understand what half of these latest ones mean, to be honest. *Skype Me, Take A Selfie*. And how about *Swipe Right*?'

'*Swipe Right* is a reference to a dating app,' said Hurst.

Cooper looked at her in surprise. He would have expected Luke Irvine to know that, but not Becky. She was full of surprises.

'Some of them aren't even in English,' said Kime. 'We've got *Totes Hilar* and *Yolo*. Apparently, that means *You Only Live Once*. But there are still a lot of the traditional messages in use. *I Love You*, or *All Mine*.'

'*Come Back to Me*,' said Cooper.

'Sorry?'

'It's a message we found among the others in Scott Brooks' house.'

Kime shook his head. 'There's never been a Love Heart with that message. They've changed quite a bit over the years. There were some old ones in the sixties and seventies which went out of fashion. Then we went for text messages.'

'Luv U 24/7.'

'That sort of thing. But *Come Back to Me*? Never.'

They stood up to leave the canteen.

'That smell,' said Hurst. 'Like burned sugar.'

'The factory is making liquorice today. When you work there, you don't notice the smell. Sometimes when I go home my wife says, "What's that smell?". But I can't smell it myself.'

They thanked Kime and left the factory, stepping back to allow another lorry load of sweets to drive out through the gates.

Cooper heard the sound of a train and looked over a wall. He knew the Sheffield to Manchester express trains passed straight through New Mills, bypassing both stations to enter the Disley Tunnel. But he hadn't realised the express line ran right under the car park at the Swizzels Matlow factory. The railway seemed to be everywhere in this inquiry.

'The Factory of Love,' said Hurst before she got in her car. 'As if love could be produced in a factory. It's not something that comes off a production line.'

'No, Becky.'

But Cooper had seen many examples of love that had been squeezed and twisted and pounded into shape. There was a lot it could survive. Even death, perhaps.

Chapter Twenty-four

At West Street Cooper was putting down the phone when DC Becky Hurst appeared in the doorway to his office.

'Dev,' he called over her shoulder. 'Mr Bateman isn't at work today. See if you can track him down for me. We need to speak to him about Mac Kelsey and that accident on the A6.'

'No problem,' responded Sharma.

Hurst dropped the package she was carrying onto Ben Cooper's desk. It landed with a thud and a rustle of old paper.

'What is this?' said Cooper.

'A cuttings book. We found it in Scott Brooks' house, in a drawer of the desk.'

It was even more faded and dog-eared than the second-hand volumes on the bookshelves in Scott's study. Cooper could see yellowed newspaper cuttings protruding from the pages, torn and folded over to make them fit.

'I don't really have time to read it now, Becky.'

'Don't worry,' said Hurst. 'You'll only need a quick glance to see what it's all about.'

And she was right. The book was full of cuttings about the fatal accident on the A6. Many of them had the familiar image of James Allsop arriving at court, and of course Ashley herself. Their dates ranged over many months, because that was how long it had taken for the trial to come to a conclusion and sentence to be passed. Scott Brooks had put a lot of time and effort into collecting these cuttings.

Later in the afternoon Cooper gathered his team for an assessment of the progress they were making with the Kelsey inquiry. It was always important to keep everyone on track and avoid duplication of effort, as well as to make sure everyone was up to speed. He couldn't remember who knew what, so a summary did no harm – especially with Becky Hurst back in the office. So far she hadn't played an active part in the inquiry, but she ought to.

'When Mr Kelsey hit the Cloughpit Lane bridge,' Cooper was saying, 'he wasn't texting by any chance, was he?'

Carol Villiers shook her head. 'No. Why?'

'It was just a thought.'

'Like the lorry driver on the A6,' said Dev Sharma eagerly. 'You think there's a connection?'

'Well, it seems possible.'

'Someone might have seen Mr Kelsey texting on his phone and decided to punish him. It would have to be someone who suffered from the outcome of the previous accident. Such as the husband of the woman who died.'

Becky Hurst looked up from her notes.

'Scott Brooks,' she said.

Cooper thought he detected a note of possessiveness. Understandable, since she'd done so much work on Brooks yesterday.

'But Mr Kelsey wasn't responsible for the A6 accident,' said Sharma. 'He was an innocent victim, who just happened to be parked in the same lay-by. The reports say he suffered a fractured wrist and scalp lacerations from the broken glass. He could easily have been killed.'

'Yes, of course,' said Cooper.

'So it doesn't make sense. Why would anyone blame him?'

Villiers had been looking from one to the other in surprise.

'Malcolm Kelsey wasn't texting anyway,' she said. 'No calls. No texts.'

'But there's still a link,' insisted Cooper.

There was silence for a moment, as everyone looked at him. He wondered who would be the first to challenge him on his statement. Somebody should.

'What link, Ben?' asked Villiers finally. 'Wasn't it just a coincidence that Kelsey found himself near Shawhead? It was a result of a satnav error and a height restriction sign missing from the bridge. That's all.'

'The suicide of Scott Brooks must be the link,' said Cooper. 'I think *he* knew what the connection was.'

'It's a shame that he decided to take the easy way out instead of waiting to explain it all for us, then.'

'Suicide is never the easy way out.'

Cooper let that sink in for a moment. It was important for them to understand the significance of what Brooks had done. Then he turned back to the facts as he knew them.

'In his job as a driver for Windmill Feed Solutions, Malcolm Kelsey didn't normally deliver in Derbyshire at all,' he said. 'I think that's an important factor. His usual route was in Cheshire – the villages out towards Macclesfield and Congleton. But the driver who covered the New Mills area is off work sick and Kelsey was covering his route.'

'So he was making deliveries to places he didn't know,' said Hurst.

'Exactly. It would explain why he might have been relying totally on his satnav and wouldn't have any idea he was on the wrong road. The usual driver wouldn't have made the mistake of trying to get a vehicle of that size under the bridge.'

'Mrs Hibbert said she gets her horse feed from Windmill,' pointed out Irvine. 'How do they normally manage to deliver to Shawhead? There's no other route but under the bridge.'

'They send a smaller vehicle. The transport manager Mr Bateman would be aware of the access problems at Shawhead. It's probably flagged up on the customer's account when they put in an order.'

'So it appears that Mr Kelsey was just badly lost and he ended up in the wrong place at the wrong time,' said Sharma. 'The other circumstances are coincidental. That would mean it was a random victim. Whoever killed him had no idea who he was. They chose him because . . . well, because he was there.'

'It wouldn't be the first time it's happened,' said Cooper.

'You'd think he would stop and ask someone for directions if he didn't know how to get to his next delivery,' said Hurst. 'But that's men for you. Just ploughing on and hoping for the best, rather than admitting they're lost.'

'That's sexist,' said Irvine.

'It's just an observation from personal experience.'

Cooper ought to stop them from squabbling again. But he was hardly listening now. He was picturing Mac Kelsey driving his enormous DAF curtainsider, leaving his last delivery at a farm near Dove Holes. There wasn't really anywhere you could stop on the A6 and ask for directions. Certainly not in a vehicle that size. Unless—

He grabbed his coat. He could send one of the DCs on this job, but he really wanted to get out of the office. The thought of sitting in that room hardly bigger than a cubby hole for the rest of the day was too depressing, and his team had plenty of tasks to being getting on with.

Before he left he caught Carol Villiers' eye.

'Carol, can you call that previous customer on Mac Kelsey's schedule again, please – the one near Dove Holes?'

'And ask him what?' said Villiers.

'Ask him what time Kelsey made his delivery. There are no approximate times on his schedule, they're an order to create a logical route.'

'No problem,' said Villiers. 'Where . . . ?'

'Then call me when you've got a time.'

And Cooper was out of the door of the CID room and heading for the stairs before anyone could ask him any more questions.

JULIANA VAN DOON was surprised to see him at the mortuary. She was still stripping off her gloves from an examination as she came through the double doors in a powerful burst of disinfectant and a glint of polished steel.

'Which case?' she said abruptly.

'Malcolm Kelsey again,' said Cooper. 'The stabbing victim.'

'Something I forgot?' said the pathologist. 'Or something *you* forgot, Detective Inspector?'

'Well, I hate to ask this,' said Cooper, 'but have you examined the stomach contents in that case?'

'Of course I have,' said Dr van Doon. 'It's part of my job. Not my favourite task, I must admit, but necessary.'

'What were the results?'

She put on a pair of reading glasses and tapped at a computer keyboard, scrolling through the results.

'That particular individual had eaten a substantial meal not long before he met his death,' she said. 'Within two hours I'd say, given the partially digested state of the contents.'

'Within two hours?' said Cooper. 'And any assessment of what he'd eaten?'

The pathologist looked at him over her glasses.

'I believe I told you that last time you were here,' she said.

'I'm sorry?'

'Burgers and chips, fried eggs and baked beans.'

Cooper gazed at her with gratitude.

'Probably with lashings of tomato sauce,' he said.

'Precisely.'

CAROL VILLIERS CALLED Cooper as he left the mortuary and was walking back to his car.

'Yes, Carol?'

'That farmer at Dove Holes. He says his animal feed was delivered early in the afternoon. Mac Kelsey arrived at about two o'clock and left three quarters of an hour later. He had to shift some bags into the storage shed by forklift, which takes longer.'

'So he was on the road again by about a quarter to three?' said Cooper.

'That's about it.'

'Thank you very much.'

SALLY WAS WIPING the counter when Cooper walked up the steps to the Snack Box again. She looked as though she was getting ready to close up for the day. Her 'The Full English' apron was spattered with specks of grease and a brown trickle of her strong tea.

'You again,' she said. 'Cup of tea in a mug, wasn't it?'

'Not today,' said Cooper. 'Thanks all the same.'

'And I don't suppose you're eating either. I can't tempt you to my Special Burger?'

'I'm sure it's delicious, but . . .'

She sighed. 'What a surprise.'

Cooper glanced over his shoulder. The seating area of the cafe was empty. The only trace of Sally's customers were the copies of the *Sun* and the *Daily Mirror* left lying on the tables, folded open at the sports pages. A red blob or two of tomato sauce on the formica, a stray fork lying abandoned on a napkin. It was like the galley of the *Mary Celeste*, after the crew had gone overboard.

'Yes, I do remember him,' said Sally when Cooper showed her a photograph of Malcolm Kelsey. 'Monday, was it?'

'That's what I'm asking you,' said Cooper.

'Yes, I think it would be Monday. I had a fresh batch of burgers on the griddle. They'd just been delivered. I get through a lot of burgers over the course of a week.'

'What time did he call in?'

Sally automatically glanced up at the clock on the wall of the cafe. It was what people always did when they were asked when something happened. They glanced at the clock, or at their watch, as if some moment from the past was preserved there for them to refer to. Cooper was reminded of a sketch he'd once heard from some old radio show. Spike Milligan and Peter Sellers in

The Goons. Milligan's character always knew what the time was, because he had it written on a piece of paper.

'It was in the middle of the afternoon,' said Sally decisively. 'I was past the lunchtime rush, but not getting ready to close up for the day. He had the all-day breakfast.'

'Burger and chips, fried egg and beans?'

'And the rest. A good blow-out, I call it.'

'He isn't one of your regulars, is he?'

'No, luv. I'd never seen him before. But his mate calls in sometimes.'

'His mate?'

'Another lad called Derek, who drives for the same outfit. He *was* delivering for the animal feed company, wasn't he?'

'That's right.'

Sally chuckled. 'I don't always remember their names, but I notice what they're driving, you see. That way I know what to get on the griddle when I see them pull up. That day I recognised the rig he was driving. But it was a different driver. He didn't usually deliver in this area, he said. But I could have told *him* that. It's Derek's patch, as a rule. And I reckon Derek had tipped him off to come here. That's usually the way it works.'

'Did he ask for directions?' asked Cooper.

'Why, yes – he did. Fancy you knowing that.'

'Where did he say he was going?'

'Oh, it was the name of a farm,' said Sally. 'Somewhere this side of New Mills. How did you know?'

'It was an educated guess.'

'Anyway, it was a place I'd never heard of. I mean, a farm? I couldn't help him with that.'

'That's a shame,' said Cooper.

'Well, I'm not an information centre. But, as it happens, he was lucky. Two of my regulars were in and they told him the way. They took him outside and pointed out the directions. Then he came back in to finish his tea and they left.'

Cooper heard the rumble of a powerful diesel engine nearby. He looked round the cafe, making sure it was still empty.

'Who were these regulars, Sally?' he said.

Sally stopped wiping the counter. 'I'm not getting anyone into trouble, am I? I've got my reputation to think about. If word goes round that I'm ratting to the police, it'll affect my business. Not that anybody gets up to no good in here, like. But I don't ask questions and that's the way people like it.'

By the time she'd finished talking, Cooper was starting to get tired of listening to her.

'Sally,' he said, 'don't you think it would do more harm to your reputation if you didn't care about helping to find who killed one of your customers?'

She thought about it for a moment or two, then began wiping again.

'Are you eating, or not?' she said. 'Because if you are, I'll need to get some burgers out. If not, I've got other things to do.'

THOUGH HE RATED members of his team highly, Cooper felt they didn't challenge him enough now on the soundness of his ideas. He needed someone to do that.

It was only when he was given a robust argument that he could properly formulate his thoughts. Sometimes being forced to think things through made him realise he was on the wrong track. But it could also cement his opinion and convince him he was right.

Without someone to pick ruthless holes in his theories, he was troubled by a feeling of uncertainty.

There was one person who could always do that. And fortunately, unlike Gavin Murfin, it was someone he could still talk to about the job.

It was why Cooper found himself sitting that evening in a gastro pub in Nottingham, the Wilford Green.

Looking out at the endless streets of suburban housing and the roads solid with traffic, it struck Cooper that his life was falling into some kind of pattern this week. He was moving backwards and forwards from the city to a medium-sized town like Edendale, then on to a smaller town and right out into the depths of the countryside to the smallest of small hamlets. Shawhead couldn't be any more different from Nottingham if it tried. The two places were at such opposite ends of the spectrum that they might as well be on different planets, or at least in different countries, rather than just fifty or sixty miles apart.

Cooper was eating a Derbyshire beef stew with dumplings. Diane Fry had ordered a butternut squash risotto sprinkled with grated cheese. When they came in he'd noticed that the bar had Deuchars IPA from the Caledonian Brewery in Edinburgh. But he couldn't risk it. It was one of the disadvantages of travelling all the way down here to Nottingham by car that he couldn't have a drink. It would be a disaster to get stopped and breathalysed on the way home to Edendale. Living near the centre of town did offer the benefit of a short walk home from the pub. He felt his Edendale local, the Hanging Gate, calling to him now. But he had to resist that too.

Fry had started by talking about her own job. She was involved in a new multi-agency task force dealing with child sex abuse gangs. It wasn't the sort of job that would have appealed to Cooper. For Fry, it seemed to be an exciting challenge. She was so engaged in describing the historical background and the parameters of the current task that she was in danger of letting her food go cold.

'Once we've done all the groundwork, we'll be putting together a major intelligence-led operation,' she said.

'In Derbyshire?' asked Cooper.

Fry looked at him, her eyes narrowing. It was the way she looked at a suspect. In fact, it was the way she looked at most people. She relaxed but only slightly. Cooper watched her shift uneasily.

'You can't tell me,' he said. 'I understand.'

'When it happens, I've no doubt we'll be targeting addresses throughout the area,' said Fry. 'But the cities tend to be the focus of most inquiries of this type. Nottingham and Derby.'

'Have you met my new DS, by the way?' asked Cooper, trying to change the subject.

'Why? Is he a child abuser?'

'No. Well . . . no, I'm pretty sure he isn't.'

'Why would I want to meet him, then?'

Cooper laughed.

'Diane . . .' he said.

'Yes?'

'Eat your risotto.'

Cooper had never really understood Diane Fry. Now he was finding that he hardly understood himself either. The way he was behaving made no sense to him. It wasn't logical. But it must have meaning at some deeper level, because it felt right.

For a long time Diane's abrupt and dismissive attitude had been vaguely irritating to him, though he'd never found her as annoying as many of his colleagues did. Frustrating and difficult to predict, yes. Pig-headed and touchy, certainly. The Diane he knew was all of those things. But she was never boring. He'd seen the real woman below that prickly exterior. Very few people had that privilege.

He could see Fry's face change as she made a very obvious effort to show interest in someone else's concerns.

'Oh, are you going to buy that house?' she said.

'I'm not sure,' said Cooper.

'Not sure?'

'Well, actually. Now that I think about it . . . yes, I *am* sure. I'm not going to buy it.'

'You've made that decision just now.'

'I think I'd made my mind up, but I wasn't admitting it to myself.'

'Yes, that sounds like you,' said Fry.

'It would be very odd, wouldn't it? Buying a house next door to where I already live. Moving just the other side of the wall. Very strange.'

'Why aren't they offering the house you live in for sale, then?'

'Number six? Guy Thomson wants to convert it back into one property before they sell it, rather than leaving it split into two separate flats. He thinks they'll get more money for it that way. And he's probably right. There's a big market for terraced houses in Edendale – they can ask a premium just for the location. There isn't the same demand from people wanting to get into the rental business. Tenants are too much trouble.'

'I bet you've never been any trouble,' said Fry.

'No, but – they get students usually, you see. Or asylum seekers placed in a rented property by the local authority.'

'And that would bring down the neighbourhood.'

'Exactly. So I couldn't stay living at number six for ever. The house won't be flats any more.'

'They can't just throw you out on the street, though. You do have rights as a sitting tenant.'

'I know, but . . .'

Fry narrowed her eyes as she gazed at him. As usual Cooper felt uncomfortably transparent.

'You don't want to stay there either, do you?' she said. 'Even if you could.'

Cooper threw up his hands. 'Guilty. Yes, it's true.'

'Well, where *do* you want to live then, Ben?'

'That's the trouble – I just don't know.'

'You've always said what a wonderful place Edendale is to live in. And you've spent plenty of time looking at houses before.'

'And yet I've actually no idea where I want to live,' said Cooper. 'Should I stay in town? Or should I move to a village, like Luke Irvine in Bamford? I have no opinion on the subject. There doesn't seem to be any point in living anywhere in particular. Not any more.'

That killed the conversation. They were both quiet for a few minutes. Cooper speared a dumpling. In the silence at their table he was aware of the background chatter in the pub, a burst of noise from the kitchen, even the normal life of the city carrying on outside. More than three hundred thousand people were out there going about their business. It made him feel suddenly unimportant.

Cooper couldn't even try to explain to Diane Fry that all his previous house hunting had been at Liz's instigation, all part of her plans for when they were married. She had known exactly what sort of house she wanted, where it had to be located, how near it should be to a good school. Without Liz alongside him, driving the search for a new home with her clear vision of the necessary criteria, he felt completely at a loss. None of the things that had mattered to her meant anything to him. Not now.

Fry looked at him closely, but didn't ask the question. She probably didn't need to. The death of your fiancée wasn't something you put behind you so easily. Especially when she'd died in a fire that you escaped from yourself. It was a knife plunged into his heart that could never be removed, a lethal wound that would never heal. Even Diane must understand, surely? Or did she just think that he was being weak and indecisive? Would she tell him to pull himself together and get over it?

In the end she did neither.

'If I can help . . .' she said. 'Well . . . you'll let me know, won't you?'

Cooper swallowed, fighting a sudden lump in his throat.

'Of course. And – thanks, Diane.'

She nodded, took a drink, stared at the barman as if she'd just recognised him as a suspect she'd been trying to track down for months. Her face suggested he might have committed a serious crime. A murderer or rapist at least. She was going to nail him for it, anyway.

Cooper smiled. Well, at least she wasn't taking that feeling out on him for once. Innocent bystanders might become collateral damage, but he could live with that.

'So you've got this murder case to deal with,' she said awkwardly changing the conversation again. 'The lorry driver?'

'That's right. His name is Mac Kelsey. Do you know the circumstances?'

'I read some of the background.'

'And there's the suicide,' said Cooper.

'A man who hanged himself from the – what was it?'

'The Millennium Walkway in New Mills.'

Fry snorted. 'I haven't been there, but I can imagine it. I've got a clear picture of New Mills in my head.'

'I bet you're picturing it wrong,' said Cooper.

'I doubt it. So what are you saying? You think it's all connected to a fatal collision on the A6 that happened eight years ago?'

Cooper smiled as he heard the scepticism in her voice. No, not just scepticism – it was more than that. Incredulity. Derision, almost. It was the familiar tone he'd got used to when he presented his ideas. It was exactly what he'd wanted to hear from her.

'It makes perfect sense when you put all the pieces together,' he said.

'Oh, of course it does. It always makes sense to *you*, though it never does to anyone else.'

'That's because it's complicated. I find it difficult to explain to other people.'

'Well, you've got Devdan Sharma, now,' said Fry. 'That should help.'

Cooper looked at her, struck by her sarcastic tone. 'What *do* you know about him, Diane?'

'Oh, no more than anyone else.'

He waited, willing her to say more, but reluctant to press her. It was a technique that worked when he was interviewing a member of the public, but it didn't have any effect on Diane Fry. If she didn't want to say any more on the subject, she wouldn't do. Fry wasn't the sort of woman to blurt something out just because you got her talking. She'd always had secrets and she didn't like to share them.

'Watch out for him,' she said. 'That's all. When one person fails, they take others down with them. But you know that.'

'Yes, I do.'

Cooper sat for a few moments, just looking at her. Diane shouldn't be the sort of woman he was attracted to. He remembered when he'd first met her, thinking that she was too lean, too angular, with her fair hair cut too straight and short. Yet she'd always had that suggestion of strength too – and, above all, a sense of unexplored depths that he couldn't resist, a mystery that he was drawn to explore.

He watched her turn her head, aware of his gaze but avoiding his eye. He caught a glint of light from the silver stud in her ear. He wondered what she was thinking. It was one of his most frequent questions and he wasn't sure he always got the answer.

Now every time he saw Fry he felt glad to see her. But it hadn't always been like that. She'd been a thorn in his side for years. The closer he'd tried to get to her, the further she'd moved away and the worse she'd treated him. He'd never found her attitude entirely convincing and over time he thought he'd come to understand why she was that way. But Diane Fry had always been able to surprise him and prove him wrong. Their present relationship was down to her. It had all been at her instigation, hadn't it?

Cooper felt a frisson of doubt, a second of uncertainty over whether he was entirely in control of his own destiny. Or was he just going with the flow? It was so much easier to do that. But you never quite knew where the current would lead you. Sometimes you felt a need for reassurance. A moment of comfort.

Cooper looked round the pub. It was much too public here, of course. But for a second their hands touched on the table. He felt that jolt of electricity, the sizzle of current that never failed to light up his nerve endings.

She left her hand there, a faint flush on her face. The touch was deliberate on his part. He had needed that contact. As far as Cooper was concerned, Diane had come to him just at the right time, when he wanted her most.

Chapter Twenty-five

Friday 13 February

BY THE TIME his team arrived at West Street, Cooper had a map of the area pinned to the board in the CID room. He could see the curious looks he was getting as he attempted to continue where he'd left off the previous afternoon.

'I still can't locate Mr Bateman of Windmill Feed Solutions by the way,' said Dev Sharma. 'But I'll keep trying.'

'Okay, Dev.'

Cooper sighed. Another one trying to keep his head down?

It was a shame, but that left only Anne Kelsey to talk to. Questioning a grieving widow wasn't his favourite job.

'So,' he said, 'let's go back to where we were up to.'

'Until we were so rudely interrupted,' said Villiers.

Everyone laughed and even Cooper smiled. 'Sorry about that. But we do have a clearer picture now.'

They settled down and leaned forward to listen.

'Okay. So on the day he was killed, Malcolm Kelsey had been delivering in the area near Dove Holes,' he said. 'A customer at a farm right here.' He indicated a point on the map. 'When he left there we believe he got straight onto the A6 and drove north.'

'Towards New Mills,' said Irvine.

Cooper nodded. 'He would have got onto the dual carriageway section at Hallsteads and driven past Chapel-en-le-Frith. Mr Kelsey had been working through his normal lunch break, because he'd decided to follow a recommendation from one of his colleagues and call in for a meal at a roadside cafe called Sally's Snack Box. And that's exactly what he did. The cafe is in this layby on the northbound carriageway of the A6.'

Cooper indicated the position of the cafe. He'd even pinned up a photograph of the Snack Box that he'd taken on his phone from the opposite side of the carriageway. Unfortunately, it had seemed a bit blurred when he printed it out. It made the cafe look as though the shipping containers it was made from were still on the deck of a ship being tossed about at sea. The cab of a lorry was just visible entering the picture from the left. A split second later and all he would have seen was the side of a milk tanker.

'Nice shot,' said Irvine.

'It's the best we've got,' said Cooper. 'Anyway the owner of the cafe confirms that a man she hadn't seen before, but who she now identifies as Malcolm Kelsey, came in at around 3 p.m. and ordered the all-day breakfast. A post-mortem examination of the victim's stomach contents confirms that was pretty much what he'd eaten an hour or two prior to his death. You probably don't want the details, but they're contained in the pathologist's report.'

'The condemned man's last meal,' said Irvine.

'It's not what I would have chosen,' replied Hurst.

'Is this case really going to revolve around the half-digested contents of the victim's stomach?' said Villiers. 'It makes me nauseous just thinking about it.'

'Think yourself lucky that you're not a forensic pathologist,' said Cooper.

'Amen to that.'

'When you went to the mortuary,' said Irvine, 'did Dr van Doon actually have the stomach contents in a bowl or something?'

'Luke, don't be disgusting,' said Hurst with a frown of distaste.

'It's a reasonable question. One day I may have to do the mortuary visit myself. So might you.'

'Maybe. But you're just talking about it to be obnoxious. It's pathetic.'

'I think the stomach contents were probably frozen by then for storage,' said Cooper, wondering how hard he should stamp on the squabble.

'I'll think about that next time I look in the freezer for some diced vegetables,' said Irvine.

'Oh, nice one,' said Hurst.

Cooper waited a moment for them to quieten down again.

'Well, this is where things began to go wrong for Mr Kelsey,' he said. 'And it's this stage of his journey that we need to concentrate on. We're going to start with two unidentified males who were customers at Sally's Snack Box and gave him directions to the farm where he was due to make his next delivery.'

'So he *did* ask for directions,' said Hurst.

'Yes, he had to do that. Remember that Mr Kelsey was a stranger to the area – he didn't normally deliver on this route. And he'd previously been in trouble with his employers for relying too much on his satnav. So he decided to play safe and ask for directions. It seems, though, that he may have chosen the wrong people to ask. In fact, these two individuals seem to have volunteered themselves to help, which I think is significant. They then left the cafe before Mr Kelsey.'

'But we don't know exactly what happened after that?' asked Irvine.

'No. Except that when Mr Kelsey continued on his way he took the wrong road and ended up on Cloughpit Lane, which is not only extremely narrow for a heavy goods vehicle, but it passes under a low bridge. Too low for Mr Kelsey's lorry. And that was where he was assaulted, while his lorry was trapped under the bridge. We need to focus on finding these men and establishing what they did when they left Sally's Snack Box. We have some circumstantial evidence.'

Cooper indicated photographs of the stolen diversion sign and the height restriction warning taken from the bridge.

'These items would tend to indicate that Mr Kelsey was deliberately lured to a point where his lorry would become trapped. It seems likely the two men at the cafe were involved in planning this and perhaps carrying out the subsequent assault. The trouble is, nobody at Sally's Snack Box is going to talk to me. Not even Sally herself. It's too public and too insular a set-up. They'll only talk to someone they trust. Lorry drivers like a chat, but only to one of their own.'

'Someone needs to go in there incognito then,' suggested Villiers.

Cooper looked round at his team. 'But I'm afraid none of you looks like a lorry driver.'

'So who do we know who does?'

'Well, I've got an idea,' he said.

LATER THAT MORNING Ben Cooper was sitting in his Toyota with Carol Villiers in the lay-by on the southbound carriageway of the A6. They were watching Sally's Snack Box, waiting as a few customers came and went from the roadside cafe.

'Here he comes,' said Cooper.

A plain white Transit van had slowed in the inside lane on the opposite carriageway, indicating to pull into the lay-by. It had no markings, but there was a ladder fastened to the roof, as if it might belong to a self-employed builder. Its paintwork was spattered with mud and somebody had written 'Clean me' in the dirt on the side panel.

'Nice wheels,' said Villiers.

'It's perfect,' said Cooper.

The van pulled into a space between two HGVs, as close to the cafe as it could get. After a moment the driver's door opened and a figure in an orange reflective waistcoat climbed awkwardly down from the cab. The driver hitched his trousers up over his stomach, sniffed the air and stretched his arms wide, as if he was stiff from spending too long at the wheel.

'Don't overdo it,' muttered Cooper, though Murfin had no chance of hearing him.

There was a long wait then, after Murfin had gone inside. Cooper tapped the steering wheel impatiently. He was in no doubt that Gavin would have taken advantage of the situation to try out what Sally had to offer. He would be ordering the all-day breakfast and claim he did it to fit in. Cooper could almost smell the aroma of bacon and sausages drifting across the road, even with his windows closed. Fried egg, mushrooms, hash browns and lashings of tomato sauce. Gavin had never worried about his cholesterol levels. It would catch up with him one day. But right now it was exactly what was required.

'Aren't some of these roadside cafes switching to healthier menu options?' said Villiers. 'I thought I read that somewhere.'

'Not this one,' said Cooper.

They waited in silence for a bit longer, hoping in vain for something to happen.

'So how's DS Sharma doing?' said Villiers finally.

Cooper had thought she would never ask. 'Oh, he's doing fine. It's all very different for him here, of course. But I'm sure he'll fit in.'

'Are you, Ben?'

'Yes. And we should all be making an effort to help him do that.'

Villiers turned away and said nothing more for a while. Cooper wondered if he'd sounded too severe. He didn't mean to be critical. It wasn't Carol's fault.

'Maybe,' she said. 'If only he wasn't so full of himself.'

'What do you mean?' said Cooper.

'Devdan. He thinks he's God's gift.'

Cooper looked at her closely to see if she was joking. But she didn't seem to be.

'I imagine his parents told him that when he was born,' said Cooper. 'From the moment they decided on his name, in fact.'

Villiers frowned slightly, then apparently decided he was talking nonsense as usual.

'You'll find I'm right,' she said.

Cooper smiled. 'Probably. But why do you resent him so much?'

'I don't resent him.'

'Mmm.'

Cooper was surprised to find himself defending Sharma, especially when he didn't really know anything about him. Perhaps

Villiers *was* right. Perhaps even Gavin Murfin was right – though both at once seemed very unlikely.

In fact, Cooper couldn't get Murfin's comment out of his mind, the cynical reference he'd made to Devdan Sharma doing his 'diversity training' by transferring to the rural territory of E Division. There was a relentless drive to create a service that reflected the diverse population it served. And the Asian population of Derbyshire was overwhelmingly concentrated in the city. Derby's ethnic minorities represented 20 per cent of the city's population, most of them Asian. In the High Peak and Derbyshire Dales the figure was around 2 per cent.

Cooper knew that police officers recruited from the Asian community were in such short supply that they were most often deployed in areas where their presence might help community relations, as well improving the public perception of the police. So why was Sharma in Edendale?

When Gavin Murfin eventually emerged from Sally's Snack Box, he was chatting happily to two men in their thirties. Cooper recognised them immediately. He turned his head away from the window and slid down in his seat a little, as if asleep.

'What are you doing?' said Villiers.

'Those two with Gavin. They know me.'

'Who are they?'

'I've no idea. But they were in Sally's when I visited the cafe yesterday. They spotted me as a copper straight away, before I could get out my warrant card.'

'Do you think they've made Gavin too?'

'I hope not. What's happening now?'

'As far as I can tell, he is telling a joke. They're laughing. One of them is lighting a cigarette and offering Gavin one, but he's refused. Now he's saying something. "See you later", I think. And he's walking back to the van. The two blokes are just watching him. They don't look happy, but they're not doing anything. Gavin has got into the van. One of the blokes is muttering something to the other, and he's nodding. No idea what that's about. I can't lip read, you know.'

'Is Gavin driving off?'

'Just a minute. Yes, he's waiting for a gap in the traffic. And he's away.'

'We'll wait and see what they do. One of these vehicles must be theirs. We can get a check on the registration number.'

THE DIRTY WHITE Transit van was tucked into a space in the corner of the Tesco car park, just off the Bridgemont Roundabout. Cooper opened the passenger door. Gavin Murfin was still wearing his orange reflective waistcoat and was eating a slice of apple pie from a paper bag. The crumbs falling on the floor probably wouldn't make any difference in this vehicle.

On his way across the car park Cooper had noticed that it was possible to walk down onto the canal bank from this side of the supermarket. The canal passed under the A6 here, just before the roundabout. By taking the footbridge he could see a few yards down, you would be able to follow the towpath past the industrial estate and the Teapot Row cottages all the way into Bugsworth Basin.

It was always surprising how the canal and the railways passed right through this area without being noticed, except by the people who actually used them. Boaters could come down the canal from New Mills and moor here to get their shopping at Tesco before going on to the basin at Bugsworth. And those hundreds of drivers passing overhead on the A6 would have no idea they were there.

'You took your time at the cafe, Gavin,' said Cooper, as he climbed into the passenger seat of the van. 'I didn't expect you to stay for the full banquet.'

'Hey, I brought my dessert with me, didn't I?' protested Murfin, with his mouth half full of pastry. 'Besides, I don't work for you any more, remember? I'm a freelance.'

'So how did you get on, Mr Freelance?'

'Oh, she's a grand lass, that Sally,' said Murfin. 'Makes a grand fry-up too. I wish I was married to her. There'd be no more flamin' diets.'

Cooper laughed and Murfin eyed him warily.

'You won't tell my missus I said that, will you?'

'Don't worry, Gavin, your secret infatuation is safe with me. Did you find out anything useful, though?'

'Well, for a start, she's not Sally,' said Murfin.

'What?'

'I mean, she's not the original Sally. Her real name is Lucy. She bought the cafe off the woman who originally set it up. Now, *her* name was Sally. Lorry drivers have always known the place as Sally's Snack Box and they pass on recommendations. That's where most of her business comes from, of course. So she decided not to change it. It was a marketing decision, like.'

'I see.'

'So people still call her Sally – even the blokes who've been going there for years and know perfectly well she isn't Sally. Do you see what I mean?'

'Yes, I understand, Gavin. You're privileged to be on proper first name terms with her.'

'It's my charm,' said Murfin. He eased his belt over his stomach and belched gently. 'You know, I might go back there again when I get the chance.'

'When did Lucy take over the Snack Box?' asked Cooper. 'Did you find that out?'

'About ten years ago.'

'She told me she was there when the fatal crash happened.'

'Yes. It was a big event. Some of the drivers still talk about that night. Those blokes *really* like a bit of gossip and putting the world to rights.' Murfin laughed. 'Don't expect any of your namby-pamby political correctness in there, Ben. They tend to be of the hang 'em and flog 'em persuasion. The courts aren't anywhere near tough enough on criminals. You know the sort of thing. They'd form their own judge and jury, given half a chance.'

'Did any of them actually see the collision happen?'

'Not exactly. There were a couple of HGVs in the Snack Box lay-by at the time. The drivers were resting in their cabs. They weren't called as witnesses for the court case, because they didn't *see* the crash, they just heard it. They woke up and jumped out of their cabs to see what was happening.'

'Like Sally herself.'

'That's right. She heard the collision, came out of the cafe and saw the wreckage on fire.'

'And she dialled 999.'

'It's what anyone would do.'

'Maybe.'

Murfin finished the last piece of apple pie and crumpled the paper bag. He tossed it onto the dashboard shelf, where it sat among a pile of existing debris.

'There were two lads you came out of the cafe with,' said Cooper.

'They're brothers,' said Murfin. 'Jason and Aidan. They work together, laying patios and tarmacking drives and such.'

'They were very interested in you,' said Cooper. 'And they were sitting in Sally's when I called there yesterday too.'

'They're regulars. She has a lot of blokes who eat there every day during the week. They said they'd been going there for ten years or more. They remembered the original Sally too. But this one's better, they reckon.'

'You didn't get their last name?' said Cooper.

'No, it's not the sort of thing you ask. Not when you're just another van driver eating his snap.'

'We waited to see which vehicle they got into when they left,' said Cooper. 'It was a Nissan pick-up truck. And Carol did a PNC check on it. It's registered to a Jason Flynn of Low Leighton, New Mills.'

'Jason would be the older brother.'

'And Flynn?' said Cooper. 'Does the name Flynn not mean anything to you, Gavin?'

Murfin frowned. 'There's a big family of Flynns in these parts. They have massive funerals with undertakers in top hats walking in front of a horse-drawn hearse. In fact, there seems to be a funeral every week, but the family never gets any smaller. They say the Flynns drop like flies, but breed like rabbits.'

'Flynn also happens to be the maiden name of Ashley Brooks,' said Cooper.

'Wasn't she the woman who was killed in the crash?'

'That's right.'

'They never mentioned that,' said Murfin. 'A bit odd, isn't it?'

'Yes, very strange. Your charm must have failed to work on them like it did on Sally.'

'Lucy,' said Murfin.

Cooper opened the door to get out. Carol Villiers was waiting in the Toyota for him. He hesitated, looking at Gavin Murfin sitting in the driver's seat of the Transit, like a proper white van man in his reflective jacket.

'By the way, I saw you talking to Dev Sharma at your leaving party,' said Cooper.

'Oh, the new DS. Yes, I told him about my job and he gave me a bit of a tip. It was quite an eye opener actually.'

'Really?'

'He says I ought to suggest to my new bosses at Eden Valley Enquiries that there's a lot of scope for using Asian enquiry agents. I mean, among the Asian community. We could expand into Derby. And why not? It's a whole new market.'

'What sort of market?'

'Asian weddings,' said Murfin.

'Are you joking, Gavin?'

'Nope. It's kosher. It's a revelation to me too, like. But Dev says—'

'"Dev" is it, now?'

'That's his name. Well, Dev says these weddings are so elaborate they cost the bride's family an absolute fortune. Maybe fifty thousand pounds, sometimes hundreds of thousands. Absolute arm and a leg. The mind boggles, Ben.'

'Yes, it does,' admitted Cooper. 'So you're telling me you're going into the wedding business, Gavin? Are you doing the dresses or the reception, or what?'

'Give over.' Murfin scowled with exasperation 'You don't understand.'

'Whatever it is, you'll have forgotten about it by next week.'

'No, I won't. My bosses are going to be really impressed when I explain the plan.'

'A gold star on your first day.'

'I reckon so.'

Cooper shook his head. What had Sharma been telling him? It was unkind to wind Gavin up so badly at his leaving party. Well, some of the other officers had been doing it all night probably. But they'd known Murfin for years. Sharma was the new boy around E Division. Baiting Gavin wasn't right.

Murfin fastened his seat belt and put the Transit into gear. To Cooper's irritation, he waved cheerily to Carol Villiers, abandoning all attempts to be unobtrusive.

'Is that a new car, by the way, Ben?' he said.

'For heaven's sake – of course it's a new car.'

Murfin sniffed, offended. 'I only asked.'

Cooper joined Villiers in the Toyota. He wasn't feeling in the best of moods. He didn't like the revelation that the two customers he'd noticed at Sally's Snack Box might be relatives of Ashley Brooks. Not only that, but it seemed they'd failed to mention the fact while Gavin Murfin was in the cafe chatting away happily to anyone he could find about the crash in which Ashley had died. For some reason the Flynns had kept their mouths shut. They had managed a greater level of discretion than Gavin.

They watched Murfin's Transit van drive up the access road past the supermarket and onto Bridgemont Roundabout. Gavin was off to start his new career on Monday.

'What next?' said Villiers.

'I want to know more about that fatal collision,' said Cooper. 'In particular, I'd be interested in seeing the post-mortem report on Ashley Brooks. It's such a pity that—'

'What?'

'Well, that we can't talk to Malcolm Kelsey about it. I've a feeling he might have been able to tell us a few things.'

Chapter Twenty-six

BY NEVER GIVING up in his attempts, Dev Sharma had eventually tracked down Charles Bateman. He reported to Cooper that they would find Bateman having lunch at an out of the way country pub in a village called Rowarth.

'Is he being deliberately awkward?' asked Cooper.

'I don't know. He certainly didn't sound enthusiastic. Did you say something to upset him last time you talked?'

'I suppose I might have done,' admitted Cooper. 'I told him he couldn't have his lorry back yet.'

'Perhaps he's sulking then.'

'I hope he's not going to be uncooperative.'

Cooper was conscious that if Bateman wouldn't talk to him, it might mean he would have to intrude on the grieving widow again.

Though Rowarth was only two or three miles north of New Mills, there was no direct way of getting to it. Cooper had to follow a circuitous route out of the town past the Pack Horse Inn to reach a crossroads on the edge of the moor, where he turned onto Shiloh Road.

That western-sounding name always created images in his mind of cowboys herding cattle across the plains of Texas. It was a picture that wasn't contradicted by the names of farmsteads along the way. Pistol Farm and Gun Farm. Often he wondered what stories lay behind the naming of places in Derbyshire. No doubt their origins were buried deep in the past and open to speculation. That was the way people liked it in this part of the world – a bit of mystery, a chance to make up your own version of history for the benefit of visitors.

At the crossroads he was surprised to see a large sign warning motorists: 'Do not follow satnav'. It was a pity Mac Kelsey hadn't been given that advice. What was it about this area that confused the communications satellites so much?

This was a more familiar type of country for Cooper. Gently sloping fields stretched out on either side, scattered farms nestled in copses of trees.

The land was better and more fertile here than at Bridge End Farm. Although it was only February, the first signs of new grass were beginning to come through – a shimmer of bright green in the landscape like a tentative hint of spring. He could see no flocks of sheep. The grazing was probably too good for them. In a few weeks' time there would probably be cows on the pasture, kicking their heels up to be allowed outdoors again. Matt would go the same shade of green with envy at the sight of such fertile land.

But by the time he reached Gun Road and the turning for Rowarth, Cooper could feel the character of the scenery changing without even looking. The road had become narrower, the grazing rougher, the farms smaller. And there were the sheep, dotted across the slopes.

Most of all, he was aware of the hills beginning to fill the horizon. The dark bulk of Kinder Scout lay along the skyline, an unmistakable presence. When he turned onto the Rowarth road, he was driving directly towards it.

He had a powerful urge to keep on driving and not stop until he reached the horizon. Cooper imagined heading right on into the high hills of the Dark Peak. The thought made him smile to himself. He would do that soon. Very soon. Nothing could keep him off the hills for long. They were where he got his energy and inspiration from. They were where he belonged.

But right now he had an interview to do. The pub at Rowarth was like nothing else in the New Mills area. For a start it had a seventy-foot-long Pullman railway carriage standing in its grounds, once used as guest accommodation but still retaining the original wood panelling and brass fittings.

Cooper found Charles Bateman sitting at a table on a terrace overlooking a large water wheel that looked as if it might have been turning until quite recently. It was quite a sheltered spot, but there was still a chill in the damp air. There was no one else out on the terrace and Cooper wondered if it was normally only used in the summer months. Bateman seemed to have chosen it to be on his own.

Yet he had obviously just finished a meal and there were two used plates on the table, their cutlery laid neatly to one side. Cooper wondered who Bateman's lunch companion had been. Mrs Bateman perhaps? Or did he travel to this out of the way location for another, more surreptitious purpose?

'I'm sorry to drag you all the way out here,' said Bateman. 'I hope you don't mind. I've been taking a couple of days off work to deal with some personal issues. But if it's important . . . ?'

'I appreciate it, sir,' said Cooper.

'This pub used to be a mill,' said Bateman, when Cooper sat down at his table. 'It was destroyed by a flood in 1930. The wheel is just a reconstruction.'

'I didn't know that. It's very convincing.'

Bateman laughed drily, his face slightly flushed.

'That sums up my life really,' he said. 'Everything was lost years ago. And all that's left is a convincing replica. Still working on the surface, but achieving nothing.'

Cooper was taken aback by the sudden outburst of self-pity. He hadn't been prepared for all that gloom and despondency. He looked at the second empty plate, wondering what the conversation had been like at the table before he arrived and wishing he'd seen the person whose seat he'd taken. It was pointless speculation, though it made Charles Bateman seem more human.

And some kind of response was required. He couldn't just sit and stare at the man in embarrassed silence after that.

'I'm sorry to hear you say that, Mr Bateman. Did you have higher ambitions in life than working as transport manager at an animal feed company?'

Bateman smiled. 'When we get older, we all have failed ambitions and crushed hopes,' he said. 'But perhaps you haven't reached that age yet?'

The one thing Cooper didn't want to do was allow the conversation to become about himself. So he didn't reply and Bateman suddenly seemed to pull himself together.

'Have you eaten?' he said.

Cooper began to say 'Of course'. And it was only then that he realised he hadn't eaten so far today. It might explain the gnawing in his stomach and the slight tremble in his hand when he'd got out of the car in Rowarth. He'd only had time for a coffee before he left the flat this morning and he'd missed lunch. Perhaps his visit to Sally's Snack Box had put him off the idea of food.

Bateman gestured at his plate. 'The al fresco menu. But it's good. Cajun chicken butterfly breast in a spinach tortilla.'

'I'm fine, thank you.'

Bateman gazed at the water wheel. 'Do you know, there's no bus service out here any more?' he said. 'The pub's owners bought their own London Routemaster bus to provide a service to customers, so they could pick them up around the area and take them back home at the end of the evening. Don't you think that's a splendid idea? A bit of private enterprise.'

Cooper looked ostentatiously at his watch. He hadn't come here to listen to Mr Bateman's personal opinions, even if it was his day off.

'Ah, I see you're back to being the detective inspector,' said Bateman sadly.

'I'm afraid so,' said Cooper.

'What can I do for you then, Inspector?'

'Mr Bateman, when we spoke at your office the other day, I believe you may have overlooked one incident in Malcolm Kelsey's history with your company,' he said.

'Oh?'

'Quite a major incident, wasn't it? On the A6.'

Bateman coughed his nervous cough. 'It was a long time ago.'

'Eight years,' said Cooper.

'About that, I suppose.'

'There was a serious collision near the Bridgemont Roundabout, when a woman was killed.'

'You're right, of course. But it wasn't Mac Kelsey's fault. An HGV driver veered off the road while texting. He was jailed for dangerous driving. But Mac was parked up in a lay-by at the time. His vehicle was stationary. He had no responsibility for the accident. So I didn't see how it might be—'

'Relevant, I know.'

'Well, it isn't. Is it?'

'In fact, I think it might be,' said Cooper. 'If only for the reason that there's still something you're not telling me.'

'About that incident?'

'Yes.'

Since Mr Bateman wasn't in his office at Windmill Feed Solutions, he wasn't able to refer to Mac Kelsey's personnel file. But clearly he didn't need to. Either the recollection of the incident was still clear in his head, or he'd anticipated Cooper's questions and refreshed his memory.

'It isn't in the file,' he said. 'That's why I didn't mention it earlier. It was a personal detail, which I saw fit not to put into the official record at the time.'

'Well, now is the time to mention it,' said Cooper.

'Perhaps you're right.'

'So what do you know, Mr Bateman?'

Bateman fiddled with his used cutlery. Then he tapped the knife sharply against the plate with a clang, a sign that he'd made a firm decision.

'As I said, the collision wasn't Mac's fault. It was an appalling incident, of course, with a tragic outcome. But Mac Kelsey was blameless. He was driving a van for us then – a long wheelbase Renault Master, a vehicle we use for deliveries to smaller customers. The main collision was between the Iveco Stralis travelling on the A6, and a small private car and a Polish-registered Volvo FH, both parked in the lay-by. Mac's van was stationary in front of the Volvo.'

'It seems the Polish lorry was shunted forward by the collision and hit the back of the van,' said Cooper.

'That's right. It caused considerable damage, but it could have been worse. The van was empty at the time, so it was light and the impact pushed it forward. Mac himself was barely injured, just a few bruises.'

'So what was the problem?'

Bateman sighed. 'It was covered by our insurers and they claimed against the employers of the responsible driver, of course. The incident itself is in our files. But not the one factor that I thought would have looked bad on Mac Kelsey's employment record.'

'Which was?'

'Just the one fact,' said Bateman. 'That lay-by on the A6? Mac Kelsey shouldn't have been there at all.'

LUKE IRVINE WAS thinking about the train Ian Hibbert had caught yesterday morning. Why the different train and the different route?

He knew what Ben Cooper would have said. *Go there and see for yourself.* By being there, you could notice things that no one would tell you, no matter how many questions you asked them. In fact, you might never ask the right question. Cooper had said that too sometimes.

So Irvine arrived at New Mills Central and waited on the platform for a few minutes for the next train to pull in.

While he waited he checked the timetable. On this line the first stop was at Strines, an unmanned station in the middle of nowhere. Then it went through a series of suburbs around Stockport. Marple, Romiley, Bredbury, Brinnington, Reddish North, Ashburys.

When the purple and yellow Northern Rail train drew in, Irvine climbed on, wondering how far he should travel. All the way into Manchester?

But he didn't have to go far. Just past Marple Bridge station, Irvine got up suddenly from his seat. The train was passing over a viaduct and right alongside he could see a stretch of water, with a boat moored at a narrow wharf and a pile of gravel on the bank for repairs. He turned to a man across the aisle.

'Excuse me, do you happen to know what canal that is?'

'Oh, it's the Peak Forest, I think.'

'Thank you.'

Irvine sat down again. It was the same canal that ended at Bugsworth Basin. And there, just nosing its way under a bridge, was the same working boat he'd seen yesterday.

IN NOTTINGHAM DIANE Fry had decided to go and speak to her boss, Detective Chief Inspector Alistair Mackenzie. He had worked in Derby before transferring to EMSOU to join the Major Crime Unit and they'd worked closely together.

'There's a murder case under way in Derbyshire,' said Fry.

Mackenzie looked preoccupied, his head bent over a thick report on his desk.

'I know,' he said.

'We should be leading the inquiry. Would you like me to go up there?'

'Not now, Diane.'

'In an advisory capacity perhaps.'

'No,' said Mackenzie. 'You have enough to do. I'd prefer you to concentrate on the job in hand.'

Fry hesitated. 'So is someone else, then . . . ?'

'Don't worry about it.'

Dissatisfied, Fry went back to her own desk. She hated it when she didn't know what was going on. But transparency wasn't a notable quality of senior officers in the police service. The higher up the command structure you rose, the more opaque you became.

She tried to concentrate on the briefings in front of her. She had to be fully conversant with the details before the planning meeting for the first operation. It was essential to be on top of your brief when you were dealing with partner agencies. You had to know what you were talking about. Otherwise it could turn into a competition, one agency trying to prove it was more on the ball than the others.

But she couldn't concentrate. There was a cold, hard knot in her stomach she couldn't ignore. She knew there must be a reason for DCI Mackenzie's dismissal of her. The one thing she couldn't cope with was the feeling she wasn't wanted, that her talents weren't appreciated. That somehow she had put a step wrong.

Fry bit her lip, as her thoughts focused on one thing she'd done. On one person. Of course she wouldn't be sent to Derbyshire for a murder inquiry now. Certainly not in E Division anyway. Her relationship with Ben Cooper was general knowledge, obviously. And at some level of the hierarchy it was considered inappropriate. She had made a serious mistake.

She remembered the moment their hands had touched on the table in the pub last night. Why she should remember that simple touch, she wasn't sure. It didn't make sense when there had been much more intimate moments in their relationship. But somehow that contact would be what she remembered – an innocent, uncomplicated connection between two people. It was the kind of moment that was hard to come by. In her life, at least.

A FEW CUSTOMERS were leaving the pub at Rowarth and Charles Bateman took another drink as he waited for them to get in their cars and disperse. It looked like white wine he was drinking, but at least it was only a small one.

'Mac Kelsey,' he said. 'Why do you think he was parked in that lay-by, Detective Inspector Cooper?'

'To be honest, the question hadn't occurred to me,' admitted Cooper.

'Well, he'd long since finished his deliveries for the day. He'd finished early, in fact. He was a good worker, was Mac. Very organised. He could get through a schedule quicker than anyone else when he wanted to. He worked through his lunch breaks sometimes to get finished quicker. Some of the other men spin the job out as long as they can. But not Mac. It was one of the reasons he was still with us after his other little incidents. He learned from his mistakes. But I did have a suspicion . . .'

'Yes?'

Bateman wiped a drop of wine from his lip. 'Well, there was a spate of it at the time. I think a lot of drivers were involved. I heard rumours from other companies and there were even some prosecutions, which made everyone nervous. One transport outfit lost its licence and had to close down completely.'

Bateman looked at Cooper and seemed to realise that he still hadn't explained what he was worried about.

'Smuggling,' he said.

'Really? Smuggling what?'

'Cigarettes usually. Large quantities of them, coming across the Channel via European hauliers. No duty paid, you see. Sometimes it was alcohol – vodka was a favourite. They could put it into water bottles and no one could tell the difference unless they opened a bottle to taste it. I even heard of a case of people smuggling garlic into Sweden, where there's duty on it apparently. Anyway large quantities of items come in from Europe illegally and when they arrive here they're switched from the European vehicle to a local driver, who sees the goods to their final destination, wherever that may be.'

'And you suspected Mac Kelsey was involved.'

'I suspected it was going on. Well, you have to be a bit suspicious in my job. I'm sending blokes out there with valuable company assets and they're on their own all day. It would be nice to have a tracking system so I can see on screen where all our vehicles are at any given moment. But the company won't do it. They're frightened of all the drivers just walking out of the yard if we tried it. So I have to be able to trust the men.'

'But you didn't have any reason to suspect Mr Kelsey specifically?' said Cooper.

'No. But it was the circumstances of that crash – the one in which the young woman died. There was no reason why he should have been in that lay-by. I had the idea that he might have been making a switch with the Polish driver. If that came out, it would have invalidated our insurance. And that's a whole can of worms that you don't want to open, let me tell you. Insurance companies are terrible to deal with – worse even than the police.'

'So you just kept quiet about it?'

Bateman shrugged. 'Luckily, the Polish driver didn't speak much English, so his value as a witness was limited. When he was released from hospital he couldn't wait to get back home to Poland. So I said nothing and no one asked. I don't think anyone even examined the contents of the Polish lorry. Why would they? It was carrying paper for a printing works and most of it was destroyed in the fire. So officially I have no idea whether there were any cigarettes in it or not. We just let it pass.'

'And no questions were asked.'

'No. It was good for everyone.'

Bateman didn't really look as though he felt it was good for everyone. Perhaps the incident had been eating at him during the past eight years. And now he was being asked about it for the first time. Time could put things into a different light.

'It's not something I'm proud of,' he said. 'But you find yourself in a position where you have to make compromises. I've always told myself there was one positive result – I helped to save the job of a good driver.'

Cooper wondered if Mr Bateman was sharing the same thought that was in his own head. That he'd saved Mac Kelsey's job for eight years, but in the end it might have cost Kelsey his life.

'Remind me,' said Cooper, 'when did Malcolm Kelsey first join Windmill Feed Solutions?'

'It was about nine years ago. He came to us as a van driver initially.'

'Yes, I remember you saying that. Do you recall who he worked for before you gave him a job?'

'He was with a local delivery company. I believe they specialised in office supplies.'

'Mr Bateman, were you aware that Mac Kelsey carried a Taser and a baseball bat concealed in his cab?'

'No, but I'm not all that surprised,' said Bateman. 'In my experience a lot of drivers feel they need some kind of personal protection. A Taser is unusual, though. It's likely Mac or one of his colleagues managed to obtain it on a run to Europe and brought it back in his cab. They're in common use among European drivers, who are afraid of robbers trying to gas them in their cabs, or illegal migrants attempting to get aboard their trucks.'

'He could have got up to ten years in prison for that alone,' said Cooper. 'Unauthorised possession of a Taser is illegal in the UK.'

'But not in some European countries. In the Czech Republic I believe their use is positively encouraged for vulnerable members of the public.'

'It's a bit academic, I suppose,' said Cooper. 'Mac Kelsey didn't get a chance to use it on this occasion.'

Chapter Twenty-seven

BEN COOPER WALKED into the mortuary at Edendale District General Hospital again. He'd been here only the day before for the result of the post-mortem on Mac Kelsey. Today he'd made an appointment with Dr van Doon to warn her ahead of time and give her chance to study the case. A post-mortem examination was required in any sudden or unnatural death, but the crash in which Ashley Brooks had died happened eight years ago.

'It wasn't my case, you know,' said the pathologist. 'It was Professor Webster's.'

'I realise that. But Professor Webster has retired.'

'Not only that. He's dead.'

'Oh, is he?'

'I'm afraid so. I had him on the table a few weeks ago.'

'Suspicious death?'

'Accidental. That was the conclusion anyway, based on my findings.'

'Which were?'

'A fractured skull.'

'But not suspicious?'

'Not really. He'd fallen off his roof trying to mend the guttering.'

'Ah. Not a good thing to do when he was – how old?'

'Seventy-eight. He'd just been awarded an MBE in the New Year honours list when he fell off that roof. It was the high point of his career.'

Cooper looked at her closely to see if she was joking. But she rarely did. Dr van Doon's sense of humour consisted of ironic comments, which often seemed cruel, though they were usually accurate.

'Well, he's dead anyway,' she said. 'Otherwise it wouldn't have been very professional to ask me to review a case of his. In the circumstances, however . . .'

'I'm very grateful.'

That was what Dr van Doon had wanted really. An acknowledgement that she was doing him a favour.

'The injuries . . .' he said.

'Multiple. She had fractured ribs, a broken collar-bone, serious injuries to the skull, causing brain lesions. Internal injuries . . . ah, a ruptured spleen, punctured lung. Fairly typical of a road accident victim. An airbag doesn't protect you in a major impact.'

'No, of course not.'

'There were serious burns too, and much of the skin tissue was destroyed. It makes it much more difficult to make an assessment. But the injuries were consistent with the collision. It was quite horrific, you know. Her car was crushed and went half underneath the other lorry, then it was caught up in the subsequent fire. The remains weren't pretty when they arrived here.'

'Could I have a copy of the report, please?'

'Photographs as well?'

'Yes, please.'

'Certainly. Much good may it do you, though. It's an old case. A man was convicted and sent to prison, wasn't he? I recall seeing it on the TV news.'

'Yes, it was dealt with,' said Cooper.

Dr van Doon frowned, suddenly anxious. 'Is there some doubt about the conviction?'

'No, it was a cut and dried case.'

She looked as though she didn't quite believe him. But she went to get a copy made for him anyway.

'There was nothing unexpected about the post-mortem results on the suicide, by the way,' said Dr van Doon when she returned.

'Oh, Scott Brooks,' said Cooper. 'I didn't think there would be.'

'Usual ligature marks, no signs of a struggle. A nice, neat job. I suppose we have the internet to thank for that.'

'I imagine so,' said Cooper.

He left the mortuary with the report on Ashley Brooks tucked safely under his arm.

IN NEW MILLS Pat Turner was just getting out of her car when Cooper's Toyota drew into the housing development and pulled up outside her house. Both her hands were full with two Co-op carrier bags full of shopping and she saw Cooper as she turned to bang her car door shut with a thrust of her hip.

'Oh hello,' she said, without any enthusiasm.

Cooper was getting used to people being lukewarm in their greetings when they saw him. He knew he wasn't always welcome. But he helped Mrs Turner with her bags as she unlocked her front door and she couldn't help but invite him into the house out of politeness.

The kettle went on automatically, but it boiled and switched itself off again while she sat and listened to his questions.

'Yes, Scott got to know her at Swizzels,' she said. 'I think he'd met her before in a pub somewhere and he fell for her right there and then. My brother was like that. Impulsive, not thinking about the consequences for himself, or for other people. He got a job at the factory after he was sacked as a teacher. He was very vulnerable at that time. A real soft touch for her. Do you know, she used to pass those Love Heart messages to him down the line at Swizzels?'

'We found some of those messages in his house,' said Cooper.

'That's typical. He got totally soppy about her. As for Ashley, she thought he was a catch, a step up the social ladder from the Flynns.'

'There was one message we found that didn't seem to fit,' said Cooper. 'It wasn't from a Love Heart. It said, "*Come Back to Me*". Do you have any idea what your brother might have meant by that?'

Mrs Turner sighed deeply. 'Personally, I never had any doubt she was just using him. Ashley went elsewhere for a bit of excitement. But he would never listen to me. As for those brothers of hers . . .'

'There was a problem between them?'

'Well, it was never as happy a marriage as Scott thought. He was very naive, you know. But I knew she was seeing someone else. You can't keep a secret like that in New Mills.'

'Who was she seeing?' asked Cooper.

'That I couldn't tell you. For all I know, there may have been more than one. She was that sort of girl. She could get away with it right under Scott's nose and he wouldn't be any the wiser. He was blinkered about Ashley. He saw her as something perfect.'

Cooper recalled the photos he'd seen of Ashley Brooks, from the posed wedding shots in Scott's house to the horrific images of her blackened corpse which were even now lying on the seat of his car. No doubt Scott would have wanted to remember her as she was on their wedding day. But even then she hadn't looked perfect. Not to Cooper, anyway. But love could completely change the way you saw someone.

'Yes, Ashley had been having an affair,' said Mrs Turner. 'I think everyone knew it, except Scott. I couldn't stand to see him being betrayed like that. He was so innocent, so vulnerable. So I took it on myself.'

'What do you mean?'

'I went to see Ashley. One day when I knew Scott was out, I called at the house to talk to her. Of course, she reacted the way I would have expected. She was quite the little madam beneath that deceptive surface. Talk about "butter wouldn't melt in her mouth". She tried to deny it at first. Got all angry and offended. But that sort of thing doesn't wash with me.'

'So you told Ashley that you knew she was having an affair?' said Cooper.

'Yes.'

'And what did you do then? Threaten to tell your brother?'

'I would have done that. And she knew I would. But she caved in when she saw she couldn't deny it, that she couldn't get out of it by blustering at me. I told her she would have to end it, or it would all come out.'

'And you think she was planning to do that?'

'Oh yes. She would have done it. I made her promise me. In the end she knew which side her bread was buttered on.'

'When you say she *would* have done it . . . ?'

Mrs Turner shrugged. 'Well, she never got the chance, to be fair. It was just before she was killed in that crash. So everything went to pieces anyway, didn't it?'

'Yes, I suppose it did.'

Cooper regarded her, reflecting that Pat Turner was a much tougher person than her brother had been. He could imagine that Ashley might have been scared of her when she was on the warpath.

'More recently, did something happen that brought it all back to your brother?' he said. 'I mean, the crash and the death of his wife.'

Mrs Turner nodded. 'Yes, Scott said he'd seen the lorry driver. I told him to forget all about it. It was time he got over the whole thing. It was eight years ago, for heaven's sake.'

'But he didn't forget, did he?'

'No, quite the opposite. It consumed him totally. I was afraid he would do something stupid.'

'Were you?'

She twisted a tissue in her hands until she pulled it apart and fragments fell into her lap. Cooper could see the build-up of tension in her. She had the look of a woman who'd screwed herself up to say something she could no longer keep to herself.

'Do *you* think he killed Malcom Kelsey?' asked Cooper.

A panicky look came into Mrs Turner's eyes. She didn't quite know what was happening now, or how she was supposed to react. That toughness had suddenly fallen apart.

'Yes,' she said. 'I'm afraid he might have done something like that. But I'm sure Scott never meant for that to happen. They misunderstood him.'

'Who did?'

She went pale then. 'Everyone. Just everyone.'

'I see.'

Cooper stood up to leave. People always thought they'd been misunderstood when things went wrong. The consequences of their actions never matched their intentions. Or so they said.

'THAT'S FAIRLY DAMNING,' said Carol Villiers when Cooper arrived back at West Street. 'If even his sister thinks he was guilty.'

'You don't have a sister, do you, Carol?'

'Well, no.'

Cooper looked at Sharma, who smiled. No matter how close your family was, your nearest and dearest could still think the worst of you. Cooper's own sister, Claire, had never understood his job, or approved of his work. She thought he was tainted by the association with crime and would eventually become as bad as the criminals he had contact with. Claire probably thought he was capable of murder, and worse.

'There's no evidence to show where Scott Brooks was on Monday night,' said Villiers. 'None at all. So he could have been at the Cloughpit Lane bridge, for all we know.'

'And he might not have been,' said Cooper. 'It's impossible to prove either way. We've had fingerprints taken from his body. But they don't match anything from the scene.'

'His suicide and the note that he left definitely suggest guilt,' said Villiers.

'He didn't do it on his own, though.'

'No. Someone brought Kelsey to him at Shawhead.'

'I think that's unarguable.'

'But surely Malcolm Kelsey was the wrong lorry driver,' protested Sharma.

'Scott Brooks must have been confused,' said Villiers stubbornly. 'He would have seen Kelsey at the trial, because he was called as a witness. Scott just got them mixed up. It's understandable after eight years, isn't it?'

Cooper recalled the cuttings book that Becky Hurst had found in Brooks' house in Peak Road. Given his obsession, how many hours must Scott have spent poring over that?

'No, I don't think he got them mixed up,' he said.

THERE WERE GOING to be a lot of frustrated drivers on the A6 today. Sally's Snack Box was closed temporarily. Sally herself had been brought into Edendale and was fidgeting irritably in an interview room. Since she'd been brought straight from the cafe, she was filling the small space with a distinct aroma of cooking fat and fried onions.

'Your real name is Lucy Armitage,' said Cooper, looking at her across the table.

'Oh, you're starting with the difficult questions,' she said with a mocking smile.

Cooper didn't respond to the jibe.

'We can get this over with a lot more quickly if you just cooperate,' he said. 'Then you can get back to your customers.'

'This is damaging my business, you know. It won't do me any good for people to start saying I'm not always there, or I just close the place up when I feel like it.'

'Tell them you were helping the police with their enquiries,' suggested Cooper.

She snorted. 'That won't help me either.'

Cooper waited patiently until she saw that he wasn't going to be provoked.

'All right,' she said finally. 'I'm Lucy Jane Armitage. Aged forty-three. Write that down. I suppose you want my address too?'

'Yes, please.'

Cooper wrote the details down, taking his time while she watched him impatiently.

'You're the owner of a roadside cafe known as Sally's Snack Box,' he said.

'You know that. That's why they call me Sally. She was the original owner. I bought the cafe from her and kept the name.'

'You recall that I visited your cafe on Thursday to ask you about the fatal collision that took place on the A6 eight years ago?'

'Yes, I remember,' she said. 'But I don't know what you want me to tell you. I didn't see the crash, I just heard it. Then there was the fire, and the fire engines and ambulances and all that stuff going on for hours afterwards.'

'It's actually what happened just after the crash that I wanted to know about,' said Cooper.

'Is it?'

Cooper watched her, observing the change in her manner. There was definitely something she'd seen. She could no longer deny it, now that he was asking the right question.

'The driver of the van,' said Cooper. 'You do remember the van?'

She sucked her teeth.

'Everybody was talking about it,' she said. 'I could hardly not know. There were two lorries, a van and the poor girl who got trapped in between them in her car. Terrible, that was.'

'You saw the van driver immediately after the crash, didn't you?'

Cooper had almost called her Sally, and had to check himself and look at the name he'd written down.

'Lucy, you saw the van driver. Didn't you?'

'Yes. I stepped out of the cafe when I heard the crash. An awful bang it was, then more crashes and all the metal flying about, and the horrible *whoosh* when the petrol went up.'

She gazed past his shoulder at the wall of the interview room as the memory came back to her. He could see the shock of it reflected in her eyes.

'By the time I got to the door, it was all over but for the flames,' she said. 'You could barely make out what was tangled up in all that mess, especially with the smoke. But then I saw the van driver jump out of his cab. He wasn't badly hurt, you know.'

'No, he just suffered a few bruises.'

She nodded. 'Which made it so hard to understand what happened next.'

'Why, what did he do?'

'It's more what he didn't do,' she said. 'He ran back to where the car was crushed and he stared at the injured girl in the driver's seat. But that's all he did. He made no attempt to get her out of the car.'

Cooper trawled through his memory of the witness statements presented at the trial of James Allsop.

'The van driver said in his statement to the police that the fire was too bad for him to get near the car.'

But Lucy Armitage shook her head as she continued to stare at the wall, seeing the scene being replayed in front of her.

'He could have got her out before that,' she said. 'I'm sure he could. But he just stood and watched that young woman burn.'

Cooper showed her the photograph of Malcolm Kelsey again. She'd seen it already when he called at the Snack Box. Yet she still regarded it blankly.

'I wouldn't recognise him,' she said. 'Was that the same man?'

Instead of answering, Cooper let her relax and put the memory aside.

'Why were you at the cafe so late that night when the crash happened?' he asked. 'Don't you close at tea time? Your business falls off by then.'

'I was cleaning up. I've got to keep the place hygienic.'

'It doesn't take that long.'

She scowled, tight-lipped, saying nothing.

Cooper thought about his conversation with Charles Bateman at Rowarth. If Malcolm Kelsey was involved in a smuggling operation, it brought money back into the equation as a possible motive.

But what if it wasn't Kelsey? Lots of foreign lorry drivers used the A6. Where more natural for them to stop than a roadside cafe? There must be plenty of storage space in that second shipping container. Enough for a few thousand smuggled cigarettes, at least. And after dark, when the 'open' sign was switched off, no genuine customers would come calling.

'The Polish driver,' said Cooper. 'His name was Artus Borzuczek.'

'I didn't know his name.'

'But you knew what he was there for. Had he stopped in the wrong lay-by? It was right over on the other side of the carriageway. How were you supposed to manage that?'

Her face had gone rigid again now. 'I have no idea what you're talking about,' she said.

There was no point in pursuing it now. But it would be something to mention to the intelligence unit.

'All right,' he said. 'You're free to go.'

Before she left, Lucy stood and looked down, leaning over him with a sudden intensity.

'He ought to have got her out,' she said. 'What was he thinking about while she burned? He could have saved her from the fire.'

'No,' said Cooper. 'I don't think he could.'

When she'd been shown out, Cooper sat for a moment and thought about what must have been going on in that roadside cafe after the fatal collision. He recalled what he'd been told yesterday. *It was talked about in here for a long time afterwards. People who come in like to have something to talk about. They have their own opinions. I can't blame them for that.*

And he found he could picture it quite clearly. He could imagine the muttering and shaking of heads over all-day breakfasts and mugs of tea in a steamy cafe during those following days, with evidence of the fatal collision still visible on the tarmac a few yards away.

Even before the hearing against James Allsop had begun at Derby Crown Court, a separate and more informal trial had been taking place in Sally's Snack Box. Solely on the grounds of Sally's own witness statement, Malcolm Kelsey had been found guilty. The jury had been unanimous in their verdict.

No one had been there to stand up in Kelsey's defence or speak on his behalf, let alone Mac Kelsey himself. Guilty, then. But who had carried out the sentence?

Chapter Twenty-eight

DENSE FOG HAD settled in the Goyt Valley by the time Cooper reached Shawhead that evening. Traffic on the A6 had been driving on headlights, cars picking their way through the fog like explorers in a cave.

Cooper slowed down as he reached the Cloughpit Lane bridge, letting the Toyota stand for a moment between the arches. The fog funnelled into the gap, swirling in an evil-looking miasma against the damp stone.

He rolled down the window and looked up at the parapet. Where there ought to be sky, he saw only a faint reflection of his headlights, absorbed and dissipated by the vapour. Dark outlines appeared and disappeared as the fog churned in the opening.

The throbbing of his engine was amplified by the funnel effect and it was uncomfortable to listen to. But he knew if he switched the ignition off, there would be no sound at all, except for the drip of moisture from the walls. He couldn't bring himself to do it.

At Shawhead Cottages Amanda Hibbert was at home alone. She was surprised to see him again, especially in the evening.

'Is your husband here?' asked Cooper.

'No,' she said. 'He's out.'

'Where has he gone?'

'He sometimes walks down to the pub for a drink. You know, the Navigation Inn down by the canal basin? It gives him a bit of exercise, gets him out of the house for a while and he doesn't have to drive home. It's good all round. And he's always calmer when he comes back. I wouldn't want to stop him doing it.'

'That sounds fine,' said Cooper. 'Except your husband doesn't go to the pub. They've never seen him at the Navigation Inn.'

She shook her head in confusion. 'I don't know what to say. It's probably just a mistake.'

'How long is it since he left?'

'Just a few minutes,' she said.

Cooper found the stile at Higher Fold Farm by working his way along the wall at the side of the road. For once Mrs Swindells wouldn't be able to see what was going on outside her house, even if she was looking through the window. If there had been a fog like this on the night Malcolm Kelsey took his wrong turning, he might still be alive. No one could see what they were doing in this.

Cooper made his way carefully, following the line of a wall rather than trying to strike across the field as the footpath did. It was too easy to lose the line of an unmarked or little used path, even in daylight. He located the stretch of collapsed wall and knew he was in the right place. It was just on the other side of here that Kelsey had been hastily buried under a heap of fallen stones.

Then the railway embankment loomed ahead of him out of the murk. He turned to the right and kept walking until he reached a small bridge. It was no more than a tunnel really, just wide enough to take the footpath under the railway and leading to a flight of worn stone steps on the other side.

The final stretch of the Peak Forest Canal had been built half-·way up the hillside to serve the limestone quarries. After a few minutes Cooper came out onto the track of one of the old tram-lines leading into the basin. He could hear the slow movement of water, the dull slap of the stagnant surface, the muffled sounds of activity on the canalside.

Mist danced in the narrow beam of light from his torch. Ten feet away his torch light smeared itself flat against a wall of fog.

And then he saw Ian Hibbert. His figure emerged from the mist, wet and glistening in a ragged burst of light spilling from the hatch of a narrowboat. His face was white and startled as he turned towards Cooper. In his hand he was swinging a short iron implement with a heavy, rounded end. A windlass.

WHEN LUKE IRVINE called, Cooper gave him directions to reach Bugsworth Basin. At least with Irvine here, he wouldn't have to walk back to Shawhead for his car.

'I found out who Mr Hibbert was visiting,' said Irvine, slightly breathless as he drew into the car park.

'Anne-Marie?' said Cooper.

'No, the name of the boat is Anne-Marie. The people are called Cartwright – Jessica and Danny Cartwright. They're itinerant folk musicians. They play gigs in pubs along the canal.'

'Itinerant? When did you start using words like that, Luke?'

'It means they move about.'

'I know what it means. Are you saying they don't have a fixed address?'

'They live on the boat,' said Irvine.

'Oh, I see. But I don't think there are any residential moorings here at Bugsworth. They need planning consent from the local authority.'

'That's right. That's why the Cartwrights move around. Even a leisure mooring can cost up to two thousand pounds a year, they told me. It's an expensive business. Since they don't have a residential mooring, they have to keep moving on. They'd been at Bugsworth too long, so they pulled up anchor on Wednesday. When I found them, they were in a mooring basin at Marple Junction, just where the Peak Forest connects to the Macclesfield Canal. They were supposed to be coming back here this afternoon, but they broke down and had to call out River Canal Rescue. It turns out their boat had a blocked fuel filter.'

'So they weren't at Bugsworth when Ian Hibbert took his usual walk across the fields on Wednesday night?'

'No. But he got hold of them on the phone and found out where they were. Then he called at Marple Junction on his way into work to pick up some supplies. That was the reason for him taking a different route to work on Thursday morning. His usual train into Manchester goes via Disley and Hazel Grove.'

Cooper's heart sank as he realised Ian Hibbert had led them to a dead end. Now he would be no nearer to the answers he needed. He'd promised Superintendent Branagh progress and there would be nothing to show her. Did no one share his sense of urgency?

'Supplies?' he said with a sigh. 'So why was Mr Hibbert visiting them at night? Not to listen to folk music, I imagine?'

Irvine smiled and gestured with his hand to his mouth, blowing gently from behind two fingers.

'It's where Mr Hibbert gets his fix,' he said. 'Their boat reeks of marijuana.'

'Smoking pot on a narrowboat with a couple of folkies,' said Cooper bitterly. 'Now that's a proper hippy.'

COOPER STOOD OVER Ian Hibbert as he huddled on a bollard by the canal. At the moment he wasn't feeling well disposed towards the man. He could happily blame him for all the time being wasted. Whatever Hibbert had been up to, he was being an idiot.

'You're seriously telling us that when you went out on Monday night and walked down that footpath to the canal, you didn't notice anything?' said Cooper.

'Yes. Well, that's the truth,' said Hibbert.

'You heard nothing? Saw no one?'

'Nothing,' he said. 'No one. Why is that so hard to believe? You've seen how quiet it is out there.'

'It wasn't quiet that night,' said Cooper.

Hibbert swallowed nervously. 'Is this concerned with the lorry driver?'

'What did you think it was concerned with, sir?'

He shook his head. 'Not . . . well, I didn't know. So it's the lorry driver? It's about what happened to him.'

Cooper didn't reply, but watched the man, waiting for him to carry on talking.

Hibbert's puzzlement seemed to clear from his face.

'*That* was on Monday night, of course.' Then anxiety replaced his puzzlement. 'Do you think the murderer was still around then? Was he nearby when I walked down the field to meet . . . I mean, when I walked down to the canal?'

How good an actor was Ian Hibbert? He was either putting it on too much, or he was actually very naive. Cooper recollected that Amanda Hibbert was a member of the amateur dramatic society in New Mills, though she only worked behind the scenes.

'I'm sorry about the windlass,' said Hibbert. 'Someone had dropped it on the canal bank. I tripped over it and nearly fell in the water. I was just trying to find the right boat to return it to. You took me by surprise when you shone that torch in my face.'

'It's lucky you dropped it, sir,' said Cooper.

Hibbert laughed bitterly.

'I wouldn't have been much good, if it had been a real assailant,' he said. 'A murderer lurking in the fog. He would have made short work of me.'

THEY PUT IAN Hibbert into Irvine's car and drove him back to Shawhead. It seemed a long way round compared to the walk over the fields. The fog was so thick that Irvine missed the turning into Cloughpit Lane and had to reverse dangerously to the junction.

When they entered the house, Cooper noticed plasters on two knuckles of Hibbert's right hand.

'Have you hurt yourself, sir?'

'It's just a scratch. I stumbled against a wall in the dark.'

'It's easily done.'

But then Cooper saw a splintered crack in the glass of one of the patio doors.

'Did you have a break-in?' he asked.

'No.'

'Somebody tried to get in here. Or threw a brick at your window. That's more than a bird strike.'

'No, it's nothing.'

Cooper looked more closely. He could see a trace of blood on the broken glass. He turned back to Hibbert.

'Did you do this yourself, sir?'

Hibbert looked embarrassed. 'Well, yes. It was just one of those things, though. An impulse. You know.'

'An impulse? You have anger problems then, sir?'

Hibbert didn't answer. He shook his injured hand, as if remembering the pain of the impact with the glass.

'What was it about?' asked Cooper. 'Did you have an argument with your wife?'

Hibbert sighed. 'She can be a bit aggravating sometimes. I'm sure you know what it's like – when you've been married for a while, I mean. You can get along fine most of the time, but just now and then it all gets too much.'

Cooper regarded him steadily. 'Even so. If it's a problem, you should get counselling before it escalates. I'd hate to hear from your wife that it wasn't just the window that felt your anger. Unless already . . . ?'

He could see the man was sweating now. Hibbert shook his head. 'No, no, I promise you. Nothing like that. You can ask her.'

'Perhaps I will.'

'I know I have a short temper. It's why I go to visit *Anne-Marie*. It helps me, you see. It calms me down.'

A FEW MINUTES later Amanda Hibbert saw Cooper to the door of Shawhead Cottages.

'You know, I didn't really think anything terrible had happened to the driver of that lorry at first,' she said. 'It's very shocking. And in a place like this too.'

Cooper resisted telling her that it was often in small communities that murders happened. Though perhaps not as small as Shawhead. He smiled at the thought that there were so few people here that they had to import a victim for a murder, instead of killing each other.

Mrs Hibbert noticed his smile before he could hide it and she frowned in disapproval.

'I suppose it's different for you when you're in the police,' she said sharply. 'You deal with it all the time. People like us, we're not used to such violence. We live in places like this to get away from it. But it seems that's not possible.'

Cooper stepped out into the fog, feeling suitably abashed. Amanda Hibbert was right, of course. People ought to be able to live in places like Shawhead without the fear of violence. They should be able to live anywhere in safety, in an ideal world.

But he knew from his job that nothing was ideal. Violence might strike anywhere. You couldn't bury your head in the sand and pretend it was just something that happened on the news, that violent crime would never reach your own doorstep.

Besides, Cooper couldn't deny the inescapable conclusion that he'd been facing from the start of this inquiry. Somehow the hamlet of Shawhead had brought violent death on itself.

INSTEAD OF RETURNING to the A6, Cooper took a back road that climbed over the edge of Chinley Churn, rising well above the remains of the fog. The lane was as narrow as the approach to Shawhead and it coiled in tight, blind curves up the hill. But there was no traffic at this time of night and he had the road entirely to himself.

He spotted a gateway where he could pull in. When he'd stopped the car, he wound down the window and listened to the silence.

He'd been remembering the way he felt on the way to Rowarth. He could feel the hills calling to him out there in the darkness now, a tempting murmur on the wind. This was what he'd been missing, the sense of the wide, open spaces of the Peak District, the acres and acres of wild, majestic country that he'd always loved. Tonight the temptation was too strong.

Cooper got out of the car and locked the doors. He could hear no traffic sounds, not even the background hum from the A6. The hillside undulated so much that he must be protected by a hump of ground, despite the height he'd reached. It was as if the landscape was holding him gently in its palm and sheltering him from the outside world.

He crossed the road to a footpath and walked a few yards up the hill onto Cracken Edge. The remains of quarrying were everywhere here – layers of rock carved into rugged faces, the remnants of buildings left by generations of quarry workers, with tracks worn between them by thousands of tired feet. This was the real Peak, a spectacular landscape that had been shaped by human hands over the centuries, until the sense of history and humanity was etched deep into the rocks themselves.

Below him to the south lay Chinley, its lights like a string of pearls along the valley floor, and the conical shape of Eccles Pike silhouetted against the sky behind it. The mass of rolling hills merged into the night as they swept away to the east, rising higher and higher as they headed towards Kinder Scout.

Cooper turned and looked to the west. Down there was Shawhead, hidden now by those comforting folds of the landscape, and sunk in the mist. Now he was able to see the place in its context instead of from the inside, the way people living there saw it. He was finally able to let air in where he'd begun to feel so claustrophobic.

He turned his face to the wind and felt it blowing through him, cleaning out the cobwebs. Soon he would be able to sweep the clammy grasp of Shawhead from his life completely.

Chapter Twenty-nine

Saturday 14 February

SATURDAY MORNING WAS quiet at West Street. Many of the offices were empty. Uniforms on weekend duty would mostly come in later on to deal with the drunks in town and the usual Saturday night incidents. So when Ben Cooper tapped the code into the keypad and opened the door, he walked into a building that echoed like the morgue.

But Carol Villiers was in the CID room, sitting in splendid isolation among a small sea of empty desks. She was the one person he could always rely on. Cooper knew he should never let himself forget that.

'Have you got something, Carol?' he said when he got his jacket off.

'We managed to get hold of some scene photos from the A6 collision,' said Villiers. 'These were never released to the press, of course.'

'Let me see.'

'Some of them aren't very pleasant.'

'When are they ever?'

It was difficult to tell anything from the photographs of the scene on the A6. The tangle of torn metal was barely distinguishable as separate vehicles.

Cooper could make out the Polish lorry from the name on the side of the cab, some European haulage company. And there was a glimpse of a white van in front of it. But the wreckage at the back was worse. Ashley Brooks' Honda was almost impossible to see between the lorries, except in the close-up shots. Of course, the fire and rescue service would have had to take the shell of the car apart to get Ashley out. Wrecked cars often looked as though they'd been in much worse accidents than they actually had, as a result of having their roofs cut off to remove an injured driver safely.

The centre of the mess was blackened by fire and the trailer of the Polish lorry had been almost destroyed. The flames had also centred around the Honda and the cab of the Iveco.

'Was James Allsop burned in the fire?' he asked.

'Slightly,' said Villiers. 'Let's see . . . yes, second degree burns to his legs and feet. He was lucky, wasn't he?'

'Yes, you could call it that.'

Police crash investigators would have spent several hours measuring and photographing the scene of the crash, trying to gather evidence about the cause and nature of the incident before they could reopen the road. They were always working under the pressure of time, just as Cooper himself had been at Shawhead. How long could you justify keeping a road closed, or stop trains running over a bridge? They were always tough decisions. And it was even more difficult on a major trunk road like the A6. Traffic would have been backing up for miles and clogging all the surrounding roads while the task was carried out.

But the Forensic Collision Investigation Unit were experienced and very skilled at their jobs. According to the crash investigators, three of the vehicles had been stationary, parked in the lay-by, when they were hit by the Iveco Stralis – first the Honda, then substantial impact damage on the Volvo lorry and the Renault van.

It was obvious that blame for the crash had lain squarely with the driver of the Iveco, who must have strayed out of his lane to collide with the vehicles in the lay-by. There were no signs of him braking until almost at the site of the first impact. There were no skid marks on the surface of the road or remains of tyre tread in the section approaching the lay-by.

Cooper recalled the witness statements taken from other drivers on the southbound carriageway who had seen Allsop veering onto the hard shoulder. It seemed fairly cut and dried. And when his mobile phone records were analysed, the case against him was strong.

He laid the post-mortem report on Ashley Brooks on Villiers' desk.

'Have you had breakfast?' he said. 'Or can you face these pictures?'

'Are they worse than mine?' said Villiers.

'Well, let me put it this way – even Dr van Doon said they "weren't pretty".'

'Oh God. That bad?'

The photos had made Cooper flinch. They showed the remains of Ashley Brooks after she had been removed from the burned-out Honda – a blackened mass, barely human in shape. Her charred arms were held out in front of her body as if she was still clutching the steering wheel. It was what they called the 'pugilistic stance', typical of a severely burned body, the result of the high temperature of a fire stiffening and shrinking the muscle fibres, flexing the elbows, knees and hips, clenching the hands into fists. It happened to a body even if the person was already dead before the fire. Some areas of the body could be protected by the stance and were burned less. But the fire had burned through the layers of Ashley's skin to the tissues underneath. Professor Webster's report had referred to 'thermally altered bones'.

Cooper put the photos back in the file when Villiers had seen them. At least Scott Brooks hadn't been expected to look at these. They were enough to disturb anyone.

'James Allsop, then?' said Cooper. 'He was the man responsible for this.'

Villiers took a deep breath and read from her notes.

'Under Section One of the Road Traffic Act 1988, James Allsop was sentenced to eight years in prison for the offence of Causing Death by Dangerous Driving,' she said. 'He was also disqualified from driving for eight years, with an automatic extended re-test at the end of his ban.'

'Eight years is in the Level One range, isn't it?' said Cooper.

The Court of Appeal has set down four levels of seriousness for the offence of Causing Death by Dangerous Driving. An eight-year prison sentence fell into the most serious range.

'Yes. The offence Allsop committed initially appeared to be at Level Two – driving that created a substantial risk of danger by a gross avoidable distraction, in this case composing a text message. But the initial circumstances were compounded by evidence that he'd been driving while knowingly deprived of adequate sleep.'

'So the Crown Prosecution Service achieved a Level One sentence by presenting them both together,' said Cooper.

Allsop was lucky, though. The maximum sentence at Level One was fourteen years. If he'd been drinking or under the influence of drugs as well, he would have been spending a few years longer inside.

'James Allsop was released on licence four years ago. His sentence expired last month. He's a free man, Ben.'

'Where did he go? He must have been living at an approved address during his period on licence.'

'Of course. But here's the thing. His life was threatened at the time of the court hearing and again when it was reported that he was going to be let out. It was a big story for the local papers, you know.'

'Yes.'

'So he's been living under a different name, for his own protection.'

'Not an anonymity order,' said Cooper.

Official anonymity orders for offenders on licence were very rare indeed. Currently there were only four, so far as Cooper was aware. They were all notorious names – Jon Venables, Robert Thompson, Mary Bell and Maxine Carr. The circumstances had to be exceptional, the risk to them very high. James Allsop wasn't nationally known like Venables and Thompson, the killers of two-year-old James Bulger. But he was recognisable locally and feelings had run high in some quarters.

'No, it's not an official anonymity order. They didn't give a new identity. But his offender manager from the Probation Service agreed to him going by a new name when he left prison on licence. It's common practice among sex offenders, so they can settle anonymously into new communities. But in this case, he hasn't been doing anything wrong. He hasn't even tried to take a job under his new name. He just took his mother's maiden name.'

'All right,' said Cooper, putting on his jacket.

'Hold on, you haven't asked what his new name is.'

'I'd be very surprised,' said Cooper, 'if it's anything else but the name I'm thinking of.'

BEN COOPER LOOKED at the yard full of vehicles, some of which would never move again. He realised what it was that had seemed wrong about Shaw Farm. It wasn't really logical, just something that came from his instinct, a result of a lifetime spent among these hill farming families. But it had led him to the right conclusion.

The door was answered by the woman he'd seen driving the Range Rover. Sarah Wyatt. She took one look at him and her face fell. Her expression suggested she was resigned to the inevitable.

'Jack,' she called. 'The police are here to see you.'

A minute later Jack Lawson appeared walking down the hallway, his limp worse than Cooper remembered it. He looked grey and ill.

Cooper didn't ask to enter the house, but permitted Lawson to steer him out into the yard. Psychologically, it meant he wasn't being allowed all the way into Lawson's life. But step by step it would all come out.

'Well?' said Lawson with a faint note of impatience. Once this moment had arrived, perhaps he wanted to get it over with as quickly as possible.

But Cooper wasn't ready to get straight to the point with his questions. It was better if Lawson was willing to tell the story for himself.

'Which of these cars do you drive, sir?' he said. 'The Range Rover looks more your style than the Panda.'

Lawson grunted irritably. 'I drive a tractor round the farm. That's my style.'

'Really?' said Cooper. 'You said you'd only been in farming a few years?'

'We bought this place when the last owners went out of business. They couldn't make it pay any more. You know what it's like.'

'Yes. So how long exactly?'

'How long?'

'How long have you been here at Shaw Farm?'

'Oh, about two years.'

Cooper turned and looked at Lawson. Would he take the trouble to lie about his past now, or was it something he was anxious to talk about, given the opportunity?

'And what did you do that before that, sir?'

Lawson regarded him for a long moment. 'I think you probably know that already,' he said finally.

'I could take a guess.'

'And I bet you'd be right with your guess. I suppose you've been asking enough questions, digging things out, putting two and two together. I was a lorry driver. I did that job for fifteen years. But not any more.'

'You're still banned from driving, I imagine? That's why Sarah and Nick drive the cars.'

Lawson shook his head. 'No, you're wrong there. My disqualification came to an end six months ago.'

'So why . . . ?'

'I just can't face it. I haven't the stomach to get behind the wheel again after what happened. I suppose you'd say I've lost my nerve.'

'How are the burns, sir? Did they leave any scars? I notice you have a limp.'

'The doctors say it's psychological,' said Lawson. 'The burns were just superficial. But some things go deeper than the skin.'

'Yes, I can imagine.'

'So how did you know?' said Lawson.

'There were a few clues,' said Cooper. 'The first was something very trivial. I thought it was odd, when Mr Swindells' sheep got out on the road, that it was the Durkins who went down to help him get them back in. Farmers normally pitch in and help their neighbours in those circumstances. You didn't.'

'No, I couldn't do that.'

'But it was really something my sergeant said. About people coming and going, and some who never went out at all. I thought at the time he meant old Mrs Swindells. And then I realised. I'd seen Sarah Wyatt driving that Range Rover and her son Nick in the Fiat Panda. But not you. Jack Lawson is the one who never goes out.'

'Oh, that's me all right. The man who never goes out. My latest claim to fame.'

Cooper watched him walk slowly across the yard towards the half-mended tractor.

'Your real name is James Allsop, of course,' he said.

Lawson's shoulders slumped. 'I could never have come here using that name. Not anywhere in this area.'

'I take it Sarah knows all about it.'

'Of course. We've never actually married, but you can't start a relationship on lies.'

'Well, that's another thing. The records show that James Allsop had no children. But nor does Jack Lawson. Nick isn't your son.'

'I call him my stepson. He's like family now anyway.'

'So what happened to Mrs Lawson?' said Cooper.

'What do you think? She divorced me while I was inside. When I came out on licence, I was totally on my own. I had no idea what I was going to do with myself. I thought about moving right away from here, emigrating to Canada or Australia. Well, I don't know what I would have done.'

Lawson stroked the huge back tyre of the John Deere, knocking off a chunk of dried mud that broke and scattered on the surface of the yard.

'Then I met Sarah,' he said. 'She's been the best thing that ever happened to me. I couldn't let anything jeopardise that. Sometimes secrecy is necessary. That's just because of the way people are. They won't let you forget something you did years ago, no matter how much you've changed.'

'Is the farm in Sarah's name?' asked Cooper.

Lawson nodded. 'She had some money after her previous husband died – Nick's father. There was a property to sell and a decent insurance policy. Yet she accepted me and understood about my past. You see what I mean? She's too good to be true.'

'But why the farm?'

'Sarah comes from a farming family and Nick is interested in the business too. When this farm came up for sale and at a price we could afford . . . well, it was too good to resist. I'm not a farmer myself, but I'm doing my best.'

'And I take it the problem is Donna Schofield at Top Barn?'

'You seem to know everything about me,' said Lawson. 'Yes, the barn conversion work was going on when we came here. Grant Swindells sold it off because he can't make a go of it at Higher Fold and needed the money. We didn't think anything of it at first. But then that damn woman moved in. Can you imagine what that was like? One of the Flynn family right here in Shawhead?'

'It must have been difficult,' said Cooper.

'Difficult? It was like my past was pursuing me. I thought I was never going to escape from what I did. Well, I couldn't risk her recognising me. The Flynns were in court all through the trial, you know. Particularly those two brothers. They shouted abuse at me when I was sentenced. They said they'd kill me when I got out.'

'And that was why you changed your name.'

'I got approval from my probation officer, so I could be known as Lawson while I was on licence. It was my mother's maiden name.'

Lawson gestured round the yard and at the house where Sarah Wyatt was waiting for him.

'I've got a new life now, a new family,' he said. 'I ought to be allowed to put the past behind me. But I don't go out, in case *she* sees me. I haven't been out in daylight since the Schofields came. I feel like a vampire. I'm Count Dracula, or some other monster. One of the undead.'

It struck Cooper as a strange expression to use. Only an hour before, he'd been looking at the post-mortem photographs of Ashley Brooks. If Lawson was the undead, she was definitely the dead. And so was Malcolm Kelsey. Which of them was the better off?

'I'd rather people in Shawhead didn't find out who I am,' said Lawson.

'I'm afraid it might already be too late for that, sir.'

Now Lawson looked defeated and Cooper began to feel sorry for him.

'You know that cab-over-engine design in most HGVs?' said Lawson. 'Some people call a cab like that a "flying coffin".'

'Why?'

'Because of its position right over the engine. When an accident happens, there's no escape for the driver.'

Cooper nodded. 'But you did escape,' he said.

Lawson flinched. 'You're not the first person to point that out. Well, the reason I escaped without serious injury was because the truck only hit a small car. It was no contest. The Honda took all the damage.'

Cooper could see that the memory still made Lawson edgy.

'I have to ask you, sir – were you involved in the death of Malcolm Kelsey in any way?'

'Why would I hold any kind of grudge against Kelsey?' said Lawson. 'I was the guilty one.'

Chapter Thirty

WITH HER USUAL efficiency, Carol Villiers had made sure the scene at the Cloughpit Lane bridge was cleared and the field provided by Grant Swindells as a parking area for police vehicles was left tidy.

When Ben Cooper encountered Mr Swindells near the entrance to his farm, he almost looked happy, so far as any farmer ever did.

'A satisfied member of the public?' Cooper asked Villiers.

'Well, it's nice to have someone vaguely on our side at least,' said Villiers. 'Were you right about Jack Lawson?'

Cooper nodded. Perhaps he ought to feel more pleased that he'd been right. But at the moment it didn't feel like a triumph.

'So we've eliminated the Hibberts and Jack Lawson, have we?' said Villiers.

'They weren't involved in the murder of Malcolm Kelsey,' said Cooper. 'I'm pretty sure of that.'

'Not exactly innocent, though, are they?'

'Who is, really?' said Cooper.

'What next, then? We're left with the Schofields and the Durkins.'

'The Schofields are having some building work done at Top Barn. They're restoring an old farm building. A byre.'

'The Hibberts mentioned that, I think,' said Villiers. 'And Luke saw that when he checked out the property. There were a lot of building materials lying around, but no one working of course.'

'They couldn't get through to Shawhead because of the blocked road,' said Cooper.

'And haven't bothered coming back since. Isn't that always the way?'

'Perhaps it was different this time.'

'What about the Durkins?' said Villiers. 'The people round the bend.'

'Oh, yes. That strange-shaped house you noticed, Carol. It isn't a former windmill. It's part of what used to be a coal mine, Clough Pit. That tower would have housed the winding gear.'

'Of course. Cloughpit House. It seems obvious now.'

'The old mineral line runs from the back of their property and passes over the bridge,' said Cooper. 'It's not clear on a map, but it's obvious on the ground. That's how the coal was transported when the mine was still working. But there are no tracks now, just the bed of the old line on top of a foundation of ballast. It makes quite a good road.'

'So they have their own route out. They could drive from their property and pass right over the bridge.'

'Yes, if they wanted to.'

'Where would they come out?' asked Villiers.

'Near New Mills Junction, where the old track meets the existing railway line. There's a signal box and a maintenance shed there.'

'But if they went that way, someone on a train was bound to have seen them driving alongside the track.'

'Perhaps they did. But I suppose people on this line are used to seeing maintenance work going on. They might notice a car in the wrong place. But they wouldn't think anything of it, if it was just another workmen's van.'

'Or a motorbike?' suggested Villiers.

'Yes. And the Durkins have a Yamaha.'

'On a motorbike you could be there and back without anyone even seeing you.'

'It's time to go and talk to Tania and Vincent again,' said Cooper. Then he remembered the monosyllabic Vinnie. 'Or to Tania, at least.'

TANIA DURKIN WAS the first person Cooper had met in Shawhead who looked almost pleased to see him. But Vincent wasn't at home today and the motorbike was gone. Perhaps the goats weren't enough company for her when she was on her own.

'Tania, has anyone else been on your property recently?' asked Cooper.

'Oh, do you mean the roofers?' she said. 'They've been working next door at Top Barn. They came one day and asked if they could get access through our field to get to the old byre. They needed to get some scaffolding up on this side so they could work on the roof.'

Cooper looked down the field at the old building with the missing tiles.

'There doesn't seem to be any scaffolding. Didn't they manage to get it up?'

'They started last week some time. Then they came back again. Maybe, with all that's been happening . . .' said Tania doubtfully.

'Did you actually see them go down there?'

'Yes, they came in that flatbed truck of theirs. Vinnie was out on the bike, but I knew who they were, so I thought it would be all right. Once they were down past the stable, I couldn't see what they were doing. Perhaps they just unloaded their stuff and meant to come back later. But then the road got blocked and they couldn't get to the job.' She looked at Cooper. 'That must be it, mustn't it?'

'Can we have a look?'

'You'll need decent footwear. It's a bit claggy at this time of year.'

'I'll be fine.'

Tania Durkin led him down the field to the stable block, where they turned and skirted a pen full of goats. At this end of the field the ground was wet and muddy. Cooper's boots slithered on the flattened grass as they reached a gateway. The entrance was churned up by hooves and he had to edge round the worst parts as Tania unhooked the gate.

Beyond the stable was another field. This one was low lying and looked more like a marsh. Clumps of coarse sedge broke up the boggier stretches. It was obvious to Cooper now why this bit of land had never been incorporated into one of the farms. It was useless for growing crops, or even grazing livestock, without a major drainage scheme.

'You can only get a vehicle down the far side, where it's drier,' said Tania.

'Yes, I see.'

They followed the line of the fence marking the boundary with Top Barn. Work had certainly been taking place on the old byre, but not from this side. Not so far as he could tell.

'That's funny,' said Tania, standing with her hands on her hips and her wellies sinking into an inch of boggy water.

But Cooper had carried on. There was another gate at the bottom. A bigger gate. Two of them, in fact, with a padlock and chain closing them. The railway embankment blocked the skyline from here.

'Those gates lead onto the track of the old mineral line,' called Tania as she watched him striding away. 'No one uses them. Network Rail are the only ones who have legal access and they haven't been near for years.'

Cooper reached the gates and examined the padlock. When he lifted it, the chain fell away in his hands. The gates pushed open easily. On the other side there were tyre marks in the mud, until the track became firm and dry a few yards in.

'Well, what happened there?' said Tania in surprise.

'Did you see the roofers leave after they came down here?' asked Cooper.

'Well, no. I assumed they must have left while I was milking. I play music for the goats. It keeps them calm.'

'I see.'

'I did think it was a bit rude, just leaving and not saying a word of thanks or anything.'

'And that was Monday, of course,' said Cooper.

'I didn't say that,' said Tania. 'But you're right. I suppose they must have gone before the bridge was blocked, then.'

'Yes, I suppose they must.'

COOPER WENT NEXT to Top Barn to see Donna Schofield, where he got a much less warm reception.

'Mrs Schofield, who has been doing the work on your old byre?' he asked.

Mrs Schofield scowled at him.

'Just Jason and Aidan,' she said. 'They're good boys.'

Cooper nodded. 'And of course, they're family.'

'Well, yes – they are,' she said defensively.

'Thank you.'

She closed the door firmly behind him. Cooper hardly reached her gate, when the figure of Mrs Swindells came into sight. Her black wheelie bin still stood on the side of the road, but she didn't make any pretence of checking it. She knew there was little chance of the binmen coming on a Saturday.

When she saw Cooper, she smiled and asked him how it was all going. He understood that she was just fishing for information, but it made quite a welcome change.

'It seems Mr Hibbert had been walking across the fields quite regularly,' he said. 'Not just on Monday night.'

'Oh, I know,' she said. 'I've seen him more than once.'

'You didn't tell us that.'

'Oh, I did,' said Mrs Swindells. 'I told the young Indian man.'

'Really?'

Cooper left Shawhead, hoping it might be for the last time. Before he got into his car, he stood for a moment and looked back at the hamlet with its silent, unwelcoming air and its almost hidden bend like a deliberate obstacle course. This road was a hazard in itself. People here were living on the edge of danger.

He wondered how Jack Lawson would feel if he knew that the Flynn brothers had been working on his neighbour's property, just a few yards round the corner. But he probably had no idea, since he never went out.

IT TOOK TIME to call the rest of the team in for the operation. But everyone responded at short notice. It was part of the job and they understood that.

A rendezvous was set up in the car park of the Tesco supermarket just outside Whaley Bridge. Cooper arrived first and parked in the furthest corner, the same spot that he'd chosen when he met Gavin Murfin in his battered Transit van on Friday morning. What a pity he hadn't arranged to have the Flynn brothers picked up then, when he knew where they were, just taken them quietly into custody while they were sitting in Sally's Snack Box.

But he hadn't known then what he did now. He hadn't been able to put all the pieces together properly. He hoped the Flynns weren't already too on edge and ready to make a run for it. Worse was the possibility that they might already have disappeared. Cooper prayed that wasn't the case. It made for much too messy an ending to his case.

Gradually, the rest of the team began to arrive. They parked their cars and gathered around Cooper for a quick briefing.

'I'd like to do this without any fuss,' he said. 'If we can take the brothers separately, that would be ideal. There will be back-up available, but only if we need it. I think we can manage it ourselves, can't we?'

'Of course we can,' said Irvine confidently. He was dressed casually and even had his hair gelled into a different style, making him look quite different from the young DC who came into the office every day. Briefly, Cooper wondered what Luke did with himself at the weekends and what he might have interrupted.

'We need to locate the Flynns first,' pointed out Sharma.

Cooper glanced at him, slightly irritated at the comment.

'Obviously, Dev. So let's get on with it.'

Cooper sent Luke Irvine and Becky Hurst into New Mills to make a discreet check on whether Jason and Aidan Flynn were home. Then they waited.

Dev Sharma fidgeted impatiently as he watched the shoppers coming and going from the supermarket. It was getting busy and cars kept crawling past looking for a parking space. Trolleys rattled over the walkways, children screamed irritably. A charity collector stood rattling a tin in the entrance to the store.

'Is it always like this?' said Sharma.

'What do you mean? Like what?'

'So, well . . . dull.'

'There's often a lot of waiting,' said Cooper. 'Isn't it like that in D Division?'

Sharma shrugged. 'I suppose so. Though you're usually wanted somewhere else if you stand still long enough.'

After twenty minutes or so, Irvine called in to report that a neighbour in New Mills had seen Jason arrive in the white Nissan pick-up and collect his younger brother.

'It looks as though they're going to work,' he said. 'It must be an urgent job if they're working on a Saturday. That, or they need the money.'

'They didn't have any overnight bags with them, anything like that?'

'It doesn't sound like it. Just tools.'

'Is there anyone else home?'

'Not at Aidan's house.'

'We need to find out where they've gone,' said Cooper. 'But the only phone number for their roofing business is a mobile. It's probably in the pick-up with Jason. We could call that as a last resort.'

Irvine's voice was muffled for a moment, then he came back on the line.

'Becky is going to try the number. She thinks she can make an innocent enquiry and give the impression of being a helpless woman.'

Cooper smiled. 'Okay. Call me back straight away if you get a result. Otherwise someone will have to visit Jason's house. He's married, so his wife might be at home.'

'Will do.'

He ended the call and they waited for a few more minutes, watching the shoppers, trying to ignore the suspicious glances.

'Jason Flynn's wife might equally be doing her shopping here at Tesco,' said Sharma.

'True. But we'll track them down one way or another, even if we have to wait until they come again from the job they're on.'

'Seriously? We'd wait that long?'

'If necessary.'

But Irvine wasn't long calling back. He sounded more excited now.

'The Flynns have been looking at a job in Chapel-en-le-Frith,' he said. 'They told Becky they would be on their way back soon. She made up an address in New Mills.'

'Great work. That means they'll be coming up the A6.'

Irvine laughed at something Hurst was saying in the background.

'Becky is upset because Jason Flynn called her "love",' he said. 'But she'll get over it once he's banged up in a cell.'

'I hope no one in New Mills tips the brothers off that you were looking for them,' said Cooper.

He could hear Irvine hesitate then. 'We can't be sure of that. It's not the most friendly of neighbourhoods. You know what it's like. We're getting the old evil eye from some of the neighbours here.'

'Okay, Luke. Fingers crossed. And thanks.'

'Let's go, then,' said Cooper when he ended the call.

'No more waiting?' asked Sharma.

'Not too much, I hope.'

First Cooper asked Carol Villiers to take up a position on the A6, where she had a good view of the passing traffic. Then he and Dev Sharma moved out of the Tesco car park and sat in the Toyota, parked in a gateway just off the Bridgemont Roundabout.

Restlessly, Cooper tapped the steering wheel and stared out at the passing traffic.

'You know both the Flynns have form,' said Sharma. 'All the way back to their teens. Assault, disorderly conduct, taking a vehicle without consent – even a bit of burglary. The older brother, Jason, spent some time in youth detention. Not the best of qualifications for someone working in the building trade.'

'People do learn to go straight,' said Cooper, though he didn't feel any great conviction in this case.

Sharma was on the radio to keep the control room up to date with their progress.

'There's back-up on the way,' he said. 'A response unit and a Traffic car in case we get into a pursuit.'

'But there's no sign of the Flynns yet.' Cooper was starting to get impatient himself now. 'We need to move on them soon. Where are they?'

Then Carol Villiers came through on the radio.

'The Flynn brothers have just left Sally's Snack Box,' she said. 'I'm no more than fifty yards behind them.'

'Be careful, Carol.'

'Don't worry. If they're fuelled up on Sally's chips and baked beans, they won't be in any condition to put up a fight.'

Cooper put the Toyota into gear and moved onto the round-about. He twisted round in his seat to look back down the north-bound carriageway. He couldn't see the Flynns' Nissan pick-up in the traffic, but he saw the blue lights of a Traffic car flashing further down the carriageway.

'Wait, they're stopping on the hard shoulder,' said Villiers. 'The passenger door is opening. One of them is out of the vehicle. He's legging it. It's the younger brother.'

'Aidan?'

'Yes, I think so.'

Cooper could see him now. Aidan Flynn was running along a narrow strip of tarmac between the inside lane and the verge, practically on the white line.

'The pick-up is moving off again fast. They're splitting up.'

'Damn, they must have seen the blue lights and panicked.'

Cooper saw Aidan stumble, his arms flailing, but he seemed to steady himself and keep on running.

When he veered suddenly into the road, Cooper couldn't tell whether he'd done it deliberately. He heard brakes screech and a horn blaring. A white van swerved into the outside lane, forcing a car to brake suddenly, its nose swinging dangerously close to the barrier.

'Was he hit?'

'No, he's still running.'

'Carol, you pick Aidan up before he causes an accident. We'll keep the Nissan in sight.'

'Okay.'

The pick-up rocketed through the roundabout, with Jason Flynn hanging grimly on to the steering wheel. Cooper accelerated hard and managed to get in behind a Ford, then followed the Nissan.

Just a few hundred yards further on the pick-up took a sudden swing across the oncoming traffic by a railway bridge and roared up a side road. Cooper could see the spurt of exhaust as Flynn put his foot down.

He managed to make the turn safely in the Toyota, but Flynn was already disappearing round a sharp bend. Cooper looked in his rearview mirror, but saw no blue lights following. The Toyota crossed the centre line as he tried to gain distance on the Nissan. Ahead he saw a village with a church and a few houses. And he was just in time to see the brake lights of Flynn's white Nissan as it made another right turn in the centre of the village.

'Where is he heading?' asked Sharma as he clung to the door.

'Bugsworth Basin, by the looks of it. If he gets over Silk Hill bridge, we might lose him in the lanes on the other side.'

The Nissan was still in view as they descended the hill. Flynn's car bounced over the bridge by the Navigation Inn. Then he must have seen the blue lights of a police car coming towards him on Silk Hill and his car skidded sideways as he braked to swing right.

He bounced off the railings along the side of the canal as he struggled to control the car. A red waste bin broke off the railings and flew past Cooper's windscreen as he slipped in behind the Nissan. He heard a bang and glanced in his mirror just in time to see the waste bin whirling off the dented roof of the response car behind him.

Clouds of dust were thrown into the air by the Nissan's tyres as Flynn accelerated away along the edge of the canal, past the row of shipping containers and horse bridges towards the old wharfinger's house. Cooper caught a glimpse of the startled faces of boaters emerging from their narrowboats moored in the lower basin.

'He's going to have to stop and make a run for it,' said Sharma.

'Maybe not,' said Cooper.

'Where does it go then?'

'He could turn into the industrial estate when he gets past the cottages. It's the site of an old mill and there's access from the towpath. But he won't make the turn at this speed.'

The Nissan fishtailed dangerously as it slid into the narrower part of the towpath past the bridges. Two walkers ducked behind the wall of the shop when they saw the car coming. Cooper had to slow down, alarmed at the possibility of mowing down a couple of members of the public.

But Jason Flynn had lost speed too as he mowed down a couple of wooden bollards at the gauging stop, where the canal became narrower. A boat was chugging down the canal towards the basin, and the steerer at the stern shouted abuse and shook his fist, as if Flynn was likely to taken any notice.

Luckily, no one was outside the row of cottages as the Nissan sped past. Clumps of grass and mud flew up as he scraped the stone walls. The turning into the industrial estate was just past the end of the row, almost invisible among the trees beyond the last cottage. Did Flynn know it was there, or not? He certainly didn't seem to be slowing down.

'He's not going to make the turn,' said Cooper. 'Hold on tight.'

'What is he going to do?' said Sharma.

'I've no idea. But it isn't going to be good.'

An elderly couple sitting on a bench gaped at them as the pick-up shot past. But Cooper knew he didn't need to hurry now. He watched Flynn's vehicle rumble over the big coping stones that edged the canalside. The wheels of the Nissan were juddering as Flynn fought with the steering. Yet still he didn't slow down.

Cooper slid to a halt. He knew there was nowhere else for the Nissan to go. He expected Flynn to stop and run for it like his brother.

But Flynn must not have seen the next bridge until it was too late. It was the modern bridge carrying the A6 over the canal, and it constricted the towpath to a width of about four feet where it swung sharply under the road. There was no way to get through.

Cooper heard the smash as the Nissan's front wing hit the concrete pillar, spilling headlight glass and shreds of bumper. The pick-up jolted sideways, until its nearside wheels slipped off the edge of the bank.

The vehicle teetered dangerously. For a breathless moment Cooper thought it was going to settle like that, wedged at a forty-five-degree angle between the bridge and the canal, its tyres hanging in mid-air. But Jason Flynn's frantic movements in the driving seat shifted the weight of the pick-up and it began to topple – slowly at first, but gathering speed until it hit the water with a tremendous splash that threw waves onto the towpath.

The open back of the Nissan immediately filled with water and the pick-up tipped gently over. It bobbed on the surface, filling the width of the waterway, its transmission and exhaust system turned up to the sky like the belly of a stranded turtle. Bubbles rose through the murky brown water as it began to creep up the bodywork. The canal was shallow here and the vehicle would be on the bottom in seconds.

Cooper jumped out of the Toyota. Automatically, he began to take off his jacket. But Dev Sharma put a hand firmly on his shoulder to stop him.

'No,' he said. 'You can't do it.'

And Sharma was right, of course. It would be suicide to jump into that water and try to get under the sinking Nissan. If Flynn couldn't free himself from his seat belt and open the door, he was going to die while everyone stood helplessly on the bank.

The response car juddered to a halt behind Cooper's Toyota and he could hear an officer radioing for assistance. But it was already too late by then.

Chapter Thirty-one

BEN COOPER AND Dev Sharma sat across the table from Aidan Flynn and the duty solicitor in an interview room at West Street.

Flynn was wearing a similar sweatshirt and perhaps even the same dirt-streaked denim jeans that Cooper had seen him in at Sally's Snack Box. His working uniform presumably. It was a bit different from Malcolm Kelsey's brown fleece and his matching peaked cap with the windmill logo. That didn't mean Flynn was any less good at his job, he supposed. But a professional look helped.

That angular, brooding face seemed even more familiar, now that Cooper had seen it in Flynn's official record. He had hardly changed since his first arrest, except there was more dark stubble, the hair on his collar was blacker and curlier.

Flynn gazed down at the table in the interview room, his eyes occasionally darting up with that intense stare.

Aidan Flynn was thirty-one years old, so he would have been just twenty-three at the time his big sister was killed in the crash on the A6. But he could hardly blame the incident for sending him off the rails. Aidan had a police record stretching back into his teens. Assault, criminal damage, taking a vehicle without consent – and even a bit of burglary. In every case he had been charged jointly with his older brother Jason.

No doubt the solicitor had advised a 'no comment' approach, but Aidan wanted to talk. It seemed to be the fate of his brother that made him talkative, but Cooper could hardly claim credit for that as a successful interview strategy.

'You lot should never have made him drive into that canal,' said Flynn. 'That's criminal. That's on you. You killed my brother.'

There would certainly be an internal inquiry into how a suspect had died during a police pursuit. The Independent Police Complaints Commission was already on the case.

But Cooper reassured himself that he'd held back, in fact had stopped before Jason Flynn made the fatal mistake of trying to get under the canal bridge. Inquiries were never pleasant for anyone, but it would have to be gone through.

Right now he didn't know what to say to Aidan about his brother's death. In fact, he wasn't allowed to say anything. If he showed any regret, a lawyer could use his words as the basis for an action against the force for negligence. So he had to sit tight-lipped and say nothing in the face of Aidan's anger.

All he could do was wait for Flynn to calm down.

So Cooper let him get a drink of water and gave him a chance to think about his situation while his anger subsided. There was no point in applying too much pressure at this stage – it would only produce negative results. But a few minutes of reflection usually worked, even on the angriest interviewee.

'I don't know what I'm going to do without Jason,' Flynn said eventually. 'I'm no good for anything without him. He always told me what to do.'

When he heard that statement, Cooper wondered if this would be Flynn's argument in court, that he'd been under the influence of his older brother. It wouldn't earn him an acquittal, but it might reduce the tariff for his automatic life sentence.

But then Aidan undermined his own mitigation straight away.

'Jason had it all figured out with the lorry,' he said. 'We worked it out to put the driver right there on tap for Scott. But when Scott saw him, he got cold feet. He tried to say it was the wrong driver. But it was too late by then. We'd come too far.'

The solicitor looked horrified and tried to intervene. But Flynn ignored him as if he wasn't there. It was often the case. When the opportunity came for a suspect to get something off their chest, it could be irresistible. The calculations about pleas and mitigation came later. Sometimes when it was too late.

'So Scott Brooks was there at the bridge on Monday night?' asked Sharma.

'We made sure he was there. But he was hopeless. Completely useless. He just walked away. No – he ran away. Jason got angry then. He went after Scott to bring him back. The driver tried to run off then, so . . .'

'So what, Aidan?'

He leaned towards them across the table, his voice suddenly earnest, almost pleading.

'I didn't know what else to do,' he said. 'I think I must have panicked. I had the knife in my hand and I reacted when he came towards me.'

'It was you who stabbed him?' said Cooper.

'I suppose so.'

'You *suppose* so?'

Cooper took a breath. He mustn't get annoyed with Aidan Flynn. After all, he had no idea what it was like to be in that situation. Was it possible to sever someone's jugular vein without being quite sure whether you'd done it or not? Perhaps it was, in the heat of the moment. If you were agitated and frightened. If you panicked.

'So let's be clear – it was you who stabbed Malcolm Kelsey, not your brother?' he said.

But Aidan shook his head and didn't answer directly.

'He tried to run. He fell down twice, then his legs just gave way. He was dead. Jason was as freaked out as me. Scott had gone by then, I don't know how he got back to New Mills. He was an idiot. We thought he might run off to someone and shop us. He wasn't really family, you know, just because he married Ashley. We never had anything in common with him.'

'You thought he might go the police?' asked Sharma.

'Well, yes.'

Cooper felt it more likely that it had never occurred to Scott Brooks to do that. He'd taken the guilt on himself. Perhaps because he *did* think of the Flynns as family.

'This was all to do with the crash that your sister was killed in,' said Cooper. 'Isn't that right?'

'Obviously,' said Aidan. 'Sally at the Snack Box described it all to us. The crash in that lay-by. How the van driver just stood and watched Ashley burn.'

'When you say "us",' said Sharma. 'Would that include your brother-in-law?'

Flynn nodded. 'He knew everything. We talked to Scott about it all the time. We used to see him around town at night, drinking on his own in one pub or another. Jason liked to find out which pub he was in, then walk up to him at the bar and tap him on the shoulder. Scott would jump out of his skin every time. It made him really paranoid. Jason thought it was hilarious.'

'So you deliberately tormented him for years,' said Cooper.

'He was really wet. We wanted him to do something – well, anything. But he didn't seem to care about what happened to Ashley.'

'That wasn't true,' said Cooper. 'He cared more than you could possibly understand. He just didn't show it in the way you wanted him to.'

Flynn stared at him as if he was talking Chinese. And he might as well have been, in some respects. Aidan Flynn and his brother had been upset about the death of their sister, but almost as a matter of pride, an insult to their family that had to be avenged. Their mentality was the opposite of Scott's. He'd cared more deeply about Ashley, but in a manner that had consumed him daily and didn't require anyone else to die.

Cooper silently corrected his thoughts. Of course, it *had* required someone to die. Scott himself.

'Did you and your brother know that Ashley was having an affair after she married Scott Brooks?' he asked.

Aidan scowled. 'What is that to you?'

'So you did know?'

Flynn fidgeted with the paper cup until he spilled the last drops of water on the table. He watched it dumbly as it trickled slowly towards the edge and began to drip.

'There were rumours,' he said. 'There are always rumours in New Mills. Jason wasn't happy. He smacked a bloke once for making a crack about Ashley.'

'Your brother was angry that Ashley might be having an affair. But you said he didn't think much of Scott either. Isn't that right?'

'Yes, but . . . well, Ashley was married to Scott. No matter how useless he was, he was still her husband. Don't you see?'

'So it was a matter of honour.'

'Something like that.'

'Did you know who she was seeing?' asked Sharma.

Aidan shook his head. 'No. If he'd found out who it was, Jason would have killed him. But the rumours didn't go that far. I think Ashley must have let something drop to one of her girlfriends. You know the way they talk. She probably just couldn't keep a secret and needed to tell someone. She had to boast about it. And when Jason found out, he went ballistic. He laid it on the line that she'd better give her boyfriend the boot.'

Cooper recalled that Pat Turner had also confronted Ashley with her knowledge of the affair. With her older brother on her case too, Ashley must have felt under a lot of pressure to end it.

But Aidan didn't seem to think it was important. He was more concerned about what had happened on Monday night – and rightly so, since it was going to affect his whole future.

'We had to finish him off,' he said earnestly. 'That driver, you know. Jason was as freaked out as me. We had to do something.'

Sharma glanced at Cooper, who nodded. So now it had become 'we' again. Aidan would take careful handling when he was in court. But with the right cross-examination, he would confess to everything that was put to him.

'We couldn't believe he died so quickly,' said Aidan. He actually sounded aggrieved, as if it was all Mac Kelsey's fault. 'I didn't know that would happen. But all that blood. Why was there so much blood?'

The duty solicitor finally stopped the interview, though he almost had to shut Aidan Flynn up by force. Cooper studied the young man, wondering what he was really thinking now.

'You cut through Mr Kelsey's jugular vein,' said Cooper. 'That's why there was so much blood.'

Flynn looked at him wearily.

'I don't even know what that means,' he said.

'WE'RE GOING TO have to interview Donna Schofield,' said Cooper when he and Dev Sharma came out of the interview room.

'Why?'

'Donna Schofield is a member of the Flynn family. She was Ashley Brooks' aunt.'

Sharma nodded. 'It would explain why she's been keeping her head down. But how long did she think she could keep that up? Until we went away, I suppose.'

'I bet she was relying on people in Shawhead having no idea whether she was at home or not,' said Cooper. 'Sometimes keeping yourself to yourself has its advantages.'

'It would never have worked, would it?'

'Well, if she held out long enough, she might have been able to slip away when we cleared the scene. Perhaps she really was intending to head for Thailand. If we search her house, we might find her suitcases packed and ready to go.'

Cooper looked at his new DS. There was one fact he couldn't let go without an explanation.

'There's one thing, Dev . . .' he said.

'Yes?'

'Mrs Swindells says she saw Ian Hibbert coming and going across the field at night several times, not just on Monday. And she claims she told you that. Is it true?'

'Yes, that's true,' admitted Sharma.

Cooper felt a surge of irritation – not at the mistake itself, but his sergeant's apparent lack of concern.

'You were selective with the information you passed on,' he said.

'Does it matter? We were only interested in that one evening. The other nights weren't relevant.'

Cooper bit his lip, annoyed that he should have to explain this to someone who had been appointed to the rank of detective sergeant.

'If we'd known it was a regular occurrence, it would have cast a different light on Mr Hibbert's activities. We might have formed a more accurate hypothesis from the start.'

At least Sharma responded to his tone of rebuke. 'I'm sorry,' he said.

'Well,' said Cooper. 'Remember that we share information fully in this team. Don't keep details like that to yourself.'

'I'll remember.'

Well, that seemed fairly painless. No sign of defensiveness. But what else might Dev Sharma be keeping to himself? Without knowing that, Cooper wasn't sure they would be able to work together. The jury was still out.

WHEN SHARMA HAD gone back to the CID room, Cooper sat alone in his office and assessed his case. He would never know what had caused Mac Kelsey to turn up Cloughpit Lane and get his lorry stuck under the bridge. Had someone placed that diversion sign at the corner of the lane, either as a joke or for a more sinister reason? Or was it simply another satnav error? The only person who could tell them whether he'd followed a diversion was dead.

The height warning had certainly gone from its position on the bridge, but that might have been wear and tear. Even if someone's fingerprints were found on the sign, it wasn't proof that they'd removed it from the bridge. They might have picked it up from the road and put it safely out of the way on the verge. He needed something more solid than that.

What he really needed was a weapon. That would make all the difference. But where was that knife?

If he was right, the Flynn brothers had accessed the old mineral line from the Durkins' property to stage the attack. They couldn't have been certain that Kelsey would drive his lorry right under the bridge and get stuck, but their plan had worked out perfectly for them up to that point. They must have been jubilant.

He could imagine Jason and Aidan getting frenzied and over-excited, dropping down onto the roof of the cab like a pair of characters out of *Mission Impossible*. Had they intended to kill Mac Kelsey? Was that part of the plan all along? Perhaps not. It might only have been an exercise in intimidation, a prank to frighten him.

Or it might have been staged as a test for Scott Brooks, the brother-in-law they'd come to despise for his weakness. They'd tried to force Scott to come face to face with the man who'd stood and let his wife die in her car. And Scott had backed down. He'd walked away and chickened out of their plan. The Flynns would have been furious. Who would they have taken that anger out on?

Well, it would be up to the CPS to assess whether a murder charge was justified and had a reasonable chance of success. And if it came to a full trial, it would be a jury's responsibility to decide the Flynns' intentions. Aidan Flynn was left to face that possibility on his own.

Carol Villiers knocked and put her head round his door.

'We've searched the pick-up truck and properties of the two Flynn brothers,' she said. 'We've seized some clothing – which has been washed, but may retain some residual blood staining, if we're lucky. There's no sign of a weapon, though. Nothing like the one used in the assault on Malcolm Kelsey. Sorry.'

'They wouldn't have taken it back home with them anyway,' said Cooper. 'It's been disposed of somewhere.'

He was thinking about the little collection of houses in Shawhead. He was picturing the Flynn brothers coming out of the yard at Cloughpit House and back into Top Barn, where they were working on the old byre for the Schofields.

What part had Donna Schofield played in their scheme? The loyal aunt, who would do anything to help out her family, even if she felt guilty about it afterwards. What role had they chosen for her?

People often chose burning as a means of disposing of evidence. But the Schofields had no open fires in their house, only oil-fired central heating. And there were no signs of a bonfire outside. The smoke would have been noticed, the remains would still be visible on the ground. You couldn't burn a knife anyway. So where might Donna Schofield have disposed of the weapon?

Cooper laughed suddenly. It was a genuine laugh, the first time he'd felt like laughing for days. It was a laugh of relief, but of amusement too. How ironic that the factor which had seemed such a headache at the beginning of this inquiry might now provide the final piece of evidence in his case against the Flynns.

SHAWHEAD LOOKED NO different. But the light was going, with the first hint of colour in the sky where the sun would set over Cheshire. They didn't have much time to get the job done today.

'If the Flynns left the murder weapon with Mrs Schofield on Monday night, it will be long gone by now,' said Dev Sharma as they gathered outside Top Barn.

'Not necessarily,' said Cooper.

He had a warrant to search the Schofields' property for the knife, but he was hoping a full-scale search wouldn't be necessary. As the rest of the team went into the house under the angry glare of Donna Schofield, Cooper turned to Luke Irvine.

'I've got a special job for you, Luke,' he said.

Irvine's face fell. No doubt he was thinking that he was being kept away from the main activity for some reason.

'What is it?'

Cooper pointed at the black bin standing at the side of the road near the Schofields' gate.

'These wheelie bins are the most public aspect of Shawhead. People have no idea what you get up to inside your own house – but if you came out and started picking through the rubbish in your own wheelie bin, someone would notice and wonder what was going on.'

'If it was this wheelie bin, Mrs Swindells would certainly notice,' said Irvine. 'She's watching us right now.'

'I hope she enjoys the show then,' said Cooper. 'Get the gloves on, Luke.'

'Oh, great.'

THE SEARCH DIDN'T take long. As Cooper had hoped, Luke Irvine was the one to make the find. He pulled out a Tesco carrier bag wrapped round something long and narrow. When he unwrapped it carefully, the blood stains were obvious to everyone.

'How did you know it would be there?' asked Sharma in surprise.

'I was betting that Donna Schofield panicked,' said Cooper. 'Obviously, she knew her nephews were involved in the murder. But she was on her own and she didn't know what to do for the best. So she dropped the knife into the wheelie bin and put it out for collection, thinking it would be taken to landfill that morning.'

'Then she shut herself in the house, refused to answer the door and tried to pretend she wasn't at home.'

'Exactly. She was hoping it would all just go away and disappear, along with the contents of her wheelie bin. She hadn't anticipated that the road would still be blocked the next day and the bin men wouldn't get through.'

'And how lucky that the bins are still standing here now,' said Sharma.

'We have the refuse department of High Peak Borough Council to thank for that. They either wouldn't, or couldn't, organise a special collection for these five properties.'

'Not for little Shawhead.'

Cooper nodded.

'Besides,' he said, 'everyone who lives in this area knows the rules about what goes in your wheelie bin. And cutlery goes in the black bin.'

AN HOUR LATER Cooper sat in his office at West Street with Dev Sharma to wind up the day as everyone else went home to continue their interrupted weekend.

'Well, that's that,' said Sharma. 'Aidan Flynn has confessed to killing Malcolm Kelsey and we have the murder weapon. Jason

Flynn is beyond the reach of justice. And Scott Brooks took his own life.'

'Yes, absolutely,' said Cooper. 'That's that.'

But he couldn't put the same confidence into his voice that Sharma did.

In fact, Cooper wasn't thinking of Scott Brooks, or of the Flynns. He was recalling Lucy Armitage's account of that fatal collision eight years ago, as she'd seen it from her cafe across the A6. She hadn't been the closest of witnesses and she hadn't actually seen the crash itself.

But at least she hadn't been moving at fifty miles an hour. And she hadn't been asleep, like the Polish driver. Her view of events had clearly made an impression on her. And despite her reticence – or perhaps because of it – Cooper believed her.

It was clear to him that Ashley Brooks had been having an affair. Pat Turner had said so, and her brothers had thought so too. Perhaps even Scott had suspected it, deep down, but hadn't wanted to acknowledge it to himself. It would explain that odd message among all the Love Heart notes. *Come Back to Me*. Maybe Scott thought he'd lost her, even before she died. He wanted her back.

And no one had ever explained why Ashley was parked in a lay-by on the A6 at eleven o'clock that night. Or why Malcolm Kelsey was in the lay-by either. There was a fairly obvious conclusion.

Cooper opened the post-mortem report lying on his desk. It wasn't the report on Mac Kelsey. It was an older report – eight years older, in fact. It was the result of the examination by the late Professor Webster on Ashley Brooks. Severe burns to the body had made it difficult for the pathologist to reach a firm conclusion. But her underlying injuries were consistent with the nature of the collision – bruising from the impact, cuts from a shattered windscreen and lethal shards of broken metal.

Professor Webster had been hugely experienced. As well as providing forensic pathology services to coroners and police forces in the East Midlands, in his later years he'd been a member of the Council of the Royal College of Pathologists and served on advisory committees. He'd published scores of papers, as well as writing a book on forensic pathology, with another in production when he died. Not forgetting that MBE, which wasn't awarded lightly. He had official approval from the Queen herself.

So it seemed disrespectful to be doubting Professor Webster's conclusion in a case like this. But Cooper knew the results of a post-mortem were always open to interpretation. Even the most expert witness could be wrong. It had happened many times.

Having reassured himself, Cooper turned to another stack of papers. He was aware of Sharma watching him curiously. Perhaps his new DS had learned by now to wait to see what happened and not to ask too many questions.

Next to the post-mortem report on Cooper's desk was Wayne Abbott's file on the contents of Mac Kelsey's cab, those items found in the DAF curtainsider jammed under Cloughpit Lane bridge. A Taser, a baseball bat and a retractable shark knife.

Cooper nodded silently to himself. Yes, Ashley Brooks' injuries were consistent with the collision, as Professor Webster said. But they could also be consistent with an assault by someone armed with a baseball bat and a shark knife.

Pat Turner and Aidan Flynn had both told him that Ashley was under pressure to end her affair. Cooper particularly recalled

Mrs Turner's words: '*Well, she never got the chance, to be fair. It was just before she was killed in that crash.*' But had Ashley just ended it? As she sat in that lay-by, had she told the man she was meeting that it was all over? Did he react the way so many people did when they were rejected – with anger and perhaps even with violence?

Reluctantly, Cooper closed the report. He wondered if that informal jury in Sally's Snack Box had been right about Mac Kelsey's guilt, but just not right enough.

One thing seemed to be beyond doubt. Eight years ago Kelsey had stood in that lay-by on the A6 and watched Ashley Brooks burn, without making any attempt to pull her from the car. That might not have been because he was a coward. It might have been because he knew perfectly well that Ashley was already dead when the crash happened.

Cooper didn't know how to prove what he suspected about that collision eight years ago. And, even if he could, what purpose would it achieve? Everyone had spent the intervening years seeing things in just one way. They would have to alter what they thought they knew, abandon notions they'd taken for granted as truths. No one found that easy. Jack Lawson in particular might find it very hard to deal with the suggestion that he hadn't been guilty of Ashley Brooks' death.

But there was one person who had never seen things in the same way as everyone else. He'd only been pretending. That one person had known the real truth all along. Malcolm Kelsey.

Justice was a strange thing. For Ben Cooper, sitting in his office in Edendale, the concept was hard to come to terms with. Mac Kelsey might have been guilty of many things. Just not the one he was executed for.

Dev Sharma couldn't keep quiet any longer. He tried to make a guess at what his DI was thinking.

'People are capable of making such a mess of their lives,' he said.

'I know,' said Cooper. 'Believe me, I know.'

Chapter Thirty-two

Sunday 15 February

'A SUCCESSFUL INQUIRY, then?' said Fry when he phoned her first thing on Sunday morning.

'I suppose so. There'll be a conviction anyway.'

Fry knew him too well not to sense the ambivalence in his tone.

'No doubt you've come up with some theory that no one else has thought of,' she said.

Cooper smiled. She didn't say it with quite the sarcasm that he was used to. Was it resignation? She'd known him a long time after all. Or perhaps it could finally be called acceptance.

'Yes,' he said. 'I think you would probably say that I have. But I don't know how I'm going to prove it. It's all circumstantial.'

'Naturally. Your best theories are always the ones that can't possibly be proved. So what do you think happened to this driver, Kelsey?'

'I think he was killed out of revenge.'

'For what?'

Cooper paused, anticipating her response before he'd even shared his idea.

'For the murder of Ashley Brooks,' he said.

'Are you joking?' she said. 'That was the woman who was killed in the fatal collision eight years ago. Haven't I got that right?'

She always had the details right. It was Cooper's interpretation of the details that was sometimes at odds with the accepted facts.

'When I read the accounts of that accident,' he said, 'I expected to find that the other lorry involved in the crash was being driven by Kelsey.'

'Which other lorry?'

'There was one parked in the lay-by at the time. Ashley Brooks' Honda was smashed into by James Allsop's Iveco Stralis. In fact, her car was crushed between the two HGVs. She had been sitting in the lay-by right behind that lorry. It was a forty-ton Volvo belonging to a haulage company in Poland. I thought she and Kelsey were having a . . . what would you call it?'

'A rendezvous? An assignation? A tryst?'

'Something like that.'

'But the Volvo wasn't being driven by Malcolm Kelsey.'

'No. The driver's name was Borzuczek. Artus Borzuczek. He was Polish,' said Cooper. 'And he'd stopped for a rest break.'

'So you were wrong.'

'Not quite.'

'How can you be "not quite wrong"?'

Cooper smiled. It didn't sound logical when Diane Fry said it. But that was exactly how he felt most of the time.

'I think Ashley was already dead when the accident happened. I believe she'd been having an affair with Kelsey and she'd arranged to meet him in that lay-by.'

'Are you sure?'

'Pretty certain. It's a pity the original inquiry was so focused on the calls Jack Lawson had been making and the texts he'd been sending. If only they'd checked Mac Kelsey's phone, or even Ashley's, we might have some proof of the relationship.'

'But there was no reason to do that at the time.'

'There didn't seem to be,' said Cooper. 'I'm not blaming anyone. No doubt it was the right call in the circumstances. But in retrospect, well . . .'

'Everything seems different in retrospect,' said Fry.

Now, that was said with genuine feeling. Cooper wondered what was going through her mind, what aspect of her life she was regretting so much. There were quite a few possibilities, he supposed. But it was better not to ask her what suddenly looked so different and so regrettable. It might involve him.

'And the lorry driver who went to prison for dangerous driving. Allsop?'

'Yes, though he changed his name to Lawson when he came out.'

'Why did he worry about it so much? He'd served his sentence. For him it was all over.'

'He was concerned about what people would think of him,' said Cooper.

'Well, that's stupid, isn't it?'

'Why?'

'There's no point in worrying about what other people will think of you,' said Fry. 'If you believe your life has been ruined because you never became wealthy and successful, never achieved your dreams, never became a great footballer or whatever, that's all within yourself. It's just you, creating your own pain. The reality is, most people don't think about you at all. They're too busy thinking about themselves.'

It was a long speech for Fry. Cooper took a moment to let it sink in.

'I suppose Jack Lawson made a mistake, that's all.'

'One mistake can ruin your life,' said Fry, with feeling.

Cooper had been listening carefully to the tone of her voice all the time they'd been talking. Sometimes it was the only way he could get an idea about what she was thinking. When she didn't say anything, that was worse. It meant she was thinking something she didn't want to tell him.

And today there was something wrong with Diane Fry's voice. It sounded brittle, restrained. She sounded as though she was choking something back, a spurt of bile that she was fighting to swallow down. What was bubbling inside her that was making her so tightly wound up?

Cooper was thinking about Love Hearts, the sweet smell hanging over New Mills, the sugar coating the windows of the factory, the saccharine messages left all over Scott Brooks' house in Peak Road. When he and Becky Hurst had stood in the house, Becky had said the messages obviously weren't intended for them. But perhaps they had been, in a way. They were part of Scott Brooks' suicide note, his explanation for what he'd done. It was all about his love for Ashley.

'Diane, we need to get out,' said Cooper.

'Out?'

'Come and get a breath of fresh air, away from the city.'

When she didn't answer straight away, Cooper thought he could almost hear the traffic noise in the silence at the end of the phone. He wondered if she was gazing out of the window of her apartment at the streets and suburbs of Nottingham, weighing up the options.

'Okay,' she said finally. 'Where are we going?'

'There's a place,' said Cooper, 'that I've been thinking about all week.'

'I can't wait.'

KINDER SCOUT WAS a daunting place for walkers. There was no easy way to scale the flanks of that brooding hump of mountain. The ascent of Kinder was the first stage of the Pennine Way, one of Britain's most popular long-distance paths.

But within a couple of hours of leaving the dale below, many walkers were left exhausted, blistered and frequently disorientated in the lightest of mists. And when they finally reached the plateau, the moorland appeared unrelentingly bleak.

But for Cooper that was the appeal of moorland. Despite its physical challenges, Kinder held a special place in his heart, as it did for all walkers. Eighty years ago this stretch of land, then out of bounds to the masses, became the focus for the campaign for access to the countryside.

There was a reason this area was known as the Dark Peak. Acres of wet, black peat were the most distinctive feature of the plateau.

Although the Kinder moorland had evolved from prehistoric times, it was surprisingly vulnerable. Overgrazing by sheep, industrial pollution, wildfires and thousands of walkers had taken their toll. The peat was drying out, threatening many species of animals and birds that lived there.

The National Trust, which owned most of Kinder, had fenced much of the moorland off from sheep, though not from walkers.

Gullies were being blocked to prevent water from draining off and cotton-grass was being planted by dropping hundreds of thousands of seed pods from helicopters.

On the top moorlands filled the horizon to the north. To the west was Manchester, with the small towns of New Mills and Whaley Bridge sitting in the valley between.

Eastwards you found yourself in a different landscape altogether. On an Ordnance Survey map the plateau of Kinder Scout looked like a spider's web of blue lines, the streams and drainage channels feeding in every direction to fill the brooks running off Kinder's slopes. Grinds Brook, Crowden Brook, Far Brook – and the River Kinder itself. Many of those streams were so close together that the result on the ground was a boggy morass under foot. The tangle of lines was scattered with black dots – hundreds of them, like tiny flies caught in the web. They were the rocks of Kinder.

It was such an alien place that it looked like something from the set of a science fiction film. This was a moonscape of freakish, isolated rocks sculpted by the weather. Boulders and distorted stone columns seemed to have fallen from the sky. With a bit of imagination, they could easily resemble monstrous creatures or massive broken teeth. Each stone had its ancient name and a legend to go it with it. The Giant's Club, The Bird Stone, The Druid's Stone, The Woolpacks, Ringing Roger, Pym's Chair, Madwoman's Stones.

It was also the area where walkers got lost and injured every year and had to be rescued from the moor. When the weather turned bad or darkness fell, Kinder Scout became a terrifyingly hostile place. Without the volunteer mountain rescue teams, there would be a lot more fatalities on Kinder.

They met at the car park just outside Edale village. From there they walked up through the village and turned on to the Pennine Way opposite the Nag's Head pub. Past Upper Booth Farm, they followed the River Noe through ancient woodland and climbed the Jacob's Ladder footpath, which had been rebuilt by the National Trust using gritstone boulders. At the top Kinder Plateau opened out. They could see the giant anvil-shaped rock known as Noe Stool, sitting amid areas of exposed peat.

'So how are you getting on with your new DS now?' asked Fry.

'Dev Sharma? He's okay. We went for a meal together in Edendale last night. We had a good chat. We've had a few teething troubles, but I think we'll be able to work things out.'

'Where did you go?'

'For dinner? The Mussel and Crab on Hollowgate.'

'Nice. I wondered where you were.'

'I'm sorry, Diane. I should have phoned.'

She hunched her shoulders against the cold. 'Actually, I'm glad you didn't.'

Before he could ask her what she meant, she was striding off again. For a moment she looked like a born hiker, setting off at the start of the Pennine Way with two hundred and sixty-seven miles of hills and dales in her sights. But then she stumbled on a ridge of peat and almost fell flat on her face. He heard her cursing peat moors, Kinder Scout, the Peak District – and nature in general. That was more like it.

ON THE WAY back down they took a different route, skirting a plantation of conifer trees on the edge of the moor. It looked like grouse shooting country to Cooper. There were probably rearing pens in the woodland.

Most of Kinder Scout belonged to the National Trust, as did 26 per cent of the national park. But they were entering privately owned land now.

You could recognise upland grouse moors from the map. If you looked for an isolated patch of woodland bordering the moor, you'd often find locations marked as 'shooting huts' or 'grouse butts'. You were likely to find snares on the edge of the woodland. They were often placed on fence lines, or against holes in walls.

Cooper immediately became more alert. In Derbyshire there were concerted efforts to achieve convictions for offences under the Wildlife and Countryside Act. It could only be done by people keeping their eyes open.

'Oh God, what's this?'

Fry had her hand over her mouth as she stared at the ground.

Cooper moved to her side. He saw a couple of dead foxes, a crow, a magpie, a hare. All piled up and left to rot.

'It's a stink pit,' he said.

'A *what*?'

'A stink pit.'

'Stink is right anyway.'

'The smell of rotting animals lures animals into the area and straight into snares,' said Cooper. 'They usually leave hares and foxes, or birds like these. But sometimes you see a sheep or a deer.'

Branches had been cut down from the surrounding trees and arranged on the ground to make a wall around the rotting animals. Gaps were left in the wall, where snares had been placed. Although stink pits were legal, they were indiscriminate as they could attract all kinds of different species as well as their main target, the fox. Any predator might be attracted, including badgers, pine martens, or even pet cats and dogs.

By a dry-stone wall Cooper found a spring cage trap. The cage was split into two and held open by a piece of wood. A dead hare had been placed on the bottom of the cage as bait. When a bird landed on the wooden perch it would collapse and the cage would close, capturing the bird. Another indiscriminate method, which could easily catch protected raptors.

For once Fry seemed lost for words.

'Don't touch anything,' said Cooper.

'I wouldn't dream of it.'

It didn't take them long to discover three dead birds of prey. All of them had been buried in shallow graves on the edge of the woodland. From the state of decomposition, Cooper guessed they'd been dead for six months. It was impossible to say how they'd died, but it was clear that somebody didn't want them found.

There had been a case recently in which a gamekeeper had staked the carcass of a dead rabbit to the ground, baited with a highly toxic poison called carbofuran. Any animal eating carbofuran would die an agonising death. For a human just touching it could cause serious illness.

Cooper took out his phone.

'I'll alert the wildlife crime officer. Some of these snares may be illegal.'

'May be?' said Fry.

'It's difficult to tell sometimes. These snares are empty, so the gamekeeper may be doing his job properly and checking them within twenty-four hours.'

'It wouldn't take twenty-four hours for an animal to die in one of these.'

'That's true,' said Cooper. 'I've heard stories of dogs getting caught in a snare and dying within forty-five minutes.'

Fry looked at the snares and then at the stink pit with an expression of intense distaste.

'In some ways,' she said, 'the countryside is much more evil and immoral than the city.'

Cooper smiled. 'You said it.'

The patchwork of farmland and tree-covered slopes to the west looked welcoming and approachable, lit by the sun. But it was full of hidden depths and unseen corners. It was criss-crossed by a pattern of dry-stone walls and it erupted here and there in the ripples and pockmarks of abandoned mine workings. It was, above all, a human landscape, settled and shaped by people and still a place where history might be expected to come to the surface, if you cared to look.

Fry was staring straight ahead at the valley below the slopes of Kinder, the small towns in the corner of Derbyshire and the sprawl of the city in the distance.

'So where do we go from here?' she said.

COOPER TOOK HER back to his flat in Edendale. It might be the last time she came here to Welbeck Street. Who knew where he might be living soon? He might move to Nottingham to be closer to her. That might work.

'I think Guy Thomson is showing someone else around the house next door,' he said, peering through the window into the street. 'I was supposed to get back to him with a decision this week, but I was too busy. He's probably written me off as a time waster.'

'Perhaps it's a good thing,' said Fry.

'Why?'

'You didn't want it anyway.'

'No, you're right.'

When they were sitting in the warmth with a coffee, he noticed that Fry had gone very silent. He'd done most of the talking in the car on the way back from Kinder and she'd hardly responded. Now she was hardly able to meet his eye. She fidgeted in her seat, clutching nervously at her mug.

'What's the matter, Diane?' he said.

At first she said, 'Nothing'. But then she told him.

Cooper thought he hadn't heard her properly.

'What?' he said. And again: 'What?'

'Well, it was never serious, was it?' she said. 'I've never been serious with anyone in my life. Not really.'

'But for me it was.'

'No.'

'Diane . . .'

But the words had disintegrated into a dry starch in his mouth with a bitter aftertaste, like a memory of a lemon-flavoured Love Heart. He didn't know what to say at all.

'Ben, it was a rebound,' she said. 'After Liz died, it was just something that happened.'

Then she'd gone, just slipped out into the cold night air.

Cooper stood on the doorstep of number eight Welbeck Street and watched Diane Fry walk to her car, as he'd watched her walk away many times before. This time she looked back once. Their eyes met and suddenly Cooper understood everything.

He had never been all that close to Diane after all. He had certainly never understood her, or known what she was thinking. He'd felt that way when he first met her in Edendale all those years ago and he still felt that way now. He'd only been fooling himself in between.

Of course, Diane Fry was a woman who could never be close to anybody. She could only pretend, at best. It was clear to him now, as if it had come out of the sky like a revelation. Why had he been so stupid?

Cooper shivered as an icy wind lashed through the streets of Edendale. The pavements were wet with rain as Fry's black Audi hissed away up the street and vanished round the corner.

Sometimes, just sometimes, this was a terrible place to live.

About the Author

STEPHEN BOOTH was born in the Lancashire mill town of Burnley, and has remained rooted to the Pennines during his career as a newspaper journalist. He is well known as a breeder of Toggenburg goats and includes among his other interests folkore, the Internet—and walking in the hills of the Peak District, in which his crime novels are set.

He lives with his wife Lesley in a former Georgian dower house in Nottinghamshire.

www.stephen-booth.com
www.witnessimpulse.com